Dirty Like Jude

TITLES BY JAINE DIAMOND

CONTEMPORARY ROMANCE

Dirty Like Me (*Dirty* #1)
Dirty Like Brody (*Dirty* #2)
2 Dirty Wedding Nights (*Dirty* #2.5)
Dirty Like Seth (*Dirty* #3)
Dirty Like Dylan (*Dirty* #4)
Dirty Like Jude (*Dirty* #5)
Dirty Like Zane (*Dirty* #6)
Hot Mess (*Players* #1)
Filthy Beautiful (*Players* #2)
Sweet Temptation (*Players* #3)
Lovely Madness (*Players* #4)
Flames and Flowers (*Players Novella*)
Handsome Devil (*Vancity Villains* #1)
Rebel Heir (*Vancity Villains* #2)
Wicked Angel (*Vancity Villains* #3)
Irresistible Rogue (*Vancity Villains* #4)
Charming Deception (*Bayshore Billionaires* #1)

EROTIC ROMANCE

DEEP (DEEP #1)
DEEPER (DEEP #2)

Dirty Like Jude

JAINE DIAMOND

Dirty Like Jude
by Jaine Diamond

First Edition September 2018

ISBN 978-1-989273-80-7

Cover and interior design by Jaine Diamond / DreamWarp Publishing Ltd.

Published by DreamWarp Publishing Ltd.
www.jainediamond.com

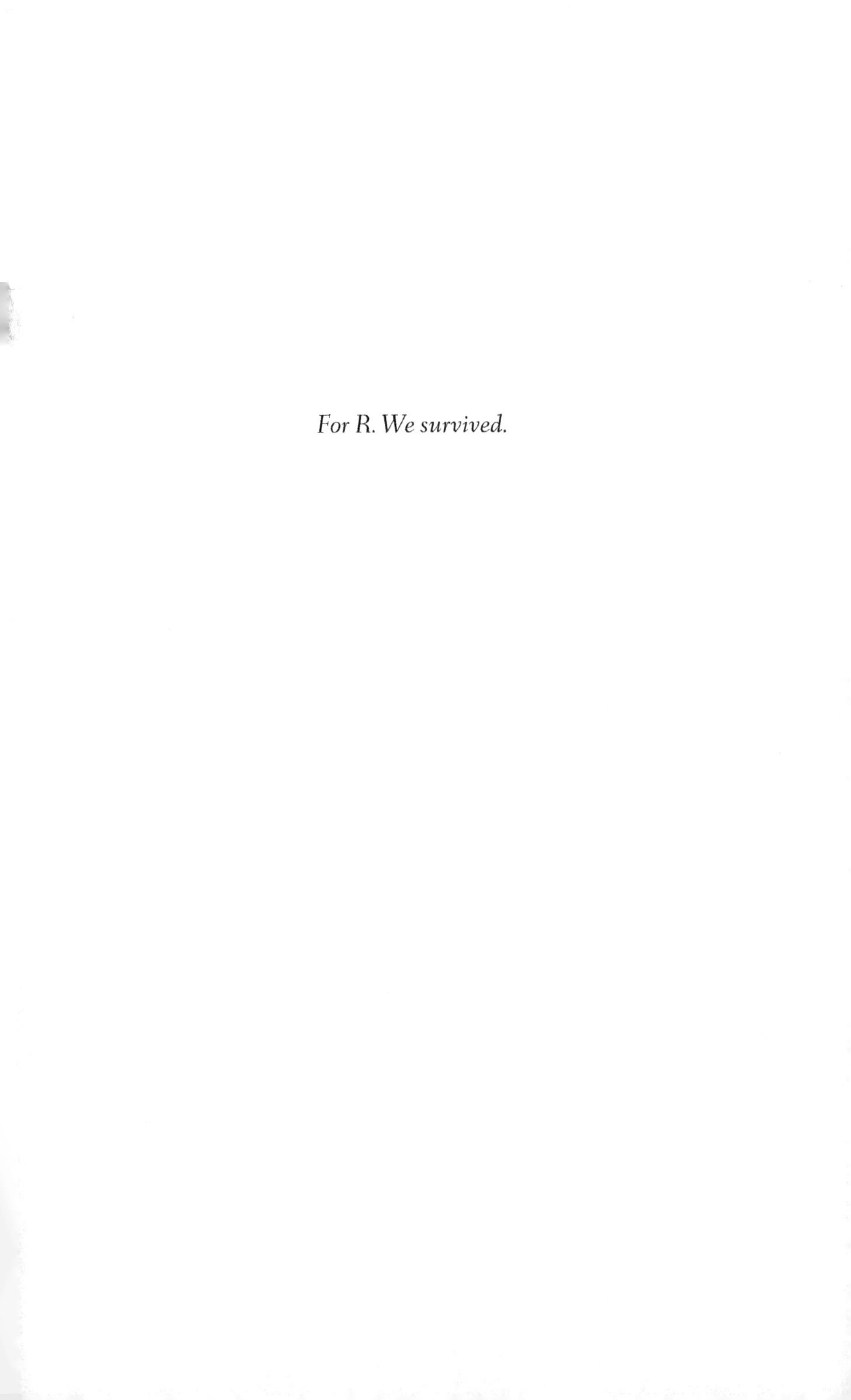

For R. We survived.

AUTHOR'S NOTE

The characters featured in this book were introduced in the earlier Dirty series books. I recommend that before reading *Dirty Like Jude* you be sure to read 2 *Dirty Wedding Nights*; there is a story within called *A Dirty Lie* which is a prequel story to this book.

With love from the beautiful west coast of Canada
(the home of Dirty!)
Jaine

CHAPTER ONE

Roni

I FELT his weight settle over me, the warmth of his naked body. His morning wood, hard and eager between my legs.

I was just barely waking up. My eyes weren't even open yet and he was already pinning me down to the bed. The head of his cock nudged into me as he nuzzled into my neck and kissed my throat... gently. He was already starting to fuck me, and even though I didn't usually let him get so damn snuggly while he did it, I let him.

He knew if he snuck up on me while I was half-asleep, I'd let him.

He filled me, deep, with a low, pleasured groan as he kissed my neck. I wrapped my legs lazily around his waist as his toned body slid against mine. His hips started pumping between my thighs, slowly.

I didn't even bother opening my eyes.

Generally, my boyfriend knew what I liked in bed, and he usually tried to give it to me. Sometimes he tried to change things up, get a little more... gentle. To lukewarm reviews. But despite his best efforts, no matter how he came at it, I wasn't totally thinking about my boyfriend when we were in bed anyway.

Actually, I wasn't thinking about Taze at all. Other than to vaguely register the fact, somewhere in the back of my mind, that I wasn't thinking about him.

Taze was blond, and I was definitely picturing someone a lot... darker.

Darker skin. Darker eyes. Darker hair.

Darker general fucking aura, by miles.

Unfortunately it had come to the point where, if I didn't close my eyes during sex, my boyfriend's sandy-blond hair was, frankly, a total and utter distraction. It jarred me from my fantasies.

Taze was also leaner than the man in my head, but he was strong and muscular enough that if my eyes were closed—or if it was at least very, very dark—I could maintain the illusion enough to reach orgasm. Quickly.

I'd never wanted to just get there so quickly as when I started totally disassociating myself from the person I was actually getting there with.

Minor problem with that: Taze liked to do it *forever*.

With the lights on.

Therefore, eyes closed.

He also liked to do it in the morning, like right now, when there weren't any lights on but the sun was starting to pour in the windows. I didn't love the morning sex. Daylight stripped the illusion away, made it harder, even with my eyes closed, to lose myself in my head.

Plus, there was the guilt. I felt guilty for always closing my eyes. Especially when he asked me to open them, which he sometimes did.

Hoping he wouldn't, I made a sleepy, pleasured sound and bit his throat as I buried my face in his neck. He was pretty busy groaning filthy shit into my ear anyway... which was another problem with sex with Taze. I loved dirty talk. *Loved*. But with Taze, I actually had to mentally drown out his voice, because it sounded nothing like the one in my head.

His voice.

Thinking—obsessively, single-mindedly—about another man

was pretty much what my sex life had been reduced to lately. Or for about the last ten months.

Basically, my entire relationship with Taze.

Maybe because right around the time I'd first hooked up with Taze, a certain dark horse from my past had reared its wicked head. And fucked me.

Literally and figuratively.

God, that fucking night... I was still having flashbacks of it.

All. The. Time.

Even when I was just in bed by myself.

Or when I was buying fucking groceries.

And one thing I was definitely not gonna do was lie to myself about it.

I'd lie to Taze. I knew for a fact that he lied to me. That there was a ton of shit about his life I'd never know.

That was the way it usually went with bikers—outlaw bikers—a breed of which I'd dated a few. And yes, they'd all lied to me. Or lied by omission. And I'd accepted those lies. I'd accepted those men as they were, and I'd accepted Taze just the same.

For now.

But what I wouldn't do was lie to myself about how I felt.

Running into my own personal dark horse—which was exactly how I'd come to think of him now—at Jesse Mayes' rock star wedding, ten months ago, had quite honestly stirred up all kinds of feelings in me.

And not just feelings. Memories. Regrets.

Longings.

All that crap.

Running into him *again* at Jessa Mayes' meet-the-baby party six days ago didn't exactly help matters.

Especially when he cornered me, alone, in the baby's room and virtually incinerated my clothing with that *look* in his hellfire eyes.

Seeing him up close, those molten, panty-melting eyes of his, the thick muscles bulging from his black T-shirt... Hearing his voice, *fuck*, that deep, rough voice of his... Fucking *smelling* him, that intoxicating alpha male smell of his... It all just reminded me of how he'd *felt*—naked, with me.

How fucking amazing his skin felt...

So smooth... silk poured over hard muscle, sliding against mine...

Yeah. I was *almost* there...

Then Taze's phone started buzzing on my bedside table and simultaneously blaring AC/DC, "Dirty Deeds Done Dirt Cheap"—and fucking shattered my fantasy.

Not unusual. Unfortunately.

Taze picked it up, also not unusual. Right when I was *that* close.

I groaned and slapped his shoulder.

I knew it was one of his MC brothers because they all had that same fucking ringtone. There was definitely too much of a good thing, and that ringtone was it.

Especially when I was so *close*.

Taze knew I was close, so he didn't stop fucking me, though his efforts were far less than half-assed as he carried on a stilted, brief conversation—mostly *Uh-huh* and *Yeah, brother* on his end—*while* he fucked me. He'd slid half-off of me, his upper body twisted to the side so he could lean on his elbow next to me as his hips kept grinding. But the angle was no good for me.

No good at all.

I groaned in frustration again as he hung up. He looked at me, his hazel-brown eyes half-lidded with sleep and sex, and blew out a breath. "I've gotta go," he said, his morning voice all raspy with pre-orgasmic tension.

I said the only thing a woman could say in this situation.

"Fuck. Off. Are you serious?"

He dropped the phone and shifted over me, pumping into me a few more times—you know, just to make things worse. At least he looked regretful, especially when I pressed up against him, panting, seeking friction. Then he swore under his breath.

"I gotta pull out, babe."

Then he did pull out. Before I could come.

I went limp in defeat as I watched him ease off the condom and pull on his jeans. "I can't believe you're fucking serious."

"Club business. You know I've gotta go."

He leaned in to kiss me, a quick, sloppy kiss, then left me there, naked on the bed. His gaze dragged over me one last time as he yanked on his ratty T-shirt and scrubbed a hand through his shaggy blond hair. He shrugged on his black leather Sinners cut and grabbed his phone. "Later, 'kay?" Then he left the room, still fighting his erection into his jeans as he went.

I flipped my middle finger at the patch on the back of his cut, the big one underneath the one that said SINNERS MC: the silhouette of a naked woman straddling a motorcycle, backwards, back arched and boobs thrust out. That bitch had fucked with my sex life more times than I cared to count.

I heard Taze leave my place and I sighed. Really, what good was a boyfriend when the one thing this particular one was good at, he wasn't available for?

I considered finishing myself off, obviously, but the mood was kinda ruined. Instead I checked my own phone, which had also buzzed while we were fucking. Yes, I'd been thinking about another man, fetishistically, while we'd fucked, but at least I didn't check my phone while Taze's dick was inside me.

I'd missed a call from Jessa.

I got up and headed into the bathroom to start the shower, dialing her back. I put the phone on the counter on speaker and stepped in under the water while it rang. And rang.

While I waited for Jessa to answer, I ducked my head under the hot water and let it lash down on me, waking me up. Washing away Taze's touch and smell.

Wishing it was someone else's touch, someone else's smell that lingered on my skin.

Jesus. *My life.*

Sex with Taze—my entire relationship with Taze, for that matter —was *supposed* to help me forget about my dark horse. Yet somehow every time I was with Taze, all I could think about was Jude Grayson.

"Roni." Jessa finally picked up. "How are you?"

"Fantastic," I said, really heaping on the sarcasm. She would know it was sarcasm. Ever since we were teenagers, Jessa and I had answered one another's *How are you?* with pretty much the opposite of how we were actually feeling. "You?"

"Stupendous. Do you have time to swing by this morning?"

Yeah. I had a little time. For Jessa, I'd make time. Especially since she'd just had a baby—two weeks ago—and had way less time for me in general.

As long as Jude wasn't gonna be there.

One unnerving, lust-charged confrontation with him while pressed up against baby Nick's crib was enough for me.

"What's up over there?"

"Just hanging with Nicky. Brody's gone to work."

Perfect. If Brody wasn't home, the likelihood of running into Jude at Jessa's place was pretty damn nil.

"I really need to talk to you," she added. "As soon as possible."

Which gave me pause. Jessa never "needed" to talk to me.

"I'll be over as soon as I can," I told her. "With coffee."

CHAPTER TWO

Jude

MAGGIE ONCE ASKED me why I rarely wrote anything down. I told her, *Old habits die hard.*

Maggie was young at the time. She was new to the Dirty team, eager, smart, but innocent. When she asked me what I meant by that, I told her my older brother had taught me not to write things down and the lesson had stuck. I also told her he was teaching me to steal cars at the time.

She never asked again.

Maggie was a quick study like that. You never had to tell her shit twice.

As I stared at the text message on my phone, I realized I was gonna have to make myself a little clearer to one of the newest members of our team.

Lex: Just arrived at Miss Webber's.

I sat up with an annoyed groan. Served me right for checking messages before I was fucking vertical.

I deleted the text and dragged my ass out of bed, rubbing the sleep away. I cleaned up and got dressed in my workout clothes, tossed some jeans and a T-shirt into my gym bag. Made myself a massive breakfast smoothie and drank the entire thing before I let myself deal with Lex.

It was Saturday. And fuck, this week was moving slow.

All week, it had been *Miss Webber* with this guy. No *V*, like I'd told him to call her over text message. No *Wild Card* in casual conversation, like a lot of the other guys I knew called her. No *Veronica*, like I sometimes called her. No *Roni* even, like everyone else in the world called her.

Miss Webber just arrived home.

Miss Webber is having lunch with Miss Mayes.

Pretty sure he assumed I had a thing for *Miss Webber*, and he thought he was gonna get extra points for being polite.

He was half-wrong.

Lex—Lexington, that was his actual name, I couldn't possibly make this shit up—had recently joined my security crew. Lexington Miller Davenport. Dude had the name of an investment company. Or maybe a villain on a soap opera—which was exactly what he looked like, from a distance, if maybe you were drunk. But then maybe you sobered up when he grinned and you glimpsed, on either side of his perfect white porcelain veneers, the shiny platinum canines that told you you'd misjudged him. Badly.

I kinda prayed if Roni noticed him, he didn't try to put her at ease by smiling at her.

Luckily, Roni didn't scare too easily.

And anyway, if Lex knew one thing it was how to disappear.

Like so many others, Lex was a good man with a dark past and a need to make a living. Enter my brother, Piper, who'd recruited him to the West Coast Kings MC, the most powerful outlaw motorcycle club in the Pacific Northwest.

Like many men on the Kings' crew, Lex was hungry for legit, legal work to supplement his other endeavors. Plus, he didn't have a record and was cleared to travel. And so, just like I'd done with several other Kings, I'd gotten Lex legit work—on Dirty's security payroll. As personal bodyguard to Dirty's lead singer, Zane Traynor.

Which had lasted about two nanoseconds. Frankly, Lex irritated the shit out of Zane, which meant I had to reassign him elsewhere.

Granted, most of my guys irritated Zane.

I sighed and threw on my hoodie, ready to get on with this fucking day. Then I dialed Lex. "Call her V," I told him the second he picked up. I hated having to repeat myself. "No more of this *Miss Webber* shit. All you gotta say when you text me is *V*. Think of it as a code and quit writin' me novels. All. You. Need. Is. One. Letter. Fucking *V*. Memorize it."

"Sorry, brother. Thought you'd wanna know I just saw Mr. Murphy leaving Miss Webber's building. V's building. Shit. Do I call her V over the phone?"

"Call her whatever the fuck you want over the phone, as long as no one hears you."

"He's, uh, on his bike. I haven't seen her leave the building yet. You want me to follow?"

Right. Because this surveillance gig would undoubtedly get a hell of a lot more interesting—for him—if he tailed that bike. But no, I did not want him to follow. I wanted him right the fuck where he was, which was as close to Roni as he could get without her noticing him.

"No. Just let me know where she's at. V, coffee shop. V, hair salon. V, fuckin' bible study. Whatever."

"Uh, I don't think she's a bible study sorta girl, brother."

"Anything more eventful than that," I said, ignoring that observation, "you pick up the phone. And Lex?"

"Yeah, boss."

"Call him Mr. Murphy again and I'm gonna shoot you in the ass."

"Alright, then." I heard the smile in his voice as he cracked his gum. It wasn't that Lex was stupid. He was just trying too damn hard.

I hung up on him.

I wondered at what point he was gonna decide that what I had him doing—running surveillance on a woman, for her "protection," when she didn't even know it was happening—was dirty as fuck, and tell me to go fuck myself.

So far, hadn't happened. I'd probably never know why. Like most of my crew, even though I knew every detail there was to know about Lexington Miller Davenport on paper—and other details that would never be written down any-fucking-where—I'd never truly know what made him tick or the exact reasons for his loyalty.

As long as he remained loyal, I didn't give one fuck.

I picked up my keys; my fingers were fucking vibrating. My nerves were twitching, muscles tense, heart slamming blood through every tissue in my body—adrenalin response.

I stood just inside my front door and took a deep, slow breath.

And wondered what the fuck Roni was doing.

And *why* she was still doing it.

Fucking *Mr. Murphy.*

Roni's fuck buddy of the month—well, the year—Tyler "Taze" Murphy, was leaving her place at seven in the morning. Again.

Which meant he'd spent the night.

In Roni's bed.

Again.

With her hot-as-fuck body wrapped around him. With her hands on him. With those jade-green eyes of hers and that thick black hair, and her smell... all over him. And no doubt, her throaty, horny, sweet-ass voice telling him what to do to her.

Because no way that kid knew how to satisfy Roni Webber on his own.

I grabbed my gym bag and slammed out the door, tossing the fucking morning paper aside on my way to the driveway. I had no use for newspapers or the entire "news" reporting industry. When you'd seen the bullshit they printed, the shit they got *wrong*, over and again, about people and things you *knew*, you knew better than to subscribe.

Some previous tenant had subscribed, and the papers just kept coming.

I kept tossing them into the neighbor's yard, and my neighbor kept leaving apples and figs from the trees along her back lane or bread from the bakery up the street on my porch in return. Once, she'd even voluntarily baked a pie for me.

Pretty sure she was hoping I was gonna fuck her, but that was never happening. Way too close to home.

I was rabid-protective of my privacy.

Too bad for other people, I didn't always feel the same about theirs.

I knew a lot about my neighbors, but not because I was interested or looking. I just knew how to read the clues without looking very hard.

When I was interested, I looked harder.

I knew, technically, that Taze was Roni's "boyfriend." Meaning they had some kind of fucked-up relationship where they regularly had sex, held hands in public and, presumably, he pretended he wasn't fucking anyone else and she pretended to believe him.

Not my idea of love, but each to their fucking own, right?

I also knew what Taze looked like naked, which was un-fucking-fortunate. Had a vivid mental image of him—and his piece-of-shit friend—fucking Roni *at the same time,* permanently branded into my gray matter.

If you asked me, Roni Webber deserved better than some twenty-three-year-old blond pretty boy wannabe-thug who'd share her with who-the-fuck-ever at a club party and cheat on her on a weekly basis.

But no one had asked me.

I got into the Bentley and peeled out of the driveway, and just like pretty much every morning, I headed west, toward Jesse's place.

Day-to-day, I was personal bodyguard to Jesse Mayes, shit-hot rock star, Dirty's lead guitarist—and my best friend. In general, I went where he went. Every morning, whenever possible, we started the day together with a jog or a workout. After that I'd take him wherever he needed to be, or we'd split and meet up later; whatever his schedule demanded.

Which was why he'd bought me this car after we came home

from the last Dirty tour and he realized I'd driven the Range Rover into the ground. I tended to do that to cars, and no way Jesse was riding bitch on one of my bikes. So here I was.

This was the only moment of my day that was kinda-sorta my own, early in the morning, before I got to Jesse's.

Before the clock started ticking in my head.

Before I'd answered whatever messages were already waiting on my phone; Lex's was the only one I'd bothered responding to yet.

Everyone else could wait while I had my morning drive.

I put on Soundgarden, "Rusty Cage," and gunned it.

As I drove across the city, I did my usual mental inventory. While I watched Jesse's back, I also managed security for the entire band. Right now, while Dirty was recording an album, that was easier to do on weekdays, when they were all in one place—in the studio. But even on the weekend or if they were scattered across the globe, I knew where they all were. I always knew where they were and what they were doing. Every member of the band—Jesse, Zane, Elle, Seth and Dylan—and my security crew, as well as band management—Brody and Maggie.

I'd checked in with Maggie last night, as usual, before going to sleep, before I could turn off the mental clock.

You need anything?

Her response was brief and the same as it had been all week: *More men.*

Maggie knew better than to write me a fucking novel.

She also knew I was working on the men. We needed a few more solid guys to work security on the upcoming tour, on salary. I also needed to round up a few more bodies, whoever was in town over the holidays, for the New Year's Eve event, if that was happening.

NYE? I'd texted her back.

Her response: *?*

Meaning she didn't have the first clue what was happening on New Year's Eve yet. I knew she'd let me know when she knew more.

Until then, I deleted the conversation.

Throughout the day, every day, I'd check in with her, with Brody, with every single guy on my security crew, or they'd check in with me, keeping me posted on wherever they were at, whatever was going on.

And then, of course, there was my other crew. The Kings.

They were always in contact, too.

And then there was my special project. My secret, admittedly fucked up project. Lex, paid out of my own pocket to run surveillance on Roni Webber.

Because ever since I'd fucked her at Jesse and Katie's wedding, I couldn't get it out of my mind. Couldn't get *her* out of my mind.

I'd asked her, right after we fucked: *You feelin' me, V?* Looked her in the eye and asked her, straight up.

Her answer? *No.*

I'd told her that was good, that she and I weren't going down that road together.

Same as I'd told her when we were young.

And she'd seemed perfectly fucking fine with that.

Problem was—I wasn't.

I told myself nothing had changed between us, that there was no use digging around in the past.

But I wasn't even sure if that was true.

The fact was, I had some kind of lingering, unresolved attraction to this girl that just didn't seem to want to fade the fuck away. And fucking her had just thrown a bucket load of fuel on that long-neglected fire.

After that night, I'd run a security check on her—because old fucking habits. I knew exactly what I'd find: that she was fucking someone else. I thought it would turn me off, I'd stop thinking about her, end of story.

Not fucking so.

When I discovered she was fucking a biker—some kid with the Sinners MC, of all fucking bikers—I couldn't let my morbid curiosity about it go. Morbid, because hearing about a woman you wanted to fuck fucking someone else could only inspire fantasies of that dude's untimely death.

Which meant that in order to avoid resorting to murder, I'd become mildly obsessed with waiting for her to ditch his ass. As if when that happened, I could finally let the obsession go. Because the obsession wasn't about her, right?

It was about the fact that she was sleeping with the fucking enemy.

And then that night. The night I received a distress call from Jesse's sister, Jessa—from a fucking Sinners party. I'd immediately called Brody and my brother and flew there on my bike. I knew Roni would be in the middle of it.

I did not expect to find her in the middle of a fucking three-way with Taze and another Sinner.

The door was open on the bedroom where it was happening, and I'd walked right in. I'd just stood there staring for a long, long moment, trying to absorb what I was looking at, not really believing my own eyes...

This is what it is.

This is what she *is.*

... And not really wanting to believe myself. Even though I *knew.*

I'd always known.

I stared at her until she suddenly met my eyes. Then she shoved both guys—who hadn't even noticed my presence—off of her, grabbed her clothes and stalked right past me, out of the room.

After she left, Taze got in my face a bit. He had no idea who I was other than some dude with a Kings cut on my back; no idea I was in that room because of Roni. But when he realized the Vice President of the West Coast Kings—my brother—was there with me and we were making nice—we were outnumbered fucking ten-to-one, so not much choice on that—he backed down.

I didn't back down. Not with Roni.

I found her in the backyard, where she was smoking up with

some chick, and dragged her aside. I asked her what the fuck she was doing. And I warned her about the Sinners.

I explained to her, very calmly, that there were good men who became bikers, bad men who became bikers, and seriously bad men who became bikers. In my experience, men recruited to the Sinners MC fell somewhere in the realm of seriously fucking bad.

She laughed in my face.

And I tried not to be so bothered by it.

I already knew shit about her new boyfriend she would not want to know, no matter how tough she thought she was—offering herself up for gang bangs and all—but I wouldn't go there. Judging from the attitude she was giving me, she probably wouldn't have believed a word I had to say about Taze anyway.

But I was bothered as fuck by what I'd just seen, the world she was dabbling in, the risks she was taking. And by *her*—acting like she didn't give a shit what I thought about any of it.

I told myself to put her out of my mind right then.

Just forget about her.

Not so easy to do.

A few nights later I saw her again, at a Dirty show at the Back Door. I couldn't even tell if she saw me, but she definitely avoided me like fuck. I had no idea if she was pissed at me or totally over me—if she'd been over me for years and I was fucking kidding myself there was anything left between us to salvage.

If she still wanted me or hated me.

If she just didn't give a damn.

I kept telling myself to leave it alone, to stay away. Just like I did back then, all those years ago.

And just like I did, all over again, when I saw her exactly six days ago at Brody and Jessa's meet-the-baby party—and she brought fucking Taze with her.

It. Pissed. Me. Off.

She basically told me to go fuck myself when I warned her, again, what a piece of shit her boyfriend was.

But even while she did that, I was sucked the hell in by my attraction to her. Again.

Always.

That overwhelming chemistry between us. Pheromones and fireworks and all that shit. That fucking electric spark that always seemed to end up burning me in the ass.

When I'd left that party early, Taze had followed me out to the driveway. Apparently, he recognized me from that night at the Sinner's party, and he was finally starting to connect the dots in his head. *What a coincidence, huh?* he said to me. *Running into you again...* But then Roni had come outside, and he took her by the hand and the two of them left.

After that, I put Lex on her. Every day this week. Without her knowing.

Because telling me to mind my own business about something I'd already decided was my business? Fucking futile.

When I'd found Roni in the baby's room at that party, alone, and pretty much cornered her so I could look her in the eyes without Taze in the room, stood mere fucking inches from her and felt what it was to be close to her again... Then I'd looked her piece-of-shit boyfriend in the eyes and saw what there was to see there, too... I'd definitely decided Roni Webber was my business.

Maybe I was doing what I could to keep her safe from Taze and all his ugly shit, but I was also looking for a way to get her *away* from Taze. Trying to figure out some way to make her leave him.

I'd totally fucking sworn to myself that when that happened, when she ditched his ass, I'd let it go, for good.

Let her go.

Thing about that was, I still wasn't sure if I believed myself.

I wove in and out of residential neighborhoods, avoiding traffic. It was about thirty-five minutes from my place in East Vancouver to Jesse's in Point Grey at this time of morning, less if I avoided the main roads. Watching the backs of people who had targets on them —both rock stars and outlaws—for the past fifteen years had made me cynical, paranoid, and sharp. So I alternated my routes.

Today, it was seventeen minutes to Nudge, Katie's sister's coffee shop. Six minutes to get Katie's coffee—there was a bit of a lineup. Becca probably would've let me cut to the front, but I wasn't that kind of douche.

Coffee in hand, another fourteen minutes would get me to Jesse and Katie's house.

Then I'd turn up my phone.

And the clock would start ticking.

The running clock in my head was an old habit, too. At any given moment of any given day, I knew I could be questioned about where I was—or where Lex or Flynn or Shady or any of my guys were—when X, Y or Z happened.

Questioned by my brother. Questioned by my best-friend-slash-employer. Questioned by Maggie, who signed off on payroll for my security crew.

Questioned by the police.

And since I rarely wrote shit down, that meant I carried it all in my head.

I was just getting back in my car with the coffee when I heard my phone vibrate. I really shouldn't have looked at it.

I looked.

V.

This time, that was all Lex's text said. Which meant he had eyes on her. He'd seen Roni.

She'd left her place.

It was seven fifty-five in the morning. Earlier than she usually left her condo. Roni Webber wasn't really a morning person, and on Saturdays she wasn't due at work until ten. I knew that.

I knew a ton of shit I probably shouldn't know.

I knew Lex would follow her and fill me in along the way, on everything she did today.

I deleted the text.

Not knowing where Roni was or what she was doing—or who she was doing—had now been officially replaced with knowing every-fucking-thing she did.

I still couldn't decide which was worse.

CHAPTER THREE

Roni

I PICKED up a coffee and some breakfast at Nudge to eat on the drive, with tea and scones for Jessa, and headed over to her place. It meant a drive into downtown, over the Lions Gate Bridge and into North Vancouver, in rush hour, then all the way back, also in rush hour, to get to work on time. It would give me only a half hour or so at her place, but I didn't mind.

Right now, I'd take pretty much any chance to hang with Jessa that I could get.

We'd become closer this year, ever since she'd moved back. As close as we'd been as teenagers; maybe more so. But with a newborn baby literally sucking her energy, I expected to fall down her priority list.

"*Please*, come in," she gushed when she answered her front door. "I'm starved for adult conversation." She was cradling baby Nicholas in her arms, and he was feeding. As usual.

This would've been Jessa's permanent social media status these days, if she were on social media: *Boob in baby's mouth*.

"Baby Nick's not much of a talker, huh?"

"Unfortunately, no."

She gave me an awkward hug as we tried not to squish the baby. He wriggled and made a slurping sound, and I told her for the millionth time how adorable he was. I didn't even have to exaggerate; Jessa and Brody's son really was the dictionary definition of adorable.

I followed her through the living room, the one at the front of the house that was rarely used, and into the dining room, where Jessa settled onto the antique couch that had come from Brody's grandparents and was her favorite spot to sit and nurse Nick. It put her kinda central in the house, where she could see both into the kitchen and out into the backyard. She had a bunch of pillows propped up to support her arms on either side of her while she cradled the baby, like a breastfeeding throne.

I put the tea and scones on the edge of the table, within her reach, and she thanked me profusely.

"Do you want some breakfast?"

God love her, she actually asked me that, right while she was smack in the middle of doing what she was doing.

"No worries, babe. I already ate. Let me get you a plate."

I started into the adjoining kitchen... and stopped in my tracks.

I was not a kitchen girl. Jessa Mayes totally was.

She had the fancy electric mixer, the knife block, the industrial blender, the giant food processor, all gleaming and lined up just waiting to be used, her pretty tea cozies and matching tea towels usually all clean and ready, so that she could whip up hearty, healthy, low-cal meals at a moment's notice, for herself, for her man, for whoever dropped by. That was just Jessa. Didn't hurt that Brody had hired on a part-time housekeeper to help keep everything spotless.

Not today.

The entire surface area of the kitchen was strewn with dishes, some clean, some not, and baby gear—clean bottles lined up to dry, nipples, milk collection bags and pacifiers and random toys. I even glimpsed what had to be Brody's underwear mixed in with the clean towels and baby linens that had been dumped on one counter, waiting to be folded.

"Holy shit. The orphanage called. They want their kitchen back."

Jessa sighed, a sound of sleep-deprived surrender.

"How many babies do you have again?"

"*One*," she said, unamused. "And until you have one, I kindly request that you do not judge."

"Not judging. Just... startled." I found a clean plate for her and tossed a scone on it, then pulled out my phone and texted my boss that I was going to be late. He wouldn't care. Sadly, he had a thing for me, so there was that. And since I didn't care enough to make a fuss if he threatened to fire me, we both knew he wouldn't. To be sure, I made it sound like a somewhat-family emergency.

Helping my sick friend with her baby. Be in just a tad late. So sorry.

Then I got to work tying on one of Jessa's cutesy aprons and searching for the surface of her countertop under the layers of what-not, despite her half-assed protests. "I'm going in. If I'm not out by Monday, call in reinforcements."

Jessa sighed in surrender again, this time gratefully. "Thank you. Just a bit, okay?"

"Where's your housekeeper lady?"

"She's not in until Monday. She does Monday, Wednesday and Saturday now."

"Today's Saturday, babe."

"Yeah. This week she switched it to Friday."

"She was here *yesterday*?" I opened the dishwasher and found it empty. I started filling it with dirty dishes, rinsing as I went.

"I thought you weren't judging," she said, through a mouthful of scone.

"I'm not. I'm not judging you. But Brody can't clean a kitchen?"

"He hasn't had time."

"Where is he?"

"He had some stops to make this morning before some meeting."

"Yeah? How's the album going?"

I assumed it was going amazing, like every other time I'd asked.

Brody managed Dirty, and they were an amazing band, pretty much end of story. Really, it was a courtesy ask, because I knew how important this album was to her and to Brody. Because this was the first time Jessa had co-written songs with Dirty since their first album a decade ago.

"Incredible," she said. "Everything I've heard is incredible. I wish I could be more excited about it, but honestly, I'm just so drained." She nodded at the baby on her boob for emphasis.

"Literally," I quipped.

She grunted, like laughing was just too much work. "How's Taze?"

I couldn't even help rolling my eyes. "The usual. He's decent in bed, usually, but honestly I'm not even thinking about him when we're together anyway." Yes, I went straight to sex, which I assumed she was asking about, because where Taze and I were concerned there really wasn't much else to discuss. "Do you ever do that? Think about someone else...?"

"Someone other than Brody?" she said, like she had literally no idea what I was talking about.

"Of course not. You're in bed with the man of your dreams." I was in bed with the man of my dreams too, but only in my head. Because in reality, the man of my dreams was kind of a nightmare. "And this is why I hate you. Because you probably actually fantasize about Brody fucking you while Brody's fucking you."

"I do," Jessa admitted. "But it wasn't always that way. I didn't always have the man I wanted. I used to think about Brody when I was with other people. I know how that feels. It's painful, not being in love with the one you're with."

It was nice of her to say; she knew I wasn't in love with Taze. But really, when had I ever been in love?

I could count the time. On one finger.

One incredibly stupid finger.

I shrugged. "Usually, it's reality."

She glanced at me, but her attention was split, still stuck on the baby on her boob. "Who would you be in bed with if you could?"

"How would I know? I haven't found anyone worth replacing Taze for yet. When I meet him, I'll let you know."

It was true enough, though it was kind of sidestepping the question.

I watched her for a minute, trying to eat her scone without dropping crumbs on Nick, fussing over his blankie, tucking in his little hands. The dishwasher was full, and I hip-checked it shut.

"And *this* is why I love you," I told her. "You're in the middle of literally keeping another human being alive with your life-fluid, and you still make the effort to follow up my casual inquiry about your man with the requisite casual inquiry about my man. As if Brody and Taze are in any way equal."

Jessa just smiled, but she was still looking at Nick. "If you care about Taze, you can consider them equal."

"Jessa. Your man is devoted, successful, wealthy, and, you know, a grownup. Mine is a man-baby with a *Star Wars* poster over his bed—"

"What?" Jessa started laughing and Nick squirmed in her arms. "Like, Darth Vader or Princess Leia in the gold bikini? Please don't tell me it's Ewoks or something."

"It's Han Solo and what's-his-name. Chewbacca?"

"You're kidding me."

"I'm totally fucking serious. Do not even get me started on the centerfolds."

Jessa wrinkled her nose. "Cliche, much?"

"Very much. Which is why we never do it at his place. I could stand looking at young Harrison Ford while I'm in bed, but the rest of it is untenable. *And* he ditched me halfway to orgasm this morning."

"Halfway?"

"Three-quarters of the way. He had to *leave*. I'm three-quarters considering never speaking to him again."

Jessa made a sympathetic sound, though I wasn't sure if it was for me or baby Nick. "He probably feels bad for having to leave. I'm sure all he really wants to do is please you, Roni."

"Where on Earth would you get that from?"

Jessa looked up. I was folding her laundry and she looked me over, pointedly. For the first time, I really noticed the faint purplish circles under her big brown eyes. Jessa was gorgeous—literally, lingerie-model gorgeous—but right now, she looked like a wilted flower someone had forgotten to water.

"You're seriously asking me that," she said, "while I'm wearing a nursing bra with milk-absorbing pads and I stink of spit-up and I haven't had a proper shower in three days? Take a look in the mirror. You're twenty-seven and a total babe. You have all that glossy black hair and epic cleavage and a manicure, and your own condo. He's twenty-three. He lives in some nasty room in his biker clubhouse, right? With centerfolds on the walls? He probably worships the ground you walk on."

I stared at her. "Why aren't you showering? What about your nanny person? What's-her-name?"

"She got sick and had to bail a few days this week and I didn't want some stranger coming over, so it's been a bit around the clock. And Brody's been so busy with the album, the upcoming tour..."

"Fuck that. Hand me that baby and go have yourself a fucking shower."

"Okay. I will." I could see the relief in her body, the total gratitude, as her shoulders softened. But Nick was still firmly attached.

I made a mental note to tell Brody to hire on some more help for her, or something. It wasn't like he couldn't afford it. And knowing Jessa, she hadn't actually told him how tired she was. He probably didn't realize how much help she actually could've used while he was working. It wasn't like she had a mom or a sister who could come around and watch the baby for an hour here or there so she could have a bath. Jessa was on her own, had always been on her own in some ways, and I knew she wasn't used to asking for help.

I also made a mental note to make myself more available. Check on her, even when she didn't ask.

"Babe. I hope you know you don't have to feign interest in my bullshit with Taze just so you can get a shower. I'm capable of holding a baby for thirty minutes for you."

"It's not that." She looked at me, kinda hopefully. "I wanted to talk to you about Dirty."

"Dirty?"

"Yeah. Here's the thing." She sat up a little straighter, like this was important... which was odd, since Dirty really had nothing to do with me, and vice versa. "They'll be finished recording the album next week, and then they start up promotion for it right away. They leave on tour in January. But Brody says they're getting restless and kinda driving him up the wall about it. It's been so long since they've played a full show live, and apparently they really want to do a show before the tour starts, just something fun, and they've been asking Brody to put something together. He says it has to be over the holidays, here in Vancouver, since that's the only time they'll all be available and they'll all be home for the holidays."

"Cool. Put me down for a handful of tickets. You really didn't need to invite me in person," I teased. "I know I'm pretty essential at a party, but..."

"Brody thinks it should be intimate," she went on, "but still kinda big. Someplace more special than the Back Door, a higher capacity venue, since they'll be playing some of the songs from the new album for the first time..."

"Sounds about right."

"No media. Just fans. And he wants it on New Year's Eve."

"Oh. Well, I can come late, after my thing." I had an event at a pub I was working that night already, so hopefully I could make it work. "What time do you think they'll play until?"

"I don't know. The thing is... the nightclub Brody was hoping to get, the one where they held auditions for the documentary series and filmed the big reveal show with Seth, is already booked."

"The Ruby." I knew the place. I knew the owner, actually. "I'm not surprised. Every decent place in town and then some will already be booked. Brody must know that."

"Right. And that's the thing... His plate's kinda already overflowing, overseeing all the promotion around the album launch, planning the tour, and now the baby... Maggie's just as busy. So they'll need a promoter to put this show together. Brody was saying he's gonna bring one on next week."

The wheels were starting to turn in my head. I could pass her a few names, for sure. But Brody definitely had better connections than I did in the rock 'n' roll world.

"So." Jessa blinked her big brown eyes at me. "Here's where you come in."

I stared at her, suddenly getting her meaning. "Me?"

"Why not you?" she said. "No one throws a party like you, Roni."

I really could not argue with that.

I'd been doing the party promotion thing, part-time, for the last three years. Ever since I realized it was a thing. That I could actually get paid doing what I loved to do anyway.

I'd always been a party girl. And I'd always thrown fantastic ones.

My milkshake brought all the boys and girls to the yard. It had just always been that way.

So, becoming a promoter was a no-brainer.

But I'd never worked with Dirty. I didn't work with bands. I promoted nightclub events. Theme nights with bubbles and pajama parties and college kids on E. I hosted a regular night at a local club, did special events at other bars around town, and worked mostly with small to mid-list local DJs, and sometimes visiting talent.

Small-time shit compared to Dirty.

I had no particular aspirations to work in rock concert promotion. My loftiest aspiration, these days, ever since meeting DJ Summer at Jessa's baby shower last month, was to work with her. It hadn't happened yet, but it would.

I'd definitely worked my ass off to get to where I was already, and I was pretty bent on making my way to the forefront of the local party scene—so I could one day promote talent of DJ Summer's calibre... and beyond. But it wasn't that easy. It took time to do it right.

It took time to meet the right people, foster the right relationships, and build a name for yourself in a competitive, challenging, and often weirdly cutthroat environment.

An environment where, admittedly, you didn't get offers like this —like Dirty, one of the hottest rock bands in the world—dropped into your lap.

But.

"It's November," I said carefully. "You want me to find a location for this New Year's Eve event—in November? Every place in town is booked solid by now. Including the bar where I'm already promoting a New Year's Eve party."

"So you hand that off to someone else," Jessa said. "I know you've been wanting to give up the day job forever. Promote bigger parties. I also know the money in real estate is good, and you have a mortgage to pay. That you need something *big* to make that leap financially."

All true.

My day job for the last six years had been doing temp work in the real estate industry. Currently I worked at the display suite office for a real estate developer. I ran the welcome desk and pretty much worked alone; it was so slow they didn't even keep an actual sales rep on staff, so I was it. It was stunning how few people actually came through the fancy office, which had a full-sized display suite in it. Most of the clientele were overseas buyers who never set foot in the display office, who bought the condos sight unseen and didn't give a fuck whether the one they chose had the black-and-gray color scheme or the sand-and-cream one, because they were never going to live in it. They were buying the condos as investments, as rental properties.

Which meant that the majority of my day was spent on my laptop, on social media, working on my true love: party promotion.

Did I actually want to work in real estate? Fuuuck no.

But...

"It's not just about the money," I told her. "It's also about my reputation and making the right moves. Leaving the steady paycheck behind would be pretty much a go-big-or-go-home situation, in all respects. I'm not sure I'm ready for that anyway."

"This is as big as it gets," Jessa said. "This is Dirty. Who knows where this could lead? You really can't turn this down, Roni."

"This is late November," I reminded her, doing the calculation in my head. "New Year's Eve is five weeks away."

Jessa looked entirely unsympathetic, in that way a new mother did. Like, *You get to sleep, what the hell are you complaining about?*

"Dirty wants to throw a party," she said. "They want to play a show. Someone out there would kill to host that show at their venue. All you have to do is find him or her, sell tickets—which will not be a challenge—and get yourself paid. You can probably negotiate a pretty decent cut. Dirty isn't doing this for the money. If they want the money, they'll play a stadium. This is a small gig for them, for shits and giggles. But it's huge for *you*."

"Five weeks from New Year's Eve," I repeated.

Jessa shifted her squirming son from one breast to the other. "So you're saying you won't do it? You won't even try? Instead, Maggie gets on the phone to every promoter she and Brody know, and someone else jumps at the chance to plan a Dirty show?"

Fuck.

And no. I wasn't about to let that happen.

"If I do this, I'll take that generous cut of ticket sales," I informed her.

"You can work that out with Brody."

I crossed my arms at my waist and stared her down. "And incidentally, why am I not having this conversation with him?"

Jessa just looked at me, and in her silence, it became clear.

"Because I don't have the gig yet."

Brilliant. She wanted me to find a venue, *then* present Brody with what I had to offer.

I sighed and took a few steps closer to her, gazing down at her baby boy. "Remind me never to underestimate your mother," I told him, nudging his little foot.

Jessa smiled. "You'll do it? Roni, this would be sooo good for you. And just think how much fun it would be if you worked with the band, with Brody... with me..."

I didn't respond to that. I was still thinking it through. Fun, sure. But I didn't love the position it put me in.

If I found a venue, it would definitely give me more to bargain with when I brought it to Brody.

But if I went around town trying to book a venue for a Dirty show... it's not like Brody wasn't going to find out. Which meant I probably couldn't *say* it was for a Dirty show upfront; not until after I actually had the venue.

"Fuck."

Jessa just beamed her gorgeous, lingerie-selling smile up at me.

I sighed again and sat down next to her. "What other intel have you got? I want every detail you know so far. Motivate me."

"All I know is the band is really keen on the show. Like *really* keen. And..." She hesitated.

"And?"

"And... this isn't public yet. Which means you can't tell anyone."

"You know I won't."

"It's gonna be Elle's last show until after she has the baby."

"Oh."

"Yeah. So it's kind of a big deal for the band, and the fans."

"Uh, I would say so." Elle was Dirty's bassist, and she was a few months pregnant now. But she'd been with Dirty forever.

"She and Seth have been really private about the pregnancy so far," Jessa said, "keeping it out of the media, but that won't last much longer. She's really starting show, and the band is planning to announce to the fans at this show, for the first time, that Elle won't be on the tour. I mean, she'll be on the tour, traveling with Seth, but she won't be playing shows. She won't even be at a lot of the shows. She told me she's spoken with her doctors about it, gone over her touring schedule with them, and they've told her that the repeated exposure to the excessive noise levels at the constant concerts, sound checks, everything, pose a risk to the pregnancy. And it's not just possible hearing loss to the baby, but preterm labor, that kind of thing."

"I see." Honestly, I'd never thought about that. I'd wondered how she was going to play with a baby belly, how tired she might be, but that was about it.

The noise thing hadn't even occurred to me.

"So, Elle's going to take a step back," Jessa said. "She already told me she was worried about how far she could take it, how much energy she could bring to the stage, to give the fans and the band and the music what they deserve. I've been through a pregnancy and I don't blame her. Even if there was no possible harm to the baby, she doesn't need that kind of pressure right now."

"For sure."

"Which means... this is gonna be a special show." Jessa gave me a slight smile. "No pressure."

"Oh, none at all," I said.

"In terms of the venue itself," she added, ignoring my sarcasm, "someplace with a similar capacity to the Ruby would probably be ideal. And I know Brody never approves of a venue without Jude's okay. Security has to meet his specifications. So you'll have to go over all of that with him, I guess."

Right.

Jude.

"Of course."

"I think security's gonna be extra tight at this one. When Brody said no media, he really meant no media. He wants this to be a special night for the fans. For the band and for Elle. So, I guess what I'm saying is... You'd be a total idiot not to take the opportunity to be a part of this, Roni. If you pull it off, they'll really love you for it."

She was right, probably.

And it would be a special night, clearly. For all of them.

For me?

I felt it sinking in; what this could be, for me. The pivotal event of my career. The event that took me from part-time party pusher to top promoter.

On the other hand, if I fucked it up, I could jeopardize everything I'd worked for these last three years—mainly my reputation, which was basically everything in my line of work. Not to mention potentially burning bridges—professionally, maybe even personally—with Dirty, with Brody, with whatever venue owner I might rope into this.

With Jude?

I didn't want this to be a factor in my decision-making, but there it was, nagging at the back of my mind...

If I fucked this up, would it also burn my bridge with Jude?

Granted, the bridge between us was a long-ass, rickety old bridge that wove in and out of the dark like a confused drunkard.

But it was a bridge all the same.

Despite whatever had happened between the two of us, I knew that if I ever called Jude up in the middle of the night asking for help, he would come. It was his nature, no matter how he felt about me.

Which meant that no matter what came of this event, Jude would still pull my ass out of a burning building; he'd do that for pretty much anyone.

No matter, even, if I totally fucked this up.

"Okay," I told Jessa. "I'll do it."

Because professionally—hopefully—it was worth the risk.

And as far as Jude Grayson was concerned, there really was no risk at all.

Jude didn't care about me anyway. He wasn't about to magically start.

CHAPTER FOUR

Jude

8:09 am.

The clock starts ticking.

The automatic gate rolled aside and I eased the Bentley into Jesse's driveway, parking alongside the sunshine-yellow Jeep he'd bought for Katie last year, to get her off her skateboard. We'd both tried to talk her out of her vehicle selection, but the girl wanted what she wanted—it was a Jeep, a used Jeep, or she kept the skateboard as her transportation method of choice.

She won.

Honestly, Katie usually won.

When she answered the front door in her paint-splattered jeans and Blondie T-shirt, a bandana in her dark hair and a smile on her rosy-cheeked face, it was easy to see why.

She took the cherry-vanilla latte I'd brought for her, her favorite coffee, and smacked a kiss on my cheek. I didn't bring her a coffee every morning, but close.

I followed her into the sunroom, her little home studio, where she was setting up to paint. She showed me the final art for the cover of the new Dirty album—*To Hell & Back*, their tenth anniversary album, which they were just finishing recording.

"Love it, darlin'," I told her.

I loved *her*. Whatever sweetness I had in me? My best friend's wife brought it out.

While I waited for Jesse to haul his ass downstairs and Katie chatted me up about the painting she was working on—a portrait of her niece—Delia texted.

Are you coming tonight?

I answered her right away, because when the wife of your MC's President texted you, you answered right away, if possible. And you did it politely.

Yes. What can I bring?

She wouldn't answer. She never did. She didn't expect me to bring anything, would probably give me royal shit if I lifted a finger to bring a thing. The wives and girlfriends took care of the food at a Kings family barbecue. Prospects took care of the booze. End of story.

I deleted the conversation.

8:27 am.

We headed out for a jog, just Jesse and me. Up Point Grey Road, where he lived, and out along the beach. He talked about the album, worked out his thoughts about the last couple of songs Dirty would be recording this coming week. I listened.

Jesse Mayes was a textbook extravert, worked shit out while he talked, got off on vibing with people. As long as it wasn't emotional shit. When it came to emotional shit, he shut right down.

I was the opposite.

I was always thinking things through in my head before I opened my mouth. But when it came to emotional shit, I cut right to the chase.

We understood each other.

It had always been like this.

We were a duo, symbiotic. Leaned on each other's strengths. Lifted each other up. Bounced shit off one another. Made decisions together. Not all decisions, but most. I'd looked out for Jesse ever since we became friends at thirteen. He'd looked out for me.

He'd never been more pissed at me than when he'd found out,

just a few months ago, that I'd failed to fill him in on the extent of things between his little sister, Jessa, and Seth, Dirty's other guitarist, when we were all teenagers.

Back then, it was all sex, drugs and rock 'n' roll—but not for Jesse's little sister.

He was trying to protect her from that shit.

I was trying to protect Jesse from MC shit. I always would. Jesse Anderson Mayes, rock star, just didn't belong in that world.

My other world.

Even Jesse didn't know what was going on right now, the extent of things, the shit that was on the table. The proposal my brother had made me, the decisions to be made.

The pressure of the clock ticking in my head.

9:38 am.

Breakfast with Jesse and Katie; Katie made pancakes and I ate one, for her. Jesse would be home with her today, wouldn't need me. If he did and I couldn't come, if I was busy with Kings shit, I always had other guys I could send in.

Jesse brought up the New Year's Eve show. "Zane's been griping about it."

I assured him, "Brody will come up with something."

I checked my messages.

Brody: Video shoot on the 11th. Church/concert concept.

The band's first video shoot for the new album was a go. It was happening at a sound stage, with a replica "church" set to mimic the church where the band wrote and rehearsed, and would incorporate a staged concert. Which meant a large crew and an audience—tight security.

I replied. *Got it.*

Then I deleted the conversation.

Flynn checked in. He was headed up the coast with Seth and Elle; they were spending the weekend in Whistler. The mountains there didn't have much snow yet. What else there was to do in

Whistler in November but rent a lux hotel room and fuck, I didn't know, so I figured that was Seth's plan.

Delete.

10:22 am.

I hit the road to Zane's place in West Vancouver. Planned to tell him how good he'd sounded yesterday at the studio. Wondered if he really knew how good this album was gonna be. If he realized how crazy this year would be, for all of us. And that he'd be right in the middle of it.

Our frontman.

The dirty voice of Dirty. The sex symbol / rock idol who was really just a mortal dude who never thought that far into the future, about what might be coming... and one of my best friends. And I was worried about him.

I always worried about Zane on tour.

About his sobriety. His fucking sanity.

And now, I was more worried about him than I'd been in a long time. It was how he'd been acting this year. He wasn't coming clean with me, and I was used to that, at times, but this was different.

It was the Maggie thing, maybe. That fucking secret-as-shit Maggie thing that he thought I didn't know.

And if I wasn't gonna be there, on tour, to keep his shit straight, I'd be even more worried about him.

10:54 am.

Zane answered the door of his multi-multi-million-dollar house wearing a cheap T-shirt that said *Drunk Chicks Think I'm Hot*, flannel pajama pants and rimless glasses. Hardly anyone knew Zane sometimes wore glasses. To read. To watch movies. Shit like that. Not so much because he hid the fact, but because it didn't fit the image of Zane that the world knew and loved—sex-crazed Viking rock god—so the world tended to disregard it, in that way that the world often chose to disregard the fact that celebrities were actually human.

We shot some pool while we talked about the album. I won. Zane was the one who owned a fucking pool table, but I always won.

He accused me of practicing at the clubhouse. I didn't. I was just good at pool.

Shady dropped by, even though he didn't have to. I'd put him on Zane, as Zane's newest bodyguard, and so far, so fucking good. Zane had a hard time handling anyone on his back as often as someone needed to be there, though I figured I'd finally found his match in Shady.

Another thing not many people knew about Zane: the way to his heart was definitely through his funny bone. At least, if you were a dude.

A veteran King, Shady was an old friend of my brother's, and every time he got telling one of his wacky stories, Zane pretty much shit his pants laughing; so far, a bromance of epic proportions had been born.

Fingers crossed on that lasting an entire tour.

Shady kicked Zane's ass at pool; Zane accused him of practicing at the clubhouse. Then Zane took a call.

Con checked in by text, said he'd see me later at the clubhouse.

Delete.

Zane got off his phone. "Maggie says I've got a bunch of promo shit, interviews and whatever, week after next."

I listened—I always fucking listened—to the way he said *Maggie*, watched the way his face changed when he'd talked to her on the phone, the way his entire fucking physiology changed when he mentioned her. And wondered why the rest of the world was so fucking blind, when some shit was so obvious to me.

Piper messaged me about the club meeting: C400.

Church at 4:00.

A totally different kind of church.

Delete.

That feeling of being ripped in two.

Not sure if I was actually going on tour with Dirty this time, or staying right here.

My brother had been putting on some major pressure this year, ever since he became Vice President of the Vancouver chapter—the mother chapter—of the West Coast Kings. Wanting me to patch over as a Vancouver King, give up my Nomad status for good.

No one in the Dirty world knew yet. Not Zane. Not Brody. Not Jesse.

My loyalty was being torn right down the middle. But if I was doing my job well, no one would see it.

It was my job to protect them, not the other way around.

12:06 pm.

I left Zane's, headed back to my place to drop off the car. One of my security guys, Bishop, who was currently assigned to Jessa Mayes as her driver, checked in; he was taking her and the baby to Dolly's, then Brody was meeting them, taking them to dinner.

Delete.

At home, I layered on warmer clothes and my leathers, my cut with the West Coast Kings patches. The one on the back, the bottom rocker, that read NOMAD.

Hopped on my Harley and rode out to see my brother. Wondered why I felt late.

All the time, lately, I felt like I was running late. Under the gun.

Running against time, when I wasn't late at all.

2:11 pm.

I arrived at my brother's acreage. My mood shifted as I parked my bike in his gravel drive. I was aware of it, fully conscious of this shift, aware that my MC life was different than my life with the band. Heavier. That I carried it differently. That I was different, from one life to the other, in some ways.

My brother was on his phone when I let myself in. He chucked a baseball at me, at my head. I ducked; he missed.

He laughed.

Why he had a baseball, I had no idea. I tossed it into one of the potted plants some woman from his past had left in the living room, clinging to life.

I watered the fucking neglected plants from a Coke bottle I found in the kitchen. It looked like Piper hadn't done his dishes in a week. The place was a mess.

In his defense, he was rarely home.

But the fact was my brother was kind of a pig, more ways than one.

I cleaned up his disgusting kitchen, a bit. Only for him.

I'd never loved someone so fucking fiercely as I did my brother, even Jesse, and I'd kill for Jesse. I loved a lot of people, would take a bullet for a lot of people, and not just because they paid me to do it. But I loved my brother most.

Spent one particular dark winter, nine years ago, hating him fucking fiercely. But that could never last. Especially when he reminded me so damn much of Dad.

My older brother, Jeremy "Piper" Grayson, was this contradiction of big and menacing, muscles and tats, scars, and this fucking angelic face. Just like our dad.

Funny how genes worked.

Piper was the spitting image of our dad—blond and dimpled, blue-eyed, all Nordic-British regal cheekbones, but our mom's full lips—and mom's personality. Passionate and whip-sharp, fierce, intense, given to flights of imagination. Dreamed big, maybe too big.

On the other side, I looked like our mom.

Mom's parents were Hawaiian and Brazilian, and I got everything that came with that. My brother got a killer tan to go with his blue eyes. He looked like a California kid.

I looked like the only half-brown boy in a lily-white mountain town, and got my ass kicked regularly because of it.

I hated growing up in that pissant town, and after our parents split, hated having to go back, spending summers at Dad's place. Lived for my new life in the city at Mom's, even though her and Piper were like oil and water by then: too much alike, too fucking incompatible.

And even though I looked like her, Mom saw right through me. Right to my dad.

She told me, often, that God had made a carbon copy of my dad's personality, and that carbon copy was me. Despite the fact that she once fell in love with the man and gave birth to his two sons, it wasn't a compliment.

I knew she was right. I had my dad's grudging sense of humor, his restlessness, his loyalty. His stubbornness. His heart.

His unwillingness to change.

Like my dad, I was a lone wolf in the middle of a pack, struggling to balance those two disparate sides of himself.

Unlike my dad, I had *two* packs to negotiate.

2:27 pm.

Piper got off his fucking phone and we rode to the clubhouse.

And these moments... On my bike, in the wind, with my brother. These were the moments that made me feel the most alive.

The most free.

2:48 pm.

I sat down to lunch with the boys at the clubhouse. The bar was packed, whole lotta dudes from nearby chapters rolling in, some for the meeting, others just for the party afterward.

Sat right next to Ben, road name Blazer. Not because he "blazed" up the road or anything like that. Because he once wore a blazer to a Kings party and no one would ever let him forget it. Good guy, old friend I hadn't seen in a while. Also the Vancouver Kings' Secretary, I gave him the respect he was due.

Did I love that I was now sitting next to a man—that I was in a room with two men, actually—who had, once upon a time, fucked Roni Webber? Not so fucking much.

But I'd been forced to make peace with that uncomfortable reality years ago.

These were my brothers.

Nothing would ever change that.

3:28 pm.

Jesse texted.

Flynn checked in again from Whistler.

Delete.

Delete.

The routine.

The timetable in my head.

The mental tally of everyone who needed me.

4:00 pm.

Church—club meeting in a room in the back of the clubhouse that we called the chapel. Fourteen men present. Not the entire club, just the local and semi-local officers.

And me.

Not local, not an officer. Just a Nomad with special privileges. Because everyone knew if I was local, if I was a Vancouver King, my brother would yank me up the ranks and slap a patch on my chest I wasn't ready for. Would maybe never be ready for.

So they put up with me, sitting in on their meetings. Because, in truth, they needed me.

They needed us all.

Heavy shit was coming down. Shit I did not wanna think about, did not wanna deal with, but had to.

I didn't need the Kings. I had Dirty. I'd always had Dirty.

The Kings needed me.

My brother needed me.

4:41 pm.

Meeting adjourned.

I passed by the photo of my dad up on the wall in the hallway outside the chapel—fallen members of the Kings MC. My dad had been up on that wall for five years. I knew it meant something to my club brothers, that it was important to have the photos there, my dad's photo there. But it was still hard for me to see it every time I was here.

Sometimes I didn't even look. It was too hard to see that face, that face that could've been my brother's, that one day would very possibly be my brother's, grinning down at me.

Today, I looked.

When I walked out into the club bar, the women were starting to arrive. To set up for the family barbecue. In summer, the party would be out back; tonight, it would be in the bar.

Seth had texted me a photo. A blurry image of a blobby thing that looked vaguely like a humanoid alien, obviously from the ultrasound Elle had yesterday.

I texted him back. *Looks just like you.*

Then I deleted the conversation.

I was aware that my cell provider could always be compelled to cough up my phone records. Not much I could do about that. But the thought of dropping my phone and some fucknut picking it up, breaking into it and seeing my friends' personal shit, like ultrasound photos of Seth and Elle's baby, and leaking it to some shitty magazine so they could slap it on the cover—*First Photos of Rock Star Baby!*—really fucking disturbed me.

Cynical.

Paranoid.

Sharp.

5:23 pm.

I stood in the bar amidst the families that had converged in this unlikely place, nursing my beer. Dinner would be eaten. The families would stay a while. Eventually, they'd leave.

The girls would pour in.

The party would go all night.

Same.

Old.

Thing.

I wouldn't drink much. I never did.

I might not stay long.

Everyone in the band was pretty much in for the night. Jesse was in for the night. With Katie. I'd officially lost my wingman. Wing*men*. I couldn't remember the last time Zane had been on the prowl.

Everywhere I looked, the single guys were dropping like flies. They'd all drank the relationship Kool-Aid.

Shady texted. He'd come to the clubhouse for lunch but left when the meeting got underway, was now with Zane for the night. Braiding each other's beards or whatever.

Bromance.

Delete.

Lex: V. Home.

It was Saturday evening. She was probably home for dinner, get ready for whatever she was doing tonight. Roni Webber wasn't the kind of girl to sit at home on a Saturday night.

Unless, maybe, if Taze was coming over.

Delete.

7:06 pm.

Brody sent a group text, with photos: *Nick spit up in my truck. There's baby milk barf between the seats.*

The responses came in pretty quick.

Dylan: GOOD BOY. (Fist pump emoji.)

Jesse: Dude. Get a new truck.

Zane: Good thing it's November.

Jesse: ??

Zane: If it was summer the heat would bake in the barf smell.

Brody: Fuck me.

The petty complaints of my wealthy friends. Brody had a healthy baby boy and the woman of his dreams—Jessa Mayes was a lingerie model, for fuck's sake—and he *could* buy a new truck, if it came down to it.

Plus, I knew a brilliant detailer who'd take care of it. If he could make DNA disappear, he could handle a little baby barf.

Me: Take it to my guy. Have Bishop swing back for you.

I deleted the conversation.

7:18 pm.

I looked around at my brothers in the bar. The harder lives lived. Men with larger complaints, but who weren't necessarily any less well-off, in terms of family. Love.

I looked at their loved ones—the women, the kids. The people who didn't want to know the half of what their men had just talked about in that room in back.

Not a life I'd want to bring a woman into, much less children.

Too many secrets.

Too much darkness.

Too much risk.

But this life, it wasn't something I could ever give up. Piper was VP now. There was a target on his back.

There always would be.

He was in too deep. I was in too deep. And I would never turn my back on my brother. Our father may have been many things, but he raised us well.

My brother taught me well.

Lone wolf.

Two packs.

Family.

11:17 pm.

I sat at the bar, not drinking, not really listening to whatever my brothers were talking about around me. Ignoring the women climbing into their laps, trying to climb into mine.

I didn't even know if I wanted to be here. If I wanted to get laid. If I wanted to be alone.

If I wanted to go to sleep and ignore my phone for twelve hours, turn off the clock in my head.

I stared at Lex's text on my phone.

V, it said. *Artemis Club.*

CHAPTER FIVE

Roni

"HAVE you ever had that feeling you're being watched?"

Talia strode through my front door, dropping her purse on the floor before giving me a quick hug.

I shut the door behind her. "Watched?"

"There was a guy downstairs," she said, "sitting on a bike, and I swear I saw the same guy when I was at JJ Bean the other day, picking up coffees for us. And both times, he looked at me. Like *looked* at me."

"A bike?" I followed her into the living room.

"Yeah." She unpacked her laptop, laying it on the coffee table next to mine. "Like one of those big-ass biker bikes, you know? Like a Harley or whatever?"

"Was he wearing a Sinners vest?" Talia had met Taze, so it couldn't have been him, but I wondered if it was one of his guys. "Or, you know... Kings, or something...?"

Would it be too much to imagine that Jude had some dude parked out there, stalking me, because he was as obsessed with me as I was with him?

Yeah. Definitely.

"No," Talia said as she tapped on her computer, getting set up.

"His jacket didn't say anything on it. I never would've noticed, actually. Totally not my type." She glanced at me. "No offense. But when I looked at him he did this thing. He like, showed me his teeth."

I felt my eyebrow raise and she grinned. "His teeth?"

"Yeah... I'm assuming you have beer?" She headed into the kitchen, not even needing an answer. "It wasn't exactly a smile, but he touched his tongue very deliberately to his canine tooth, and it was like, silver."

Nope. No one I knew. I did not know any dude with silver canines.

I leaned against the kitchen door frame. "Maybe he wanted you to know he's got a silver dick?"

"Sadly, I don't go for anything less than solid gold." She helped herself to a beer from my fridge.

"And why should you?" I teased, flattering her. Talia was gorgeous, a peppy little blonde-Italian ex-cheerleader type, and if I was a dude, I'd totally want to sink my teeth into that.

"Neighbor of yours?" she teased back.

"Is that hope I hear in your voice, or trepidation?" I held out my hand for a beer, and she passed one to me.

"Both?"

"I've never seen him. So probably not." We cracked open our beers and headed back into the living room. "What if the teeth are platinum or something?"

"Well, damn. Now I've got myself a dilemma." She grinned, getting comfy on the couch. "So. What're we working on?"

"Something big," I said. "Potentially huge." I took a swig of beer and wondered how to... well, pitch this to her. Talia often worked with me on the events I was promoting. She worked *for* me, really; I hired her on as an assistant when I needed one. But when it came to Dirty, she was definitely the authority in the room.

Talia had been working with Brody and Maggie, on and off, for the past few years, as one of their many managerial underlings-slash-slaves. She'd worked a lot of Dirty events and she definitely knew a shit ton more than I did about the inner workings of the Dirty world.

Honestly, I'd really never paid all that much attention to the inner workings of the Dirty world before. It really wasn't my world.

Until now.

"Oh?" She blinked at me, waiting for more.

I settled in on the floor, cross-legged, across the table from her. "You can't tell anyone yet. It's top secret until we're sure it's a go."

"Okay."

"It's... Dirty."

She stared at me. Then she cocked her head a bit. "What? How?"

"Jessa brought it to me. She told me the band wants to play a New Year's Eve show, in town, and Brody's looking to put it together. Have you heard anything?"

"Yeah. Of course. But I thought Maggie was on it."

"I guess not? Jessa said Maggie and Brody are both too busy. She said they need a venue, basically, and suggested I find one and make it happen."

Talia sat back, considering that. "Wow."

"Yeah. So I really want to make a go of this, obviously."

"You have a venue?"

"No. Which is why I need your help."

Talia's pretty face immediately tightened, in that way a person's did when they really didn't want to have to break the bad news to you, but knew they had to—because you had a giant tarantula on your head or something.

"Roni..."

"I know, I know. Everything in town is booked. But there has to be some way. Let's just put our big, juicy lady brains together and see what we can do, okay?"

"Okay..." she said, sounding not at all optimistic, but at least willing.

"I've started a list, of all the places I'd love—"

"Don't bother," she said, clicking around on her laptop. "I've got the only list you'll ever need." She turned the laptop toward me. "These are the only places in town Dirty will even consider playing. This is Brody and Jude's approved list."

My stomach dropped as I took a look at her list. There were exactly seven venues on it, with data about each venue and contact information. "Jude?"

"Yeah. Jude. He's a real hard-ass when it comes to security. On the road, Dirty only plays major venues. At home, they love playing smaller shows, trying out new material and just having fun. But it always has to meet Jude's standards for security. He's very protective of Jesse and Zane, especially. You know I wasn't even allowed to *meet* Zane until the fifth show I'd ever worked for them?" She rolled her eyes. "I promise you, these are the only venues Jude will approve. And Brody won't even consider anything Jude won't approve."

"Great." I closed my list, which was obviously a total waste of time, with a dramatic jab of my touchpad. Then I took a big-ass swig of beer.

"I'm telling you," Talia said, sympathetic. "You think rock stars are difficult? Try working with Brody and Jude."

I scanned her list again. "Booked, booked and booked. Every venue on there is booked. I've already checked."

"Yeah." She sounded the least bit surprised.

Shit.

I knew I could pull this thing off—in theory. I had the main skill that was needed: the ability to negotiate. I knew I could negotiate this event into being, *if* I had a venue to negotiate *with*.

At the look on my face, Talia squared her shoulders and turned her laptop back toward herself. "Let's just look at these venues again."

"Maybe there's no point." I flopped back against the couch and pushed my hands into my hair. "Unless there's any wiggle room on that list of yours, there's no point."

"There's no wiggle room. But let's just look at each place, at their New Year's Eve events. In case anything stands out."

"Like what? Someone's already managed to book Dirty there since this morning?"

She grinned. "Nope. I would've heard. But let's not throw in the towel yet, right?" She was typing on her laptop. "Don't even bother with the arena or the stadium or Pacific Coliseum. Not happening. Let's look at the smaller ones."

"Jessa said they want something more intimate for this show anyway." I thought through Talia's incredibly short list… "That leaves the Ruby, Pandora Ballroom and Elysium Theatre. And the Back Door, which Jessa specifically told me Brody doesn't want for this."

"I'm looking at the Elysium now. You do one of the others."

"Is this the part where I tell you that I already talked to the Ruby today, and they confirmed that they're committed to four out-of-town DJs and the event is already almost sold-out?"

"Yeah, okay. So cross them off the list."

I sighed. "Pandora it is." I opened Google and searched *Pandora Ballroom Vancouver - New Year's Eve.*

"The Elysium is booked with Harper Sloane," Talia informed me. "And some special guests. *Ugh.* Folk rock. Zane calls it 'snooze rock.' Not happening."

"Are the tickets on sale already?"

"Yeah."

"Scratch that off." I'd pulled up a flyer for the New Year's Eve event at the Pandora, where I'd already discovered, earlier in the day, that DJ Summer was on the bill. "*A Pandora New Year's Eve,*" I read aloud. "*Featuring DJ Spyyder, DJ Summer…* and some other small-time DJs I'm not even gonna bore you with… Fully booked."

"I *love* DJ Spyyder. We should totally hit that party."

"Yeah. Tickets aren't on sale yet. I'll see if I can score some from the venue. I know the new assistant manager." After all, if this Dirty show wasn't happening, I'd be looking for someplace to get good and drunk that night after I was done with my lame-ass pub event.

"I'll see if I can score some from Summer," Talia said.

I looked at her, considering. "How well do you know her?"

"Not that well. I mean, I have her number."

I had her number, too. Didn't mean I had the courage to use it, unless I had something to offer her. DJ Summer was, unfortunately, a little out of my playing field—both personally and professionally.

But then again, so was Dirty.

Talia was typing and clicking, and frowned. "How come when I go to the Pandora website, Spyyder's not on the bill?"

"What?"

She spun her laptop toward me again. Her browser was open to a page on the Pandora Ballroom's website—info about their New Year's Eve event. Featuring DJ Summer, several other, smaller DJs... and: *More to be announced.*

"That's weird." I glanced up at Talia. "Which one do you think is correct?"

"I'm gonna go with whatever's on the venue's official webpage."

"Me too. Does Summer like you?"

"I think so? She always invites me to her parties when I talk to her. But I think she invites everyone to her parties..."

I doubted that. She'd invited me to one, so far, and since I hadn't been able to make it, I hadn't received another invite. Yet.

"Can you message her?" I said. "Ask her about the show."

Talia pulled out her phone and wrote a text. "What if she doesn't answer—?"

Ding. Talia's phone chimed with an incoming message before she'd even finished talking.

She stared at her phone, beaming. "Hey. DJ Summer just messaged me."

"Imagine that."

"She says, *Hi hon.*"

Ding.

"Now she says, *Spyyder bailed on the show. Promoter trying to pull out.* And a really sad face emoji."

Ding.

"She's at the Artemis Club tonight," Talia informed me, turning her phone toward me, showing me the message Summer had just sent her. "She's on at eleven. Just sayin'." She grinned at me.

I grinned back. "I knew there was a reason I kept you around all this time..." I was already searching the promoter on the Pandora Ballroom's New Year's Eve event, the gears in my head whirling. "Okay, hear me out on this. What if we buy the other promoter out? I mean, I'll buy him out. Pay him off to get him to hand the party over to us. He's based in Chicago, just like Spyyder, which is probably why he wants out of the show. It's not worth it for him to deal with this show in Vancouver if Spyyder's not on the bill. They're probably friends."

"Right..."

"We talk to the venue, let them know we're on it. Then we get rid of the smaller DJs, book them out to other events that night. Instead, we book in a smaller band, someone *hot*, to open for Dirty. And..." I looked at her hopefully. "I give you the other New Year's Eve party, the one we were gonna do together?"

Talia's eyes kinda widened; the thrill of running her own event. She hadn't done that yet. "You can try that," she said, "but you probably won't end up making much money on your event. Depending how much you have to pay the other promoter."

My phone buzzed. It was Taze, at the front door of my building.

I sighed and buzzed him up.

"I don't really care about making money on this one," I told Talia, realizing it was true. "I just want Dirty to be happy."

Jude.

Jude was in my head when those words came out of my mouth.

Which meant... Was I hoping to make *him* happy with this?

Was I hoping to make him happy with *me*?

Was that what this was really all about? Looking good in front of Jude?

Oh, for fuck's sake.

"And what about Summer?" Talia asked as I got up to unlock the door for Taze.

"Let me work on it." She was getting to her feet, and I told her, "You don't have to go."

"I really do." As she was packing up her laptop, Taze walked in. "I would hit the Artemis with you later but, I'm not gonna lie, I've got a super hot date with a pile of books. Got a paper due Monday."

"No worries." I hugged her. "Thank you." Besides working with me and Dirty and several other bands around town, Talia was in school. The girl was only twenty-two and definitely going places.

Frankly, I was just hoping she'd hire *me* when she got there.

Taze slung his arm around me and kissed my neck as Talia picked up her purse, which was pretty much at his feet. "Hey, Tal," he said, in his lazy, overly-familiar way, even though he barely knew her. He also looked her over in an overly-familiar way, though honestly that was how Taze looked at anyone with breasts. Especially anyone as pretty as Talia.

"Hey, Taze," she said, politely. Then to me she said, "Call me," and left.

Taze shut the door behind her. "The Artemis?"

"Yeah. I think I'm gonna head down there tonight."

"Yeah?" He backed me up against the wall. "You thinking about inviting me?"

"To the Artemis? It's not really your scene, Taze."

He kissed me and I let him, for a minute. Then I planted a hand in the middle of his chest and pushed him off a bit. "I'm working, okay? I have some calls to make."

"Uh-huh." He slid his hand up my shirt and inside my bra. "But first, why don't we finish what we started this morning..."

"I don't have time."

"You don't have time for dick?" He kissed my throat and squeezed my breast. "Since when?"

"Since I have to work tonight."

"You can work. After."

Right. We fucked, then he got to leave.

Convenient.

And I possibly missed my chance to talk to Summer tonight.

I extracted his hand and pushed him off. "So, let's see... When you need to work, it's all, 'I gotta pull out, babe,' and when I have to work you're all up in my bra?"

He pulled back. "What, you want me to go?"

"I never asked you to come over, Taze. I don't have time to service the needs of your dick right now. I'm working."

"It's Saturday night, babe."

"Yeah. And sometimes I work on Saturday night. Since when is this news to you?"

I really couldn't say why that pissed him off like it did, but apparently he didn't love my tone. "Maybe next time *you* need to be *serviced*, I shouldn't be so quick to come over here."

"Whatever."

He made a pissed-off noise and stared at me for a minute. Maybe he was waiting for me to apologize and drop to my knees.

When that didn't happen, he turned and walked right out the door, with a grumbled, "Call me when you're off your rag."

Dick.

I locked the door behind him.

I really, really needed to break up with him. It was inevitable, right?

All we did was irritate the fuck out of each other... and fuck.

So why hadn't I done it yet?

Jude.

Jesus. What was that man becoming—my reason for *everything*?

I shook it off and went to get changed into an outfit worthy of a DJ Summer show. Black leather leggings and suede booties, a flowy, shimmery sleeveless top.

I fixed my hair and makeup.

Then I made a few calls. Telling myself all the while that I could do this. I would pull this off. I would book the most killer Dirty show and New Year's Eve party known to man.

It was about my career.

It had nothing at all to do with my fucked up feelings for Jude Grayson.

When I arrived at the Artemis, DJ Summer was deep into her set.

The club was at capacity and the party was going strong. Summer wasn't headlining this show, but she was definitely holding her own, pumping up the crowd for the visiting headliner.

She was onstage above the crowd, wearing a black bodysuit with knee-high faux fur boots and a wicked crown of skulls, fur and twisted horns. She was playing a killer Florence + the Machine remix with a lively, sexy beat, and the crowd was right into it.

I slipped into the dark alongside the dance floor, though most of the club was pretty much one giant dance floor. I stood back and just took in the show, though I couldn't resist dancing a little right on the spot. The groove of Summer's music was just too damn infectious.

And as I watched her do her thing, if I squinted just enough, I could almost imagine it was *me* up there—if, you know, I was a shit-hot DJ. Summer was a couple inches shorter than me but, like me, she had dark hair and a figure that probably got her a lot of attention from men.

That was where the similarities between us pretty much ended, though.

Frankly, I was born white trash. Literally in a trailer park. I had to claw my way up through the world. Summer, on the other hand, was from Elle's walk of life. Which meant well-educated, well-traveled, and she grew up with money.

Where Summer's confidence probably came from her total ability to win at life—and probably from a young age—mine came from sheer force of will. An unwillingness to be pushed down, pushed aside.

As she finished her last song and the crowd screamed their appreciation, I could feel her affect on the audience. I could feel that DJ Summer was on a mission to make people feel good around her, feel good about themselves—and tonight, she was definitely succeeding. It was this talent that made her queen of the local party scene; a fucking killer DJ.

Me? I'd never concerned myself overmuch with how other people felt. Their feelings, their business.

Yes, I knew how to charm, how to seduce, and how to negotiate. Key factors in my line of work—both of them—and in my relationships with men. I knew how to get what I wanted, most of the time.

Jude Grayson aside.

I had a feeling, though, that Summer Avery Sorensen got what she wanted *more.*

By now, I'd Googled her. And Wiki'd her, and social media stalked her. I knew her personal stats, her fondness for exotic cars and overpriced designer handbags, her history of relationships with strapping, beautiful dudes. On paper, DJ Summer and I had little in common—but I could definitely get in bed with her taste in men.

Unfortunately, I wasn't here to talk about boys.

Even if the most beautiful one she'd probably ever dated—in my humble opinion—was suddenly standing right in front of me.

"Ash," I said, startled. He'd kinda loomed out of nowhere. And he was definitely looking a little... unsteady on his feet.

Drunk. He looked drunk.

But yes, beautiful. With ink-black hair and blue eyes, Ashley Player was all edgy rock star charisma and couldn't-give-a-fuck attitude in his tight black jeans and a sleeveless T-shirt that said: *Who needs cash when you got a dick like...* with an arrow, pointing straight down.

I kinda froze as he put his finger under my chin, leaned in... and kissed the tip of my nose.

"Roni," he said.

Then he pulled me in for a hug, just like that. Like he'd never come *this* close to screwing me... and then totally bailed on my ass. Leaving me literally naked in the night, at Jesse and Katie's wedding.

I'd run into Ash a few times since then, but we'd really never talked much since that night. I wasn't exactly crushed about it. Honestly, I figured he'd circle back around, eventually. Single dudes on the prowl pretty much always did. I had a Tinder account full of messages from horny dudes to prove it.

I never took those messages personally, just like I wouldn't take *this* personally.

For one thing, Ash was very obviously inebriated. For another, I was going to assume that this—the nose kiss and the hug—had at least something to do with his best friend, Dylan, falling in love with Amber, a girl they'd *both* been sleeping with; Jessa had recently filled me in on the latest Dirty drama and how MIA Ash had been lately.

Even so, when he hugged me, I hugged him back. His body definitely pressed up against mine a little longer and a little harder than it needed to, but I couldn't say I minded, exactly. Ash was hot.

But I did not like men who played games.

Especially games that I couldn't win.

I extracted myself from his arms, and after he'd told me how good I looked and gushed over me a bit in that way he did—kinda absently, like he was just putting the flattery out there and not really caring one way or another if I flattered him back—I let him know I was here to see Summer.

I really didn't want to miss my chance to talk to her. The next DJ had already taken over, and for all I knew she'd beelined straight out the back door the second she went offstage.

"Summer?" Ash said, both eyebrows raising.

Then he took my hand, sliding his fingers through mine and yanking me through the crowd. He pulled me right past the bouncer at the entrance to a hall that shot behind the stage, a hall that was lined with people talking and drinking, some with staff shirts and others with that *I'm with the DJ* air about them.

Ash knocked on a door along the hall, then tried the knob. He opened the door, telling some dude who was standing next to it and staring at us, "Five minutes," then yanked me inside. "*Suh-uh-uh-mmerrrrrr*," he sang out in his husky lead singer's voice, even though Summer was right in front of us, standing alone in the small room.

She was taking off her crazy horned crown thing and turned to us, shaking out her thick, dark hair. "Roni," she greeted me, pulling me in for a quick cheek kiss, which I returned.

"Hey, Summer..."

Before I could say more, Ash pulled Summer to him, his arm locked around her waist—pretty much like he'd done to me. He kissed her on the neck. Loudly. Repeatedly.

She shoved him off. Playfully—sort of.

"I found this lost kitten looking for you," he told her, looking me over. He seemed to like the leather leggings.

Summer cocked an eyebrow at me. "Yeah, Ash is really good at rounding up the lost pussy," she informed me, dryly. Then she told him, "Go herd yourself some kittens."

Ash did an obedient little salute thing, then stumbled out.

Summer shouted after him, not so playfully, "And stop drinking!"

When he'd gone and shut the door, we looked at each other. I thought, for a moment, that she might say something about him. Something apologetic? Sympathetic? Something clever to gloss over the slight discomfort in the room.

Or maybe it was just me.

I knew Ash was Summer's ex-boyfriend. Clearly, he was sloppy drunk tonight. And who the hell knew how she felt about him or what she thought I might've been doing with him before we'd walked in here? Not me. But I was here to win her over, and now I wasn't so sure if Ash getting me in to see her was a smart move or not.

Though if he hadn't, I wasn't sure I would've even gotten in. There were a hell of a lot of people outside that door, waiting to party with DJ Summer. Many of them men who could offer her way more interesting companionship tonight than I could.

I was about to say something, maybe open with a compliment—but she spoke first.

"Welcome to my queendom," she said, "and by that, I mean my mess." She gestured around at her "dressing room," which was, like the rooms reserved for talent in the backs of many clubs, pretty much as she'd called it—a mess. Random, somewhat broken furniture had been jammed awkwardly around a giant wall mirror and a makeup counter, where enough makeup for a dozen women had been laid out.

"Great show," I said. "They should've had you play longer."

"They should always have me play longer," she said, as she sat down to slip off her furry boots. "These things are hot as shit." She sighed with relief as she kicked them aside. She had that mildly dazed, distracted, exhausted-but-wired look about her that a lot of performers did when they came offstage. Luckily, she didn't look high, like some DJs did when I spoke to them during or after their sets; I really didn't want to have this conversation with her while she was less than totally coherent.

"Ah, but they look hot, too," I said, speaking the truth.

"Thank you."

"I spoke with the promoter on your New Year's Eve show," I informed her, as she slipped on a pair of black leather boots. It was only a white lie; so far, I'd spoken with his assistant. "Sounds like he's going to let me buy him out. Which means I'm taking over the event, and my plan is to book the other DJs out to other parties in town."

She glanced up at me. "You want to book me out too?"

"No," I said, kinda surprised she'd even think I wanted to. Since meeting her, I'd been keeping in touch, dropping in at her shows, and she knew I was hoping to put a show together for her sometime next year; I'd made that pretty clear. The only issue was I hadn't yet worked with a DJ of Summer's calibre, and she knew that, too.

In short, I hadn't won her over yet.

But I'd never really had anything to offer her before.

"You're still playing," I told her. "I hope."

She considered that as she got to her feet, then turned toward the mirror and started digging through her makeup. "What other DJs are you bringing in?"

"None. I'm bringing Dirty."

She stopped digging and looked at me in the mirror. "I've heard better ideas."

"You've played with them before," I pointed out.

"I can't open for Dirty with this kind of notice, hon," she told me, as she blotted the shine from her face with a tissue. "It takes preparation. I'm booked solid over the holidays, and I'm sure they're busy. This idea needs proper planning and promotion."

"Which is what I'm here for."

Summer shook her head as she pulled out a powder compact and a fluffy brush. "The crowd will be wrong. The vibe will be wrong. You put me in front of a Dirty crowd without the proper promotion, it'll be a blood bath. For me." She tapped some powder onto her brush and set to work touching up her face. "You bring Dirty into a DJ Summer party? Could go sideways for Dirty, which is not what they deserve. You need the right audience. You need time and you need to finesse these things." She stood back from the mirror and checked her face, smoothed her hair a bit with her fingers, not looking at me. "We took half a year planning the first show I ever played with them, where we did a partial set *together*, and that was at a festival, electronic music and rock. Totally mixed crowd. Open crowd. You can't just throw together an intimate New Year's Eve party with me opening for Dirty and expect it to work."

"It will work."

She met my eyes in the mirror, looking incredibly doubtful. "And you know this because...?"

"Because you won't be opening for them."

She turned to face me. She seemed to gauge that I was serious, and made a sound akin to a laugh. "You're gonna ask Dirty to open for me? You've got a solid steel pussy, hon." She turned back to her reflection. "Brody is gonna eat you for a nice, light snack and leave your pretty bones by the side of the road."

Well, there was some imagery.

"Or," I said, as she touched up her lip gloss, "I get a hot electronic rock band to open, warm up the crowd. Then Dirty takes the stage in all their rock star glory. They play from say, ten, ten-thirty, whatever they like, until midnight. At midnight, they count in the New Year. Everyone's happy. Everyone's half-trashed. The venue is open until three on a special license and the bar pours until two. After the New Year countdown, Dirty heads offstage to drink champagne and fuck or whatever rock stars do after midnight on New Year's, and DJ Summer takes over, presiding over the party until the wee hours. Just the way, I assume, she likes it."

Summer quirked an eyebrow at me but said nothing. I knew I had her interest, so I went on.

"You want to play for three hours straight, you can. You want to switch out with another DJ, bring in some friends to spin with you, special guests, whatever. It's all on the table. They don't even have to be on the bill. We can work it out."

"You're offering me top billing?"

"No. You know there's no way in hell I can do that. But I am promising you equal billing with Dirty."

At that, she looked doubtful again. "With an equal cut of ticket sales?"

"Equal. Your set is twice as long, but you get equal. This is Dirty we're talking about. If I were you, I'd take the offer and run."

"You're not me," she reminded me, turning to face me again. "And I will take the offer. If you can get Dirty on board with that plan." She looked at me like she wasn't yet sure what to make of me. If she trusted me. If she even liked me or not. "I'm assuming you haven't spoken with them yet, or I would've heard something from Elle."

"I'll get them on board."

"I'd love to see it."

So would I.

"If you don't mind though, hon, I have people waiting." She picked up a glass that was sitting on the counter, a cocktail I hadn't even noticed, and took a sip.

"Oh. Of course." I shifted out of her way as she moved toward the door.

I took a breath and tried not to dance around. Because shit, yes. I'd convinced her. More or less.

I was *so* pulling this off.

When her hand landed on the door handle, she glanced back at me. "Are you coming?"

I blinked at her. It took a mere half-second to dawn on me that DJ Summer, party queen, was inviting me to party with her.

And there was only one response to an invitation like that.

"Absolutely."

CHAPTER SIX

Jude

12:04 am.

The Artemis Club was packed, and I didn't exactly have a ticket or a pair of tits, but I did know one of the bouncers, so getting in wasn't a problem.

Blending in was a little more of an issue. Which was why surveillance was never gonna be a realistic career fallback for me. I wasn't exactly a dude who could blend into a crowd. Any crowd.

Not like Lex could.

So I just stood back in the darkest corner I could find, and watched. I watched Roni watch the show.

I'd let Lex go for the night when I arrived, taking over for him. When he'd texted me that Roni was here, I'd removed my Kings cut, tucked it away in a saddlebag on my bike, hopped on and drove for an hour, all the way into downtown Vancouver, and walked straight into this club.

Why? Fuck if I'd totally figured that out yet.

All I knew was Roni was here and now, so was I.

And Taze wasn't.

Lex had made that clear; Roni had gone out, on a Saturday night, to a club—alone.

Without her degenerate boyfriend in tow.

Which meant—yeah, maybe I was optimistic as fuck, but just fucking *maybe* it meant that even though she'd kept him around for the last ten months she was finally getting tired of him.

Just fucking maybe this was my opening.

My chance to drive a wedge between the two of them—somehow.

I'd already tried to warn her off Taze, twice. And failed. She'd seemed to take my words of warning about Taze as seriously as shit-all nothing. I could've coughed up evidence; something to show her rather than tell her what a piece of garbage her Sinner boyfriend was. Undoubtedly, that would've gotten my point across.

But going that route would've endangered Roni, so it was never happening.

Which meant I really only had one other card to play. The only real leverage I'd ever had with Roni.

That fucking combustible spark between us.

I knew for a fact—an uncomfortable, painful fact—that, despite what a "Wild Card" so many of my friends insisted on labeling her, Roni Webber was not the type of woman who would cheat on her boyfriend. No matter what a piece of shit he was.

But maybe she'd seriously consider ridding herself of him if a better option came along.

Obviously, I was that better option.

It wasn't like I was gonna offer to be her boyfriend. I'd made it pretty clear to her the last time we fucked that that was never gonna happen.

But I could definitely fuck her better than Taze could.

I could be fuck buddy of the century, if that's what she needed to rid her mind and body of any fucking memory of Taze Murphy.

The more I thought about it, the more my instincts told me that if I walked right up to Roni in this crowd, got close, put my hand on the small of her back or on her hip as she danced, put my lips to her ear to tell her how fucking sexy she looked in those leather pants, how fucking good she smelled—*fuck*, that goddam sex kitten smell of hers, I could almost smell it from way over here... Yeah. She'd be leaving here with me tonight.

And the more I thought about it, the more it gave me a raging fucking hard-on.

But my instincts also told me to stand back and watch. So that was what I did. I watched Roni watch the end of the show, dancing all the while, just like she did when she was sixteen—slow, sexy and free, like she didn't care who was watching—her attention locked on the stage.

And then I watched Ashley Player walk right up to her.

My chest tightened until I could barely fucking breathe... as I watched him kiss her, then hug her—for way too fucking long.

And I remembered...

I remembered how Roni flirted with Ash at Jesse's wedding. How she made out with him at Katie's stagette party; how she danced with him on the coffee table in her bikini. How she wore that hot-as-hell red dress to the wedding reception, looking for his attention. How she'd sat next to him at the fire pit afterwards—and I'd gotten the fuck up and left. And when I'd seen her later that night, how she'd acted like she didn't even care he'd blown her off.

I remembered how she chased after Ash the entire wedding, but late that night she'd ended up with me instead.

So, what? Did she really want Ash this whole time?

Was she fucking *him* now?

Or all along?

Jesus. And fuck.

I watched Ash take her hand and drag her off backstage, my jaw so fucking tight I couldn't believe I didn't break any teeth.

And I decided, right here and now, that I did not fucking need this.

This fucking stupid-ass pet project of mine, this misguided-as-fuck mission to save Roni Webber from Taze—or from her fucking self—was a surefire one-way ticket to Crazy Town, population fucking me.

12:16 am.

I walked out the door of the nightclub wanting to kick my own ass. Made my way back to my bike, got on, and rode.

I rode through the city, right through my neighborhood and just kept going. Headed back out of town. To Piper's place, maybe, back to the clubhouse, wherever. I just needed to ride.

Because what the fuck was it about this woman, this one woman, that had burrowed its way the fuck under my skin when I was nineteen and never left?

And now had me acting like some obsessed teenager?

I'd raced to that nightclub in the middle of the night, at a moment's notice, to seize some imagined opportunity to rescue her from her boyfriend?

Riiiiight.

Who the fuck did I think I was kidding, and when, exactly, had I started lying to myself about my feelings for Roni Webber?

Today? This year?

Fucking years ago?

And when was I gonna get it through my damn head that she wasn't mine to protect?

12:50 am.

Or something...

In retrospect, there was no fucking way, if I didn't have my head so far up my own ass over a woman I was stupidly obsessed with, who was fucking every dude I'd ever met—other than, you know, me—I never, ever would've pulled into that fucking gas station lot.

For a cream soda.

All I wanted was a cream soda.

Ninety-nine percent of the time I ate well, treated my body as something of a temple, avoided junk food. I didn't drink to excess or smoke pot to excess or use other drugs.

But when I was alone and I was agitated about something—like really fucking agitated—cream soda was my vice. I tried not to let my brother or Jesse or anyone else who knew me too well see me drinking it, because that meant they knew I was in a weak state.

And I was in a weak-ass state.

I never should've been so distracted, over a woman who wasn't mine and a fucking cream soda craving, of all things, that I didn't even notice the sketchy-as-fuck van pulling into the lot right behind me—until it was too late. Until it had pulled up alongside me, blocking me from the rest of the gas station, and the first guy had already walked right the fuck up to me.

And another one shoved something hard and cold into my left kidney.

If it was a gun, it was totally fucking unnecessary. Especially since there were three of them and the dude standing right in front of me was none other than Taze.

Roni's boyfriend.

Pretty fucking obvious this wasn't a friendly social call.

The third guy had already joined the party by the time I'd done a mental inventory of every weapon or weapon-like object on my bike. I had nothing on my body, wouldn't have risked it at the door of the club, but I had what I needed in a hidden compartment on my bike.

No chance of reaching it, though.

The four of us took a stroll around the backside of the building, away from the security cams. Which would've looked suspicious as fuck—if anyone was actually around to notice it. The whole way, the prick behind me kept his weapon jabbed firmly into my back.

I went along, cooperative as fuck. I was not getting my internal organs blown out behind a gas station off the Trans-Canada highway in the middle of the night by some dumb fuck who hadn't graduated middle school.

I got a look at him, and I knew who he was.

The Sinners called him Brag, and of all his shitty qualities, my least favorite of Brag's personality flaws was how cozy he was with Taze. Cozy enough that Taze shared his brand new girlfriend with him at a Sinner's party in a romantic little threesome I was lucky enough to witness.

"On your knees," he said, "and hands behind your head."

Clearly he'd watched too many episodes of *Law & Order* while chain-smoking weed and studying to be a badass.

I complied.

The other kid stood in front of me. I knew him only as Topper. He was a bruiser, one of those guys that the other guys kept around mostly because he was handy in a fight. But when I looked in his eyes, he looked fucking nervous.

I was on my knees, and *he* looked scared.

As he fucking should.

The three of them were crossing an ugly line right now.

At least they weren't so stupid they didn't know it.

"Fool me once, shame on you, huh, Jude?" Taze started talking. "Fool me twice... shame on me, right?" When I looked up into his face, he was standing over me, off to my right side, watching me carefully. "Took me fuckin' long enough, huh? But I figured you out. I got you. You got a thing for my girl, is that it? That's why you keep showing up uninvited. When I'm fucking her. When we're meeting her friends' babies. And you keep giving her that fuckin' *look*. Lemme guess. She turn you down, you can't take no for an answer, something like that?"

Topper shifted, and I glanced at him.

"I'm asking you a fucking question. You got a thing for Roni?"

I looked at Taze again and said nothing.

Honestly, he looked scared, too. That fucking vein in the middle of his forehead. He looked pissed, but backed-into-a-corner pissed. Impotent pissed, like a dude who'd just had his dick cut off and handed to him.

Yeah, he was scared.

And he was jealous. Threatened. Not sure what my relationship with Roni really was.

Trying to look tougher than he was for his brothers.

I wondered whose idea this was.

Theirs?

His?

He lowered himself down on his haunches and looked into my face.

"I get it. You're Mr. Protector. The security guy, right? Bodyguard to your best friend, the rock star... what's his name? Jesse."

Jesus. Christ. Was he seriously threatening Jesse to me?

This kid was way the fuck stupider than I took him for.

Then he leaned closer to me and said, "I know about the dude with the pretty teeth. Lex, right? Had my boys follow him home from the club tonight. Know who he is. Know where he lives. Know he's been watching Roni. Know you're the one who put him there, watching her, that right?"

He waited, but I didn't answer.

He knew I was never gonna answer a question like that, right?

"Good looking guy," he went on. "Probably not so much, though, after Topper plucks out all those pretty white teeth. Those silver fangs, I'd definitely have to keep those. Make myself a necklace or something. Trophy kill, right?"

Right. So maybe he wasn't that stupid.

He was sharp enough to figure out that a death threat to one of my club brothers, or anyone else I cared about, was the surest way to get my attention.

But the kid definitely had some kind of death wish, pulling what he was trying to pull right now.

Did they teach him nothing in that joke MC of his?

I glanced at Topper again. There were huge sweat stains under his armpits.

None of them were wearing their Sinners shit.

There was a thick, nervous energy crackling in the air between them. They felt to me like three yahoos who'd cornered a lion on a safari to take selfies and didn't know at what point the lion was gonna turn around and bite their faces off. Just knew it was gonna happen, if they didn't work quick.

Then Taze's gaze shifted to Brag, behind me—and something hit me, hard, in the lower back. Fucking kidney shot.

Left side, up under my ribs.

I went down like I'd been struck by lightning, the pain shooting through my body. I was already on the ground and curling up like a snail when I saw the weapon; not a gun but a tire iron, in Brag's fist. He was standing over me, but I couldn't pull my shit together to get up. Pain was spreading through my body again in a residual wave of fire. I couldn't find air in my lungs.

Fortunately for me, he didn't take another shot.

Taze hit me once, in the face, with a closed fist.

"Forget. About. Her." Close to my ear, his voice. But I couldn't quite see through the haze of pain.

Then he kicked me in the side with his booted foot, hard.

Then they were gone.

Forget.

About.

Her.

It took a while, but I managed to get myself upright and around to the front of the building, moving kinda like an extra from *The Walking Dead*. Luckily there was no one around, but the lights were blazing over the gas station. I sat down on the curb in the shadow of my bike.

I searched for blood, but other than a shallow scrape on my cheekbone from Taze's pussy-assed punch, I seemed to be in one non-bloody piece. I was aching and queasy, and my kidney still felt like someone had shoved a rusty steak knife through it.

1:19 am.

I called Brody.

"Roni's at the Artemis Club," I told him as soon as he picked up. My voice sounded gruff and weird, even to me.

"Okay?"

"I need you to go get her."

"Now?"

"Yes. Now." I knew I'd woken him up. I knew he had a new baby. I also knew he'd do what I asked. "Try her phone. If she's not there, she might be with Ash."

"Ash?"

"Yeah," I growled, "Ash." The image of Ash pulling Roni into that hall behind the stage was burned uncomfortably into my brain. "Just find out where she is and go get her. And don't say I asked you to. If you can't find her, get Bishop to help you, but be discreet about it. Bring her back to your place, keep her there overnight and tomorrow morning until I can get there. Tell her Jessa needs help with the baby, whatever you've gotta say to keep her there."

I heard the sound of shuffling as he got up. "Can I get a fucking 'please' on that?" He was talking quietly, probably trying not to wake up Jessa and/or the baby.

"Fucking please."

"Is everything okay?" Clearly he knew it wasn't.

"It's fucking fine. Just get her there."

"Alright, brother."

"I'll see you tomorrow."

I hung up, then called Lex and filled him in. I told him Taze had made him, knew he'd been tailing Roni. "Watch your back," I told him. "And stay the hell away from Roni."

"Right. You good?"

"Yeah." I realized I probably didn't sound so good. "Not a word to anyone."

I hung up and got to my feet. I got onto my bike, with difficulty, my lower back fucking screaming at me, and eased slowly out of the gas station lot.

1:42 am.

I pulled off onto a quiet road about twenty minutes from my house, in front of a fenced school yard.

No fucking way I was gonna make it.

I parked under a tree in the dark between the streetlights. Sat down on the curb.

Then I called Con to come get me.

He was still at the clubhouse, but I knew he wasn't drinking heavy tonight. He was one of the few Kings who never crashed at the clubhouse, would always make sure he was sober enough to drive home at the end of the night.

"No bike," I told him, spitting blood out onto the pavement at my feet. "Bring a car and come alone. Bring some cash. Can you get a couple grand?"

"Yeah. Okay. I'll be there in about... forty-five."

"And Con?"

"Yeah, boss."

"Not a fucking word to anyone."

"The fuck happened to you?"

I opened my eyes.

2:36 am.

I looked up to find Con standing over me with a white-toothed smile, blond hair rimmed in the streetlight like a bloody halo.

"Jumped."

He laughed uneasily. "Shit. Who the fuck jumps *you*?"

"Coupla kids." I spat pink, bloody spit on the ground at my feet. My tooth had cut into the inside of my lip when Taze hit me, apparently, and it was still bleeding. "And a tire iron."

He sat down next to me on the curb, looking me over. "You okay?"

"Not really fuckin' sure."

"Who the fuck was it? Where did this happen? You want me to call this in?"

"No." I looked him in the eye. "We're not telling anyone about this."

He stared at me a minute, processing that. "Even Pipe?"

"Especially my brother."

Con was silent for a minute.

"I'm gonna assume the cash is for the doc, then?"

"Like to make sure my kidneys are still functioning," I said.

3:19 am.

When we arrived at Dr. Singh's clinic, he was already there. He let us in with a smile. The man was incredibly upbeat for a dude who'd been woken up in the middle of the night by a couple of bikers, one of whom was spitting and pissing blood.

Dr. Singh always wore a smile and the man had crazy eyes. He looked to me like he was always on some kind of uppers. Or maybe he was just high on life. Or the cash the Kings steadily siphoned his way.

Or all of the above.

He looked me over and took some X-rays, asked me not one single thing. Other than what had hit me in the back. When I told him it was a tire iron, he said, "Lever? Or like a four-way lug wrench?"

"Lug wrench," I said. "L-type."

"Ouch," he said, with a smile.

While we waited for the results, Con came at me a few times about the "kids" who'd attacked me, wanting to know what the fuck really happened.

"I told you," I said. "I was jumped."

"For what? Your fucking wallet?" He looked pointedly at my wallet, which was in my hand, and the wad of cash I was pulling out of it.

"Next time I tell you to bring two grand," I said, "bring two grand."

He just grinned as I added two hundred from my wallet to the eighteen hundred he'd brought.

When Dr. Singh returned and showed me the X-rays he assured me, with a smile, that there was no breakage. Bones, organs, or otherwise. Just one hell of a gnarly bruise.

There was that pesky blood in my piss, which he told me not to worry about—unless it got worse. Then he hooked me up with some painkillers.

Con paid the man and drove me home, where I planned to piss some more blood and sleep for a year.

"Have a prospect pick up my bike and deliver it here before the sun comes up," I told him when he dropped me off.

"Yup. We sticking to this story about the world's stupidest kids jumping you for no good reason?"

"Yes," I said. "We are. And... I need you to do something else for me."

CHAPTER SEVEN

Roni

WHAT FUCKING TIME IS IT?

This shitty feeling, in the confusion before I was fully awake.

Where was I, and what day was it?

Wake the fuck up...

Sunday morning. *Late* morning.

Fucking 11:03 am.

Home.

Bed.

This shitty feeling, lingering. That my life had been reduced to an endless accounting in my head. Every moment filed away for later recall, in case of the need to provide an explanation, to produce an alibi. And as it was filed away, the moment was already gone, so when was I ever really living it? Was I here?

What if I really wanted to be *there*?

Her.

I almost reached for my phone, almost checked for a message from Lex, almost forgot he wasn't tailing her anymore. Almost forgot about last night.

Fuck, last night.

Roni.

Ash.

Fucking Taze.

The pain in my lower back as I climbed out of bed, as I got dressed.

Breakfast smoothie.

Painkillers.

I checked my phone—found texts from Brody. He'd brought Roni to his place last night, like I asked. But Bishop drove her home in the morning, after she promised Brody she'd come back.

Found texts from Jesse, wanting to know where the fuck I was.

Shit.

I texted Jesse back, let him know I wasn't coming over, that I was heading to Brody's. That I'd check in with him later.

I texted Con with a simple question mark, meaning: *send me an update.*

I called Piper, told him, "I need to pull Hazard or Bane for Dirty crew. Today."

"Today?" My brother did not sound happy about it.

"Today."

I'd already talked to him, and to both Hazard and Bane—both Kings—about joining Dirty's security crew this year on the road. Piper had approved of me hiring on one of them, not both, and not until the tour started in January.

But thanks to Taze's bullshit play last night, I was not gonna be able to wait that long.

Piper sighed and said, "Take Bane. Fucking guy annoys me anyway."

"I owe you one."

"You owe me more than one, little brother."

I hung up and sent a quick text to Bane. *Call me.*

Then I called Brody. "Roni went home?"

"She went home to shower and change," he said. "I tried to keep her here, but I couldn't exactly make her stay."

"Bishop's bringing her back?"

"They're back already. She's having lunch with Jessa. Said she has some kind of business proposal for me."

"Stall," I said. "Don't talk to her until I get there."

"When will you be here?"

"Soon," I said. "Just fucking stall."

When I hung up, a text came in from Con. *Not yet. But this shit will be easy.*

I threw on my leather jacket, grabbed my keys. Found my bike parked in the driveway, where whatever prospect had left it.

Fucking newspaper.

I got into the Bentley, awkwardly. The painkillers were kicking in, but I felt stiff all over.

Morning drive. Metallica. "Die, Die My Darling."

The mental inventory in my head.

11:52 am.

I arrived at Brody's place, headed straight into his office. Endured his stare-down, aimed at the damage on my face. It wasn't that bad. Just a small bruise and scrape on my left cheekbone from Taze's fist.

"What happened?" he finally asked, flatly, like someone who didn't really expect to get an answer.

"Nothing you want to know."

I sat down on the couch, ready to go the fuck back to sleep. I was walking normal by now and I was no longer pissing blood, so that was something. Maybe a few hundred more hours of sleep and I'd be like new.

There was a knock at the door, which was half-open, and Jessa appeared.

"Hey..." The smile fell right off her face when she saw me. "Jude! What happened?" She pushed the door open; baby Nick was snuggled in the crook of her arm, half-asleep.

Roni was right behind her.

Roni's face fell when she saw me, too, though probably for an altogether different reason.

"Nothing," I said. "Had a little disagreement with a door."

"A door? You want me to believe you walked into a door, and it gave you *that*?" Jessa frowned at the scrape on my cheek. Then her gaze flicked over to Brody, and her shoulders dropped. "Alright. Whatever." She brought Nick over to me as I got to my feet.

I ruffled his silky little tuft of hair with my fingertips and offered the obligatory, "Cuter every day, huh?"

"Yes," she said proudly, kissing his head. "Your uncle Jude's a badass," she whispered to him in her super-sweet mommy voice, "and you are never, ever riding one of his motorcycles. No... you're not."

"His dad get a say in that?" I glanced at Brody.

Brody just rolled his eyes.

"Nope," Jessa said. "He's not riding Daddy's motorcycles either."

"Right," I said.

Jessa flashed me her bratty face.

"Come in, Roni," Brody said, gesturing for Roni to join us. She was standing way back, just inside the door, arms crossed.

"We're not staying," Jessa announced, heading for the door with Nick. "I need to feed Nicky." She gave Roni a quick hug. "Don't take no for an answer," she told Roni, then she threw Brody a sharp look over her shoulder and left.

I stared at Roni.

It was the first time I'd been this close to her since the meet-the-baby party a week ago, and my guard was way the fuck up. The ways I felt about this woman... were incredibly conflicted. That was never more obvious to me than when I was face-to-face with her.

I was definitely pissed about her choices. Taze, for one. And last night... whatever the fuck was going on with Ash.

But at least I wasn't pissed about the past anymore.

Mostly.

Either way, I'd definitely told myself I was never gonna be with her. Which pretty much meant never being in the same room with her, apparently.

Because as soon as me and Roni Webber were face-to-face, I could *feel* it... how the entire dynamic of our non-relationship shifted. Her relationship to me shifted—from someone I needed to stay the fuck away from, to someone I *had* to get close to.

Fucking dangerous, this woman...

She looked at me, barely, as she took a couple more steps into the room.

Her black hair was smoothed down past her shoulders, parted to one side. She wore it long all over, without the bangs she'd had as a teenager. She still had a preference for black eyeliner, just a lot less of it. Back then, she looked kinda like a doll. Now, she looked like a total sex kitten, even when she dressed for business.

She wore a fitted black skirt with tall leather boots and a collared blouse. The blouse was a deep green with a bit of a shine to it—totally fucking gorgeous with her green eyes—and it was tucked into the skirt, so her full breasts pressed against the fabric. The top couple of buttons were undone, though not enough to show cleavage.

She'd dressed to impress, but not to seduce.

"Thank you for meeting with me," she said—to Brody. If I wasn't mistaken, she seemed to be waiting for him to ask me to step out. But of course, he didn't. I could've sat in on any band-related meeting in existence. Brody never asked me to step out.

And if Roni had any kind of "business proposal" for Brody, it had to do with the band.

Dirty was Brody's business.

And mine.

He offered her a seat in front of his desk.

We all sat.

"Jessa mentioned to me that you're looking to book an event for Dirty on New Year's Eve," she said, still talking to Brody, and only Brody. "As you know, I've been doing event promotion for a while now, so I thought I might put something together."

Brody's eyebrows raised. He sat back in his chair. I couldn't tell for sure if he was pulling away, totally fucking against the idea, or just surprised.

"I've got the Pandora Ballroom," she added quickly, before he could say anything. "And DJ Summer on the bill, after midnight."

Brody just stared at her for a few seconds. Then he glanced at me.

I said nothing, but the gears were turning in my head.

DJ Summer. That's what that was last night? Ash pulling her behind the stage at Summer's show...?

She was there to talk business with Summer?

Brody looked at her again. "You want Dirty to open for DJ Summer?"

"Not open. They'd have the prime—"

"But they'd play before her."

"In the prime spot," Roni said. "Right before midnight. They'd do the New Year countdown—"

"And then Summer would take over."

Roni sat back. "Are you really gonna tell me that Dirty wants to play until three in the morning?"

Brody said nothing.

"It would be a double bill. Best rock band in town. Best DJ in town. *Best New Year's Eve party in town.*"

I sat back, watching. Listening.

Impressed.

It was a good idea, and a good venue.

Dirty would like it. Zane would like it, and that was the main thing. If Zane was happy, no one else was likely to bitch about much. They'd be happy to play to a packed house, pretty much wherever we—Brody and me—sent them.

They trusted us like that.

But more than that—I was impressed she'd actually gone ahead and gotten the ball rolling on this, brought it to Brody.

I was also more than a little surprised. Because she had to know working on this event would mean working with my ass.

"Uh-huh," Brody said. "Dirty won't take the stage before Summer without a warm-up. Who've you got to open? The Pushers?"

"The Penny Pushers aren't right for this. Pushes the balance too far in the rock direction." I listened carefully to her answer, and I liked it. If she'd wanted Ash's band for this, I was gonna go ahead and assume she really *was* fucking him. "I'm thinking more of an electronic/pop rock vibe," she said. "Someone who vibes with both Dirty and Summer."

I watched Brody. Closely. I could see that she was starting to win him over. Somewhat.

"And you've got someone like that on the line?"

"Not yet, but I'm working on it. I'll come up with someone perfect."

Brody looked skeptical as he pretty much stared her down. He also looked like a new dad; like a dude who hadn't gotten more than a few hours' sleep per night the last two weeks and had no time for bullshit.

"I came up with DJ Summer and the best venue in town for this party," she reminded him, unflinching as she stared him right back down. "With five weeks' lead time. For New Year's Eve. I can come up with an opening band."

Brody took that in. Then he leaned forward on his elbows on the desk, seeming to relent. I knew he'd fucking love to have this event off his plate. But we both knew we couldn't just hand a Dirty show over to anyone. "What do you need from me?" he asked her.

"I need your agreement that Dirty's in," she said. "I need promo images of the band. Any requests you have on behalf of the band. A look at some previous contracts you've had with local venues would be nice, if you'll let me see them. I'll need to know what you need for sound check and security. And I'll get a contract drafted, for you to review."

Brody's gaze shifted to me. "That work for you?"

Roni didn't even look at me. She looked fucking annoyed as shit, though, that he'd turned this over to me.

"Should be fine," I said, "but we haven't played the Pandora in a few years." I met Roni's green-eyed gaze as she finally looked over at me. "We'll need to go over some things."

The Pandora was fine by me. Great staff, I knew the owners, and they had huge bands play there all the time. We'd never had a problem there.

But she didn't have to know all that.

"I'll get to work on the contract." Roni stood and extended her hand to Brody.

Brody stood and shook her hand, still not looking totally sure about this.

I stood and Roni turned on her heel, sailing straight out the door without another glance in my direction. Just a whiff of her faint sex kitten perfume, then gone.

I looked at Brody. "You think she can handle this?" he asked.

"I'll make sure she does."

I could literally see his relief. He did not want to babysit Roni or anyone else right now. His hands were more than full.

"Let me know what you need," he said.

"Alright, Bro."

As I left, he added, "Don't walk into any more doors, yeah?"

When I headed out to the foyer, I found Bishop waiting to drive Roni home. We waited together while Roni said her goodbyes to Jessa and the baby. Then I walked her out.

Bishop got in his car when I waved him on, and I pulled Roni aside, alone.

"We need to discuss security," I said. "You've got a big band going into a small venue. I cover Dirty, you'll need to bring in an outside security agency to cover crowd control, work with the venue staff. I can give you a few names."

"Fine," she said. "We can schedule a call tomorrow."

"A call won't do. We need to meet." *And fuck tomorrow.*

"A phone call will do."

"A phone call will not do." Because in a phone call, I couldn't see her jade-green eyes and her perfect tits. "We'll do dinner."

"It's concert security, not rocket science," she said, taking a little dig at my profession. "What can't be discussed over the phone?"

"You ever promoted an event this big?" I dug right back.

She didn't respond. But the answer was no, she'd never promoted an event this big, and we both knew it.

She sucked in her cheeks as she drew a breath, and pushed out her full, round lips, looking annoyed.

Jesus *fuck*, those lips.

"We'll set something up," she finally agreed, fucking vaguely, and got into Bishop's car.

I watched them drive off, knowing exactly three things.

One, I was gonna see Roni again *soon*.

Two, until I did, Bane would watch her back.

And three, there was no way in fuck Taze was getting anywhere near her, ever again.

I was right in the first place; I had to protect her from that dumbass piece of trash.

Bane had already called in, and I'd given him Roni's address and his instructions. He was taking over for Lex on my little surveillance project. He'd be at Roni's place by the time Bishop dropped her there. Watching. Reporting in to me.

Con had another brother, Maddox, helping him with his task.

And Lex was on standby.

I was gonna deal with Taze, and Lex was gonna help me do it. That comment about the teeth? Not going unanswered.

Contrary to what most people might assume by looking at me, I was not a violent man. I didn't have half the temper of my brother or a lot of the other bikers I knew. I didn't particularly subscribe, without exception, to the "an eye for an eye..." mentality of dealing with grievances.

But I was a King.

A death threat against a member of my club could not go ignored.

Taze had crossed one hell of an ugly line last night. Me dealing with it without telling my brother, my club President, and the rest of my club was crossing another ugly line. But I would not bring violence down on my brother, in any way. I was not gonna let Taze start a fucking war over this bullshit.

The Kings had enough bullshit to deal with.

So I was gonna deal with Taze myself.

I was definitely gonna deal with Roni first, though.

Not sure yet what that was gonna entail other than feeling her out and going from there. This New Year's Eve event gave me an opening, but getting a throbbing hard-on in the middle of a business meeting didn't really go hand-in-hand with keeping things professional.

Well, fuck professional.

I pulled out my phone and sent her a text.

Meet me at Cardero's. 8pm.

CHAPTER EIGHT

Roni

MEET *me at Cardero's. 8pm.*

I kept staring at the text on my phone, like I was making sure it wouldn't just evaporate or I hadn't hallucinated it. It had come in as soon as I left Jessa's place, from a number I didn't recognize.

But I knew who it was from.

I saved the number to my contacts and programmed in his name: *Jude Grayson*. All the while, I tried to ignore the little thrill of knowing I now had his number in my phone.

Of course, I used to have it. But that was years ago.

Mid-afternoon, I finally replied.

Me: How did you get this number?

Did he seriously still have my number in his phone? After all these years?

He didn't respond. All day.

I knew, with his silence, that accepting his invitation—which was more of a command than anything else—would only start the ball rolling on a very dangerous game. One I'd seriously love to play —if there was any possibility I could win.

Either way, I went to meet him.

I wasn't about to do anything that might jeopardize the New Year's Eve event, now that Brody had entrusted me with it—more or less. Even if that meant sitting through a dinner with Jude.

All day I'd been mentally pinching myself about the whole thing. I'd convinced Brody to take a chance on me. There was now a shit-ton of work to do, of course, but I'd gotten things this far. I'd gotten the venue. I'd gotten DJ Summer. I'd gotten Dirty.

And now I had a dinner meeting with Jude.

I knew it wasn't a date. Yes, he'd asked me to meet him at a restaurant, in the evening, but this was normal in my line of work. I often met with people professionally, at all hours of the night, in restaurants or bars, to talk shop.

And yet... this did not feel like that, either.

Cardero's was on the waterfront in Coal Harbour, and I made sure to give myself enough time to find parking and not be late. I walked up the walkway and through the door fashionably early, because I was a professional, and I wasn't about to let Jude glimpse a single chink in my armor. There was a reservation in his name, but when I was shown to the table, he wasn't there yet.

Minus one point for Jude.

Or maybe it was minus one point for me? As I settled in, I wondered if maybe I should've arrived a *little* late, made him wait.

Not half a minute after I'd sat down, though, someone approached the table. The first thing I saw was his arm as he reached past me to set a glass of white wine on the table in front of me—and there was no mistaking who that arm belonged to.

The full black sleeve tattoo of a big, twisted tree and the long, gnarly roots that wound down over his hand.

The silver skull ring on his middle finger.

The warm, burnt-toffee tones of his skin and the thick curves of his muscles.

I looked up at him. His built body towered above me as he gazed down, looking me over. He wore a charcoal-gray, long-sleeved T-shirt with the sleeves pushed up and fitted black jeans. The shirt clung to his thick pecs, the jeans to his thighs, and my tongue pressed to the top of my mouth as I fought back some primal response that would have me drooling if I wasn't careful.

His almost-black hair was thick and short-ish and, as usual, casually, haphazardly styled. His dark eyes were a deep, bottomless molten brown. His lips were full and oh-so-fucking-kissable.

And those *dimples.*

Good fucking lord, the dimples. He smiled at me now, halfway, and it really wasn't fair. Those things were weapons of mass destruction.

How did I convince myself I could handle this, exactly?

He moved to sink into the seat across from me and I caught his scent. One part faint, woodsy cologne mingled with his sexy man-musk, one part fresh air and the leather of the jacket he had slung over one arm and now tossed on the back of the seat. One-hundred-percent pure alpha male.

He set his drink in front of him on the table. If my memory served, it would be whiskey.

He'd remembered what I liked to drink, too. When I took a sip, it was a Pinot Grigio or something similar, light and just a touch sweet.

"You're late," was the first thing out of my mouth. I glanced at my phone. "It's eight-oh-four."

"Sitting at the bar," he said. "Saw you walk in."

And with that, his wicked, hellfire eyes moved slowly, deliberately over every inch of my body that he could see above the table.

"So, how are you?" I asked, when his gaze finally met mine again. It was the way I might start a conversation with any professional associate, whether or not they'd just eye-fondled my breasts. And whether or not they had a fresh, raw bruise and a scrape on their face from a collision with a "door"—like he did, right now.

Though I really wasn't sure how I'd handle his answer; how I'd handle any information about Jude or his life—a life that didn't include me in it.

"Hungry," he said, picking up the menu and, predictably, avoiding answering me in any meaningful way. He looked me over again, completely ignoring the menu in his hand.

Also predictable. I didn't exactly wear business suits to business meetings.

I dressed according to how I wanted to feel.

And sitting down with Jude, I wanted to feel wanted.

My halter-style top was bronze-colored silk, with a plunging neckline, worn without a bra, and from certain angles a little braless cleavage might be glimpsed. When I moved, there would definitely be some suggestive jiggle. The shirt tucked into the high-waisted black lace pencil skirt that hugged my hips and butt, and the strappy nude suede shoes had bronze spiked high heels. I wore clothes that I felt good in, powerful in, always. I dressed for myself. Tonight, I'd also dressed for a meeting with a man I was deeply attracted to.

To see what I'd see in Jude's eyes when he looked at me.

Appreciation. That's what I saw.

And, yes; hunger.

"How're you?" he asked.

"Fine." I figured a non-meaningful answer deserved a non-meaningful answer.

"How's Taze?"

I felt my eyebrows go up, because really, I was surprised as shit he would ask. "Also fine," I said, which was unfortunately the truth. Taze was nothing if not fine.

He definitely wasn't drool-inducing, mind-melting, or totally fucking heart-shattering.

He wasn't Jude.

"Yeah?" He put the menu, which he still hadn't looked at, down. "Why're you with him?"

I laughed a bit, but it came out as an incredulous scoff. Maybe because a mere week ago, Jude had warned me off my boyfriend. Told me he was "a bad dude." If he was intent on more of the same, I'd call Taze down here right now and fuck him on the table.

Nobody told me who to date, or fuck, much less a man who wouldn't lower himself to do either.

"Really?"

"Really."

"Because I feel safe with him," I said, in all honesty.

Jude seemed to find that funny, though not ha-ha funny. A dark, disbelieving smile pulled at his lips. "You're fuckin' kidding me."

I sipped my wine, unmoved. "Don't ask the question if you don't want the answer."

"I want the answer."

I waited a moment, maybe giving him a chance to take that back, to change his mind.

He didn't.

So I answered.

"He's a biker with an outlaw motorcycle club. He wears club colors and he carries a gun. He thinks of me as his, and if anyone tried to hurt me, he'd have a large-size problem with it."

"That it?"

"Like I said. He makes me feel safe."

Jude stared at me with those gorgeous dark eyes of his, and I just tried not to squirm.

"He's younger than you. He make you feel safe like that?"

"Like what?"

"Like someone who'd never leave you because he looks up to you. Because you're better than him."

"I never said I was better than him."

He sipped his drink. "He do what you want him to? Do everything you say?"

I laughed. "Hardly."

"And yet."

"And yet, *what*?" I was getting irritated with this line of questioning. Me, sitting here defending my relationship, which was none of his business. Instead of discussing the business we were supposedly here to discuss.

"And yet," he said, "you are better than him."

I feigned disinterest, glancing at the menu myself. "And what do you base that on?"

"Everything."

"Everything? Could you be more vague?"

"You want a list?" He leaned back in his seat, dark gaze fixed on me. "You have a legitimate source of income and a career. Two careers. You own your own home. You're older."

"We've established that. And we all get older, so I won't fault Taze for his year of birth."

"You have more money."

"And you would know that, how?"

"You're smarter," he said, ignoring that. "More well-spoken. You're kinder. More confident. Classier." His eyes drifted down to the exposed slice of skin between my breasts. "You have better style. You smell better."

"Says you," I said, completely cool. How or why he'd ever been close enough to Taze to smell him, I wasn't sure, and also wasn't sure I wanted to know. "That all?"

"Mmm," he said, sipping his drink. "That's a start. You're better looking." His gaze roamed over my face. "You have prettier eyes."

"Is this your idea of flirting?" I asked. "Comparing me to a man you don't like?"

"Wasn't flirting," he said. "Just speakin' the truth."

A waitress appeared with a bottle of white wine, which Jude had apparently ordered. It was the same wine I was drinking, and she topped up my glass before placing the bottle on the table. Jude just sipped his drink as she ran through the night's features. We ordered, and when she'd departed, he said, "You're stronger than him, too."

I said nothing.

He lifted his glass. "Congratulations. Putting together a Dirty show is no small feat. Impressing Brody, even bigger feat."

I clinked the rim of my glass to his. "I'm not sure I've actually impressed him. Won his trust, for now, maybe."

"With Brody, that's pretty much the same damn thing, darlin'."

Christ. Already with the *darlin'*.

This was gonna be a looong meal if he was already flashing his dimples and pulling out the *darlin'*.

Next thing he'd be calling me V, like no time had passed between now and then, and my panties would be around my ankles.

We sipped our drinks and his dark eyes never left mine. And I remembered what happened the last time we'd toasted each other—the night of Jesse and Katie's wedding. Late in the night, just the two of us, on the deck of the lodge.

The night we last fucked.

I wondered if he was remembering the same thing.

"You always discuss your security needs with promoters in person, over dinner and drinks?" I asked him.

"Promoters don't always look like you," he answered. "You always leave your bra at home when you meet with security?"

I glanced down; my silky halter had draped open a bit too far on one side, exposing a rather generous curve of breast. My nipple was still covered. I could've casually smoothed the shirt closed, covering the rest.

I left it right where it was and looked him in the eye.

"I've never had to meet with security before. As you know, I've never done an event this big. Does my lack of bra offend you?"

"Long as you don't mind me staring, darlin', I don't mind your clothes comin' off."

Later, when the food had long been cleared away and I'd hit the bottom of the wine bottle, and Jude was on his third or fourth drink, I asked him, "Are you seeing anyone?"

It wasn't like it had never occurred to me to wonder. I would've driven myself into a mental ward long ago if I'd ever allowed myself to dwell on that topic, though.

Right now, the way he kept looking at me, the way he'd flirted with me all through dinner, the way every conversation kept leading back to some sort of compliment about me... I just suddenly needed to know.

"No one regular," he said, vague as fucking possible.

"Anyone special?"

"Special to me? No."

"Anyone who'd be bothered by you being here, right now, with me?" *And looking at me like that...*

His eyes narrowed slightly, and he didn't answer right away. So I amended the question.

"Anyone who you'd *care* would be bothered by you being here, right now, with me?"

His gaze drifted down my chest. My nipples hardened under the slinky, silky fabric of my shirt, and I truly hoped he saw it. Not because I wanted him to know how his heated glances affected my body. Because I wanted him to remember how my breasts felt in his hands. How my nipples felt in his mouth. How they tasted.

I wanted him to relive every steamy, raunchy, X-rated moment that had ever passed between us—and eat his fucking heart out.

Cruel, maybe.

A tease? I'd never been called that. But Jude, for sure; I'd tease him in a heartbeat.

Why? Because he'd rejected me, not once, but several times in my life, and yes, deep down in places I would never tell a soul, it still stung.

A lot.

"No," he said, finally.

"Anyone who makes you feel safe?"

At that, he licked his lip. His eyes twitched a little, though I couldn't tell if he was amused or considering the question. "Safe. How?"

"That thing you said about Taze. Someone younger or someone lesser than you, who looks up to you and makes you feel secure."

"Thought you weren't doing that with Taze."

"I didn't say I was. You said it."

"No," he said. "No one like that."

"You don't date women who make you feel powerful?"

He didn't answer that for a moment. Then, "No."

"You date women who make you feel weak?" I challenged.

"Not what I said." He sipped his drink, slowly. "I don't date women to 'make' me feel anything. I date women I want to date."

I finished the last of my wine, staring at him.

He stared back.

We really hadn't talked all that much about business, in the end. Over dinner he'd laid out his expectations for me, in terms of security for the New Year's Eve event. It wasn't exactly anything earth-shattering. Nothing he couldn't have filled me in on over a brief phone call. But the entire time, he seemed more focused on me, on staring at me and flirting with me, than anything else. And one bottle of wine in, I was definitely focused on him.

The fact was, Jude Grayson was the one that got away.

That had always been true.

Though most days I just didn't allow myself to think about it. I didn't dwell.

If I'd ever allowed myself to dwell I would've been, frankly, heartbroken, and I didn't want to live like that, plain and simple.

So I just. Didn't. Think. About. It.

Ever.

Until he'd suddenly come back into my life.

And now that he was in my life again—suddenly fucking everywhere—I hadn't quite figured out how to deal. I'd had a minor pathetic freak out around Jessa's meet-the-baby party, but thank God that was over. I just wasn't yet sure what my next move should be.

Ignoring him wouldn't work. Not when I was now going to have to see him, repeatedly, in the planning and executing of this event.

Fucking Taze also didn't work. Unfortunately. That had really seemed like a two-birds-with-one-stone situation—get laid *and* get over Jude—but no such luck.

So maybe facing him down was the way to go?

Worth a try, right?

"Did I make you feel powerful?" I asked him.

He didn't answer.

"Did I make you feel weak?"

He didn't answer that either, but he also didn't break eye contact, even when the waitress came by to ask if we wanted anything else. He ordered us two shots, then when she was gone, he said, "You made me feel a lot of things."

"Like what?"

He stared at my mouth. Then his gaze dropped lower again. The way he looked at me, there was no doubt in my mind that he remembered exactly how I felt, how I tasted.

Then he locked eyes with me again. "You playin' games with me, darlin'?"

He'd asked me that once before. So long ago...

"I never play a game that I can't win," I told him.

"Neither do I."

"Then I guess that makes us both sore losers."

After the waitress returned with our shots, he slipped her a credit card. His dark eyes met mine as we clinked and downed our shots.

I asked him, "What if you realize, at some point, that you're losing the game?"

"Then I change the fuckin' rules."

CHAPTER NINE

Roni

AFTER DINNER, the night pretty much deteriorated, professionally speaking.

It wasn't that we were drunk. We were, probably, but that wasn't the cause. It was that Jude was, apparently, bent on tearing my relationship with Taze up at the root and stomping it into dust.

And when I let him take my hand and pull me into the back of that first taxi, I knew I was going to let him.

We ditched our vehicles and headed from one bar to the next. I stuck to one drink per bar, so I didn't get totally shit-faced. Though I was definitely partway there.

I insisted on paying for drinks in every bar we went into, because he was kinda sorta like my client, this was supposed to be a business meeting, and no way was I letting him get some imagined upper hand by being all chivalrous and generous with his wallet.

I even opened my own doors.

Though Jude got pretty surly-looking about both the money I forked over for the drinks and every door I opened—for him.

I made sure to check a few mirrors along the way, and I didn't *look* shit-faced, which was probably the important thing. I looked a little flushed. My eyes were shining. My wavy hair was a little tussled, wild and sexy around my face.

Honestly, I looked pretty damn DTF.

Unfortunately, so did Jude.

By the time we'd walked into the second bar, his hand was on the small of my back, on my bare skin. By the time we sat down in the third, we'd smoked a joint I had in my purse, together, I was feeling incredibly warm and fuzzy and, well, *loose*... and his hand was on my thigh.

I knew I had a boyfriend. He wasn't here, and since I wasn't about to break up with anyone by picking up the phone at midnight and telling him, *Hey, guess what? It's over*, I was still going to have a boyfriend when I woke up in the morning.

A boyfriend I didn't love.

A boyfriend who didn't love me.

And another man's hand was on my thigh.

The man.

The man I'd always wanted, would probably always want, no matter how many times he rejected me. Because—dare I acknowledge it to myself?—I'd gone ahead and fallen the fuck in love with him, years ago, and that love had just kinda stuck around.

Even though he hadn't.

His hand felt heavy, possessive and presumptuous, on my thigh. Daring. He was daring me, really, wasn't he?

My lace skirt ended just above the knee and he wasn't touching my skin, but I could feel his heat soaking through the fabric. He knew I was with Taze. I told him Taze made me feel safe. And here he was, his hand on my thigh, offering—no, threatening—to rip that all to shreds.

It was as if he was saying with that hand, *He's not here, darlin'.*

What are you gonna do about it?

At one point, when I was telling him about the party I'd thrown at this bar last month, he removed the hand from my thigh. He was leaning into me, close, with his ear to my mouth so he could hear me over the loud music, and it was all I could do to keep from touching my lips to his ear, his neck. From licking his skin. I just kept talking, a kind of half-drunken rambling, because I felt like I had to talk about something, as if talking about something could erase the fact that he'd just had his hand on my thigh.

When I was finished talking, he looked at me.

He slipped his arm around my waist, drawing me closer against him, then leaned into my ear and said, "You look gorgeous."

When he drew back enough that I could see in his eyes, I said, "Did you hear anything I just said?"

"I heard everything you just said, V."

Oh, fuck.

Why did it make me melt when he called me V?

Because it felt intimate.

Because it felt like a term of endearment.

He was still holding me, his arm around my waist, and my back was arched as I leaned up into him. My head was tilted back so I could see into his face, and his was tilted down to mine. We were inches apart.

He put his other hand on my ribs, just lightly.

His eyes stayed locked with mine as he ran his hand up my side... and grazed my breast through the silk of my shirt.

My breath caught.

His hand lingered there, and his thumb skimmed over my taut nipple.

A shiver ran through me.

He said nothing. He just watched me, watched my face, my eyes as he did it again... his thumb touching my nipple, slowly, drifting over and then around... as the delicious ache spread through my entire body.

I watched his eyes darken as whatever guise of respectable professionalism we'd both brought to this "meeting" evaporated... along with any hope in hell of me remaining faithful to my boyfriend tonight.

After we left that bar, we got into another cab. I was just finished telling the driver which bar to take us to next, when Jude leaned in and laid his warm mouth over mine, just like that.

His lips parted and mine went with them, and then his tongue slid into my mouth and his hand went around the back of my head, gripping my hair. He groaned into my mouth… and it was all over.

Desire swept through my body as his tongue ravaged my mouth. I let him do it, kissing him back, sort of, but I barely moved. I barely breathed.

When he broke away, he told me, "Message Taze. Tell him you're done."

I blinked at him. "You want me to break up with a man via text message?" No matter how sacred my relationship with Taze wasn't, I would not do that to any man I was involved with.

"Right now."

"I'm not doing that."

He kissed me again anyway.

Deeper.

Hotter.

He took my hand and pressed it down on his cock. He was hard in his jeans, and his dick was, just as I remembered, more than a handful. I didn't squeeze him but I didn't exactly resist as he held my hand against himself, tight, and slowly rocked his hips, grinding his hard-on into my grasp—so there was no mistaking what he was offering.

When his mouth broke away from mine again, I was panting softly.

"You want that dick?" he murmured against my lips.

I did. I did so want that dick.

But I was dimly aware that I still had a boyfriend. Which meant I was still trying, really *trying* not to participate in this.

But I did not stop him when he fisted my hair, pulling me tighter against him, and squeezed my hand around his shaft.

"You want that dick, deep in your mouth, V?"

Oh, God. He lapped his tongue deep into my mouth, hot and slow, for effect.

Then he left my hand in his lap and drifted his hand up, skimming his fingers over my nipple through my shirt. "I want you in my mouth." He drifted his mouth over to my ear. "I want you to sit on my face... feed me that beautiful pussy." He brushed his mouth over mine. "I remember..." he told me between kisses, "I remember how fuckin' beautiful..."

After that, we didn't make it to the next bar.

We were kissing as we stumbled through my front door. If you could call it kissing. We were feasting on each other, Jude's mouth totally dominating mine and mine trying to dominate his... and *fuck*... I'd missed his kisses.

I'd been dreaming about Jude's kisses since I was sixteen years old, and unfortunately not much had changed since then. He still kissed me like I was his whole world.

I still knew that I wasn't.

In the moment, I just didn't care. Not enough to stop this.

My purse landed with a thud on the hallway floor as he pushed me up against the wall. He smashed his lips against mine as our tongues fought for dominance. Our bodies fused together, my hands in his hair, his hands in mine, his hips slamming against me. His thigh pressed between my legs, my tight skirt preventing him from getting where I wanted him.

I wanted him to throw me right down on the floor and fuck me. I didn't care that it was hardwood. I didn't care about what came after this... or didn't.

I didn't care about Taze.

I just wanted Jude Grayson to lose his shit over me, right now, and fuck me on the floor.

When we'd left the restaurant and climbed into that first taxi, it had started to feel like a game of chicken. Both of us gunning it at each other, holding strong—waiting to see who ditched out of the way at the last minute.

Except no one ditched.

So now it was more like a car crash. Like a head-on collision—see who came out alive on the other side...

Me.

It definitely had to be me.

I wasn't going down in flames over this.

As soon as we'd clawed our jackets off, I tore his shirt off over his head.

He gripped my shirt and ripped it down over my shoulders, tearing it right down the middle, exposing my breasts. "This fuckin' shirt..." he said.

Okay, so he won that one.

I went for his jeans next, popping the button and flipping up the tab on the zipper so I could rip them right open.

He pushed up my skirt and pulled me right down to the floor—and onto his face.

Jesus. He was so winning this battle...

He didn't even take off my panties first. Somehow, his tongue was in me. His thumb was digging in, dragging my panties more or less out of the way, as he fucked me with his tongue.

"*Omigod...*" I moaned, mostly to myself. His dick wasn't in me, but his tongue sure as fuck was, and this was definitely cheating territory.

We'd crossed that boundary somewhere between that last shot at the restaurant and his hand taking mine. I knew that.

I was still fighting it.

It wasn't even about Taze.

It was about *me.*

He rolled, taking me down with him. He laid me out on my back on the floor, pushed my skirt up farther around my hips, and dragged my panties down and off. Then he hiked my thigh up and went to town on my pussy with his mouth.

I laid back and took it. His swirling tongue, the heat of his mouth, those soft lips of his... all the while, the guilt swimming in my head... along with the liquor and the weed and the desire.

I was vaguely aware of his jeans coming off and the condom going on, and when he prowled on top of me, much like that first night we'd ever had sex... I knew where this was headed. When I glanced down he was suited up, stiff and ready, and when I looked up—his eyes said it all.

Brace yourself, darlin'. That's what that look said.

Shit.

"Wait." I held him off with one hand on his naked, rock-hard chest.

His dick was about a millimeter away from obliterating the view I'd always had of myself—of a girl who didn't cheat—while I managed to grab my phone out of my abandoned purse and write a text to Taze.

I was pretty sure it said something like *We're breaking up. It's over.* No doubt it was riddled with typos. Maybe it was totally fucking unintelligible.

I sent it. Hopefully Taze could decipher it.

"There," I said.

Jude ripped the phone from my hand and tossed it across the living room rug, and in the next second, he was in me—in one forceful, animal thrust.

He fucked me the way he always had. Deep. Dominating.

So I'd feel it for days.

He fucked me on the hallway floor, halfway between the living room and my bedroom. It was my home, I'd had sex here many, many times, but I'd never been fucked right here, in the hall, on the floor. It felt dirty and amazing, and the only thing that could've made it any better was if he'd really let loose.

But something was holding him back.

It was subtle. But he was holding himself up over me, on his arms, and he was definitely holding back.

"Fuck me harder," I urged him.

He did, but he was still holding back. Maybe he was afraid of hurting me on the hard floor?

"Come on, Jude," I groaned. "Make me feel it."

"Jesus, V..."

But he fucked me harder. He adjusted a couple of times, repositioning himself, for what reason, I had no idea. Every which way he came at me felt fucking perfect.

Not only was he fucking gorgeous, the sexiest man I'd ever been with, the one I was the most attracted to, but Jude's dick was huge and filled me in a way that just drove me fucking crazy. Every part of his body just lined up perfectly with every part of mine.

Physically speaking, we were fucking *made* for each other.

"Don't stop..." I clutched at his ass, clawed his back, tried to pull him down on top of me, desperate for his weight. But he grunted and kind of locked up, and that's when I realized something was wrong. Or at least, it definitely wasn't right.

I was hurting him. Or something.

"You okay? What's—"

He pulled out suddenly, and got to his feet, taking me with him.

"Are you alright?"

He kissed me, silencing me, and started pushing me up the hall. By the time we'd made it to my bed, we'd peeled every remaining stitch of clothing from each other's bodies. He pulled me with him onto the bed, laying back as he drew me over his hips.

I straddled him and took him inside, and when I started fucking the hell out of him, he grunted again. "*Agh.* Shit. That's worse."

"What's wrong with you?" I asked, softly, but he just rolled me off, put me on the floor again, on the rug by my bed, and started pounding into me. He held my hips with one hand, the bedside table with the other, and gave it to me. He pounded me so hard my eyes watered from the intensity.

Not pain; emotion.

A swell of lust and gratitude, relief and affection, desire and satisfaction... So many emotions at once, I couldn't separate one from the next. It was all just one astonishing blur of... *pleasure*.

I screamed as the pleasure gripped me, thrashing beneath him as I came.

I whacked my head on the bedside table.

A vase fell off the table and smashed on the hardwood floor, narrowly missing us.

It was like two-thirty in the morning.

I didn't even care.

"Roni," he breathed, "you okay, darlin'?" He'd stopped pounding, and as the slight pain rang through my head, I looked up at him in a daze.

"Come," I said. "Jesus Christ, don't stop."

So he dragged me a safe distance away from the table and kept at it.

"*Fuck*," he groaned. "Fuck, you feel so good..."

"Yeah," I moaned right back, "*yeah*, that dick..." And I came again, totally losing it beneath him.

"Yeah, V..." He pounded into me with short, deep thrusts as I rode out my orgasm. "Gonna fuck that pussy..." Then he lost all his rhythm as he fell apart. He came with a growl, and as I felt his release, his muscled body locking up and his cock firing inside me... then his body going limp as he panted over me... it was pure fucking glory.

I did that.

I turned him on like that.

I made Jude Grayson totally lose his shit on my bedroom floor.

It wasn't until after he'd come that I glimpsed, in the mirror on my closet door, the horrendous black bruise on his lower back.

"Jude!" I gasped, as he eased himself off of me. "What the hell happened to your back?"

"Nothing." He eased the condom off and kissed me.

"But—"

"It's nothing..." Then he kissed me many, many times, until I got the message and stopped asking.

CHAPTER TEN

Jude

MONDAY NIGHT.

11:03 pm.

I fell into bed, spent.

Stared at the fucking ceiling, spread out on the king-sized mattress that no one ever slept on but me. I was a king-sized dude. It never occurred to me before that that was weird. That no one had ever laid in this bed with me.

This bed that I'd never shared with a woman. Had never thought about bringing a woman home to.

Had never laid in by myself, either, jerking off and longing for a *specific* woman... until recently.

Until her.

This morning, I was late to meet Jesse. Combination of being out late, drinking with Roni, fucking the hell out of each other at her place until almost four in the morning, then dragging my ass home... and the residual discomfort of my injuries.

Taze. *Fuck*, that little shit.

I'd tossed the painkillers this morning thinking I could go without them, and I was feeling it, but it wasn't too intense. Just exhausting as my body struggled to heal while I instead punished it with shots of bourbon and wild-ass sex.

I didn't need anyone to know how wrecked I was, though, so I downplayed the damage on my cheek and I definitely didn't tell anyone about my back.

I'd spent the day at the recording studio with the band, but all the while Bane had kept me posted on Roni's whereabouts. She'd gone straight home after work and stayed in for the evening, and Taze hadn't reared his head.

After getting her breakup text late last night, twenty-four hours after he'd pulled a tire iron on me, he was probably worried that I'd gotten to her.

Good start.

But I wanted to be sure she'd stay the hell away from him. I had no idea if she really would. Just because she dumped him last night, via text, when I was a nanosecond from fucking her, didn't mean it was gonna stick.

She didn't message me.

I didn't message her.

I wondered if she wanted me to give chase.

I wondered if I would.

Soon after I met her, Roni had told me, casually, that she never went back for seconds. She told me that many times. Just one of those flirtatious, ridiculous things she used to say.

She told me the same thing, again, the *third* time I'd fucked her —the night of Jesse's wedding.

But then she went and got herself a boyfriend.

I said I didn't want a relationship with her. Told her that. Told myself that. But now here I was, home alone in bed, without her—wanting more. I was thinking about how to seduce her when I told myself, long ago, I'd never do this.

Veronica Webber hurt me. More than once.

I swore I'd never look back.

But now I was looking back. Trying to see things as they were. Through mature eyes, rather than the limited vision I had back then.

How fucking little I understood about women then.

But I *always* knew myself.

Over the years, I'd had my share of women, but I'd always cared. No matter how little I knew them, no matter what strangers they were to me in that moment, I always had to care. Couldn't turn that part of myself off like some guys could. Had to look a woman in the eye and give a shit how she felt about it during, afterward.

Had to look Roni in the face ten months ago, right after we'd fucked, stare straight down the barrels of those two jade-green eyes of hers and ask her, *You feelin' me, V?*

Because I didn't mislead women. I didn't lie to them to get them into bed or afterward. I was straight with her, just like I was with every woman I'd ever been involved with, however casually.

You and me, darlin', we're not goin' down that road.

I'd meant it when I said it.

At least, I sure fucking thought I did.

But the truth was I wasn't done with her. I knew that about two seconds after she walked out of that lodge, and in the days and weeks and months that followed, when I couldn't stop thinking about her.

Wondering about her.

I wanted to fuck her again. Obviously.

I'd always wanted to fuck her.

But I was not sure where this road went, and that made me incredibly fucking uncomfortable. With her, I'd never been sure.

And I wasn't sure I liked that feeling. At all.

Fact was, I *had* always dated women who made me feel powerful.

And never had a woman brought me to my fucking knees the way she did.

I was nineteen when I met her.

In my apartment.

I'd just walked in the door, and the Doors were playing over Brody's stereo. "Love Her Madly." She was lying sprawled on my bed in the living room, her legs tossed up against the wall, her too-small plaid skirt up around her hips, and I could pretty much see her pussy, covered only by a thin strip of baby-blue lace panties.

Wasn't exactly an unusual scenario to walk into in this apartment, which I shared with Jesse, Brody and Zane.

She was looking at a copy of Zane's *Penthouse*, so I couldn't see her face.

"Wrong bed, darlin'," I told her.

It was a one-bedroom apartment and I shared the living room with Zane, mainly because I was the only one who could handle sleeping a few feet from Zane. Though I didn't love it when his sexual conquests spilled over onto my futon.

Which they did, regularly.

She lowered the magazine. Pretty. Little upturned nose, black hair in two long pig tails and a thick fringe of bangs over jade-green eyes with too much black eyeliner. And she was sucking on a lollipop.

"Who are you?" she said, looking me over, slowly, from head-to-toe and right back up again. She made absolutely no move to adjust her skirt or cover her barely-lace-covered pussy.

"Jude!" Jessa came out of the bathroom, surprising me. She was all bedazzled in a sparkly pink tank top and jeans—both way too tight. The girl had a generous rack since she was about twelve, and Jesse would've flipped if he saw her in that shirt. "Hi!" She gave me a hug and I hugged her back.

"Hey, bratface," I greeted her. "Where's your brother?"

"Don't know. We're going shopping." She motioned for the other girl to get the hell up, at which point it dawned on me that the chick spread out on my bed was not some random piece one of the guys had dragged home, but a friend of Jessa's—Jesse's fifteen-year-old sister.

A high school girl?

I watched the girl ditch the *Penthouse* and get up, smoothing her pig tails, her black-rimmed eyes on me the entire time, even as I noted the definite smell of booze Jessa had tried to hide with perfume and mouthwash. Was no secret to me that Jessa often swung by her brother's apartment when he wasn't home because four men shared it and there was always booze to be found.

"Shopping," I said as I watched them pull on their shoes. "At eight o'clock on a Wednesday?"

"The mall's open for another hour," Jessa said, grabbing her friend by the elbow and yanking her past me, out the door.

"Nice to meet you, *Jude*," the girl said, licking her lollipop and really working the Lolita vibe.

I didn't even know her name.

Three days later, when I saw Jessa at a band rehearsal, I asked her, "Who was that girl with you at the apartment the other night?"

"That was Roni," she said.

"You mean Wild Card," Zane said. "That's Jessa's new friend from school." His eyebrow arched in a way that told me he'd met her, too.

Jessa rolled her eyes. "Her name's Roni."

Zane mouthed at me: *Wild Card*.

Within a week, I'd found out all kinds of shit about Veronica Webber.

First of all, the "Wild Card" thing: Zane's invention. And unfortunately, it caught on. Even though she was new to Jessa's school, Roni Webber was already making something of a reputation for herself around the neighborhood. She was a junior, a year ahead of Jessa—and obviously, lightyears more sexually mature.

I found out she lived with her mom and her mom's boyfriend in a crappy old house about ten blocks from the house where Jesse and Jessa had grown up, where Jessa now lived with their mom. I also found out that Roni used her mom's piece-of-shit car to go to parties. And that she was starting to take Jessa to those parties with her.

Parties neither of them should've been at.

Jessa seemed to like her, was always hanging out with her.

Jesse didn't love her. Definitely didn't want any of her "wild card" ways rubbing off on his baby sister.

I was reserving judgment.

I didn't dislike her, that was for sure.

The Lolita thing didn't really do it for me, but something about her did.

I'd always been pretty selective with girls. Usually, I was attracted to older women. Maybe it was my own insecurity, or maybe I was just wired that way. But I'd never understood my brother's fascination with club sluts. I was never drawn to the fangirls who hung out like flies around my dad's motorcycle club, now also my brother's motorcycle club, *or* around the band.

I preferred women who offered a little challenge. Smart. Classy. Maybe a little mysterious.

Women who wouldn't touch men like my brother with a very long and sterile pole.

I wasn't usually drawn to younger girls, in general. When I was sixteen, I was already sleeping with twenty-year-olds.

But I was curious about Roni.

And the few times I crossed paths with her, when she was with Jessa, she kinda stared at me. She flirted a little. She asked me about my name.

"*Jude*," she said, the third time I met her, stressing the U sound. "Juuude. I've never met a guy named Jude. Is that like the Beatles song?"

"It's not unlike the Beatles song," I said.

She smiled. She had round, pouty lips, and she definitely knew how to work them when a guy was looking at her. It was the first time she'd smiled at me, and I liked it.

Then she showed up at a band rehearsal with Jessa, literally the next day—and flirted up a pheromone storm with Zane, right in front of me.

And with Dylan.

At that point, I pegged her as a groupie. Disappointing, sort of. But it wasn't like I was surprised. I was so familiar with the routine that it had already become numbingly boring. The way some girls looked right past me to my brother, or Zane, or Jesse, or whoever.

I knew the type.

Call me crazy, but I preferred women who actually saw *me.* Who actually gave a fuck about me.

Who were drawn to me and only me, despite all the other available dick in the room.

I figured I knew everything I ever needed to know about Roni "Wild Card" Webber, right then.

But then a few weeks later, Jesse asked me to pick Jessa up one evening. Not unusual. As it turned out, though, she was at Roni's place.

I happened to get there a few minutes early, parked on the road in front of the house, and when I got out of my car, I saw something I shouldn't have. Something neither Roni or Jessa ever knew that I saw.

I saw Roni standing in the front door of the house, which was open, talking to her mom's boyfriend, who was standing just inside. Arguing with him, maybe.

Then I saw him push her right out the door.

She stumbled and fell, and once she was already off her feet, he shoved her right down the stairs and shut the door.

Right in front of Jessa, who was standing at the bottom of the stairs.

It happened so fast, it was over before I could react. I couldn't do anything about it.

But I saw Roni, from that moment on, in a totally different light.

That brief glimpse into her life would shape how I would always view her—as a girl who'd been pushed around but worked so hard to show the world she was anything but a pushover. A girl who took what she wanted and moved on—before she could get hurt.

And it didn't take a degree in psychology to realize why she sought out the attention from men that she did.

It bothered me, long afterward.

I didn't say anything to Roni or Jessa when they got in my car that day. They both acted like nothing had happened. They didn't know I saw.

But seeing Roni treated like that hit me deep. It tweaked every protective urge I had, and I had a major protective streak.

I'd always been that way.

I'd been in way too many fights in my life, sometimes fights I had no business being in, because I felt like I had to protect my brother. Never mind that Piper was bigger than me, five years older than me, had always been a better fighter, and our dad was a biker. It was my *nature*. I looked out for my own. For anyone I gave a damn about.

Hell, I looked out for anyone who needed it, if I could.

It bothered me enough that a few nights later, I jumped a guy coming out of a convenience store. Not just any guy; Roni's mom's boyfriend.

His name was Jed. Fucking *Jed*.

Just sounded like the name of an asshole who shoved his girlfriend's teenage daughter literally on her ass.

I shoved a knife up next to his ribs under my jacket and told him, "Walk."

He walked. I took him around behind the store where my brother, Piper, and a friend of ours was waiting. They were both Kings, but they didn't wear their colors. Neither of them knew who this guy was or why we were here, but they stood by, stood watch, as I beat the crap out of him. Piper would've done anything for me; he didn't ask. He had his piece in the front of his jeans, shoved into his waistband, and the guy on the ground saw it. The gun was never drawn. It didn't need to be.

I left him lying there, bruised to hell and no doubt scared as shit, drooling blood, and whispered in his ear, "You leave Roni the fuck alone."

He had no idea who I was, but that message got through.

Within a week, Jed had broken up with Roni's mom and taken the hell off.

Good riddance.

One afternoon, not long after that, I was with Jesse at his mom's place. We were down in the basement, picking up some of his things; he still stored some music equipment there. I heard Jessa come home, and the sound of Roni's voice.

And I felt a nervous stab of guilt.

Obviously, she needed that guy out of her life. But I hadn't seen her yet, since what I did. I wasn't super proud of it. I wasn't really a violent person. At least, I never thought I was.

I'd seen plenty of violence growing up.

As a man, I rarely resorted to it myself. But some situations, maybe they just called for it. I'd no more let that asshole hurt Roni and be able to sleep at night than I'd be able to hurt her myself.

That was how I stomached it.

After a few minutes, I made some excuse to slip upstairs. I wanted to say hi to Roni, but they were in Jessa's bedroom. The door was open and I heard them talking. I didn't exactly hover outside like a creeper, but I stopped in the living room. They were talking loud enough I could hear every word.

Obviously they had no idea I was there, because Jessa was talking about some guy she liked, and she never talked about that shit in front of me or Jesse.

"Just tell me who it is," Roni was urging her. "You know I'm gonna find out anyway."

"No," Jessa said. "I don't want to talk about it."

"Are you gonna fuck him?"

"Ew. No. I mean... not yet."

"Why not?"

"I don't know. I mean, we're not there yet. I don't even know if he likes me that way."

"Of course he does. If I were you, I'd hit that before some other girl gets her claws into him."

Jessa sort of sighed and laughed uncomfortably. "It's not that easy."

"I never said it was easy. You *know* I've got my own personal sexual bucket list. It's okay to have goals. But not every guy is a sure thing from moment one, no matter how hot you are."

Jessa snorted. "You and your sexual bucket list."

"I mean, just because Piper is at the top of the list, doesn't mean I'm gonna screw him, like, tomorrow."

A bolt of discomfort stabbed through me as I heard Roni's words. I heard them, but it was like I was in shock.

"Believe me," she went on, "I would screw him tomorrow, if I could. But sometimes, when the guy's really worth it, you have to wait it out. Which is why you're going to introduce me to him the first chance you get, and then I'll start working my charms..."

After that, I took off. I didn't want to hear more. I headed back downstairs to help Jesse, then got the fuck out of there.

But it really fucking floored me.

Maybe I'd really started to feel something for this girl? Because I was not taking this whole sexual bucket list thing too well—especially when I found out my older brother was at the top of her list of sexual goals.

Fucking ironic or something.

Roni had no idea I'd driven off her mom's boyfriend. No one did. Even Piper didn't know or care who the fuck Jed was. Which meant Roni didn't know Piper had helped me do it, either; he hadn't even *done* anything to win her over. It didn't even sound like she'd met him yet.

And now she had a thing for him?

Fucking typical.

It was that day that I told myself to forget about Roni Webber.

For the first time of many.

And just like all the other times, it wouldn't stick.

I didn't see her until a few weeks later, at a party Dirty was playing outside of town, at Shady's place. The party was in the big barn in the side lot, it was pretty packed, and I was talking to Brody near the small stage in back when he fucking freaked out. His eyes locked on something across the barn. "Fuck, no," he growled, and then he bolted through the crowd.

I went after him.

It was Jessa, and she was there with Roni. And I knew why Brody was flipping out. For one, he had a massive hard-on for Jessa

Mayes, which he tried to hide from Jesse *and* me. But since I was pretty sure he was also head-over-heels in love with her, would never actually touch her and would probably die before hurting her, I let it slide. I didn't tattle on him to Jesse. But I did help him bounce her ass out of parties like this one—which was filled with bikers and other people none of us wanted Jessa anywhere near.

I followed Brody right up behind her.

"What. The. Fuck," was all he said, loud enough for her to hear it over the band; Dirty was onstage, and hopefully Jesse would never have to know his little sister was here.

She turned around and put on a forced half-smile. She wasn't any happier to see us than we were to see her.

"Hey, Brody," she said.

"The fuck are you doing here?" he growled.

"You've got five minutes," I said, looming over her. The quickest way to diffuse the situation—and Brody's ticking time-bomb temper—was to get her the fuck out of here.

"Five minutes until what?" she asked, as if she didn't fucking know.

"'Til I bounce your ass out of here," I said. "Say your hellos and goodbyes and let's get going."

Roni had lingered, listening in, but now she flipped her hair, giving me a bored look. "I'm gone," she told Jessa. "Call you later, 'kay?" Then she smiled at me. "Later, jailor."

"Keep an eye on that one," Brody said, bumping my arm as Roni headed off through the crowd.

"Why?"

"'Cause she's sixteen. She gets to drinking, bounce her ass home."

I snarled my irritation and glared at Jessa so she knew I was pissed—though that never did much to scare her away, anyway—then stalked off after Roni.

"Good luck with that!" I heard Jessa call after me. Whatever. Forget minutes; five *seconds* and Brody was gonna have her out the door.

I didn't love it, but I did what he asked me to. Because he was right. Roni was Jessa's friend, and Jesse was gonna lose it if she got shit-faced at this party and ended up underneath some asshole. He was already worried enough about Jessa. None of us needed her or her underage friends at these parties. Least of all me.

I'd been in charge of any kind of security we needed as the band gradually got bigger, but managing Jessa's safety was becoming a fucking headache. One way or another, that girl was growing up, and Jesse was gonna have to get used to it.

Still, I followed Roni through the crowd.

She was wearing a black strapless shirt, super tight, with push-up cups. It was velvet, looked like no underage girl should legally be allowed to wear it, and fuck if I knew what it was called—a corset? Her jeans were skin-tight, low-cut on the hips, with a line of sparkly rhinestones right up the crack of her ass. They kept catching the light, snagging my eyes, like a g-string winking at me in the dark.

She ignored me, at first, but she knew I was there. When she stopped to watch the band, I came up beside her. She pretended not to notice.

"Piper's not here," I told her.

She gazed up at me, with the put-on innocence of a stripper doing a nun routine. "Who?"

"Piper," I said. "My brother. You're here for him, no?"

"I'm here for Dirty," she said sweetly, blinking up at me. "But I'll hang out with you, if you want."

Like I'd asked her to hang out with me.

She said it *so* sweetly I could almost buy the innocent act. Maybe. If I'd never met her before, or overheard all that shit about her sexual bucket list.

But since I knew that if Piper was around he'd be her first choice, I was not falling for it.

"I mean, unless you want to leave," she said, turning toward me. She shifted her hips so her tits jiggled in the cups of her velvet jail-bait top. "You wanna take me for a ride on your bike?"

I was nineteen years old. My dad and my brother were patched members of an MC. I'd been riding motorcycles all my damn life. And I worked with a rock band. Which meant I met women *all the time,* and I'd definitely had a lot of them ask for a ride on my bike.

I'd *never* had a woman—or for that matter, a girl—ask for a ride on my bike with that much innuendo.

"No."

She immediately pouted, dropping the innocent act. "Oh, come on. It would be fun. I'm an incredible passenger."

Again, the innuendo.

And I had to wonder...

If she knew what I'd witnessed, fucking Jed shoving her down those steps... would she be acting this way in front of me?

No. She'd be different.

Would she be angry?

Embarrassed?

I grabbed her by the shoulders, right then, and I kissed her, shocking the saucy-teen-seductress look right off her face.

The truth was, I'd been thinking about her, a lot. Ever since the first time I saw her.

Despite my efforts to forget her after I heard her talking about my brother.

And I needed to know: What the fuck was this?

Was it real?

Was there anything about this that was real, that was worth pursuing?

Or should I just forget her?

It took her a moment to get over the shock. A *short* moment. But within a heartbeat, she was kissing me back. Her mouth was as soft and juicy as it looked and the kiss was tender, hot.

Then it got hotter as she pressed into me, her mouth opening. It got deeper. Dark and brutal... and by the end, it stole my breath.

It seemed to steal hers, too.

I pulled back, not wanting to hurt her. Not even sure if I hadn't already.

I stared at her and she stared at me. Her lips were flushed and swollen. Mine felt bruised.

I didn't even know how to feel about any of it.

My head was fucking spinning.

"You want to fuck?" she asked me.

"Yeah."

I didn't even know in that moment if I was going to. If I was actually going to fuck her.

I knew she was sixteen.

I knew she wanted my brother. My twenty-four-year-old brother.

I didn't know what I was gonna do.

I just felt...

I took her hand and we worked our way through the crowd, slowly, together. At one point, I had to stop in the crowd to talk to someone. Roni got pulled away to talk to someone else; she broke away. She got farther and farther away in the crowd.

I looked at her across the room. I watched her dance.

She looked back at me.

And late in the night, when my back was turned, she left.

CHAPTER ELEVEN

Roni

I PUT in my hours at the display suite office on Monday, and while I did, I worked on the New Year's Eve event as much as I could. I kept working on it over Indian takeout at my dining room table, after work.

And all the while, I put Jude and what we'd done last night completely out of my mind. Or almost completely.

Because I was determined to keep the New Year's event and what happened last night *separate.*

Work. Play.

Work was serious.

Play was not.

The last thing I needed was to get serious about screwing Jude Grayson.

Brody had already emailed me some sample contracts, and by the time I'd finished dinner, I'd sent a detailed outline of the terms I needed drafted into a contract to my lawyer. I'd worked out a rough schedule for the day of the event, beginning with the time security and crew needed access to the venue, and including the tear-down in the hours after the show.

And I wondered, as I stared at the schedule on my laptop, if that night—as we finished up with the event, the crew packing the gear out of the venue and Jude sending his guys home—would be the last time I ever saw him.

I'd had so many moments in my life that I'd thought would be the last time I ever saw him. And yet... somehow, he just kept coming back.

Or I did.

When I walked into my bedroom, it was so empty of him it actually hurt. When I woke up this morning, he was already gone. Actually, he was gone long before morning came. But he'd been here, in my home. When I woke up, I could smell him on my sheets.

I could smell him on *me*.

I didn't even want to take a shower this morning because of it.

I did.

But yeah. Not good.

I sat down on my bed and stared, for a while, at the glass of water on the bedside table.

So strange, how a man and a woman could act like such animals together. Naked and raw and so ridiculously intimate, and afterwards get dressed and go about all the polite niceties of life.

After Jude fucked me so hard and so good my eyes watered and a vase on my bedside table smashed on the floor and my neighbors probably hated me, he sat on the edge of my bed and asked me if I wanted a glass of water.

Then he went into my kitchen and poured me a glass of water. He put it on the table by my bed, where the vase had been, then went into the bathroom to clean up.

The water glass was a generic tumbler with an ugly pattern of yellow flowers on it, which I'd held onto somewhat ironically when I moved out of my mom's home for the first time. It was one of those glasses they used to give out for free at the gas station at the end of our street when you filled up your tank with gas. I was proud the first time I could afford to fill my mom's gas tank all by myself. I'd brought the tumbler home to her.

That very same night, her boyfriend used it to drink whatever shit he was drinking, got drunk, and broke it. Not on purpose, but just as a side effect of generally being an idiot and a drunk.

One month later, when I could afford to, I filled up the tank with gas again, got another tumbler, and kept it in my room. It was a symbol of a whole lot of shit to me at the time; my independence, my ability to take care of myself, the places I was headed in life with or without my mom's help. I barely even noticed how ugly it was.

As it sat on my bedside table where Jude had put it, I wondered if he noticed how ugly it was. I wondered why he picked that one ugly glass from a cupboard filled with much more beautiful glasses.

After I got ready for bed and finally slipped under the sheets, naked, I couldn't quite sleep. I checked my phone to see if Jude had texted me, too many times.

He didn't.

Then I ended up masturbating, thinking about him. I thought about last night, about the sex, obviously. And the build-up to the sex.

I thought about him kissing me, like I so often did.

I tried to draw it out, make it last... but Jude just got me there too quick. Even when he wasn't in the room.

Afterwards, I still couldn't sleep. I kept thinking about how he'd asked me—no, told me—to text Taze before he fucked me. How he wanted to break us up.

Like he wanted me for himself.

For more than one night?

It definitely didn't *feel* like a one-time fuck. It felt like a fuck that led to other fucks... and from there... probably nowhere.

Just like every other fuck we'd had.

Every other amazing fuck.

And still... I would fuck him again. I knew that much.

I was going to work my ass off on this event and I was going to fuck Jude any chance I got.

If I got the chance.

Fine plan.

But what happened when he decided we were done, like he did before?

I did not like making myself vulnerable to him. I really didn't need any more Jude-induced heartbreak in my life.

I was perfectly fine without him.

But since when was "fine" good enough?

I did not want fine.

I wanted epic, frantic, desperate, intense, brutal, no-compromise *alive*. I wanted what I felt when I was with *him*.

I wanted Jude.

I wanted him...

But I didn't text him. I didn't call.

On the edge of sleep, I was still thinking about him kissing me in the cab last night. And I was thinking way back to when he kissed me eleven years ago, at that party.

The best first kiss I'd ever had.

The feel of his lips on mine for the first time; that surprising kiss. The foreign taste of him that quickly became familiar, the heat of him and the rhythm of his mouth...

That kiss that was my secret.

So unexpected. So brutal.

So soft.

That kiss Jude stole; that little piece of my heart that he took from me that night, and never gave back.

Even after Jessa told me what happened to her that night—that Brody had kissed her outside that party before he drove her home—I didn't tell her Jude kissed me. It just felt too intimate. Too private, even though it happened right in the middle of a crowded party.

Plus, I didn't really want anyone to know.

So I never told anyone.

I was after Piper, I *wanted* Piper, and that didn't change.

For one thing, I'd already declared to every one of my girlfriends, repeatedly, that I was going to make Jeremy "Piper"

Grayson *mine*. I was committed to my mission, and I wouldn't back down. It wasn't my way. I just wouldn't do it.

Not until I got what I wanted.

And I *knew* what I wanted.

I also knew the way things worked in the biker world, more or less. From what I'd gathered while interrogating Jessa for everything she knew about Piper Grayson, he was tight with his brother. Which meant if I messed around with Jude first, the odds of Piper going anywhere near me were slim.

For another thing... I was sixteen and stupid.

I thought, from my limited experience with men, that I could get whatever I wanted. That I *should* get whatever I wanted.

I was just plain wrong.

I'd made my choice, but I'd made the wrong choice.

I just didn't know it yet.

Somehow maybe the universe knew, even if I didn't, that it should've been Jude. Maybe Jude knew it should've been Jude, and he was telling me so with that kiss.

Maybe he was just gonna hold onto that little piece of my heart until I figured it out.

And fool that I was, stubborn as I was... maybe I convinced myself that I could live without it.

It happened at a crappy house party.

Well, the party was okay. The house was owned by some Kings hang-around—some guy who wanted to be a King, hadn't yet been invited to prospect for the club, but had a house on a property way out in Cloverdale and threw decent parties that usually promised to include at least a few Kings.

Piper was there that night, I was there, and I was on a mission. He was drunk, he was single (after a brief, inexplicably lingering semi-relationship with a girl I was sure was half as pretty as I was, though twice as slutty) and when I started pouring him shots, he started paying attention.

It had taken me a long, long time to get Piper's attention. I'd been chasing him for a *year*. Granted, there were a lot of girls vying for his attention, so maybe it was only fair I had to wait in line. I was only seventeen, and he didn't seem to go for girls my age.

Which only made me more committed to turning his head.

I was almost eighteen anyway. I was mature. And I was *the girl* for him. He just didn't know it yet.

These were the things I'd been telling myself for the last year.

Eventually, that night, I did turn his head long enough to get him alone in the kitchen for a few hot minutes.

But his attention really didn't last long.

And afterwards, he sent me on my way.

It didn't bother me as much as it maybe should've, considering I'd been hoping to make him my boyfriend, had idealized him in my mind and fantasized about him for so damn long. But the whole thing was so incredibly anticlimactic, so... just... nothing at all... it didn't even seem to matter.

Kinda made me feel, for a few minutes, like I didn't matter.

On the edge of some minor emotional crisis, I took my ass outside, where I could be alone. I was planning to leave, but figured I should get myself together before I drove. I wasn't drunk, hadn't even been drinking, wanted to be sober when I talked to Piper. But it wasn't like we did much talking anyway.

I was sitting on the back stoop of the house by myself in the dark, kinda half-smoking a joint, when I realized a man was standing over me. He startled me, but when I looked up and discovered it was Jude, I relaxed.

"Hey, V," he said, looking at me in that silent way he did. Like he was reading the situation.

Reading *me*.

It was the first time he'd called me V. He'd never, ever called me "Wild Card" like Jessa's brother, Jesse, did, or like Zane and some of their other friends did. Jude called me Roni or Veronica. And now, V.

He was wearing his leather Kings cut with the too-clean Prospect patch on it. He'd started prospecting for the Kings that year. Jessa had told me that Jesse was hellbent on making it big with Dirty so they could take Jude on the road and keep him out of the MC, but I was pretty sure, by the looks of things, even if Jesse's band made it huge, Jude was still gonna be in the MC.

He did work with the band a lot though, as a roadie, bouncing parties, that kind of thing. Which meant I often ran into him, because I went to as many band parties as I could. He'd always been nice enough to me, but he'd always kept his distance, too.

Other than that one night he'd kissed me.

Piper was also distant, but as Jude sat down beside me on that stoop in the dark and looked at me, I could feel the stark differences between them.

Maybe I'd convinced myself Piper just hadn't had a chance to discover how fabulous I was yet; that he'd come around when I got my chance to seduce him.

It wasn't that.

Piper was distant because he just didn't care. Frankly, he probably thought he was better than me. Not that I really kidded myself that Piper thought about me at all—especially after that night. More like he barely even noticed me because, in his eyes, I wasn't someone worth noticing. I was just more slutty white noise, which, for a brief moment in that kitchen, for whatever reason, he chose to tune in more clearly.

Then tune right back out.

But Jude... Jude kept himself at a distance from me deliberately. I knew that because even while he stayed distant, he *watched* me.

And it was pretty obvious to me why, on that night of all nights, he got close. Because I was sitting in the dark, alone, at a biker party, and when I looked up at him I had tears shining in my eyes.

I'd watched him, too, and even though Jude was quieter than

Piper, I'd figured a few things out about him. One thing I knew for sure was that Jude cared about people. More than that, actually; he felt responsible for people. I'd seen it again and again with how he looked out for Jesse, the rest of the band... and Jessa. How protective he was. How he was always breaking up fights and kicking people out of parties when they got out of hand.

He didn't want people getting hurt on his watch.

And that night, I'd been hurt. As much as I didn't love to admit that to myself. It wasn't exactly that Piper had hurt me. In reality, I barely knew Piper, and he definitely didn't know me.

It was that I'd set myself on a year-long course to get hurt... for nothing.

Nothing but a few hot minutes in some dude's kitchen at a party.

Jude's shoulder brushed mine, maybe because the stoop was so small and he was so big—he'd gotten bigger since I first met him. He felt warm next to me, and solid. It just made me feel small and cold.

"You got any more of that?" he asked me, flicking his chin at my half-finished joint. As if he couldn't get weed from his brother or anyone in that party?

"Take it." I handed it to him. He took it and smoked, but he didn't hand it back to me—which was when I realized he wasn't smoking it because he wanted to smoke it. He was smoking it so I couldn't smoke it. "How old are you now?" he asked me, exhaling smoke.

I was pretty sure he knew how old I was, which meant he was asking the question for *me*. My defenses went way up, along with my attitude.

"*Seventeen*," I said, like he was stupid for asking. "And so what? I can't have any bad habits?"

He considered that. Even in the dark I could kinda see his eyes, searching my face. "This a habit?" He held up the joint.

"No. But we can't all be perfect like you, Jude Grayson."

His dark eyebrows raised. "Perfect?"

"You know. Some of us have vices. Bad habits. Weaknesses. It's called being human," I informed him, with the confidence of someone who thought she knew way more about life than she really did.

He was only three years older than me, but surely he knew how little I really knew.

"You think I don't have vices?"

I made a bitchy, skeptical sound.

"Cream soda," he said.

"What?"

"Cream soda," he repeated. "Got a major cream soda vice. When I feel shitty, I go straight for the cream soda."

I stared at him. "That's the stupidest thing I've ever heard."

"Stupid, maybe," he said. "But true."

"Why cream soda?"

"Don't know. Tastes good." He was silent a minute. "Reminds me of summers when I was a kid, before my parents split up. Just tastes like memories."

"Good memories?"

He shrugged. "Good. Bad."

I considered that, looking him over. He was wearing a T-shirt under his Kings cut, and his muscled arms weren't exactly dripping with fat. He didn't look like someone who overindulged in cream soda. "You feel shitty a lot?" I asked, still skeptical.

"Not a lot. Sometimes." His dark eyes narrowed at me a bit. "Everyone feels shitty sometimes. It's called being human."

I made another bitchy, unimpressed sound. I would never show him I was impressed with his anything. His cleverness, his muscled arms, whatever.

I was still kinda sore, maybe, that he'd kissed me at a party, once, and never tried it again. Even though it would've complicated things and I'd told myself it was Piper for me, not Jude... It felt like rejection, and I didn't do so well with rejection.

"You know," he said slowly, his dark eyes never leaving mine, "you're a pretty girl, Roni, under all the makeup. Some girls aren't. And you're smarter than most people probably take you for."

"Is that so," I said, trying not to feel good about the compliments.

He nodded at the house behind us. "There're weapons in this place, drugs..."

"Wait a sec," I said, really cranking up the bitch, "are you talking Kings secrets with me? You know I have a vagina, right? Aren't you worried they won't patch you in if you go talking to me like that?"

"Not secrets," he said evenly, still watching me. "All that shit's out in the open, right on the coffee table."

"So?"

"So, what are you doing here? You don't need this."

"Maybe I don't," I said. "Maybe I *want* it." I stared at him, all seventeen-year-old attitude and defiance.

He stared right back at me with those hellfire eyes of his. That deep, molten brown, just watching me. He'd been watching me like that for a whole year. From a distance.

I told myself it was because he watched everyone like that.

But then he leaned in, just a little. All it took was a little; we were that close. I could feel his breath on my face. He paused, then touched his lips gently to mine.

And it was the softest, softest kiss.

Oh, *damn*... when had a man's lips ever felt that soft?

It was exactly like I remembered it, like the first time he'd kissed me. His lips felt the same. I'd sometimes told myself I must've misremembered it, because no man kissed like that.

Jude did.

He also kissed in the most brutal, demanding, head-spinning way—but he wasn't doing that now.

He was waiting, maybe. Waiting for me to kiss him back.

I didn't. Instead I pretty much froze.

It wasn't his fault. He didn't know he had the world's worst timing, that his brother had just screwed me in the kitchen and I didn't want to be kissed by anyone right then. I knew he didn't know about that, because if he knew, he wouldn't be okay with it. I really wasn't sure how Jude felt about me, but I knew he wouldn't be okay with that.

And he definitely wouldn't be trying to kiss me right now.

He stopped and I drew a shaky breath, shook my head just a little... *No.*

He pulled away.

His fire-and-brimstone eyes burned into me for a minute.

I wanted to say something, to... explain? To let him know that it wasn't a forever no, just a right now no. But I didn't know what to say.

Sorry, your brother already hit that, and I'm not in the mood?

I'd never felt such shame as I did right then, sitting there next to Jude, unable to speak.

He looked away. He took a drag off the joint, tossed it down and crushed it with his boot.

"Go home, Roni," he said.

Then he went inside the house.

And since there was no way I was going back inside that house, I went home.

Soon after that party, Jessa's mom died.

Jesse had planned to take guardianship of her; that's what she always said. But when the time came, he was so busy with Dirty that it was decided he couldn't provide a "stable home" for his sister. So Zane's grandma, Dolly, got guardianship instead and Jessa moved in with her.

I didn't mind; Dolly's house was actually closer to mine.

Dirty brought in one more member, a rhythm guitarist and songwriter named Seth. Jessa told me that Seth had been more or less homeless, just kinda couch surfing, when Zane met him. He started crashing in Dolly's garage, where the band rehearsed, on and off.

Jessa had taken her mom's death hard; I totally knew she had, even if she wouldn't talk about it much. She wrote a lot, but she never let me read anything she wrote, either. She started spending a lot of time with Seth, hanging out with him in the garage, even when the rest of the band wasn't there, and they started writing songs together.

Then Dirty moved their stuff out of Dolly's garage. They got a bigger, more professional rehearsal space, a room in a building that rented out to bands. They were playing more clubs, getting paid better, and starting to play original songs, not just covers.

Everyone knew there was something special about this band.

I went to as many shows as I could get into. I also hung out at rehearsals when Jessa brought me, and when I was there, I often saw Jude.

Sometimes I sat with Jude, listening as the band practiced some new song. We talked about what we thought about the songs and applauded when required, went outside to smoke up together, and hung out.

Over time, we developed an easy, teasing banter that I came to crave. I looked forward to it. I looked forward to our moments together.

I thought he did, too.

On those days when I knew I was going down to the rehearsal space or going to some party or show where Dirty was playing, my footsteps got just that little bit lighter. Life seemed just that little bit brighter.

Sometimes, at parties, Jude sought me out and hung out with me, talked to me. Other times, he didn't come over, but he always said hi. He always acknowledged me. He always seemed to have an eye on me. He even smiled at me, sometimes.

So unlike his brother.

Piper had gone back to forgetting my existence, about two seconds after he'd pulled out.

Jude treated me with respect, kindness if not warmth, and a reserved sort of affection.

But he never even *tried* to kiss me again.

I kept seeing other guys. But it never felt like it did with Jude. More and more, I had a better time just talking to Jude than making out with whatever guy I was seeing.

Eventually, I started talking to him about the guys I was seeing. He listened. He didn't always say much, but he listened.

And somehow, he became this anchor point in my life. This stable place where I could ground myself and find true north, no matter what drama was going on at home or with the guys I was dating.

I always knew what I was going to get with Jude. He always treated me the same. He wasn't hot and cold like some guys were. He was never too busy for me if I wanted to talk to him. He never denied me if I asked him for a joint. He never looked down on me. He never brushed me off to go talk to some other girl.

There were other girls. I saw him with them.

But he never treated me like I was lesser than.

With Jude, there was no drama.

I'd had plenty of sex. I'd dated plenty of guys, both boys and men.

I'd never really felt like someone *cared* about me like he did.

The thing was, I didn't realize that care was missing until I felt it coming from him. And it wasn't just pretty packaging to deliver his dick to me in. He never even tried to get in my pants.

Never.

At some point, it became clear to me that Jessa, who'd never been into pot, was smoking up with Seth. I knew she'd been sneaking out to see him, going to parties, and I figured they were screwing around. Drinking. Whatever. Seth was hot, so I was happy for her. Until I found out she was smoking up. It just seemed odd to me. She'd never been into it, had been scared of it, I thought, and wouldn't do it with me.

But she was doing it with Seth.

I asked her if she was screwing him.

She said no.

But she kept hanging out with him—a lot more than anyone else knew. She said her brother would disapprove and it would cause drama with the band. So I kept her secrets.

Often, I covered for her.

I lied to her brother for her.

And I chatted up Jude at parties to distract him, throw him off her scent.

Sometimes it didn't work. Sometimes maybe it did. It was hard to know with Jude. He would give me his attention, even his undivided attention, even at crazy parties and even when he was working. But he never let me in on his secrets, and I was pretty sure he never would.

I figured that out about him early on.

And then I noticed, one night, when he was looking for Jessa at a party and he said to me, "Let me know before you leave," that he'd started looking out for me, too, the same way he looked out for her.

And I liked it.

I'd never had a man look out for me before. My mom's string of useless boyfriends definitely never cared that much.

"I will," I promised him.

That night, he walked me out to my mom's car. He gave me that bouncer stare-down of his, like he was making sure I wasn't gonna cause trouble. "You been drinking?" he asked me.

"Nope," I said. "I never drink and drive." I didn't. He knew that by now.

He still stared me down.

Then he opened the car door for me and when I was inside, he said, "Drive safe, V."

No one called me V. Only him.

I drove home with a weird buzzy feeling in my chest. The truth was I had a mad crush on Jude, even though I didn't want to admit it to myself.

Partly because of the Piper thing. I had no idea if Jude knew or didn't know what had happened between me and his brother in that kitchen, and if he did, I was afraid how he might feel about it—and about me.

And partly because he just kept hooking up with other girls—women—at a lot of those parties I saw him at, and never made a move on me.

Which made me wonder if I should really be so happy to be treated like Jessa after all.

Did he see me as another little sister type? Because no way would Jude ever make a move on Jessa Mayes. He called her *brat-face*, for fuck's sake.

Less than a week later, Dirty left town on their first official tour.

They were going across western Canada and down through the western States in an old bus, playing clubs and a few festivals. Just the band, Brody, Jude and a couple of crew guys they'd brought on for the tour. The day they rolled out, I went by their rehearsal space to see them off.

Well, to see Jude off.

When I got there, the bus was parked outside, already loaded up and ready to go. Jessa wasn't there; for some reason, she didn't want to come with me to say goodbye.

I glimpsed Jesse disappearing up the steps into the bus, and from the noise coming out of it, I assumed most of the guys were already onboard. The only people who weren't on the bus yet were Brody and the two crew guys; they were talking over by the bus.

And standing there on the curb at the edge of that parking lot, I felt hopelessly insecure in a way I didn't often feel. I didn't know the crew guys, I had no idea what Brody thought of me, and I wasn't sure they'd even tell me if I asked where Jude was.

But then I saw him coming out of the building, locking up the door behind himself.

I just stood there, watching him, unsure of what to do.

He started across the parking lot toward the bus, but then he saw me and halted. He turned and walked toward me instead, a slight smile pulling at his full lips.

He had a few days' dark stubble and wore a sleeveless hoodie over a long-sleeved shirt and loose-fit jeans. It was nice to see him out of his Kings cut. He wore it a lot those days, part of his duty as a prospect.

It was a spring morning, kind of chilly and dewy, and I was cold in my short skirt. But when Jude's gaze dropped to my bare legs for a moment, it was worth it. He rarely checked me out like that.

Or at least, I rarely caught him checking me out like that.

"What're you doin' here?" he asked when he got close, but he didn't seem unhappy to see me.

I smiled. I couldn't help it. "Just wanted to say goodbye." He looked so cute, kinda cuddly in his hoodie, his dark hair a little sexy-messy in that Jude way of his, and I felt weirdly nervous standing there with him.

Nervous that I wasn't good enough for him, for this part of his world.

I held up the stupid can of cream soda I'd brought because I knew he liked it. "I brought you this."

He took it and smiled, his dimples popping.

"I mean, I hope you don't feel shitty... but just in case."

"Thanks, V."

Then he leaned in to hug me.

I bit my lip and my knees kinda quivered as he slipped his arms around me. Since I was standing on the curb, his face was close to mine. He looked so, so handsome, I was just staring at his face and kinda bumped my nose clumsily against his cheek. I hugged him back, awkwardly. But with the heat of his body and his soft clothes wrapped around me, I softened into it. I clung to him, tight.

And a wave of emotion rolled through me, so strong, I bit down on my tongue and squeezed my eyes shut.

I was surprised, maybe, by how sad I was to see him go. Maybe I was a little sad he wouldn't be around to look out for me anymore. But more than that: I was going to miss him—like crazy.

I'd miss hanging out with him. I'd miss our talks. I'd miss his brown eyes, his watchful gaze, his abrupt, reluctant chuckle. I'd miss making him laugh. I'd miss flirting with him and just feeling *safe* with him.

I'd miss looking forward to seeing him.

I had never had such a long friendship with a guy before, any guy, and not had it turn sexual. Usually, they turned sexual pretty much right out of the gate.

This one hadn't.

His arms loosened around me and he drew back a bit, and when I looked up at his face again, his eyebrows drew together. He was looking into my eyes... and then he was looking at my mouth.

And then he kissed me.

His lips brushed mine, dragging my bottom lip down, and I gasped, surprised that it wasn't just a platonic kiss... My lips parted to meet his as he crushed his mouth down on mine. His tongue moved between my lips; I lapped my tongue against his, and as I tasted his wet warmth, that unique Jude taste of his, I felt it all the way to my toes. I arched into him and he held me, gripping my waist as I teetered on the curb, his can of cream soda digging into my back.

And I realized, dazedly, as he kissed me, that it wasn't that our relationship wasn't sexual. Just because we'd never had sex didn't mean it wasn't intensely, deeply sexual.

With that kiss, he taught me things I'd never understood.

Made me wonder things I'd never thought to wonder about.

He made me *want* him.

He made it stunningly clear to me how much I needed him in my life.

Whether he knew it or not, with that kiss, Jude Grayson was taking another little piece of my heart.

"Don't go." The words whispered out of me, powerless, when the kiss was over. I knew he had to go, but I said it anyway.

He just stared at me with that steady, dark look of his. "I have to go, V." Then he kissed me again, on the forehead this time, lingeringly. "I'll be back."

Then he turned and left without looking at me again. In the moment, it felt like rejection. Later, I would tell myself, over and again, that it was because it was just too hard for him to look at me and have to walk away.

We were friends. I knew he cared about me.

But I never knew if he needed me like I needed him.

He had his brother. He had lots of brothers, really. He had Jesse. He had the band, his other friends.

I'd never had a sister or a brother, and I'd never had a friend like him.

Somewhere along the way, I'd come to realize that not only had Jude become my friend... he was, kinda sadly, the best friend I'd ever had.

That, and as I stood there watching him get onto that tour bus, I knew I'd gone and totally fallen for him.

CHAPTER TWELVE

Jude

"WE'VE GOT YOUR PACKAGE," Con told me when I picked up the phone.

I really should've been happier to hear those words.

"Fuck." I stood in my bedroom, leather jacket in hand. "That was fast."

"You wouldn't believe how easy this shit was, brother. Kid is not smart."

I glanced at the time on the clock by my bed. Fucking 7:17 pm. "What's your ETA?"

"'Bout an hour."

"Meet you there."

I hung up.

Fuck was right.

I'd just gotten out of the shower, put on a snug black sleeveless shirt, a pair of jeans that Katie had recently informed me made my ass look "smackable," and some cologne... Way too much effort for the guys I was now about to spend the evening with.

I'd been looking pretty fucking forward to seeing Roni tonight. After jerking off thinking about her last night, I'd decided *Why bother, when I could have the real thing*... Or at least, I had a chance of having the real thing.

I'd texted her this afternoon, asked her if she'd meet me tonight for dinner. She said she was busy, already had plans, but could meet me afterwards for drinks. Which was in about forty-five minutes.

Bane confirmed that she was home, that Talia had gone into her building and stayed for over an hour, and left about half an hour ago. So I knew Roni wasn't lying to me or having dinner with some other guy. She'd already told me Talia was helping her out on the New Year's Eve event.

Right now, she was probably getting ready for our date, just like I'd been doing.

Shit.

I tossed my leather jacket on the bed and layered on a long-sleeved fleece shirt and a hoodie instead. I'd spent the afternoon texting with Roni, back and forth, fucking flirting, and this was definitely gonna throw her for a loop. She'd probably think I was playing games. But I didn't have the luxury of worrying about that right now.

Right now, I had three guys committing a serious offense—several offenses, actually—on my behalf.

So I pulled on my Kings cut and sent her a text.

Me: Sorry, sweetheart. Can't meet tonight. Make it up to you.

I should've called her, probably, so she knew for sure I wasn't just blowing her off.

But I couldn't talk to her right now.

Adrenaline was already coursing through my body, my heart thumping as I got on my bike and hit the road. Seventy minutes, straight out of town, to the dump.

8:33 pm.

I pulled off the sketchy dirt road onto the edge of the clearing.

It wasn't an actual dump, but just what we called the place. Was pretty sure no one even knew why.

The property had belonged to a long-time King, a retired brother now, for-fucking-ever, and the stories about how the dump came to be called the dump were all over the place. Jokes about dumping bodies; those were obvious. A tradition of dumping old bike parts; that was true, but not so interesting. A story about a certain King bringing all his girlfriends here for a final screw before he dumped them.

Dumbass shit like that.

Wherever the name came from, it fit. This stretch of land was used for all kinds of shit, but mostly, if you didn't have a place to do something or didn't have a place to put something... the dump was your answer.

It was big, secluded, private, and varied to meet your needs. It even had a few random, creepy-ass buildings, if that happened to be what you needed.

When I pulled up in front of the shed, Maddox's van was already parked, headlights shining on the small, weather-beaten and slightly-sunken wood building.

Maddox and Con stood in the beams of light, waiting as I parked my bike.

Lex came around from the back of the shed as I got off and strode over. "This place gives me the skeevies," he said.

"Then quit wanderin' around," Maddox said.

"Had to take a piss."

"Inside?" I nodded at the shed and Con nodded back. I started toward the door. "Keep the chatter to a minimum."

"You goin' in alone?" Maddox asked.

"Yeah."

"Okay, brother," Con said.

I opened the door, which creaked exactly like you'd expect it to. Really, in the daylight, the land around the shed was a rolling meadow. Even had some flowers. Kings had had family picnics here. But at night, the shed felt like someplace they shot one of those horror movies with the gnarly-ass torture scenes.

There were a couple of battery-powered lamps hung up on hooks on the wall. Otherwise the place was dark. The floor was a bunch of rotten boards with weeds growing right through. There was a single rusted chair and a couple of random buckets in the corners. One big wooden post stood in the middle, from floor to ceiling, about a foot thick.

Taze sat on the floor, facing the door, his back against the post and legs splayed out in front of him. His hands were bound behind his back and he'd been tied securely to the post.

There was a piece of duct tape over his mouth.

Some blood had dried around his left nostril and he was looking a little roughed up, but nothing serious. Lucky for him, I'd told the boys to use no more force than necessary.

Also lucky for him, I'd already seen enough violence in my life to last me several fucking lifetimes. And like all the ugliest shit in my life, at thirty years old, I was already beyond fucking weary of it.

My other friends, outside the MC, liked to joke about it. *You need someone taken care of, just tell Jude to bring his gun.* Har har. Those were the jokes made by people who had the luxury of joking about violence and darkness because it had never really touched their lives.

But violence was not an interest of mine, and to me, it wasn't a joke.

Taze's eyes met mine, and I could see his chest move with his breaths. His nostrils flared; that bloody nostril and the duct tape were probably making breathing a bitch. He was rattled, for sure. Pissed off.

Scared, obviously.

He definitely had no idea where the fuck he was, but even though none of my brothers had worn any Kings patches when they nabbed him, he sure as shit knew who'd brought him here.

And why.

I shrugged off my cut, slowly. I took hold of the chair, dragged it a few feet in front of him and turned it around. Draped my cut carefully over the back of the chair, so the back patches were facing him.

Then I watched him as he looked at it. Watched his chest working. My brothers hadn't been gentle pulling his arms behind him and tying him there. He did not look the least bit comfortable.

And I took my time, fucking studying him.

It wasn't like I couldn't see what Roni saw in him. It was pretty fucking obvious. Women liked the cocky blond thing, right? Definitely seemed to work for Piper and Zane. I'd never known any man to attract women like those two did. And Taze was definitely a blond pretty boy with cocky written all over him.

That shit Roni said about his piece, his colors, his affiliation with the Sinners, making her feel safe? Maybe that was true, too.

Maybe he was even doing something right in bed, to hold her interest as long as he did.

But that was about as far as I could take it in my mind. The kid had fuck all other redeemable qualities that I could find, and I'd been watching him for the better part of a year.

"The other night," I said slowly, "when you and your brothers forced me off my bike with a tire iron in my back, and you mouthed off to me and threatened one of my brothers... did you have any idea what I was thinking?"

He looked at me as I moved slowly closer. Just a few steps and I was right in front of him, so he had to tilt his head back to look up at me.

"I was asking myself, 'Is he really this fuckin' stupid?'"

He stared at me, and I could read the fear in his eyes.

I stared right back until he looked away.

"But then I remembered the shitbag MC you belong to, realized maybe it's not your fault. Maybe none of your degenerate brothers ever took the time to properly educate you on how things work in the life."

I pointed at the back of my cut.

"Or maybe you saw that 'Nomad' rocker I wear and misinterpreted my importance, my position in my MC."

I let that sink in.

"So tonight, I'm here to educate you, Tyler Murphy, on who you are, and who the fuck I am."

I squatted down in front of him. His eyes met mine, and yeah, he was definitely scared.

Good.

He needed to know, if he didn't already—if he'd really managed to kid himself fucking otherwise—that an attack on me was an attack on every King. A threat against Lex was a threat against the entire club. Didn't matter that he and his brothers took off their Sinners shit and tried to make it personal.

Wasn't personal.

But he was damn lucky it was me he'd forced behind that gas station.

If it had been any other King, fact was, he might be in the ground already.

Retaliation for that kind of shit would be fast, and it would be furious.

So I started his education.

"I'm the guy who *could* get on my phone right now and call up my brother," I told him. "You know my brother. Piper. VP of the West Coast Kings. Maybe I tell my brother what happened the other night. You remember. You and your brothers and your tire iron. And Piper... he gets pretty upset. He gets on the phone to our President, who gets on the phone to your President, and fills him in. What do you think happens next?"

He stared at me, but he couldn't answer me, of course, so I kept going.

"I'll tell you what happens. Because you... are nobody. You're a fucking thug. Your MC cuts you the fuck loose, strips your patch for moving on a King without sanction, and my brother swings around and picks you up. And I gotta tell you, Tyler, my big brother's got some big love for me. How do you think your alone time with him is gonna go down for you?"

I let him think about the answer to that as I stood up and walked slowly around the shed.

"But maybe I'm not that guy," I said, once I was standing in the shadows behind him. "Maybe I don't tell my brother a thing. Maybe instead I tell my brothers outside." I paused; the sounds of my guys outside could be heard, the shuffling of boots in the dirt, a muttered comment. "Those guys are not the VP of the West Coast Kings. They're foot soldiers, like you. Soldiers who do whatever the fuck I ask. Who scooped *you* up off the street, threw your ass in a van and dragged you... way... out... here."

I got close behind him, just off to the side, and crouched down.

"How do you think they'll take hearing about what happened the other night? Maybe I leave them in here with you a while, they can let you know how they feel about it."

I let that sink in. Then I got to my feet again.

"So, which of those two guys do you think I am?" I moved to stand in front of him again. "Tell my brother...? Tell my brothers outside...?"

Here was the beautiful problem with that question: the answer didn't matter.

Either way, this ended the same for him.

And Taze knew it.

Basically, I was the guy standing in-between him and a very bad ending, and he was definitely starting to realize it. By now, he'd sweat right through his shirt. I could hear his raspy breathing getting shallow.

"I know. Tough choice when you really don't know shit about me and you're really not all that fucking smart, Tyler. But let me help you out. Personally, I always look at it like this: when you're deciding between two options, even two good options... even two terrible-as-shit options... there's always a third."

I paused again, and I heard his dumbass voice, threatening me, in my head.

Forget. About. Her.

"So let me tell you who I am."

I crouched down real low, getting eye-level with him. This time, he didn't quite meet my eyes, looking somewhere near my chin.

"I'm the guy who doesn't tell my brother a thing. I don't tell my brothers outside a thing, either. I'm the guy who lets you walk out of here. Lets you go back to your sinkhole of a clubhouse. And you're the guy who forgets about Roni Webber."

I let him chew on that for a long moment before I spoke again. Eventually, his eyes met mine.

"You don't go anywhere the fuck near her. You don't make any attempt to communicate with her. You delete her contact from your phone. You unfriend her on fuckin' Facebook, you left swipe her on fuckin' Tinder, whatever the fuck you've gotta do to wipe her existence from your brain. You stay the fuck away from me. You stay the fuck away from Lex. And the second that changes, the second I hear you forgot to forget about Roni or Lex, you're sniffing around Roni or causing trouble of any kind for any of my boys, I become a different guy, Tyler. A guy who tells my brother and my Prez exactly what you and your boys did, how you threatened Lex and your brother clubbed me in the back with a tire iron. All because you were trying to stake some bullshit claim over a woman who isn't yours to claim." His eyes widened a bit, and I leaned in real close to drive home my point. "She's. Mine."

I stood up. Stood over him for a while. Just letting him wonder if I was gonna knock him in the face with my fist or kick him, like he'd done to me.

But pain was not my weapon of choice.

All I needed was fear.

"Forget about her," I said, once I'd let him sweat it out a while—how close he'd come to getting his ass kicked, or worse, in some fucking creepy-ass shed in the middle of God-knew-where.

Let him *feel* exactly who had the power here.

Then I walked out.

CHAPTER THIRTEEN

Roni

I SPENT THE NIGHT WORKING, mostly at the little desk in my dining room, the one that faced out the big window.

Today, I'd booked our opening act for the New Year's Eve event. Fabulous. I should've been a lot more excited than I was. I wanted to share the news with Jude, actually... but like hell I was messaging or calling him.

Not when he'd brushed me off.

After I'd read his text, I'd put my phone aside and dug into my work. I'd had a brief meeting after work with the manager of the Pandora, and another meeting with Talia to go over some things. My lawyer was working on the contract and promised to have it to me tomorrow. I was aiming to have tickets on sale by the start of next week, if all went according to plan.

Lucky for me, the potentially hardest part of my job, on this event, would be the easiest—because ticket sales would not be an issue. I still had a careful publicity plan worked out, which I'd go over with Brody the day after tomorrow. But he'd already assured me Dirty would sell the place out, easily and probably immediately. And I knew both Dirty and DJ Summer would deliver on performance, so really, this gig was just getting sweeter and sweeter the more I pulled all the pieces together.

But then there was the bullshit with Jude.

Canceling on me, like forty minutes before he was supposed to pick me up for our date tonight. I'd been putting on my makeup and I already had my lacy-as-hell push-up bra and thong on—you know, the one I was hoping he'd rip off with his teeth after we had a few cocktails. And then he sent me some lame-assed text to cancel our date.

Nothing to make a girl feel irrelevant like putting a bunch of effort into getting sexy for a guy she's about to see, only to have him blow her off like she meant exactly zero to him.

Though I was pretty damn sure, after the other night, he wasn't blowing me off because his dick had magically lost interest.

Which meant he was blowing me off because he had something else to do—and he wasn't telling me what that was. He didn't even make up some random excuse about having to meet Jesse or something.

Which could mean only one thing.

Club business.

And I knew what *that* meant.

I'd dated a few bikers over the years and I knew whatever he was up to, if it was *club business*, he was not gonna tell me the where, what, why or with whom. No matter if I begged, threatened or threw a hissy fit.

Fair enough, really. I understood enough about the Kings and the Sinners, in general, to know why they wouldn't tell me anything. Their protection. My protection.

Fine.

But I also knew "club business" was therefore also a convenient cover for anything at all they didn't want me to know about. I was pretty sure when Ben, a King I'd dated years ago, cited "club business," that business often involved fucking a stripper named Lissa. I was also pretty sure that when Taze cited "club business," it sometimes involved something similar. However, because, you know, "club business," I could never exactly prove it.

It bothered me, but probably not as much as it should. Maybe because it wasn't right in my face and I could just kind of ignore it?

Maybe because I was never in love with either of those men.

Maybe because even though I was faithful to Taze, I still kept a Tinder account and flirted with men online, and in person at nightclub events, and honestly had never really stopped *looking*.

Looking at other men.

Looking for something better.

But the mere thought of Jude blowing me off because he might be at his clubhouse with some other woman in his lap?

It made me feel mildly homicidal with jealousy.

I sat at my desk, looking out at the slice of water and the sparkling lights of downtown, which I could see through a gap in the high-rise buildings across from mine. My phone lay in front of me, the little light blinking to tell me I had new messages. I'd left the sound off for the last couple of hours while I worked on my laptop.

And maybe because I was avoiding him.

What if he messaged with some lame-ass explanation (i.e., lie), and/or blew me off more permanently?

What if he didn't message at all?

I never play a game that I can't win.

That's what I'd told him, and I'd definitely meant it.

Especially when it came to *him*.

Neither do I.

That was what he said, and I believed him.

Was I just a game to him, then? A game to be played and won, or manipulated however he liked, or worse—abandoned as soon as things didn't seem to be working out in his favor?

And if so, where did I really fall on his priority list?

Dead last?

When I finally checked my phone, there was no new message from Jude. Just some random Tinder dudes and Instagram messages. And Jessa, asking me if I'd hang out with her on Friday night, after my meeting with Brody.

I texted her back: *I'll bring the wine and ginger ale.*

Since she was breastfeeding, I knew she wouldn't drink with me, but hey, I could drink alone, right?

When I finally went to bed, all I could think about was how hard I'd fallen for Jude Grayson, once upon a time. I really didn't think about it, ever. But now it was all coming back, the memories sharp and painfully fresh. As if they'd been waiting all along. As if being ignored for so long had only made them *stronger*.

Kind of like my feelings for him.

Yes, I'd had a sexual bucket list. But I would've tossed the entire bucket out in a heartbeat for Jude.

Because I was in love with him.

I thought I was. It wasn't like I had any other experience to guide me or compare the depth of my feelings to. I'd never been in love before.

I'd never known how far I could fall.

I really didn't know how it would feel until it happened.

I also didn't know how it would feel to be loved back.

For a few oddly painful days, I'd really thought he did love me back.

It turned out I was wrong, anyway. At least, about his feelings for me.

I made that mistake with Jude once and it was, in a word, devastating.

Was I really so willing to risk making the same mistake again?

Dirty had returned home from that first bus tour more or less in one piece.

Jesse's ego seemed a little bigger, maybe. Zane was louder, if that was possible. Dylan was hotter, Elle had turquoise streaks in her platinum-blonde hair and Seth was... sketchier. He looked thinner and pretty baked when I saw him.

And as soon as they were back in town, Jessa vanished. Suddenly she was back hanging out with Seth 'til all hours of the night, going to parties and getting high and probably screwing his brains out.

The band was back in town for six days before I saw Jude.

I tried to run into him, dropping by the rehearsal space pretending I was looking for Jessa. That kind of thing.

No luck.

But then I found out there was going to be a party for Dirty, a family barbecue, at Dylan's place. He still lived with his parents and two of his sisters and I'd never been to his house, but Jessa promised I could come to the party with her. She was so distracted all the time, she probably had no idea why I was so eager to go.

It wasn't like I told her that I'd spent the last seven months basically pining over Jude Grayson and stalking him on Facebook. He had an account but he never posted anything, so that was kind of a dead end. But Dirty had a band page, which Brody mostly managed, and often there were photos posted from gigs, sometimes backstage, and sometimes Jude was in them.

And when I looked at those photos, which I did a lot... I knew.

I knew I'd fallen *hard* for Jude.

I messaged him, sometimes, sending him stupid little random thoughts and photos of me and Jessa and asking how the tour was going. He always answered, eventually.

But he never messaged me first.

I had no idea how front-of-mind I was with him, and yet he'd totally taken over my thoughts. I didn't even see anyone else while he was away. I didn't go on a single date. I barely flirted with anyone. I just didn't care about anyone else.

I wanted *him*.

It was kinda like I was a virgin all over again, and I was saving myself for him. I just wanted him to be the one.

The only one.

I'd never felt that way before. Not about any guy I'd ever been with, or wanted to be with. Not about Piper, even when I'd weaved all kinds of fantasies about the two of us getting together and chased him for a year.

Only Jude.

When Jessa and I arrived at Dylan's party, I hoped like hell for only three things. One, that Jude was there. Two, that he wasn't there with some other girl. And three, that he wanted to see me.

I figured I could take the rest from there.

But when I got there, I didn't see him. Maybe because the house and the yard were overrun with people—Dylan's extended family, which turned out to be huge, the band and all kinds of people who knew the band. I saw some familiar faces and talked to a few people, keeping an eye out for Jude while I sipped my drink—a stupid fruit punch, of all things, which had been put out for the "kids" and Jesse had poured for both Jessa and me. She was seventeen, I was eighteen, and the legal drinking age was nineteen, but really.

"You know," I told her, "your big brother the rock star really needs to loosen the hell up."

"*Don't* let him hear you say that," she said, rolling her eyes. "He's not a rock star yet."

Then a pair of hands came down on my shoulders. Gently. A man's hands, big and warm, fingers curling into me.

"Bratface," Jude said, right behind me, in that low, rugged voice of his, and shivers prickled down my spine... and right between my legs.

Jessa rolled her eyes again; she'd been really crabby lately. "Jude."

"Dolly's here," he said. "She's lookin' for you." I sucked in a breath; his hands were still on my shoulders.

Jessa's "bratface" softened. "I'll go find her."

She took off, leaving me alone with Jude and my cup of fruit punch. Which, as I turned to face him, spilled all over him.

It wasn't totally my fault. His hands dropped from my shoulders as I turned, he probably didn't know I had the cup in my hand, and there was an awkward mid-air collision of his knuckles and my cup... which resulted in punch all down the front of his shirt.

"Oh. My. *Shit*," I stammered, horrified.

The fruit punch was bright red. Luckily, Jude was wearing black.

"I guess that means you're happy to see me?"

When I peered up into his face, he was smiling a bit. His dimples flickered and my knees went rubbery.

"Crap. I'm really sorry."

"No worries. I'll find another shirt."

"Oh... good." I stood there awkwardly, not sure what to do or say as he stared at me, that hint of a smile on his face.

Then he grabbed my hand, lacing his fingers through mine, and pulled me toward the house. My heart swelled, like in some cartoon, and I hurried to follow him into the kitchen where Dylan's mom and a bunch of aunts were prepping food for the barbecue. When she saw Jude, Mrs. Cope immediately pointed us in the direction of Dylan's bedroom and told him to find a clean shirt.

Jude kept hold of my hand as he led me down the basement stairs and into a bedroom where it looked like a small bomb had gone off, long ago, and no one had bothered cleaning up, so the disarray had just kind of feasted on itself.

Jude let go of my hand and I waited while he fished a clean T-shirt out of Dylan's closet. I watched him slip his leather jacket off. He glanced at me, and I did my best to look absorbed in perusing the posters on the walls. Dylan had weird taste in music, though. I didn't even know who or what *Thin Lizzy* was, but they had horrible fashion sense.

Out of the corner of my eye, I saw Jude strip off his shirt and pull on the clean one.

I looked at him again when he'd pulled his jacket back on.

Then we both just stood there, with Dylan's giant unmade bed between us. It wasn't exactly awkward, but it was... something.

"Sorry about your shirt," I said, again.

"It's kinda in my jeans, too."

I glanced down at the front of his jeans. They were black, and I really couldn't tell if they were wet, but I could definitely see the bulge of his man parts, and my stomach got all fluttery.

I met his dark eyes, which were fixed on mine.

"Sorry."

"I'll live with it." His dimples flashed again.

I smiled a bit.

"So..."

"So."

"I missed you." He said it at the exact same moment that I said it.

I grinned slowly, unable to stop myself. "You missed me?"

"Yeah. Imagine that." He was staring at me and, as usual, I couldn't totally tell if he was teasing me, flirting with me, or just giving me tough-guy attitude.

I shrugged, feigning indifference. "I mean, you're okay to have around."

He kept staring at me. His eyes flicked down over my shirt; it was black and off-the-shoulder on one side. Then they drifted down over my jeans, before meeting my eyes again. Heat crept through my body as he looked at me that way.

God, the shit I wanted to do with this guy... naked and right now.

"What're you doing after this?"

I glanced around Dylan's room. "After... this?"

"After the barbecue."

"Oh. I... uh... drove Jessa here. So..."

"So, we'll drive her home."

I stared at him.

"Then I can take you for that ride on my bike."

I wasn't smiling anymore. I was very careful not to smile, to hold onto some dignity about this, when all I really wanted to do was jump up and down. And jump on him. "What ride on your bike?"

"One you asked me for, forever ago."

"You said no."

His dark eyes held mine. "Changed my mind."

That night, after Jude followed me across the city on his bike and I dropped Jessa at home, then dropped off my mom's car at my place, I got on his bike. He had an extra helmet in his saddlebag that fit me well, but I didn't really want to think that he kept it there for all the random chicks he took on his bike. Instead I let myself believe he put it there that day because he wanted to take me for a ride that night.

It wasn't the first time I'd been on the back of a guy's motorcycle while we ripped through the city... but it was the *best* time. My chest pressed to his back, my thighs snug around his hips, my arms wrapped tight around his waist as the bike rumbled beneath us. A few times, when we stopped at a red light, he put his gloved hand on my thigh, his thumb stroking back and forth... and that small caress made my heart race faster than the rush of racing down the street on his Harley in the night.

After we'd driven over one of the bridges into Richmond and down a bunch of the empty roads between the farms that bled right into the city, and then back over the water into Vancouver, he pulled over and asked me, "Should I take you home?"

It was getting late, probably near midnight. I had to work tomorrow. But I said, "No."

So he took me to his place instead; the apartment he still shared with Jesse, Brody and Zane.

"The guys are probably still at Dylan's," he said as he held the door open for me and we stepped into the dark apartment.

"You kept this place while you were on the road?" I knew they had; Jessa told me they'd sublet it to some guys they knew, and reclaimed it as soon as they came back.

"Yeah," he said, dropping his jacket and keys on a table. "Just seemed easier than having to find a new one and store all our shit somewhere. The rent's decent." He turned on a lamp in the living room. There was a pair of panties on the lampshade, and he tore them off and whipped them at Zane's bed. "Fuck." He threw me an apologetic look.

I just slipped off my jacket and dropped it next to his.

Then he went to wash his hands, which was both cute and probably a good idea.

"Sorry it's not much," he said, when he rejoined me in the living room.

"I don't care." I didn't. If he only knew what my house looked like... It was barely a step up from the dumpy trailer we'd lived in until I was sixteen and we'd moved into the city. "It's got good energy."

He chuckled as he cleared some clothes off his futon. "What, like the smell of dudes and the ghosts of old takeout boxes?"

"No. Like good male energy." I looked at him; he was staring at me and I just shrugged. "I like it."

He gathered some takeout containers off the coffee table and dropped them in the kitchen. "This shit is Zane's and Jesse's. I'm really not this much of a pig."

"I know." I could see that much.

Where Zane's corner of the living room was pretty chaotic, his blankets tossed on the floor, pictures of naked women torn out of magazines tacked to the wall, his bedside table crowded with baggies of weed, dirty ashtrays, a giant bong and some empty beer bottles, Jude's was much neater and cleaner. No naked girls on the wall, just a Harley-Davidson poster featuring a gleaming motorcycle. He'd even made his bed, sort of, the blanket laid hastily overtop.

"You still into Good Charlotte?" he asked as he went over to the stereo. The tone of his voice told me there was no way in hell he had any.

"You still into Rage Against the Machine?" I replied.

He glanced at me. "Meet somewhere in the middle?"

"Sure." I sat down on his futon, glancing at the band posters on the opposite wall, in the little dining room area that was crowded with music equipment. "Just no Pink Floyd. It makes me sleepy."

He smiled as he thumbed through a row of CDs on the bookcase.

"Hey. You have any White Stripes?"

"How do they make you feel?" he asked.

"Incredibly warm and fuzzy, actually. Especially if you've got 'Little Cream Soda'."

He glanced at me and I grinned. He popped in a CD and "Little Cream Soda" started thumping through the speakers.

"Love this album," I gushed. "Best album of last year." I sank back into the futon. It was folded up like a couch and I leaned against the back, pulling my knees up in front of me.

Jude was looking around, poking through some stuff on the bookcase. "We have candles somewhere..."

I smiled at him. "Are you trying to romance me?"

I could've sworn he looked kinda self-conscious as his eyes met mine. "I might be."

"I like candles," I said quickly.

He dug through a closet in the front hall while I enjoyed the music. Eventually, he produced some little green votives that had obviously never been used. "Christmas gift from Dolly," he explained. "Pretty sure it was a hint after Zane brought her over and she saw his mountain of dirty laundry. They're scented. 'Key Lime Pie.'"

"Yum." I watched him light a few and put them out on the coffee table. Then he turned off the lamp and we were left in the flickering light of the tiny flames.

He sat down next to me on his futon, just as the song switched. The CD must've been on random, because "Conquest" started playing next. I looked at him. He looked at me as Jack White sang the opening lines about, well, a conquest. Of the sexual variety.

"Jesus," he said, his dark eyes widening a bit.

I almost laughed, he looked so stricken.

"Is this over the top? I'm not tryin' to get in your pants, Roni. I just wanted to hang out."

I was grinning. "Okay."

He chuckled again. I loved that guarded, reluctant laugh of his. I'd rarely heard him laugh out loud, and only around the guys. It was a tiny, delicious thrill to me that I could make him chuckle. "Want me to change the song?"

"I really don't care. I'm not here for the music."

He stared at me. He picked up the remote and turned the music down. Then an awkward silence stretched between us.

I'd been in guys' apartments before, in their bedrooms. When I wanted to be. I knew when they were making moves on me, and I was pretty comfortable with it.

I was far more uncomfortable with Jude's lack of making a move.

"You really missed me?" he asked.

"Yup. You missed me?"

"Yeah. Don't go diggin' for compliments, though."

I rolled my eyes. "I figured there'd be so many girls on your rock star tour, by the time you got back, you wouldn't even remember my name."

"I'm not a rock star," he said.

"You look like a rock star."

He stared at me a bit more, as my heart drummed in my chest.

Then he leaned back against the futon, right next to me. He was still wearing Dylan's *Pearl Drums* T-shirt and his bare arm pressed to mine. He had tattoos all down his arm and he felt warm and firm, muscular. And his skin was so, so soft.

"Ver-o-ni-ca," he said, slow, drawing out the syllables with that low voice of his and that slight, soft drawl. I wasn't sure if it was because they'd grown up in some tiny town in the interior, but both he and Piper had it. The dropping of some g's and the soft a's. "How could I forget a name like Veronica?"

I smiled at that. "It's just a name."

"No," he said. "It's just like you. Pretty. Sexy. Unforgettable."

I quirked an eyebrow. "Are these the lines that usually get you into girls' pants?"

"Told you," he said. "I'm not tryin' to get in your pants."

"Oh. Right. I forgot."

"If I was tryin' to get in your pants, I'd be in your pants."

I laughed, loud. "Wow. You are... confident."

"It's got nothing to do with confidence. I just know."

"Know what?"

"That if I tried, you'd be okay with it."

I was so floored by that, in so many different directions, I didn't even know what to do with it. "I can't even figure out if I should be offended by that."

His eyebrows went up. "Didn't mean to offend you. Just meant, I can tell."

"How?"

He seemed to be thinking about how to answer that. His eyes looked like black lava in the candlelight, and I felt the heat of his gaze all the way to my deepest depths; like he could see right into me. It almost made me want to hide. "It's the way you look at me," he said. "The way you smile at me."

My heart thumped harder in my chest as his gaze slid over my face. "Is that so?"

"Yeah. It's so." His eyes searched mine. "You used to smile at me differently. Like I was just a guy. One of a million guys you could tempt and toss away. You don't look at me like that anymore."

I felt the slight smile on my face gradually fading.

"I think you like me, Roni Webber."

Well, fuck. Now it felt like he had the upper hand, and I didn't like that at all.

"I think if you tried to get in my pants right now, I'd smack you silly."

He grinned, dimples and all. "That a challenge, darlin'?"

"Nope. Just warning you. I've got a mean right hook."

"Yeah? Where'd you get that from?"

"Summer when I was twelve. I had this sixteen-year-old neighbor who thought he was all that. You know how it goes." I shrugged. "I had a good butt for a twelve-year-old."

His smile faded. He said nothing about the neighbor thing. "Just when I thought I'd actually figured you out."

"I guess you thought wrong."

He stared at me.

I smiled, and his gaze dropped to my lips.

"I wouldn't wanna feel that right hook..."

"You probably won't," I admitted.

His eyes met mine again. They twitched, and I knew I'd thrown him for a loop. "You playin' games with me, V?"

"What kind of game?"

"Like the one where you pretend you don't like me, but you do."

"I like you. I wouldn't be here in your smelly boys' apartment if I didn't like you."

Now it was his turn to smile. "I thought the key lime pie scent was really helpin' things along."

"The candles smell nice," I agreed. "You smell better."

His eyes flared.

Yeah. I had game.

He stared at me for a long, long moment. "Why can't I figure you out?"

"What's to figure? I thought you had me and my pants all locked down."

"Yeah, well. I like to think I know a little about everything and a lot about women, but sometimes that's the furthest thing from the truth."

Well. I liked that.

I little humility in a guy was sexy. Jude was definitely all that, but he was humble about it. Thing about him was, I didn't think he really believed he was all that.

But he was all that and then some.

"I'm not that mysterious, Jude."

"Says who?"

"Try," I said.

"Try what?"

"Try to get in my pants. See what happens." Then I stretched my legs out in front of me, giving him access to my jeans if he wanted it.

He watched the motion, his gaze moving down my body. When he met my eyes again, he asked me, "You want me to?"

Damn. How sweet was he?

"Yeah, Jude. I want you to."

He started to move, finally, but he didn't go for my jeans. Not exactly. He put his hands on my knees as he went down on his knees on the floor, right in front of me, and spread my legs wide. He knelt right in-between my knees and took my hands, drawing me toward him until I was sitting up straight.

Then he peeled my shirt off over my head and tossed it aside. He looked at my bra; at my boobs kind of spilling out of the push-up cups. Then he reached out and unhooked the front closure, peeled the bra open and down my arms.

My nipples hardened and my breath caught in my throat as he looked at me.

He gathered up my breasts in his hands, and the warmth of his touch spread right through my body. I arched into him. He smoothed his thumbs over the hard peaks of my nipples and I shivered; a shiver of lust and want, as my pulse thudded through my body and heat gathered between my legs.

I watched his face as he touched me, the pure lust in his dark eyes. There was an unmistakable hunger there, a rising need, but the way he looked at me... his gaze was almost worshipful.

Had any guy ever looked at my body quite like that?

Then he leaned in and flicked his tongue over one nipple, softly, and I just about died.

"Oh my God," I gasped, pushing on him a bit to hold him off, to stop him from doing that again. "Jude. Please tell me you're gonna do me tonight, because I don't think I can handle the torture if you don't. If you're just gonna do that weird thing you do..."

He was looking up into my eyes. "What weird thing?"

"That thing where you stare at me from across the room like you want to fuck me, and then you don't. That thing where you don't let me near you."

He stared at me for a few hot seconds as my heart pounded in my chest.

Then he slid a hand around the back of my neck and pulled me closer, and he kissed me. His tongue delved into my mouth and for once, I knew this kiss wasn't going to abruptly end and the both of us go our separate ways.

So I kissed him back, with all the hunger I'd felt for him for way too long.

As he kissed me, he crawled up over me. He moved over me like a beast on the prowl, and I fell back on the futon beneath him. He ripped his mouth from mine and kissed his way down my neck to my breasts. He cupped them, one, then the other, lifting them to his mouth so he could wrap his tongue around my nipple, nibble, suckle, and generally drive me fucking crazy.

Every time his tongue touched my skin, my entire body throbbed.

Then suddenly he pulled back.

"Shit. Darlin'. Just a minute..." He untangled himself and got up. "I don't want anyone walkin' in on this."

Gah. *Sweet.* He was so, so sweet.

I watched him cross the room to the front door, open it and then close it again.

"What did you do?" I asked as he returned.

"Hung the 'No Dogs' sign on the doorknob," he muttered, like he was embarrassed. "It's our code for *Fuck off and come back in half an hour*."

"Half an hour?" I teased. "We'd better get busy."

He practically dove on top of me. We started making out again and I plastered my body against his. He drove one thigh between my legs and hiked it up tight, putting pressure on my clit and pushing me higher up the bed. He rocked his hips into me as he kissed me, until I made a very unsexy little squawking sound.

"Ouch! My hair's caught in the arm thing," I said.

He helped me free my hair from the arm rest of the futon.

"I'm sorry this is so fuckin' ghetto."

"It's fine..."

"You deserve something better."

"I'm not a princess," I told him. "I'd do it with you in the dirt."

His eyes met mine and something darkened, deepened between us. Either the comment about the dirt had given him certainty that I wanted this, or it turned him on so much that he forgot to worry about it, and he kissed me, harder. Together, we managed to peel off his shirt. He shucked off my jeans and started kissing his way up my body. He devoured my nipples and sucked on my breasts until I was panting in heat.

I tried to get his jeans open, I really did, but he was tall. His body went on forever and a day, and every time I'd managed to get a hold of his zipper, he shifted his hips out of my reach.

Then he grabbed my wrists and pinned them above my head with one hand like it was nothing at all, while I wriggled under him, useless, squirming in reaction to his kisses.

"Please," I eventually begged him, "take your dick out. I wanna touch you."

He looked at me and grinned a bit. Then he let go of my wrists and kneeled up over me, slowly, and he took out his dick.

And all I could think as I watched him do it was *Holy shit*.

I didn't care what some of my girlfriends said about cocks looking weird. Those girls were *wrong*. Or maybe they'd just never seen Jude's cock. Because if they'd seen his, they obviously would've understood that the male sex organ was a thing of beauty.

It was hard in his hand and, just like the rest of him, it was big and gorgeous.

And just like the rest of him, I wanted it all over me.

He stroked himself a little, running his hand slowly up and down his shaft as he gazed down at me, all abs and flexing muscles and tattoos. His jeans were still on, but kind of down around his hips, and it was hands-down the sexiest thing I'd ever seen.

"How do you want it?" he asked me, his voice, like his eyes, kind of dazed and sex-hazed.

I answered by asking him right back, "How do you want it?"

"I could kiss you all night," he said, still stroking himself.

I groaned. "You like torturing me."

"That could be fun," he said. "But I'd rather make you come. You want that?"

"I don't really think I have a choice," I said, swallowing. Because

I really didn't think I could resist coming with this man on top of me, no matter what he was doing.

"Mmm." He lowered himself over me again and for the next God-knew-how-long he did torture me—with his mouth and his hands, his teeth and his tongue. He peeled off my panties and kissed, licked and sucked on every fucking place on my body—*except* my pussy.

It was almost getting to the point where in the back of my mind I started to wonder if there was a problem. Like, was he one of those weird guys who didn't like to go down? Because if so, I was gonna have to remedy that somehow. After enduring the full-body tongue bath, I wanted his face between my legs so bad I could've screamed.

I was already screaming softly, into his mouth, as he worked his fingers between my legs... then gradually slid a couple of them into me. He worked me like a man who was very comfortable with the female body. And I always kept myself neat and tidy down below. So what was the problem?

"Jude," I gasped when he broke our kiss to feast on my breasts, again, "can you please go down on me? Just for a second? I'm like aching here. Or at least put your dick in my mouth. You're fucking killing me."

He chuckled a bit and bit down on my nipple lightly, before dragging his beautiful lips up my chest and kissing me again. "Sweetheart," he whispered against my lips, "I go down on that sweet pussy you've got and I'm gonna come in my pants." It must've been a figure of speech, since his dick was already out of his pants, but I got his meaning; his fingers were still inside me and he undulated them around as he spoke.

I cried out. "*Fuck.* Okay. Then take your stupid pants off already."

He laughed.

"Are you on drugs or something? How do you have so much patience?" Seriously, I didn't think I'd ever made out with a guy half as long as this before he blew his load.

"Told you," he said, as he slipped his fingers out of me and finally kicked off his jeans, "I could kiss you all night."

He crawled up over me again. It was probably one of the sweetest things a guy had ever said to me, but I was still squirming with impatience. "Do you want me to beg?" I ran my hands down his stomach and grabbed his cock, just gently, and stroked him as I spoke, loving the way it made his eyelids lower and his breathing get heavier. I giggled from the strange tension. I really wasn't used to this brand of sexual tension with a guy. "Because I will beg..."

"No," he said, sliding his fingers into me again. "I don't want you to beg, V."

Then he started fucking me with his fingers, for real, and I almost went right over the edge. I dug my heels into the futon and squirmed up and away from his hand, alleviating the pressure of his thumb or his knuckle or whatever the fuck was bearing down on my clit.

"Put on a condom," I ordered him. "Right now."

So he got up and found one, and when he came back to me, he rolled it on. I watched, mesmerized by all his sexiness, just kinda grounding myself in the moment. The fact that I was here, on Jude's bed, and we were about to be together for the first time.

He spread my thighs around his hips, and he was pretty gentle about actually putting it in. I was super wet, but he was big, and those first few seconds when he pushed into me were a blend of pleasure and discomfort. He took it slow, easing in, until I smacked him on the ass. "You won't break me."

He grabbed my wrists and pinned them down above my head again. Then he shoved in farther, making me gasp. "This what you want?" he asked, his dark eyes on mine.

"Yeah. That's what I want..."

But once he was in me, the torture didn't lessen.

It just got worse.

He fucked me so fucking *slow*. Deep but slow, holding my arms pinned above my head, his hips churning slowly between my thighs, his weight pressing me down.

"That good for you?" he asked me, when he'd hit a steady, deep rhythm.

"Yeah," I breathed. "Yeah, Jude, it's good for me."

All the while he kept looking at me. He studied me, locked onto my reactions. While he did that, he also kissed me. He dragged his lips over mine. He nipped my ear with his teeth. He sucked on my neck.

And all the while, he had me right on the edge. My entire body was a whirlpool of ecstasy. My orgasm swirled in the dark, threatening to take me under.

But it never did.

I pushed up against him, meeting his thrusts, but he just kept at me in such a slow rhythm... if he didn't speed up or increase the pressure... I didn't think I'd be able to get there.

Torture.

"I thought you said... you were gonna make me come..." I panted after a while.

"I will," he said. "When I want to."

Holy fuck.

"In the meantime..." he murmured between kisses, "how about you just take what I give."

So I lay there and took it as his beautiful body worked against mine.

I'd never been one to do *this* during sex. Just lie back and let the guy take charge, take over, dominate me. My very first time ever, yes, I'd been pretty passive; I was super nervous, it kinda hurt, and I didn't know exactly what to expect. But by the second time, I'd pretty much figured it out.

I'd figured out the power I had over men.

Over their dicks, anyway.

But with him...

I felt a different kind of power. Not in taking control, but in lying back and feeling him moving over me, waiting to see and feel everything he wanted to do to my body... and just giving him permission to do it.

I was much more used to racing to the finish line, trying to make a guy come first because it thrilled me how excited I could get them. I'd found that most guys cared about getting me off, even if I got them off first; even if they didn't care all that much about *me*, their ego cared about getting me to the finish line, too.

With Jude, it wasn't a race.

With Jude, I kinda wanted it to last all night and day.

Even if it was killing me.

Shivers ran all over my body as he fucked me. His skin was the color of peanut butter in the glow of the candlelight. I wanted to lick him all over, but he really wasn't letting me.

By the time he finally started picking up the pace, breathing harder, fucking me harder, I was so ready to come apart, all he had to do was look at me and say, "Yeah, darlin'? You wanna come on that dick?"

I was pretty much hyperventilating by that point, and I took his words as an invitation to grind my hips against his and bear down on his cock with everything I had. When I did that, he pounded into me, hard, a few times—which totally threw me over. I screamed and gasped and writhed around. He went still, his dick pressed deep inside me. My pussy fluttered all over him and my head spun.

I'd never had a guy make me come so fucking hard.

"Yeah, V," he breathed above me. I felt his hand tighten on my wrists as he held them above my head. He groaned and shoved into me a couple of times, and I felt his release. I felt his cock spasm and I felt him let go... really let go for the first time all night.

Then he groaned again and slumped against me, his hands loosening on my wrists.

As he caught his breath, I tuned in to all the sensations I hadn't noticed before. The sweat all over his body, making him slippery against me. His heartbeat, thudding hard beneath the surface of his soft skin. The softness of his hair as he pressed his face into my neck and kissed me again.

He rolled off me, kind of, but there was barely anywhere for him to go. He lay on his side, right up against me, his legs tangled up with mine. He draped his heavy arm across my stomach, lay his head against mine and sighed.

And I probably could've died happy.

I'd waited for him for a long, long time. In my eighteen-year-old mind, it felt like I'd waited for him forever.

And he was so, so worth the wait.

That night, he made me feel like the only woman in the world. The only woman who'd ever mattered to him.

For the first time in my life, I knew I was in love. In that moment, I had no doubt. If Jude Grayson had asked me right then, *Will you marry me, darlin'?* I would've literally screamed with joy and told him *HELLS TO THE YES*.

But I was young.

I thought I knew a lot more about men, and the world in general, than I did.

And apparently, I thought he felt a lot more for me than he did.

Afterwards, he drove me home on his bike and kissed me goodnight.

And I waited for him to call me. I really thought he would call.

The next day. Or the day after that.

So I waited.

And I waited.

I waited for him, but he never called.

CHAPTER FOURTEEN

Jude

THE WAY I SAW IT, Roni Webber wasn't necessarily a flowers type of girl. But she was definitely a grand gestures type of girl. And when I walked into the girly, frilly teahouse where she was having lunch with Jessa, Katie, and Katie's best friend, Devi, carrying a giant bouquet of lilies and roses and whatever other shit the florist threw in there, it was definitely a grand gesture.

Especially for a woman I wasn't even in a relationship with.

I knew I had to make up for missing our date last night. I wasn't brushing Roni off, but who knew what the fuck she might be thinking right now.

After the business at the dump, I'd ended up crashing at Con's overnight. Drove back into the city this morning and picked up my car. I'd texted Roni on my way to Jesse's, but I knew that wasn't gonna cut it. She hadn't even texted me back.

Bane told me where to find her, so as soon as the band was settled at the studio and I could take off for a bit, I showed up where she was, flowers in hand.

Turned out I was the only man in the room, and I was still wearing my Kings cut. Which, in retrospect, I maybe should've left in the car. It was so second nature to me, I sometimes forgot I was wearing it, but the world never let me forget.

As I walked through the room, between the little tables with the fancy tablecloths and all the girly tea cups and tiny sandwiches and whatever, the way every woman in the place looked at me... eyes widening as they looked me over—or tried not to—I couldn't even say for sure if they were terrified or turned on.

Sometimes it was hard to tell.

When the girls at Roni's table saw me, the reactions were easier to read. I knew these women. Katie looked confused, like maybe I didn't know where the fuck I was and she might need to offer directions. Jessa looked surprised, but then kinda not surprised. Devi said, "Now there's a man looking to impress," looking impressed.

"There's a man looking to get laid," Roni corrected her, crossing her arms under her chest and sitting back. She wore one of those softer-than-an-angel's-ass sweaters of hers, light pink, with a hint of cleavage. Smoky makeup on her eyes, her black hair half-wavy and loose.

I seriously would've considered fucking her right there on the table if Katie and Jessa weren't there to get a front row view of it—and I wouldn't get an earful from Jesse and Brody about it later.

Anyway. Roni accepted the flowers. She even agreed to let me pick her up later, for dinner.

"If you're one millisecond late, I'll be unavailable for the next millennium," she informed me.

"Understood."

She lay the flowers on the table. "Too bad you broke my only vase."

Well, shit. Kinda forgot about that.

"I have one you can borrow," Jessa offered.

"Perfect!" Katie put in supportively. Devi sipped her tea, and no one said another word.

I stroked Nicky's chubby little cheek with my finger; he was dead asleep in his baby carrier thing.

Then I got out of there.

"You done with Taze?" I asked Roni at dinner. We'd just ordered our food. I'd picked her up on time. Made sure I was early, actually.

I'd driven her to the restaurant where I'd made a reservation, pulled out her chair for her, ordered us a couple of steaks and cut right to the chase.

She looked at me over the wine glass that was halfway to her lips. "Yes," she said. "I'm done with Taze." Then she took a sip, set the glass on the table between us and squared her shoulders like she was preparing for an attack.

"That on my account?"

"It was on account of the fact that you were a millimeter away from sliding your dick into me, yes," she said, looking straight in my eyes. "And I'm not that girl."

"What girl?"

"The one who lets another guy fuck her while she has a boyfriend."

"I know you're not." I did know. She'd made that pretty damn clear to my ass seven years ago.

She left that one alone.

"Anyway. It's not like Taze and I were getting married anytime soon."

"You were right to break up with him," I told her.

"Hmm."

"You know he had other women." It was a statement, not a question. I wasn't gonna insult her. Roni was sharp; she had to know what Taze was about.

She said nothing for a long moment as she sipped her wine. Then: "And you don't?"

"I'm not your boyfriend."

"And if you were?"

"I don't cheat."

She looked totally unimpressed with that. "Easy for anyone to say. Harder to live."

"What's hard?" I said. "The thought of looking into a woman's eyes, a woman who thinks I'm faithful to her, and lying to her... it's fuckin' disgusting."

"You've never lied to a woman?"

Well, fuck. She had me there.

I didn't usually lie to women.

I didn't *like* to lie to women.

But fuck yeah, there were times I'd been dishonest with a woman. For a whole fucking plethora of reasons having to do with Kings business, the band, security, my privacy, other people's privacy.

And my own fucking protection.

I had a right to protect myself, didn't I?

"Are you lying to me about Taze?" she asked.

"No. You want proof?"

"You have proof?"

"I can get proof, you want it."

"What, like pictures?" she said. Playing tough, when she was clearly uncomfortable with the whole subject. When Roni was comfortable, she got all curvy and sexy. Right now, she could've had a steel rod right up her butt, she was so stiff.

"Whatever proof you want."

Instead, she changed the subject. "Have you ever lied to me?" She stared at me like she was waiting for me to say no, just so she could catch me in another lie.

"Most definitely," I said.

That caught her so off-guard she actually laughed, sort of. "What have you lied to me about? And don't say MC stuff because I know that and I don't care. I mean important stuff."

I didn't agree with her that "MC stuff" or the lies that went with it were unimportant. But I let that go.

I took a sip of my drink and considered how to answer.

"One time, at a party, you asked me if Piper was coming and I said he wasn't, but he was."

She cocked her head a little, jade eyes narrowing at me. "Why would you lie about that?"

"Because I didn't want you hooking up with him."

She stared at me.

I stared right back.

"Maybe a few months after we'd met," I said, "you asked me if Zane ever said anything about you when you weren't around. I told you he didn't. That wasn't true."

She just kept staring at me. She didn't ask me what Zane had said about her, but I told her anyway.

"He said you had cocksucking lips."

She broke eye contact. She stared at her wine, tapped her fingernails on the glass. They were a deep burgundy, almost black, but classy-looking, different from the flat black she'd worn on her nails sometimes as a teenager. I remembered those details about her more than I'd thought I did. I'd always paid attention to the details when it mattered, and being close to her, they were all coming back.

Wasn't sure if I liked that yet or not.

"You didn't want to tell me that?" she asked.

"Fuck, no."

"Why?"

"Because it pissed me off."

Finally, she looked at me again. "Why?"

"You sure you want honesty, darlin'? Some people say they want it, they don't."

"I don't ask questions I don't want the answers to. When I ask you a question, yes. I want an honest answer."

Okay, then.

"I wasn't sure if he meant it as some fucked-up compliment, or if you'd actually sucked his cock. Either way, like I said. It pissed me off."

"I didn't suck his cock," she said, her voice kinda small.

It was pathetic, probably, how relieved I felt to hear that. I knew she'd been with Zane, once, years after that. But if she'd actually sucked his cock at that point, it would've meant she'd done it when she was sixteen and barely knew him, and for whatever reason I really didn't want that to be true.

The server approached and laid out our meals. When he was gone, she said, "This looks good."

I ignored the food. I hadn't taken my eyes off her, and she was starting to look uncomfortable with the attention. Her posture had softened up a bit, but she still looked tense.

"You once asked me if I wanted to fuck you," I said.

Her eyes flashed up to mine.

"Actually, you asked me twice. The first time, I said yes. The second time, I said no. That was a lie."

Her gaze dropped. She picked up her fork and started poking at the veggies on the side of her plate. "I'm sensing a pattern here." She sounded bored, and like she wanted me to stop talking.

"I once told you I'd never get over you."

Her eyes met mine again.

"I said 'some guys' would never get over you. Some bullshit like that. But by 'some guys' I meant me. I figured you knew that, though."

She stared at me.

"But that was a lie, as it turned out," I finished. "I got over you."

Yeah, so maybe I was needling her.

Poking her.

Wasn't her fault that sitting across a table from her had me so off-kilter. But I wasn't sure I wanted to make it all that comfortable for her, either.

Had enough time since we fucked a couple nights ago to think things through. Think about how I wanted to fuck her again, yeah. But also, think about a lot of other things. Like the way things had gone down between us in the past. Things I'd learned about her—the hard way.

Time had passed, yes.

We'd both changed, maybe, and maybe we'd both stayed the same.

But she wanted to be in my life now, in any way—even just working with Dirty—I was gonna make damn sure she knew she wasn't gonna play me.

She put the cloth napkin that had been on her lap on the table and said, "Maybe this dinner was a mistake."

"Why?"

She stood, and I reached for her. I wrapped my hand around her wrist. She looked away, her jaw hardening.

"Roni."

She looked down at me, at my hand on her wrist. "*This*," she said, and her eyes flashed to mine. "Between us. This is just sex, right?"

"Sit down."

She sat, but she shook my hand off her arm.

"Maybe we should be clear," I said. "Maybe I gave you the wrong idea."

"What, the flowers and the dinner and the creepy conversation? What kind of wrong idea could I possibly get from that?"

"Not the dinner. The other night. I should've been clear, up front. I'm not looking for more than sex."

And yeah, that was a lie.

I could feel it every fucking moment I was in her presence; the girl was getting under my skin.

Again.

Yes, I'd gotten over her. Eventually. When she was finally out of my life. Over time, I'd managed to forget all the things that were so impossible to ignore when I was in a room with her.

Almost.

But then I saw her again, at Jesse's wedding, and within forty-eight hours I had my dick in her.

So there was that.

Truth was, I hadn't yet decided what I was looking for when it came to her. But while I figured it out?

Sex would do just fine.

She stared me right down with her gorgeous green eyes. "You give all your casual fucks flowers and a meal?"

"I give them respect. Thought the flowers were warranted, given that I stood you up. And we both need to eat."

"This doesn't blur the 'just sex' line for you?"

"Why? Because we're both human and we ate a meal together? No. Does it blur the line for you?"

"No."

Christ. It was like we were feeling each other out before a fucking cage match.

I did not want to knock her on her ass, but I didn't want her killing me either. And between her asshole boyfriends and her sexual bucket lists and her *Fuck me harder... Make me feel it...* this woman was definitely gonna be the death of me, one way or another, if I didn't keep my head.

"Then let's eat," I growled.

We ate.

We kept the peace, somehow, while making small talk about Dirty, about her job in real estate, about the New Year's Eve event.

After dinner and a few drinks, I realized she was maybe getting drunk.

Again.

We'd already been here, done this, two nights ago, and I really didn't need to drink half a bottle of whiskey to get it up for her. I'd take the sex, but the hangover could go.

"Easy," I told her as she downed another glass of wine. "Wouldn't want a guy to take advantage."

"I am not afraid of you," she informed me, setting her empty glass aside. She fixed her green eyes on me. "I'm not scared of you, Jude Grayson."

"No? What scares you, Roni Webber?"

"Me," she said, shocking the hell out of me. "Myself. Sometimes I don't trust myself and that is so, so scary. You ever have that feeling?"

I stared at her. It still surprised me how this girl could be so open, so fearlessly honest, and then two seconds later so fucking impossible to read. "No."

"You always trust yourself?"

I gave that some thought. "Yes."

"So... then what happens when you make a mistake? When you realize you were wrong?"

"Then I get pissed at myself and kick my ass."

She stared at me, and a soft smile curved her gorgeous lips. "Cream soda?"

She remembered; my dumbass vice.

"Yeah," I said. "Cream soda."

"Hey. Have you ever had a Bartender's Cream Soda?"

"The fuck is that?"

"Oh, it's so good." She was waving her hand in the air, trying to get our server's attention. "It's got cherry whiskey and banana liqueur..."

"Sounds disgusting."

Within a few minutes, we had two tall cocktails sitting in front of us. We sipped, and she was right.

"Shit. That does taste like cream soda."

"I know. It's dangerous."

I watched her sip her drink, her gorgeous lips wrapped around the straw. They were red and shiny as fuck. I could've sworn she'd slathered on more lip gloss when she went to the ladies' room.

Lip gloss that said *Insert dick here.*

"You know, you really don't have to get wasted to have sex with me, darlin'."

"What?"

"Or do you?" I watched her sip her drink and gnaw on the straw a bit with a slight smile. "Am I that bad?"

She laughed. "No, Jude. You're not that bad."

"There something you need to tell me? Am I one of those guys who always hurts a girl or has no rhythm but no one ever tells him?"

Her smile faded. "No. You're not that."

"Good."

"Drink," she said.

"You don't have to get me drunk either," I told her. "Or high."

"No?"

"All you've gotta do is say the word, and I'll be your fuck buddy, V."

"My fuck buddy?"

"Yeah."

"And what does that mean, exactly, in your mind?"

"It means anytime you want it, whenever, wherever, you tell me, and I give it to you. No drama. No games. No booze necessary."

"Hmm," she said.

Then her eyes darkened and her face flushed with a look that was pure sex, as whatever-the-fuck went through her mind... and my dick throbbed.

"How about right now."

Fuck, yeah. "Where?"

She thought about it, catching her full bottom lip in her teeth and twisting a bit. "In your car."

"Yeah. Just let me clear up..."

While I got my wallet out, she said, "I want you to take me somewhere. I don't care where." I looked up at her; she wasn't touching me across the table, just watching me with sex in her eyes. "I want you to park. I want you to take out your dick and let me blow you."

Yup. My dick was all for that.

She got up from her seat, came around the table and slid right in next to me, perching on the edge of my seat, her hot, curvy body in her little black dress pressing right up against me.

"Before you come," she breathed in my ear, "I'm going to stop. Then I'm gonna start again, so slowly, and I'm gonna do it again and again until you're pretty much ready to die, and then I'm gonna make you come."

Fuck me. My dick was aching in my jeans. "Is that so?"

"Mmm."

I looked into her eyes. "That what you want, darlin'?"

"That's what I want."

I'd driven maybe four blocks from the restaurant when I caved. I spotted an empty parking space along the street and pulled over. It was a metered spot, but I wasn't getting out to plug it.

Roni's hand was already in my jeans and she was working my zipper down.

I'd planned to take her somewhere more secluded, but that wasn't happening. We were in Gastown, it was raining a little, and this part of downtown Vancouver was dark as fuck at night when it was raining, the streets and sidewalks black and seeming to absorb all the light. There were people on the sidewalks, but most of them were in a hurry to get out of the rain, ducking in and out of the restaurants and bars along the street.

Honestly, I didn't really care all that much how private this was or wasn't—for myself. But call me old-fashioned; I didn't love the world seeing what Roni was about to do to me.

"Take it out," she said, the second I turned off the car.

I took it out. I was already totally fucking hard and she went down on me immediately but slow, sliding those perfect cocksucking lips of hers over my head, wet and tight.

"Fuck, V..." I groaned, easing back in my seat. I glanced out the windows but I was pretty sure no one could see much through the rain on the glass anyway. "Yeah, babe..."

She eased herself down, taking me in halfway, twirling her tongue around, then sliding back up to the tip.

Fucking teasing me.

Then she did it again, deeper, but not all the way to the base, sliding her tongue around as she went. Getting me wet. Taking her fucking time.

I gathered up her soft black hair and wrapped it around my fist, holding it out of the way so I could watch. I watched her devour my dick, slowly, over and over, working her way a bit deeper each time. Her hand wrapped around the base of my shaft as she fed me into her mouth.

Until she suddenly had my cockhead jammed into the back of her throat.

I groaned, a fucking grateful, pleasured sound.

"*Hmm.*" She moaned a little and eased off again, and I ran my free hand gently down the back of her neck.

I don't deep throat.

That's what she'd told me, fucking years ago. Right before she deep-throated me. Well, I deep-throated her. Pushed my dick deeper into her than she'd ever let another guy do. Pretty sure I made her like it, too. Made her touch herself while she did it. Made her make herself come.

I ran my hand all the way down her back now, over her tight ass in her dress... but I couldn't quite get to her pussy. In response, she scooted off her seat onto her knees on the floor.

"Babe—"

She deep-throated me again, making my brain explode... then slid her mouth back to the head, spoiling it with attention. I felt the climax building, fast, the pressure gathering in my balls.

Then she stopped. She glanced up at me.

I was breathing hard as I watched her.

She wrapped her hand around my shaft and gently kissed my cockhead.

Then she went down on me again, devouring me in a slow, steadily-building rhythm until I was right on the edge.

Then she stopped again.

"V..." I groaned, but then she started up again. She sucked me off slow, until I was right on the edge, a few more times... and every damn time, she stopped.

Just like she told me she would.

My dick was like fucking granite in her mouth as she worked me over, moaning softly all the way. And that sound of her soft, throaty voice, muffled by my cock... I had to come, *soon.*

Had to have her, too. Her soft, tight pussy, on my dick, in my mouth... couldn't stop thinking about the other night, when I'd made her sit on my face.

"You wanna hop on, babe...?"

"Mm-mmm..." she hummed, her mouth still full of cock.

"I've got condoms..."

But she just kept riding me with her mouth, sucking me right to the edge again.

"No...?" I gasped.

She kept sucking, long and slow, then gradually faster, rolling her tongue over my head and making my eyes roll the fuck back.

"All you want... is that dick in your mouth...?"

She answered by increasing the suction and wriggling her tongue around the underside of my cockhead. I groaned, squeezing her hair tighter in my fist.

And I gave up. I gave in.

I stopped trying to hold back, to control it.

She took me deep again, slow, and I felt it fucking everywhere. Sparkling little pinpricks of pleasure all over my body. In my scalp. In my nipples. In my balls...

She swept her soft fingers over my swollen sac and I growled, low in my throat.

I stared at her.

One thing that was obvious whenever she had my dick in her mouth: Roni fucking loved giving head.

Who was I to complain?

"That's good, darlin'," I encouraged her instead. "More... like that..."

But she eased right back and released me with a soft, wet popping sound.

And licked me like a fucking lollipop.

She looked up at me, and those green eyes hit me like a lighting bolt to the spine. Heat flooded me. Her fingers smoothed over my balls again, slithered around the base of my cock and squeezed lightly, teasingly, as she kept her lips just out of reach.

Fuck...

It was like the tenth time she'd totally fucking stopped. I'd lost count, but it was definitely way too many times. My balls ached and my whole body felt like it was about to explode.

"Roni... babe," I breathed.

She flickered her tongue over my slit, lapping up the pre-come that had leaked out.

Then she pushed down, taking me deep, and the rush started.

"Fuck. I'm gonna come, babe..."

"Mmm." She slithered her tongue all over my dick, squeezed the base and pulled... and it was all over. I gripped her hair and held her down as the orgasm rocked me. As I came in her tight, wet mouth, my dick jerked what felt like a hundred times. While I shot into her, my brain smashed around in my head and the whole world went dark. There was nothing but her, me, her hair in my fist, her fucking mouth.

"Jesus Christ," I heard myself say when I finished shooting. Her mouth was still on me, gently working, easing me back down. Then she released my dick with a sexy, wet sound—right before it became too fucking much.

I relaxed with a rough sigh.

I watched her lick her lip.

I released her hair and smoothed it gently back from her face, just catching my breath.

"Fuck... was that okay?" I'd pretty much held her there as I jerked in her throat, out of my mind with lust, like some fucking caveman. "Was that too rough?"

She just kinda smiled at me, cocking her head. I knew that look.

I like it rough.

She'd told me that, too. Long ago. But some girls said that, didn't really mean it. And some girls' definition of "rough" was different than other girls'.

"Answer me."

"It was hot," she said, sliding back up into her seat.

"Where you goin'?" I reached for her, hungry to do the same to her as she'd just done to me. Slowly and for-fucking-ever.

Girl thought she knew how to inflict torture?

She'd barely met my tongue yet.

But she resisted.

"C'mere," I said. I took her face in my hands, pulled her toward me; that gorgeous fucking face with her lips all swollen. "Come give me that pussy. I wanna taste you, V..."

She broke away before I could kiss her. "No."

"You *don't* wanna sit on my face?" I asked, disbelieving, as she slid away onto the farthest edge of her seat.

"No. Thank you." She flipped down the visor to get at the mirror, and started touching up her lips with her fuck-me lip gloss.

I blinked at her, confused as shit. "You're just gonna call it a fuckin' night?"

"Yeah. I'm done." She gestured at my dick. "That was for the comment about my 'cocksucking lips.'"

"Huh? What comment?" I did up my jeans with some struggle and blew out a breath; fucking sensitive. Wasn't sure my dick was ever gonna be the same. "That wasn't even my comment, sweetheart. That was fuckin' Zane's comment."

"Either way." She finished glossing her gorgeous lips in the mirror, then looked at me, making a bitchy kissy face.

"You serious? You pissed about that?"

"I'm not pissed."

I ran my hands through my hair, catching my breath. The blood was creeping back into my brain, fucking slowly. "You should be. Zane's an asshole." He was. He was one of my best friends, yeah, but when it came to women? Asshole.

"Goodnight, Jude." She hopped out of the car before I knew what was happening.

I got out my side, clumsily; the blood wasn't exactly back in all the right places yet. "The fuck are you going?" I called to her across the roof of my car. "Roni! Get back in the car."

"I'm going home." She strode toward the street corner in the rain, where a taxi was happening by. "Alone," she tossed over her shoulder.

"I can give you a ride!" I called after her as she flagged the cab down.

"I think I already gave you one!" she called back, strutting right over to the cab with a little too much bounce in her step.

Was she fucking enjoying this?

"Then let me return the fuckin' favor!"

"It was my treat!"

Fuck me. "And for the record, you do have cocksucking lips!"

She turned and grinned at me, then dropped into the cab.

Could not believe I just yelled that down the street. But fuck, this woman.

It was a downtown street at night, where no one gave a fuck, other than some drunk college boys smoking outside a pub. They hooted and shouted back some shit I ignored.

I glanced at the truck that was parked just inside the back alley, about a dozen feet from me, as its headlights popped on. I could just make out the face of the driver as he smiled at me. Fucking Bane.

I flipped him my middle finger. Fucker probably saw the whole thing. At least, Roni's head disappearing into my lap for like a half-hour.

Fucking hottest half-hour my dick had ever experienced.

I got in my car. Watched Bane pull out, following Roni's taxi.

And I felt like a fucking creep.

I sighed. My dick was still fucking throbbing, my heart still beating too hard in my chest.

I picked up my phone and sent her a text. Two texts.

Me: I lied to you more than I should have.

Me: I'm sorry.

I started up the car, then picked up the phone again and sent one more text.

Me: I liked you. I should've said that more.

Then I drove home.

CHAPTER FIFTEEN

Roni

THE NEXT NIGHT I had my meeting with Brody, in his home office, to go over the whole promotional strategy for the New Year's Eve event. He liked it, added in a few suggestions of his own, and done.

Promoting this event would be a serious no-brainer.

Dirty, DJ Summer, New Year's Eve. Best party in town.

Not a Dirty show. Not a DJ Summer show. It was a double bill, and it was gonna sell out in nanoseconds.

All I had to do was get the word out to the right people.

As soon as we were done, Jessa was waiting to yank me up to her and Brody's bedroom.

"Nicky's asleep," she informed me, "but he often wakes up about an hour after going down for more milk. So let's do this."

No sooner had she shut and locked the bedroom door behind us than she had Katy Perry rocking on her iPhone, "I Kissed a Girl," and cranked it through her BlueTooth speaker.

I raised an eyebrow. "Is there something I should know?"

"It's to keep Brody away," she said, heading into the walk-in closet. "Katy Perry scares him. If my Girl Time playlist is rocking, he's afraid we're talking about our periods or something."

"Are we talking about our periods?"

"No. I'm probably not having one for like the next two years anyway."

"Huh?"

"While breastfeeding," she said. "It probably won't come back."

"Oh." I put on a forced, pleasant-neutral smile and said, "How interesting." Which had become my stock response for all the shit she told me about motherhood that freaked me out.

I lay on my stomach on her bed, playing on my phone and sipping my wine, checking messages and all my social media accounts while she set to work digging through her lingerie drawers. She'd put Nick to sleep in his little bassinet, which was down in the party room with Brody, and while Jessa and I had our "girl time," Brody was on baby duty.

She'd already asked me to babysit tomorrow night, to come over and hang with Nick while she and Brody went on their little date. Two hours; she'd promised me that was the longest it would be, because apparently neither Nicky or her boobs could stand to be apart from each other any longer than that.

"I need you to tell me which one I should wear," she said as she started pulling lingerie and laying it out on the bed around me. "I feel like I've already forgotten how this all works."

"It's easy. Whichever one makes you feel most bangable."

She started peeling off her clothes in the walk-in closet and I went back to my phone. Taze, the little shit, had blocked me on Instagram. Unfortunate that I noticed that, but I did. It was the only social media account he kept; his account was private, and he mostly posted pictures of his motorcycle, but I'd still followed him.

Now, he was just gone from the list.

"I'm not even sure these are gonna fit my milk boobs..." Jessa was wiggling into a black lace teddy, struggling to arrange her bloated boobs into the cups.

"All the better," I said. "Here's the thing you've never seemed to grasp about men, my dear friend. Brody is not gonna complain if your boobs are falling out."

"Right," she said, like she was trying to commit that little tip to memory for future use.

"What are you so nervous about? Brody's seen your boobs before."

Jessa walked out of the closet, and all she needed was a glittering runway and a fan to blow her hair back.

"*Damn,* girl. You still got it."

I expected her to smile, or laugh, or tell me to shut up.

"I'm proposing to him," she blurted instead.

I stared at her. "What?"

"Yeah." She giggled nervously.

"Holy... shit." I got up and flew to her, giving her a hug. She clung to me. I could *feel* how excited she was. How... nervous.

"I just want it to be... you know... romantic and everything."

I held her out at arm's length. She gripped my arms and her nervous, excited energy seemed to buzz right through me.

"Everything's about Nicky right now, obviously," she gushed, "and Dirty, and we're both so tired. That's why I'm doing it now. Because I want to surprise him, and this is the last thing he'll expect. He thinks we're just going for a little drive tomorrow, you know, get out of the house together and grab a fro-yo or something." She grinned. "I booked us a hotel room."

"For like an hour?"

"Yup."

"*Girl.*"

I looked her over. My friend the lingerie model, who'd just had a baby, dressed in a gorgeous black silk-and-lace teddy, with her quadruple-E's or whatever and her curves all over the place... "Jessa. No straight man on Earth would say no to this proposal. I'm pretty sure if you proposed to your brother wearing this, he'd consider it."

"Jesus, Roni." She made a barfy face. "Really."

"Just trying to dispel some of this tension..." I shook her a bit by the shoulders, gently, and she released her death grip on my arms.

"I know Brody's not gonna say no," she said, biting her lip a bit. "I just want it to be perfect."

"It will be."

"You can't tell anyone. No one knows. I asked you to babysit because I was too nervous to tell Maggie or Katie... Just in case they accidentally let it slip or something? Or Brody suspected something? I don't know. Paranoia?"

"Jessa. You know he'll get nothing out of me."

"I know," she said.

I felt kinda flattered, actually, that she'd picked me. I would've thought for sure Maggie or Katie would be her first choice for anything like this.

"You're gonna knock it out of the park," I told her, settling back on the bed as she checked herself out in the wall mirror. "But if you really want to get married... why don't we make him propose to you?"

"It's not about making him ask or waiting for him to do it. I don't need him to ask. It's not about me feeling wanted." She looked at me with her big brown eyes. "He's been waiting for this his whole life. He's been waiting for *me*. So I'm going to give it to him."

Wow. I actually felt tears prick in my eyes, and it took a *lot* to move me to tears. "Jessa. Fuck. I'll marry you, if you keep talking like that."

She grinned and dashed back into the walk-in, peeling off the teddy. "We'll tell everyone soon, as soon as it's official," she said. "We'll have a little party."

"And your secret is safe with me until then."

It was. I'd never told anyone—even Jessa—about how I'd seen Zane, naked, in Maggie's cabin in the middle of the night, the night of Jesse and Katie's wedding. Why? Not because of my undying loyalty to Maggie. She and I weren't really that close.

Because Maggie and Zane fucking was none of my business.

Jessa planning a surprise proposal for Brody? Also none of my business.

I'd take all that shit to my grave if necessary.

Talking about other people's love lives was bullshit. I definitely didn't appreciate it when other people gossiped about mine. As the subject of gossip from a young age, I knew how it felt.

"I just don't know if I should go super-sexy with this, or more... romantic," Jessa said, and when I looked up again, she was sliding into a royal-blue lace bustier. The matching panties were already on, and *damn*.

"Well, what reaction are you going for?" I asked her.

"Reaction?"

"Do you want him to treat you like the mother of his newborn baby, or like some dirty whore he just picked up in an alley?"

"Ew. Roni, gross." She stepped out of the walk-in to peruse herself in the mirror again. She was definitely blushing a little when she turned to me and said, "Okay. The whore thing. We haven't had sex since Nick was born and I don't even know if I *can* yet."

"How... interesting," I said quickly, my pleasant-neutral smile in place—before she could elaborate on any details about *that* I really did not want to know.

She took the hint and moved on. "*But* I wanted this night to be, you know, X-rated. I don't want him to think our sex life is over just because of the adorable little cockblocker who sleeps two feet from us."

I kind of snort-laughed, which was not something I did in mixed company. "Jessa Mayes. After all these years... you surprise me."

"I'm serious."

"So am I."

"That's what he calls Nicky. 'Our little cockblocker.'"

"Adorable." I tossed a black garter-belt-and-babydoll ensemble at her. "Try this one."

"Okay." She headed back into the walk-in to strip down. "Hey. How's Taze?"

"Oh. Didn't I tell you?" I didn't even look up from my phone. "I broke up with him."

"When?"

"Few days ago."

"Are you okay?"

"Of course." I glanced up to find her sympathy face staring at me from the closet doorway. "Come on. It was inevitable."

"How did he take it?"

"Not well? He hasn't messaged me or called at all. I don't know... Maybe he doesn't even care? Maybe he thinks I wasn't serious, or I was just mad at him. That I'll take it back in a moment of horniness?"

She raised an eyebrow at me. "Will you?"

"No."

No fucking way.

Maybe it was having sex with someone else, someone I was so deeply attracted to, that had clarified for me what that whole relationship really was—and wasn't.

But it was more than that. It was what Jude said about Taze. It wasn't even that he'd cheated on me as much as it was the fact that I'd chosen to be with a man who had, apparently, played me like that. Again.

"Jude told me Taze cheated on me."

Jessa stepped out of the closet and stared at me. She didn't say, *How would he know?* Because we both knew how Jude would know.

"Do you think he cheated?" she asked carefully.

"I don't know. I kind of assumed, though," I admitted. I glanced at the black babydoll she'd put on. "The blue thing," I said. "Definitely the blue thing. I give it five boners out of five."

"Roni." Jessa actually put her hands on her hips. "You deserve better than that."

I rolled my eyes. "Obviously, Mom. But it's not like he put a ring on my finger. It was never that serious."

"And that gives him permission to cheat?"

"He didn't really need my permission to do anything."

"That's the thing, Roni," she said. "The right man..." She hugged herself, getting all dreamy-eyed as she probably thought about *her* man. "When you're with the right man, you'll want to give him all the freedom in the world. And he'll want to give you all his loyalty in return. You don't have to live in fear that he's going to cheat. The right guy would probably rather have his balls cut off than hurt you like that."

"I dunno, Jessa. Guys are very protective of their balls."

"You know what I mean," she said.

"I guess."

She went to change and I perused the offerings on Tinder. It was a habit, but one I wasn't sure I cared to keep up. These days, they were all left swipes. *Not Jude. Not Jude. Not Jude...*

Swipe.

Swipe.

Swipe.

The Girl Time playlist was still going strong, Tegan and Sara girlying up the place with "Closer" when Jessa came humming out of the closet in yoga pants and a T-shirt, her supermodel hair in a bun on her head.

"Speaking of Jude..." she said, throwing me a not-casual unassuming look, in the most awkward segue in history.

"I didn't realize we were."

"Come on." She flopped down on the bed next to me. "He barged in on our lady lunch. *With flowers.* I understand you maybe didn't want to say anything about it in front of everyone. But it's *me.* I texted you twice, left you a demanding voicemail, and *nothing.*"

I quirked an eyebrow at her. "And?"

"And... I believe our friendship demands an explanation, Roni Webber."

"Yes. Because you were so forthcoming in your undying love for Brody Mason all those years."

"Roni, come on. *Jude* showed up at a *teahouse* with *flowers.* If Brody showed up at a *teahouse* with *flowers* for me, I would've explained."

Uh-huh. Did she expect me to believe that?

"You want me to explain Jude Grayson?" I said. "Good luck waiting on that to happen. You'll be old and gray before I ever have the first clue."

"Okay. So just tell me *something*. Did you guys go to dinner that night?"

I rolled my eyes. "We're fucking, Jessa. Is that what you're trying to ask? We're not teenagers anymore. You can say the dirty words."

Her big brown eyes went Bambi-wide. "You and Jude?"

"Yes. Me and Jude."

"Since *when*?"

"Since nine years ago, officially. With a few giant hiatuses in-between."

Her mouth dropped open. To be fair, I'd never told her I'd had sex with Jude, ever.

But hey, it wasn't like she'd ever asked.

"Do you like him?"

"I've always liked him."

"Roni!"

"Oh, don't start freaking out like all the guys."

"What guys?

"These guys." I held up my phone. "Let's just say I haven't been as active as usual on Tinder and the dudes are sniffing out that I might be going off the market, and they're freaking out."

"Freaking out...?"

"Pleading their cases. Doing everything but dropping down on one knee. Guys who've been flirting with me for *months* suddenly fear the pussy might be unavailable to them and they all step up their game. They're sending requests for dates, fucking poetry, dick pics, you name it. Dick videos, actually, that's the latest thing."

"Um. What happens in a dick video?"

"Oh, babe. If you've gotta ask, you really don't wanna know."

"Roni." She poked my shoulder. "Should I be getting excited about this?"

"About the dick videos?"

"About *Jude*. And you. Are you going off the market?"

"I don't think I've ever really been off the market before. I don't even know what that is."

"Well... is it serious? The thing with Jude?"

I glanced at my phone again. I had seven new messages in the last, what, three minutes? All from men. Snapchat, Instagram, Facebook, Tinder, text message. They all knew where to find me. They popped up all over the place, like Whac-A-Moles. There was even a message from my hopefully-soon-to-be-ex-boss, casually inquiring what I was doing tonight. While his wife was who-knew-where.

Not one message from Jude.

After he'd texted me last night, with his *I liked you. I should've said that more*, I'd texted back with *Yes, you should've.*

Since then, not a word.

I tossed my phone aside and told Jessa, "It's really not."

He messaged me at 1:07 am.

I was out at a club with Talia and a couple of her girlfriends. She'd messaged me on Snapchat before I left Jessa's, and of all the invites I'd received tonight—it was Friday night, so there were several—Talia's cutesy selfie of her and two of her girlfriends with a kitten face filter won out.

The club I met them at was packed, like sweaty-wet-as-you-climbed-over-people-trying-to-get-to-the-bar packed, definitely over capacity, and the girls were drunk when I arrived. And let's just say that a group of hawt twenty-two-year-old drunk chicks at a bar drew the dudes like horny flies, so while we spent the night dancing, we were pretty swarmed.

I really wasn't feeling it, so I was serving up a steady stream of *I have a boyfriend*, that universally polite kiss-off that usually did the trick. If it didn't, the guy was a creep, and I didn't have to be polite about it anymore. Those were the rules as far as I knew them.

But I definitely didn't mind bumping and grinding my twenty-seven-year-old hawt *single* self in the vicinity of a bunch of hawt young dudes—as long as they kept their body parts to themselves.

That's what I was doing at 1:07, so I didn't actually get Jude's message until 1:18.

Jude: Hey beautiful.

That was all.
Maybe that was all it took.
Because I texted right back.

Me: Hey yourself, gorgeous.

That was the booze talking. We'd been doing Blow Job shooters and drinking cider (both horrible ideas) and I was telling myself how awesome it was to be *on the market*, while all the while I kept sneaking peeks at my phone, hoping to hear from *him*.

Jude: You out?

That came in at 1:23, at which point I decided, *It's on*.

I was totally aware that a guy who texted a girl at 1:07 am was definitely thinking *Where should I put my dick tonight?* as opposed to *Where's that lovely lady I want to bring home to Mom?*

But tonight, I could live with that.

Me: Out with Talia. Where r YOU?

And how soon can you be underneath me?

Jude: Jesse's. Want a ride home?

Then he sent a motorcycle emoji.
And it gave me a ridiculous thrill.

Me: Yes. I want a ride.

Jude: Might be cold.

Me: You'll keep me warm.

Then I sent every emoji I could think of that represented a cock. Eggplant. Lollipop. That sushi emoji that looked like a hotdog.

Granted, he might've just thought that meant I was hungry.

I had about twenty minutes to kill before he showed up, so I partook of the round of Blow Jobs the girls were sucking back at the bar. Then we danced some more.

Then I saw Jude standing up at the bar at the edge of the dance floor, watching me bump 'n' grind with Talia. Since he was watching, I gave him a bit more of a show, then told Talia, "My ride is here," kissed her cheek, and sashayed on over to him.

No exaggeration, four different guys pawed at me as I made my way off the crowded dance floor. Our little crew of babes had stirred up a lot of attention, and the boys seemed pretty bummed I was leaving—without them.

I just grinned and pretty much fell into Jude's arms.

He pulled me close, and when I tipped my head back to look at his face, his eyes searched mine. His narrowed a little. The hint of a smile tugged at his lips.

Then he kissed me. Sweet and warm, lingering. No tongue. Just a kiss.

And little sparkles of happiness tingled through me.

Dangerous.

And the feeling of walking out of that club with him... holding his hand as he led me through the crowd...

Pure joy.

Well, horny joy.

We walked to his bike, me snuggled up under his armpit. It *was* cold out. Lucky for me, he'd brought me a sweater. A giant black hoodie that smelled of him. I pulled it on with a dumbass smile on my face, inhaling his scent.

Jesus Christ, the smell of this man.

I got on his bike, right behind him, and I didn't exactly hate that the hoodie had the Kings' insignia on it. No words, just the wicked, skeletal king of spades design, black-on-black, that anyone who lived on the west coast of Canada would recognize a mile away.

Kinda felt like a marking-his-territory thing, even though I knew he really wasn't.

Still. I didn't mind the feeling.

At all.

We helmeted up, and once we were heading out of downtown across the Cambie Bridge, he opened it up a bit. When we stopped at the next light, he revved the engine, sending tingles through me.

"Are you flirting with me?" I asked, over the roar of the bike.

He just let go of the clutch, so the bike jolted forward and I had to grip him tighter—then took off at what felt like the speed of light.

By the time we got to my place I was throughly wet and ready to screw his brains out. Admittedly, motorcycles had always gotten me weirdly hot.

I was definitely one of those girls who creamed when a Harley tore by.

Didn't even care who was on it.

But when Jude was on it?

Holy hell.

"C'mere," I said as soon as we got inside. I pulled him over to my couch and shoved him down as we both peeled off our jackets and sweaters. He went, willingly, sitting back and spreading his knees wide, so I had to spread mine even wider—like super wide—to straddle him.

I grabbed his face and kissed the hell out of him.

When my hands ran down his chest, he slid his hands up into my hair. I continued my exploration down to his crotch, and as I teased my fingers over the hard length in his jeans, he said, "You plannin' to blow me and run again, darlin'?"

"Don't think so. I had enough Blow Jobs at the bar."

He pulled back, his dark eyebrow rising sharply.

"Shooters," I said.

"There's a shooter called a Blow Job?"

"Yup. It's got whipped cream on top."

He chuckled. "'Course it does."

"And you've gotta pick it up off the bar with your mouth and suck it back without using your hands."

"There's a visual..."

"I think that's the point."

"How many of those you have?"

"Mmm... four?"

"Hmm. You gonna puke on me, I put my tongue down your throat?"

"Jude. I'm a grown woman. I can handle four Blow Jobs."

He gave me his dead-eye security-guy look, and I grinned.

"Sweetheart," he said, as I grabbed his hair and dragged his head back, so I could kiss my way down his throat, "one of these days, you're gonna fuck me sober..."

"I wouldn't say I'm drunk..."

"You're not *not* drunk, darlin'."

"Mmm. Good point."

I was kissing a path down his chest, right over his T-shirt. Slithering down between his legs until I was on my knees on the floor and his T-shirt was up and I was licking my way down his fabulous abs.

"Nope." He grabbed my arms, stopping me in my descent. "Uh-uh."

"What?" I swirled my tongue around his belly button.

"You're not gettin' that dick in your mouth, V."

"What?" I laughed. "Why?"

"Because I don't trust your ass. You're gonna do that shit you do with your tongue and make me lose it and then you're gonna bounce my ass outta here."

"And why would I do that? What's in it for me?"

"Dunno. Fucked up sense of power?"

"Aw. Jude. Did I suck out all your power? You want it back?"

I stood up in front of him and undid my jeans, watching his eyes turn into two dark pools of lust as I did it. I shimmied them off, peeled off my thong, and straddled him again. While I did that, he dug a condom out of his jacket and took out his cock. He worked his jeans down just enough, rolled the condom on, and I was on him.

I took him slow, looking in his dark eyes, watching the way they changed when he slid into me.

I angled my hips and rode him, slowly, until he was all the way in and it felt so... fucking... *good.*

Then I just kept fucking him—however fast or slow I wanted. However I wanted.

He slipped my strapless top and bra down to my waist and palmed my breasts, feeding one and then the other into his mouth. He sucked on me and ran his hands up and down my back, until I couldn't take his gentle touch anymore and I suddenly came, my whole body spasming as he wrapped his arms around me.

"Yeah... *fuck,*" he groaned. "So beautiful, babe..."

He held me tight against his body, his arms pressing my hips down against him as he joined me in ecstasy. I wrapped my arms around his neck. And as we came in each other's arms, kissing and slowly rocking together, I had no idea who had the power.

Both of us? Me? Him?

No one?

I did not care.

For the first time since I'd started fucking him—again—I just didn't fucking care.

CHAPTER SIXTEEN

Jude

IT WAS A MONDAY, a week after Dirty finished recording the new album. They'd spend the rest of December doing some promo for the album—photo shoots, interviews and a few scheduled appearances—but other than that, they'd be in rehearsals for the tour.

Today, we were filming the video for the first lead single off the album—the title track, "To Hell & Back"—which would be released in early January, right before the tour began.

One of Dirty's all-time favorite directors, Liv Malone, was directing the video. Dylan's girlfriend, Amber, who was a photographer—and Liv's sister—was shooting stills, backstage and whatnot. Elle's little sister, Angie, was hanging out, painting Elle's nails. Zane's grandma, Dolly, was backstage. Katie's sister's coffee bar, Nudge, had provided the coffee.

And so, like most Dirty projects, it had become kind of a family affair.

But we were also shooting in a giant sound stage with a ton of people in attendance, which meant security was tight and I had a large crew to manage. It was a "concert" shoot, with a staged concert, and the film crew had built an entire "church" interior for it—a homage to the church that was the band's sacred rehearsal space, the location of which we'd never make public in order to film a video shoot there.

Lucky for me, the "concert" shoot came complete with an audience of superfans—and all the BS that came right along with that.

Like overenthusiastic fangirls angling to meet the band, thinking if they just shoved their tits in my face, I'd give them access to Zane Traynor's lap.

That bullshit.

The ones who thought they were classy because they wanted to meet Seth or Dylan and were above trying to meet Jesse or Zane; those were my favorites. Saw them coming a mile away. The more elaborate the story, usually, the more bullshit it was.

I'm a songwriter and I just really want to meet Seth so I can tell him how much he's inspired me.

Sure you are, sweetheart. That's why your tits are falling out of your shirt.

Yeah, I was jaded with this shit.

The creeper guys who were gonna try to touch Elle's baby bump? Had to watch out for those, too. Groupies came in all forms.

And I was definitely not averse to tossing someone out if they gave off the slightest whiff of crazy or disrespectful.

Truly, the members of Dirty were way nicer to the fans than I ever was.

Which was why they needed me.

If it were left up to them, they'd be eaten alive. Drained dry from stopping to "be nice" and talk to every damn fan who ever tried to talk to them.

Here was the problem with being nice. Once you got to a certain level of fame, you just couldn't afford to be *that* nice anymore. It'd bleed you dry.

When it came to the fans, the members of Dirty were grateful, appreciative and gracious. Which was exactly how they should be. They knew if it wasn't for the fans, we'd have nothing.

Literally.

Zane, Jesse and me would still be living in that crap-ass apartment. Or maybe I'd be living at the Kings clubhouse or, if I was really lucky, I'd be in prison or dead by now. Zane would probably be drowning at the bottom of a bottle and Jesse would be playing dive bars and delivering pizzas, still believing he could make it, even if he didn't. Dylan and Elle would've stayed at home with their parents as long as they could, gotten more education and maybe some soul-sucking desk job. Brody would be living in his mansion, because Brody was rich as fuck without us, but would he ever have ended up with Jessa? And Seth... I didn't even want to think about where Seth would've ended up.

Without the music and the fans who loved the music, we'd all be nobody.

I knew that as well as any of us did.

But I was wary of everyone always trying to take a piece of them. It was my job to keep the members of Dirty safe, which meant sane, too. It meant doing my best to keep them *whole*.

Sometimes, that meant protecting them from themselves.

"Five minutes," I told my guys, when we let a dozen or so carefully chosen fans backstage to meet the band just before we started shooting. It was good for the shoot to dole out a few passes, let a few people back to talk to the band and get excited about it, bring that energy back out into the crowd. But I was selective as fuck.

Picked a handful of girls and guys who actually looked like they might be decent conversationalists, not just groupies who'd be begging Zane to bend them over.

Even Zane was getting weary of that shit these days.

Just before the band hit the stage to start shooting, I was hanging with Jesse backstage when he asked me, "So, you meet someone or what?"

"What?"

"You've been sending guys to fill in for you a lot lately, at night. Every time I ask you to come down, someone else shows up. I'd say I miss you, but even when you're around lately, you're shit for conversation anyway."

Really?

"Yeah," I said, because what was I gonna do, lie to Jesse's face about it? "Met someone."

"Yeah?" He gave me his brilliant, superstar smile, and I actually felt kinda bad for being so secretive about it. "When do I get to meet her?"

"I'll let you know if it becomes important."

His smile dropped a few watts; maybe he was really that jazzed that I was seeing someone? Probably wanting me to do date nights with him and Katie.

Yeah... really didn't think Roni would be up for that anytime soon.

"Alright, brother," he said.

I clapped him on the shoulder and went to check on everyone else. But even after I'd said those words and walked away, they tasted bad in my mouth.

If it became important.

Like Roni wasn't important to me?

Then, out of nowhere, Brody got up my ass.

"So what's going on with you and Roni?"

When I glanced at him, his blue eyes narrowed at me, and I knew he knew... something. Maybe this was payback for me giving him a hard time for being such a ragey bitch when Jessa first came back to town. Or maybe Jessa had told him how I'd showed up at that teahouse with flowers for Roni.

I had no idea.

So I just evaded the question.

"Roni? Yeah, Roni's hot," I said, distractedly, like maybe I hadn't even noticed before, or I hadn't heard him all that well. Then I made myself busy talking to Seth.

It wasn't like that was a lie, either.

Roni *was* hot.

If she happened to be my fuck buddy, whose business was that?

Just because my friends were nosy as shit, didn't mean I had to tell them anything.

Thank fuck Liv called the band out to the stage like two seconds later, and Brody got busy out front.

I hung out by the side of the stage, and as soon as they started rolling, I texted Roni. *Plans tonight?*

Because I planned to be her plan for tonight, if I had any say in it.

For the last week-and-a-half, we'd been fucking like maniacs. Almost every night I was at her place. Usually late, after we'd both done all the other shit we had to do. We fucked, then I went home.

Other than the night when we'd fucked on my Harley instead, parked in the dark of an empty parking lot, halfway back to her place from some bar I'd picked her up at. Was cold as shit out, but she'd insisted; something about a fantasy she'd had for years. Who was I to kill her dreams?

And, other than the night she'd replied to my fuck request to tell me she was on her "moon time." I didn't even know what the fuck she was talking about for about five minutes.

When I'd figured it out, I texted her back to tell her, *Doesn't bother me.*

She'd texted me back, *I'll be in my jammies by 6:00.*

And I'd texted back, *Perfect.*

When she didn't reply, I called her and she told me, "I'm emotional. I don't see men when I'm emotional."

To which I replied, "You're kiddin' me."

And she basically hung up on me.

That night, I'd arrived at her place around nine-thirty—uninvited—to find her in her jammies, looking surly. I walked right in anyway and managed to get her on the couch under a blanket, where we cuddled up and watched a movie. I kept my hands to myself, and I even let her pick what we watched. She chose the latest *Thor* movie, which I was pretty impressed with until she informed me she'd chosen it "because Chris Hemsworth."

Before the end of the movie, she was asleep. I watched until the end, then slipped out.

Then I left her alone for a couple of days, because that seemed to be what she wanted.

The next time I saw her, we were both at Brody and Jessa's engagement party, but not together. Apparently Jessa had proposed and they'd already set a wedding date—next summer, during a scheduled break in the tour. Everyone was happy for them, including me. Brody was pretty much glowing.

The whole night, I'd managed to be a gentleman and not put my hand on Roni's ass or something that might've pissed her off, since we were just fuck buddies and all.

Then I took her back to her place and fucked her on her dining room table. And in the shower.

And I wondered how long we were gonna keep this up.

I'd been wondering that a lot.

Over the next few weeks, I'd be prepping my security crew and working with Maggie to get all the details set for the tour. There was a lot of paperwork for my guys and bullshit that Maggie helped me take care of, and I liked to map out a whole plan of who was doing what and where and when, even if it sometimes fell to shit once we got on the road.

I liked to be prepared, as much as possible; when it came to security for the band, I didn't like surprises.

Which meant I also needed to prepare a whole alternate plan—one that laid out what was gonna happen if I wasn't on the tour. Minor problem with that was I still wasn't sure who I'd have lead my crew in my place.

And if I did go on the tour... I didn't even want to think about who was gonna take my place here—with Roni.

Being her fuck buddy and the one guy she'd let near her when she was feeling "emotional"? Those were roles I wasn't thrilled about handing off to anyone else.

Late that night, once the video shoot had wrapped, instead of heading over to Roni's place for sex, I picked her up where she was—at a bar with some friends—and I took her to my place.

It was the first time I'd ever brought her to my place, and as we walked into the house, I saw it more or less through her eyes.

The general lack of furniture. The giant TV and leather couch that pretty much dominated the living room. The dining room that had no table. The huge black-and-white photo on canvas of me and my brother as kids, with our dad and one of his motorcycles—the only decoration on any wall.

The house was old, plain, in decent repair, but it really wasn't all that much to look at.

Roni still looked, carefully, as I gave her the incredibly brief tour.

As she looked around, maybe it should've made me uneasy. Her condo by the water in Olympic Village was much newer, and like her, it was beautiful, stylish and inviting.

But it didn't make me uncomfortable.

I knew why I never brought women here. Because this was my private space. My sanctuary. My one escape from both the MC and the band.

I had a lot of love for a lot of people, but at the end of the day my introverted ass needed to shut it all down and turn off that fucking ticking clock or I'd go insane.

There were pretty much four things I needed in life, in order to maintain my sanity.

My routines.

My workouts.

Keeping my diet as clean as I could, even on the road.

And my space.

The best places to get the space I needed were on my bike, and in my home—a place that was mine alone, where I checked all the drama at the door.

I'd only had this place since coming home from the last Dirty tour. Pretty much every tour, I gave up whatever rental I'd been living in, and when the tour ended I just found another one. If I didn't count the six-week tour for Jesse's solo album last year, I hadn't been on tour for almost two years; it was the longest gap we'd ever had between Dirty tours.

And in these last two years, being more or less home from the road, it wasn't like there'd been any woman in my life who I'd wanted to bring into my sanctuary.

Just Roni.

I wasn't even sure why it suddenly felt so important to me to bring her here, except that I felt the need to do it. So here we were.

"Your dad," she said, as she gazed up at the photo on the wall of the empty dining room. "He died, a few years back." She glanced over her shoulder at me. "I heard about it. Still run into people from the club, from time to time."

"Yeah. I was away on tour when it happened. Dirty's second world tour. We were in Australia. Almost didn't make it back for the funeral in time. Jesse flew back with me, had to miss a couple of shows."

"I know," she said. "I was there." She looked up at the photo again. "I came to the burial. But there were a lot of people."

She was there?

That stunned me; that she'd cared to be there.

Yeah, there were a lot of people at the funeral. But I couldn't believe I'd missed her.

"You should've come over," I told her. "Said hello."

"No. You were grieving. I didn't think you'd want to see me, anyway." She glanced at me, then wandered right on into my bedroom.

I followed her, watching as she looked around.

"No visible signs of other women... Check." She turned in a slow circle. "Unmade bed, but the sheets look clean... Okay. No *Star Wars* posters... Check."

I raised an eyebrow.

"I'll stay." She dropped her purse on the floor and shed her jacket.

"You find that in the bedrooms of other men?" I asked her, genuinely fucking curious. "*Star Wars* posters and signs of other women?"

"Not all men are as classy as you, Jude Grayson."

"That's true."

I walked over to her and spun her around by her hips. Then I unzipped her sexy little black dress and slipped it down to the floor. I slid my hand up her back, over the tattoo on the back of her right shoulder; it was the only one on her body. A girly, swirly pattern of leaves and flowers. Pretty, like the rest of her.

I pushed her forward, so she was bent over my bed, and tore her panties down her thighs.

"I'm not always classy," I informed her.

Then I licked two fingers and shoved them into her pussy.

She gasped. "Replace that with your dick... and I won't be so classy, either."

I was already undoing my jeans, and fumbled around for a condom in the drawer by the bed. Took me a while to find one. I stopped finger-fucking her long enough to roll the condom on, then gripped her hips and slammed into her.

She cried out, a raw, animal sound, followed by a string of curses and encouragements, and for the next however long we fucked like feral monkeys.

After a while, she started to squirm like she was restless or something, so I moved myself onto the bed and pulled her with me, peeling off her panties and bra as we went and shedding my own clothes.

Then I pulled her on top and watched as she fucked me. I held her wrists tight behind her, making her back arch and her tits thrust out.

I pulled her forward so I could take her nipples in my mouth and tease her. One thing I knew about Roni: she hated being teased and touched in any gentle way during sex.

But that was only because she loved it.

"Jude... *augh*," she complained-moaned, as I suckled one nipple, then the other. I licked and nibbled as she rode me, her nipples slipping in and out of my mouth as she bobbed up and down.

Then I just watched her for a while, her black hair falling around her shoulders, her head tipped back, her mouth open. I listened to the sexy sounds she made, how she moaned and swore the hotter she got. How her body started to shake as she bore down on my dick.

I rolled us over, taking her under me. I fucked her hard, then slowed right down, teasing her. I kissed her sweet, cocksucking mouth as her hands moved over my back and her nails dug into my ass. And I could feel her want for me, so strong.

Then my head went to a strange place.

I started burning up with fucking jealousy...

Star Wars posters.

Signs of other women.

Other mens' bedrooms...

I pulled out, leaving my cockhead just nudging her slit.

"You want this, babe?"

"Yeah. Yeah..." she moaned, clutching at me.

But I held it back, just out of reach.

"Then no other dick."

Her gaze snapped to focus, meeting mine. "What?" she gasped.

"You want this dick," I said, sliding back into her, "no one else."

"Uh..." She seemed to be scraping her thoughts together. "You... you want me to be... uh... exclusive with you? Like... exclusively fucking you?"

"Yeah, that."

"Oh..."

Didn't love that response. I pulled out again, almost all the way. "That a problem?"

"No... No. I haven't been... anyway..."

Good girl.

I slammed back into her.

"*Fuck*, Jude..."

"No one else?"

"No one else," she breathed. "Since we became..."

"Good." I took her hands, pushed them into the pillows above her head, and increased the power of my thrusts. The bullshit on my back had fully healed by now, and I was planning on making up for any previous lack in performance. "You feel that?"

"Yeah..."

"Get used to it. 'Cause that's what you're gettin' from now on..."

And that's what she got, until she came beneath me, screaming.

Then I slowed it down and built it right back up until she came again.

Then I did it a few more times, because witnessing Roni Webber losing it like that was a thing of fucking beauty.

So beautiful... she finally took me down with her.

I was gradually getting the feeling back in my extremities as I laid back on the bed, sweat-drenched and pretty much panting, watching her gather her lingerie off the floor and slide it back on.

Then I realized what time it was.

"*Shit...*" How did this girl always make me lose track of time? It was like every clock in the world—including the one in my head—ceased ticking the moment I was in a room with her.

"What?" Roni stood in the middle of my bedroom in her panties and bra, doing up the bra behind her back, her hair falling over one shoulder. Black hair, pale skin, black lingerie.

Fucking perfection.

I sighed. "It's four am. I've gotta be up in like three hours. You mind if I get Bishop to drive you home? He's not far from here."

"Bishop?" she said. "Won't he be sleeping? I can just call a cab."

"Like fuck." I was already on my phone, texting Bishop. "Bishop's already getting paid. Let the man earn his keep."

"In the middle of the night?"

"He's on call, twenty-four-seven."

"For Jessa," she protested.

I gave her a look. "For me."

She just shook her head as she plucked her dress off the floor. "What if he's not available?"

"He's available if I say he's available."

"Oh, yeah?" She cocked her sexy eyebrow. "And what if he's getting laid?"

"Too bad for him."

She narrowed her gorgeous eyes at me. "So that's it? Everyone in your life is just at your beck and call, huh?"

"I wouldn't say that."

"What a charmed life you lead, Jude Grayson," she mused, as she shimmied back into her sexy dress.

Twenty minutes later, when I walked her out to the driveway and put her in Bishop's car, I asked her, "You wanna hook up with this exclusive dick tomorrow?"

"I'm working with Talia tomorrow night. I might not have time for your dick, too."

Huh?

I searched her face but she appeared to be totally fucking serious about that. After the string of orgasms I'd just given her.

Clearly, *she* wasn't gonna be at my "beck and call."

"Yeah?" I challenged. "You gonna make time?"

"Maybe," she said, then she gave me a goodbye kiss that made my cock stand right the fuck back up. "Call me and find out."

CHAPTER SEVENTEEN

Roni

TWO NIGHTS LATER, I was out at a brew pub for beers and girl talk with Jessa, Katie and her BFF, Devi, and Dylan's girlfriend, Amber. And of course baby Nick, who was sleeping in his carrier on the booth seat next to Jessa while we talked.

Because it was the number one thing they had in common, Katie, Amber and Jessa got talking about their men, and before long, Katie turned to me. She'd invited me to this girls' night herself, and when she asked me, "How's your boyfriend, Roni?" with her big, blue-green, ultra-innocent eyes, I knew why.

Obviously she was dying to know why her husband's best friend had walked into that teahouse with flowers for me and asked me to dinner—when the last she'd heard, yes, I had a boyfriend.

I glanced at Jessa. Clearly, she hadn't spread the news.

"We broke up."

"Oh?" Katie said.

"Yeah, you know, right before the flowers-in-the-teahouse incident."

"*Oh*."

"What flowers-in-the-teahouse incident?" Amber asked.

"Jude showed up at a teahouse where we were having a lady lunch, with flowers," Devi filled her in. "For Roni."

Amber looked at me and I could tell she was trying hard not to appear, well, stunned. "Jude?"

"Mmm," I said noncommittally, and sipped my microbrew.

"Please tell me there's more," Katie said, gazing at me imploringly.

"Not really," I said carefully. I glanced at Jessa again. She knew every one of these girls better than I did, so I tried to tell her with my eyes, *Jump in here anytime you want.* "We've been working together on the New Year's Eve event for Dirty."

"Oh, yeah," Amber said. "How's that going? Dylan's excited about it."

"It's going great." It really was going great. Here we were, only two-and-a-half weeks to New Year's Eve, and the event was sold out. And pretty much everything was all set for the show. "I assume you're all coming?"

"I am," Amber said, smiling. "It'll be my first Dirty show."

"Girrrl. Your man's gonna be wearing a kilt," Devi informed her, "so you might wanna bring extra panties."

"*Devi,*" Katie said.

"What?" Devi sipped her beer. "I've *seen* Dylan Cope in a kilt."

Amber just smiled, looking a little embarrassed.

"Brody's got a bunch of tickets set aside," I told them, "and I have some too, so if you need a ticket, Devi—"

"I've got one for her," Katie said. "From Brody. Already talked to him."

"Perfect."

"Now," Katie leaned on her palm and gazed at me again. "Tell me more about Jude..."

"Katie, can't you see she doesn't want to talk about it?" Devi wore a hooked smile, and clearly she was daring me to talk about it.

"There really isn't much to say," I repeated.

"Come on," Devi prompted. "We're all girls here. I've always been so curious about Jude. Like is he all bulldog on the outside and cuddly little puppy on the inside?"

Well. He'd definitely cuddled me on my couch while I had

period cramps, and been a total gentleman about it. Even brought me a chocolate bar when he showed up at my door, unannounced and uninvited. Which was pretty much the only reason I'd let him in.

"Uh... Sometimes..."

Jessa kinda laughed into her beer. She'd ordered a Guinness because she said her part-time nanny had told her it was good for her breastmilk. That theory worked for me.

"So... Does this mean we can double-date now and stuff?" Katie asked me. She glanced conspiratorially at Jessa. "Or triple date?"

"No," I said.

"Oh." Katie's shoulders actually dropped, and I kinda felt bad disappointing her.

"I mean, it's not that serious."

"Sure it's not," Devi said. "Maybe for you. We saw him at the teahouse. He is all over that."

"It's not really like that."

"Like what?" Katie said.

"He's just... you know, a biker."

They all stared at me. Then glanced at one another.

Apparently, they didn't know.

"Let's just say I've been with guys like Jude before," I explained. "They're just possessive like that. Think they own you even when they don't, like they can just walk into a teahouse where you're having lunch with your girlfriends and give you flowers because they feel like it."

"Own?" Amber scrunched up her nose.

"Yeah," I said. "Own."

She stared at me, like she was waiting for me to explain further.

I didn't.

"I think I get it," Katie said. "Jesse can get pretty possessive. He definitely doesn't like me flirting with other dudes."

"Yeah," I said. "Not like that. I'm not with Jude. He's not my husband and he's not even my boyfriend. We've just agreed to be exclusive, sexually, which means... he definitely thinks he owns me. At least, that part of me."

The girls seemed to be processing that.

"Well..." Jessa offered, "Brody definitely thinks he owns that part of me. No way he'd be sharing that with anyone else."

"It's not necessarily about sharing," I said. "It's about *owning*. Different thing. Taze definitely thought he owned me, but he was okay with sharing me. Sometimes."

"What's that like?" Devi asked.

"Hot," I said. I looked straight at Amber, who definitely knew what it was like, given her three-way relationship with Dylan and Ash.

Or her *former* three-way relationship.

"Yeah," she said softly, and sipped her beer. "It's that."

"Oh my goodness," Katie said. "I could never share Jesse. Two guys sounds kind of hot, but I think he'd have an aneurysm before he'd share me. Like his brain would just implode or something."

"So how do you know he wants to 'own' you?" Amber asked. "If he's not your boyfriend?"

Now there was a good question.

It was the demand of exclusivity, in Jude's case. It was also the way he'd taken me back to his place and fucked the hell out of me on his bed while he did it. It meant something to him.

I could *feel* it.

"Hard to explain," I said. "Just a feeling. I guess after being around so many bikers over the years, I just know the subtleties, and the not-so-subtleties. The differences between the way a guy treats you when he wants to lock you down, and when he couldn't give a fuck."

As I heard myself say those words, I considered where Jude fit on that spectrum. Definitely somewhere near the lock-it-down end of things. Though he still hadn't made any attempt to lock *me* down.

So far it was only my pussy he'd placed under lock and key.

But yes, he'd definitely been acting possessive of me. He'd told me to break up with Taze. He'd contacted me almost every single night since we started being "fuck buddies." He'd come over to my place at the end of each of those nights, no matter how late it was, and rocked my world.

Other than the night he'd cuddled me to sleep on the couch instead.

And now he'd even taken me back to his man cave.

If I didn't know better, I'd say he was in hot pursuit. Something had definitely shifted forward between us.

And it felt good.

But I was still proceeding with caution, still trying to protect myself. Because he still hadn't suggested changing the terms of our little "just sex" arrangement, which meant that neither would I.

"*Hey*. You texting your man in the middle of girls' night?"

Katie was playing with her phone under the table, and her best friend had busted her.

"I thought this table was a husband-and-boyfriend-free zone," Devi said.

"It is," Katie protested, "but he was just checking to see if I needed a ride or anything. He says he's just finished up with Jude and they're splitting up."

"Jesse's out with Jude?" It bothered me how instantaneously bothered I was that she knew what Jude was doing tonight, and I didn't.

"Yeah. Well, they were having a beer. But Jude took off to a Kings party, so Jesse's heading back home. He's got the Ferrari," she said, getting all lovey-dovey-eyed as she tucked her phone away, "which means he's probably horny."

"And he thought of you?" Jessa teased. "How sweet."

"Yeah. He's romantic like that." Katie snickered. "Don't worry," she assured Devi. "I'm not going anywhere. Not until you divulge about that model guy you hooked up with last night."

"What model guy?" Amber asked, and as Devi filled the girls in on her date of last night, my mind got stuck in a loop. A loop where I obsessed over the fact that Jude was heading to a Kings party... and he wasn't taking me with him.

He didn't even ask me if I wanted to go with him.

Secretly, I'd been really hoping to see him tonight. Last night he'd called me like I told him to, but I'd ended up working pretty late with Talia, tying up a bunch of random loose ends on a couple of events we were planning for January, and I didn't end up seeing him. I didn't mind brushing him off *once*. Keep him on his toes, right?

But when we'd texted earlier today and casually talked about hooking up later tonight, he didn't mention he was going to a Kings party. He didn't mention a club party at all.

And all I could think was: *Taze would've taken me.*

And just like that, all the old wounds ripped right open.

Jude showed up at my place that night, just like he said he would—but half an hour late.

Toward the end of girls' night, he'd finally texted me, putting out his usual feeler. The *Wanna fuck?* feeler. And yeah, I wanted to fuck. So I told him we could meet up at my place.

But then he arrived late. And by then, I was feeling raw all over again. And whatever warm and fuzzy feeling his texts had given me while I finished off my beer had frosted right over.

"Hey, fuck buddy," I said as I opened the door to him.

His eyes immediately narrowed as he caught my tone. He stepped inside, and as soon I'd shut the door behind him, I walked right into the living room. No hug. No kiss. No welcoming ass-grab.

Nothing.

I stood in the living room with my arms crossed as he made his way slowly into the room. His dark eyes scanned me, head-to-toe.

"You alright?"

"Been better. Not feeling so much like fucking tonight, buddy."

"Okay." He slid his hands into the pockets of his jeans and stood there, staring at me. "You got somethin' you wanna say?"

"Oh. I didn't know we were actually allowed to have a conversation in the middle of the night. Usually we just fuck, then you go home."

His eyes narrowed at me again, and he took a long fucking time to start talking. "If our arrangement isn't working for you, V, you've got every right to say so."

"It's not working for me."

"Okay."

Okay? That was it?

Okay?

"I mean, I know I agreed to this whole 'it's all about sex' thing," I said, cranking up the bitch. "But I guess I didn't realize that meant I'd just be your convenience fuck whenever you're horny after partying with club sluts all night."

"What?"

"You thought I wouldn't find out you were at a Kings party tonight?"

He considered that, then said slowly, "It wasn't a secret, Roni."

"You think I don't know what it means?"

"Tell me. What does it mean?"

"Jude. I'm not some regular 'citizen' girl who doesn't have the first clue what goes on at those parties. I'm not even a regular girl who has some vague idea what goes on at those parties. I've been to those parties. I *know*."

"You know what?"

"I know why you'd go to one without taking me."

He cocked his head a little, like I was suddenly speaking some foreign language he couldn't understand. "You want me to take you?"

"Not if you don't want to."

"Jesus." He scraped a hand through his hair. "I don't know what the fuck you're gettin' at, Roni. So get at it already."

"You *said* we were exclusive."

"Yeah," he said. "Which means until I tell you otherwise, or you tell me otherwise, we are."

"Glad we made that clear. Because actually, what you told me was that I had to be exclusive with *you* if I wanted your dick. You never actually said you'd be exclusive with *me*." Kind of an important detail I'd only realized tonight, while I stewed.

"I told you," he said, looking right pissed, "I don't cheat."

"Well, there are only two reasons you wouldn't take me to a Kings party."

"Enlighten me."

"One, because you're messing around with other women—"

"Thought we just went over that."

"Or two, you don't want me around your brothers."

He went silent, and I fucking knew.

"You don't want me around Piper? Or Ben? Or your other brothers? Or *all* of them?"

"Never said that."

He didn't have to say it. Clearly he didn't want me at the clubhouse, around his club brothers, and I wasn't even sure why.

He was ashamed of me?

Or he just didn't give that much of a fuck about me? Enough to put his dick in me almost every night, but not enough to be seen with me in public.

I couldn't even stand to voice the former, so I said, "Then I guess I'm just not someone you'd want them to see you with."

He stared at me, his dark gaze weighing heavily on me. "We agreed, V, that this was just about sex."

"Yeah," I said bitterly. "We agreed."

Yes, I was being stubborn and guarded and ridiculous.

So was he.

He was being stubborn and guarded and oh-so-Jude—reminding me way too much of twenty-one-year-old Jude. The Jude who hurt me. Badly.

And it terrified me.

"So that it?" he asked. "You changin' your mind?"

"Yeah. Maybe I am."

I knew I was pushing him away. But I just couldn't stop myself.

He stared at me for the longest minute in history.

Neither of us said another thing.

I watched as he turned and walked out, slamming the door behind himself.

Then I sank onto my couch and just sat there, kind of numb.

I knew why I was acting jealous and crazy.

Because I'd gone ahead and fallen for him again.

It really didn't take much.

Or maybe the truth was I'd just never picked myself back up after the first time I fell.

Because Jude Grayson was the one.

He was my man; the one I'd wanted forever and a day.

And I still didn't know if he could ever feel the same about me.

CHAPTER EIGHTEEN

Jude

SATURDAY.

11:00 pm or whatever.

I sat at the bar at the clubhouse, nursing a beer that went warm long ago. Piper sat next to me, talking shit about whatever. Some girl whose name I couldn't remember sat in his lap.

A friend of hers had tried to slither into mine, but I wasn't having it. She had black hair and was pretty enough, but everything about her screamed *fake*, including her black hair.

Other than a few of the wives, most of the women who came through these doors seemed fake to me.

I wasn't totally above it. It wasn't like I'd never fucked around with anyone at the clubhouse. But it had been a long while, and with Roni on my mind, it wasn't happening.

I probably couldn't have gotten it up for another woman right now if I'd tried.

I just wasn't wired that way.

My dick was hardwired to my head, and right now my head was all the way up Roni Webber's ass.

Piper had straight-up asked me where my head was at when I'd turned out to be the world's worst conversationalist tonight. And since I wasn't interested in beer or pussy, he was at a loss for what to do with me.

Eventually, he'd told the girl with the black hair to put a smile on my face.

"Not tonight, darlin'," I'd told her, because no reason to be rude. Wasn't her fault she wasn't Veronica Webber.

"What's eatin' you?" Piper asked as she wandered away with a pout. "Not like you to turn down good pussy."

It was definitely like me, actually, to turn down club pussy. Which just went to show that my brother didn't pay all that much attention where me and women were concerned.

He never really did.

"Just not feelin' it," I said.

I could've said, *I'm feelin' Roni Webber. Remember her? Yeah, her. I've got a thing for her the size of a Mack truck and it just keeps running me the fuck over, so I'm just gonna sit here for a while and look like this.*

But I didn't say that.

I hadn't said it to anyone, even Jesse.

I hadn't told any of the guys, the Kings or the band, that I'd been seeing her almost every night.

Because we were just fuck buddies, right? Didn't seem like I needed to send out formal fucking announcements to everyone I knew.

Right.

We were more than fuck buddies. We were exclusive fuck buddies, which was really fucked up.

And it was all my idea.

I was the one who'd suggested the whole fuck buddy thing. I asked her to be exclusive. Told her, actually, that she *had* to be if she wanted me.

And now she thought I didn't want her around my club brothers.

Maybe I didn't.

Fuck.

No wonder she was pissed.

Roni was gorgeous, sexy, witty and fun to be around, and any guy should be happy to show her off, show up anywhere with her.

I pushed my way out of the bar, outside, to get some space. To get air. The stink of booze and smoke and perfume faded and I took a deep breath. Sat my ass down on the rotten-ass old picnic table off to the side of the gravel lot. No one used it for picnics. It was so carved up with brothers' signatures, no one wanted to put it out to pasture at the dump like we probably should've years ago.

I could see my name, JUDE, carved into the tabletop near one corner, where I'd carved it when I was, what? Fifteen?

And then when I was twenty-one, the big *R* I'd carved right into the opposite corner while I was seething over Roni, just days after I'd first had sex with her.

When I was avoiding her. Hiding out at the clubhouse so I wouldn't have to see her.

Now, she'd accused me of not wanting her around Piper and the Kings, and she was right. Just not for the reason she seemed to think—that I didn't want to be seen with her. Like she wasn't good enough or something.

Obviously, she was good enough.

Maybe I just hadn't figured out how to drag my heart totally out of the past yet.

I eased my Harley into my brother's garage with an anvil in my chest.

The garage sat behind the house where Piper lived with a couple of other Kings. He'd wanted me to move in when I finished high school and moved out of Mom's, instead of moving in with Jesse and those guys.

I didn't.

The house was decent, nothing special, but the garage was huge. Though it was a disappointment to my brother, I didn't share his love of restoring motorcycles. I was more like our dad that way; preferred to ride and let someone else do the mechanical work. But I didn't mind tinkering, helping him out and tuning up my own bikes. Mostly because it meant spending time with my brother.

Not that day.

That day, I wasn't there for bro time.

I was pretty damn sure Piper wouldn't give a flying fuck that I'd hooked up with Roni last night, *but*. After I'd driven her home in the middle of the night, kissed her good night and basically grinned to myself all the way home, I'd run into Jesse. The guys were back from Dylan's party; Brody was in bed, Zane was in the bathroom, and Jesse was in the kitchen when I walked in. He'd taken one look at me and asked, with a shit-eating grin, "Where'd you disappear to?"

All I said was, "Took Roni for a ride," and for sure, the fucker could read it all over me.

He raised an eyebrow. Then he said something that kinda stopped my heart. "Pipe okay with that?"

Of course Piper was okay with it. He had no interest in Roni.

But then it stayed on my mind all night, and what started as an uncomfortable, tight feeling in my chest grew into a motherfucking anvil by the time morning came.

So I got my ass on my bike and went to see my brother. If there was gonna be any kind of problem, the sooner I got this over with—and hopefully defused the bomb—the better.

I just had to make sure Piper saw Roni Webber the same way I saw her, in one respect.

Available.

To me.

Because if there was one thing I'd learned about my brothers in the MC—including Piper—it was that they were territorial as fuck about women. If they wanted to be.

No matter if they had a right to be or not.

Which meant that even if he wasn't involved with Roni, Piper might somehow still see her as his territory.

Fucked up, but that's just how it was.

I'd never thought of Roni as Piper's territory, even when she was chasing after him—but then I'd never fucked her before, either.

It wasn't like I was gonna let my brother tell me I couldn't have her. But if there was any territorial line to be drawn, I needed to draw it. Right now.

I shut off my bike, and that Bob Marley remix with Steven Tyler and Joe Perry was playing over the stereo system. And you know when a great song gets fucking ruined for you?

That song.

That day.

We made small talk for about five seconds, while I pretended to be interested in the '57 BMW R26 he was restoring, the one our dad had given him. Then I came right out with it.

"You know Roni Webber?"

"Who?"

I stared at him. *Seriously?*

"Roni," I said. "Webber."

My brother looked back at me blankly, swiping his blond hair out of his eyes.

"Black hair," I said slowly, figuring that was one of her more distinguishing features. Her other distinguishing features, I really didn't wanna get into with him. "Jessa Mayes' friend..."

"Right. Roni. Wild Card, right? The one with the tits." I took a deep breath, steeling myself for this. The anvil was just getting heavier. "Yeah, I know her. She's pretty tight, but not really my speed."

Something hot and terrible that felt a hell of a lot like jealous fury rose through me.

"Tight?"

"Yeah. Fucked her on the kitchen counter at a party out at Crusler's... Remember that party where Shady went through the fuckin' coffee table?"

My whole body lit up like a struck match.

Yeah, I remembered that party. The one where, when I'd arrived, I found Roni alone on the back step in the dark with tears in her eyes.

And I kissed her.

Fuck, no.

I found my voice. "Just once?"

"Yeah, I mean I wasn't really into her. She just kept puttin' it in my face. You know the type."

"What type?" My voice was way low. I knew, when he said what he said, he had no idea I'd had sex with Roni last night, or that I liked her.

It didn't make me any less furious.

He stood up, wiping his hands on a rag, his eyes narrowing at me.

"A slut," he said. "That type."

My fists clenched so hard at my sides, my knuckles cracked. "Take that the fuck back."

"Why?" He tossed the rag aside. "You got a hard-on for her? She's a piece, brother—"

My fist connected with his face faster than either of us seemed to know it was gonna happen. He staggered back into the BMW, but it didn't fall over. Then he bounced right back off it and slugged me with his iron fist, right in the gut.

I doubled over with a grunt and fell to my knees.

Piper shoved me down on my side; I was in the fetal position and he stood over me, barely breathing hard. I was a pretty big dude by then. My brother was bigger.

More important than that, he was a stronger fighter. He could've destroyed me, if he ever wanted to.

We both knew it.

"Cool off," he said, cracking his jaw. "The fuck is your deal?"

My deal?

My fucking deal was, I was *crushed.*

In that moment, the wind was so knocked out of me, I didn't even have the will to get the fuck up, to stand up like a man.

I never knew Piper had sex with Roni. I knew she had a crush on him or whatever. Her dumbass sexual bucket list. But I'd never asked him about her before. I'd never seen him pay more attention to her than a few words here or there at some party. He never seemed interested, and I'd somehow actually convinced myself that nothing had ever happened between them.

That he'd never touched her.

How fucking stupid was I?

"You pissed 'cause I fucked her?" Piper asked. "Or 'cause I bounced her ass? Girl never goes back for seconds anyway. Said so herself, right after we fucked and I told her to get goin'."

I rolled over with a groan. "Just shut up."

Roni had said that to me, too. Told me, many times. Just something she said to save face and act like it didn't bother her when some guy had brushed her off. *Whatever*, she'd tell me, *I never go back for seconds anyway.*

The fact that she'd said it to my brother... after he'd given her his infamous fuck 'n' go?

We already fucked, sweetheart, time for you to go.

How many times had I heard him say that to some chick at the clubhouse when he was done with her?

And now I had it in my head that he'd said that to Roni... after he... at that shitty party...

I just lay there on the floor staring up at him, fucking hating him for the first time in my life, as he stared down at me, waiting for me to speak or stand the fuck up.

"What?" His eyes narrowed at me again. "*You* fucked her?" He laughed a bit. "You *like* her? You wanna go back for seconds?" He shook his head, like he felt sorry for me. "Sorry, little brother, I don't think she's that kind of girl, but hey, knock yourself out. You'll learn."

I got to my feet, slowly.

"The fuck does that mean?"

"It means, I don't know what the fuck you're thinking, but you can't have a girl like that around the club and think she's *your girl*. She's a groupie. You'll never be able to trust her around the club or the band. None of the guys will respect her. She'll just cheat on your ass—"

I got on my bike and tore out of the garage before I could hear any more.

I was pissed the fuck off that he'd put his hands on Roni. That he'd fucked her. That he'd used her like that.

That maybe he'd hurt her.

That he thought she was just some slut.

I was fucking destroyed, actually.

But worse... I was pissed because I was afraid he was right.

Right about her.

Right about what would happen if I let myself care about her... and think she might be mine.

After that, I didn't call her. I didn't see her around, because I made myself busy at the clubhouse and avoided every place she might be, including Dirty rehearsals.

I thought about her, though.

I thought about how, when I'd left on tour with Dirty, she'd come to see me off. How she'd seemed so bummed that I was leaving. I thought about that goodbye kiss we'd had and how I'd started to believe she really cared about me. I thought about how, while I was away on tour and missing her, I'd spent so much time thinking about how much I cared about *her*.

I always did care, really, just denied it to myself because I never really thought she felt that way about *me*.

Then when we came home from the tour and I saw her at Dylan's party, the way she looked at me... The way she looked at me while we had sex that night... I was so fucking sure the feelings between us were mutual.

But now I knew the truth.

I was her second choice.

I was *always* her second choice. The choice she only made because Piper had already fucked her and rejected her.

I managed to avoid her for exactly a week, until the night of a Dirty show at the Back Door.

The bar was packed and it was a big night; everyone had been going ape shit over Dirty's new original song, "Love Struck," and

Brody was talking about cutting a demo, this year. He'd convinced a bunch of local industry people to come to the show, including some big record producer. So it was an important show, and luckily Brody had managed to fill the room with a hot crowd of Dirty's ever-growing local allegiance of fans.

The band was excited.

I was happy for them, of course.

But I wasn't happy.

And my night only turned from shit to worse when I saw Roni.

I was making my way through the crowd with Brody, and the place was so packed I didn't even see her until she'd appeared right in front of me.

I walked right past her, and she was so expecting me to stop that she had to kinda spin out of the way to avoid getting plowed down.

She didn't quite take the hint, though.

Two minutes later she popped up in front of me again. I was standing at the back of the bar, my back to the wall, talking to Jesse, but as soon as he saw her he clapped me on the shoulder and took off.

Some wingman.

All he knew, though, was that I'd taken her for a "ride" last weekend. Which meant he probably assumed I liked her. I didn't even bother telling him the rest. I was afraid I wouldn't be able to get the words out of my mouth without puking, or killing someone.

She stood right in front of me in her skintight, incredibly low-rise jeans and midriff-baring shirt. "Hey," she said, kinda bouncing on her toes as she hooked her thumbs in her jeans. She even smiled at me.

I didn't smile. "Hey."

"Where've you been?"

"Clubhouse."

She quit bouncing, her smile faltering at my lack of basic manners. "Cool. Did you bring your bike tonight? Maybe we could go for a ride after the show..." She looked me over, maybe reading my body language, and amended, "Or maybe a cream soda?"

"I'm working," I said. "How'd you get in?"

"Oh. Ben got me a fake ID."

"Ben?"

"Yeah. You know... Blazer?"

I knew Ben/Blazer. He was a King and one of my brother's best friends. And apparently, he'd gotten Roni a fake ID at some point while I was away on tour.

Yeah, you fuck him too?

The words were right on the tip of my tongue, but I bit them back.

Her eyebrows pulled together and she chewed a little on her sexy bottom lip. "You're upset about something..."

Perceptive.

I should've maybe just disappeared backstage, but I wasn't gonna run and hide from her or spend the rest of my life avoiding her at every party in town. *She* sought *me* out. That was her mistake, not mine.

"I'm busy," I said. The band was on in about half an hour, and I could've been busy, but all I did was stand there. Of all things, "Cold Hard Bitch" was playing, and it was fueling my fucking fire.

"What's wrong?" she asked, her green eyes going wide. She looked concerned—about me.

It only pissed me off more.

"Thought you said you never go back for seconds," I said, with all the cold-ass prick I could summon.

She stared at me. Then her backbone went rigid and she stopped pushing her tits toward me. "Well," she said, "what if I want to, with you?"

"What if I *don't*?"

She drew back like I'd slapped her. But then she fired right back, "What the hell happened? What changed since I saw you, like a week ago? You took me to your place and lit candles and kissed me for like three hours..."

"So?"

Her plump lips twitched in a legit pout. "So... So we had sex and now you're just trying to blow me off?"

Yeah, that was about it.

Could she not get the fucking message?

She had to be able to fucking feel it. My skin was practically crawling with disgust. I knew I was acting different. I was even looking at her differently, like she was beneath me or something—like I couldn't even stand looking at her, and that was the fucking truth.

But there was a shitload of pain behind it that I was not gonna let her see.

Too bad for both of us, Roni Webber was not a girl to back down from a fight or a man, even a pissed-the-hell-off one. She had way too much experience for a girl her age. And right now, all of it was fucking eating me.

Every time I looked in her green eyes, the want I had for her just churned in my stomach with the revulsion.

"It's just not gonna work," I told her, as dead-cold as I could manage. I'd never been a cold dude, but it was the only way I knew how to deal with her.

Just shut her out, completely.

"I... I thought..." She was struggling, really struggling to pull together the pieces in her head. "I thought... this was the real thing. You know, like... *real*."

She stared at me, at a total fucking loss when I said nothing.

"I thought you felt... the same. We spent so much time, and... I thought we both wanted... I trusted you. I *confided* in you."

I stared back at her, silently fucking furious, because she was right.

I did want.

I did start to trust.

And *she screwed my brother*.

She sure as fuck never confided in me about *that*.

She was still standing there, in my face, and I needed her gone.

So I took her hand, pulled her close to me and twined my fingers through hers, holding her there. Her nose was an inch from mine when I told her, slowly and deliberately, "You and me, we're not goin' down that road."

She stared up into my eyes, looking hurt and damn confused. "Why not?"

"Because, *sweetheart*, you tried to go down that road with Piper first."

She ripped her hand from mine.

"You think I wasn't gonna find out?" I said, low and fucking accusing, letting some of that hateful fire that had been simmering in me all week burn right through the cold.

She was shaking her head slowly, staring at me, and tears were starting to brim in her eyes. And all I could hear in my head was my brother's voice.

You know the type.

You'll never be able to trust her...

"I was wrong about you, Jude Grayson," she said, and the tears started rolling down her face. "You weren't falling in love with me. You never cared about me at all. You were just using me for a place to put your dick. Just like your brother."

Then she turned and took off.

CHAPTER NINETEEN

Roni

IT WAS SATURDAY NIGHT, and I was spending the next few hours with a super cute boy.

Baby Nick was all swaddled up in his blankie in my arms, and I was settling in to cuddle the hell out of him. Jessa's date with Brody had gone so well two weeks ago—what with the marriage proposal and all the sex—they decided to have another one. So I was at their house, in the party room, rocking Nicky in the big, cozy glider rocking chair they'd put in so Jessa could comfortably nurse the baby in the middle of whatever party was going on.

Jessa had left her Girl Time playlist quietly playing for us, which apparently put Nicky to sleep like nobody's business. At the moment, we were rocking to Gwen Stefani, "4 In The Morning."

And *damn*, Jessa and her Girl Time music...

I wanted to know I was safe, too.

I wanted to have a really true love.

I never wanted to have to give Jude up.

"I hear ya, Gwen. Sing it, girl," I said softly, rocking baby Nick. He was warm, cuddly dead weight and I figured my arms would soon be asleep, but I didn't much care. Looking into that tiny, serene, perfect little face, I felt all kinds of affection for Jessa's baby boy.

I felt protective of him, too.

Jessa had mentioned getting a regular babysitter, maybe one night a month for now, so she and Brody could have a proper date. I'd immediately kiboshed that plan. As long as I had some notice and we could arrange it on a night I didn't have an event, I told her I'd be happy to do it. It would only be a few hours at a time anyway, and honestly I didn't mind the alone time with Nick. I wanted him to know his Auntie Roni.

You know, the cool aunt.

I was definitely a big fat load of envious, though, watching Jessa head out the door on Brody's arm to have another romantic night with the man she loved—a man who loved her right back.

While the man I loved wasn't even talking to me.

Because I'd pushed him away.

As usual, it wasn't like I didn't have other options for dates. I just didn't *want* other options.

My phone was constantly buzzing with incoming messages from other men. But I never answered them anymore. For the first time, I really wasn't interested in juggling a bunch of prospects, keeping them on the line *just in case.*

Just like that first time Jude went away on tour… I felt like I was saving myself for him. Waiting for him to come back to me.

Really, I was no stranger to waiting… even if the man I was waiting for never came back.

I tucked the little stuffed toy I'd given Nicky shortly after he was born—the purple monkey—into his blankie with him. One of my mom's boyfriends, the only one I ever actually liked, had given it to me. After he'd left—or maybe my mom drove him away—I'd longed for him. I wanted him to come back.

Sure, I'd probably idealized him in my mind. I knew this, but I didn't even care. I needed a father figure, even if that father figure was a fantasy based on a real person who'd given me a glimpse of kindness, and I'd run with it.

He was the one who would one day come back and be a real father to me.

Of course, he never did, but at least I had the fantasy.

The purple monkey he'd left behind was a symbol of hope and that man's kindness to me, however brief. It was the only tangible evidence I had from my youngest years that any sort of father figure had ever cared about me.

In my fantasies, the purple monkey was a talisman, a protective charm, purposely left behind to keep me safe by someone who cared.

I knew it was silly, even when I was young.

But it still meant something to me.

He gave me the monkey when I was a baby, and he left when I was five. My mom told me, many times, that he wasn't my real dad—as if that somehow made his leaving irrelevant. And after he'd left, when I cried about it for days, she couldn't even seem to understand why.

He's not your dad, Roni girl, she told me. *And I told him not to come back. I don't love him. You want me to spend my life with a man I don't love, to make you happy?*

That, or some version of that, was what she'd said every time I cried or asked if he would come back to see me.

So eventually, I stopped asking, and I stopped crying about it in front of my mom. But I still hoped.

For years, actually, until I was about twelve or so, I hoped.

Which was why I put the monkey in baby Nick's crib. Because no matter what happened, he'd always have his Auntie Roni looking out for him. And the monkey would be my assurance that even if I wasn't here to give him a hug or tell him everything would be alright, or listen to whatever had made him upset, he'd have his purple monkey to hold onto, just like I did.

Whoever said I wasn't sentimental didn't know jack shit about me.

I could be sentimental as hell.

I still had, of all things, the ticket from that Dirty show at the Back Door where Jude stomped on my heart.

Why? Tangible evidence.

That little bit of something I could look at and touch was proof to me of everything that had happened between us and what we'd almost had... even if it had ended badly.

Even if it was going to end badly all over again.

It had been three days since we'd fought and Jude had stormed out of my place, and I had no idea how long he'd be gone this time.

Days?

Years?

Maybe I couldn't even blame him for disappearing. But I was *not* about to go running after him.

I just couldn't. Not after everything we'd been through. All the times he'd pushed me away... I couldn't put myself out there again and risk him rejecting me, again.

I was strong. I'd always been strong. Maybe because so many early experiences in my life had abraded me until I had to be outwardly tough to survive. Something like that. But I really didn't want to stand there, face-to-face with Jude Grayson, ever again, and have him turn me down, push me away.

Because maybe it would be that push that would be the one that would shatter my heart, irreversibly.

To that end, I knew I was holding myself back, even when I was with him.

Protecting myself.

Drinking too much to give myself an excuse to lose my inhibitions with him. Flirting instead of being straight with him. Using sex and our whole stupid "fuck buddy" arrangement to get close to him without actually getting *close*.

He was protecting himself, too.

I knew he was.

I knew I'd hurt him too, long ago.

And so, we were both playing the game. A game neither of us was willing to lose.

Making carefully-calculated moves.

He stepped forward, I pulled back. And vice versa.

But we still weren't actually having a relationship with one another.

I wondered if we would ever be able to make any kind of a real relationship work, or if he'd ever even wanted to.

I wondered if it was already over before it had begun.

Just like the last time.

And all the times before that.

After Jude took my hand in that bar and told me *we're not goin' down that road*, you better believe I stayed the hell away from him.

Days became weeks, and then months passed.

Almost two *years* passed.

At some point, I started dating Ben, one of Piper's best friends and a King who went by the road name Blazer. Unlike Piper, Ben had pursued me. It was fun, sometimes, but we weren't always the world's best match. We were on and off and on again. He treated me with respect, mostly, but like my other relationships with men—other than Jude—it wasn't deep.

Meanwhile, Jessa had kept doing whatever she was doing with Seth. But things between them seemed rocky and about as on and off as Ben and me.

Dirty had landed a record deal off their demo. Even when it happened, I didn't realize what a life-changing thing that would be for them.

Or how much farther it would take Jude away from me.

Brody had gotten some huge inheritance when his dad died, and he bought a house in North Vancouver which became the band's party palace. But I never went to those parties. Dirty's debut album, *Love Struck*, was released and they had a number one hit right out of the gate with "Dirty Like Me," a song Jessa had co-written. She'd co-written the entire album, but she didn't seem to want to stick around to reap the benefits; she refused to go on tour with the band in support of the album even though her brother wanted her to go and I told her she was crazy.

We actually fought about it; she cried.

She seemed dead set on modeling instead and left for the summer to model overseas. Then she came back to start college in the fall, and while she was in her first year of college and I was working at a store in the mall, just trying to scrape together enough money to make rent on the apartment I shared with two roommates and borrowing Jessa's study materials—she was studying media and public relations, something I would've liked to do if I could figure out how to afford it—Dirty left on their first world tour.

And Jude went with them.

I would've liked to see the band before they left, but by that point there was really no getting close to Dirty unless you knew someone who could get you close. They'd moved into a new, private rehearsal space and Jessa never hung out with them anymore, didn't go to shows and didn't hang out at rehearsals or anything. And I was hardly gonna show up and rely on Jude to let me in.

I hadn't seen him even once since that show at the Back Door—the one where he ripped out my heart and served it to me on an ice-cold platter. If he ever showed up at some party I was at with Ben, which happened on occasion, I turned around and left the party just as fast.

I wanted to be able to put on a brave face and wish him and the band well when they left town. But it still hurt.

So I settled for messaging Jesse. I never saw him anymore either, but I had his phone number, so I texted to wish him well on the tour and left it at that.

Months later, the band came home for a break from the tour. There was a party at Brody's house, and to my surprise, not only was Jessa going but she asked me if I wanted to go with her.

To my surprise, I said yes.

She'd also invited a friend from college, Maggie, and I soon realized the only reason Jessa was even going to this party was because Maggie wanted to work in the music industry and Jessa said she'd introduce her to Brody.

Jessa also brought some skeezy guy she'd been dating; a dude who offered us cocaine and crank while we drove to the party in Maggie's car.

I declined, and was relieved as fuck when both Jessa and Maggie did too. I wasn't against a little experimentation in the right circumstances, but this dude was *dirty*, and no way was I ever trying meth.

The party was great. Tons of people, tons of booze, hot guys, drunk girls, the usual. I hung out with the band a bit, mainly Jesse and Seth, who'd always been nice to me. I made sure to say hi to Brody and thank him for having me and all that. And I did my best to keep an eye on Jessa and her skeezy date.

Jude, of course, was at the party.

I didn't talk to him, at first.

He didn't talk to me either.

The first time I saw him, he and Brody seemed to be in a mood. I saw them pull Jesse aside, and a short while later I watched as Jude escorted Jessa's date right out the door and tossed him in the street. Then Jessa and Brody got in a screaming match. Well, Jessa screamed. Brody just kind of stood there, ashen-faced and looking like he wanted to strangle her. Then she stormed off into the house and I went after her.

I found her at the bar in the party room, where I helped her polish off an army of shots. Mostly, she did the polishing. I just had a few. I felt way more nervous than I thought I would seeing Jude, especially when he barely looked at me, and I was scared of getting wasted and doing or saying something horrifying in front of him.

Every time I caught a glimpse of him, I tried not to stare and just ended up staring.

Then, at some point in the night, he started staring back.

And my heart fucking ached.

Never mind that I was currently on again with Ben; I had a boyfriend, yes, but he'd never made me feel like *that* across a room.

Or even right close up.

Late in the night, probably a good hour or so after I should've cut Jessa off and gotten us the hell out of there, she got into a fight with Seth about God-knew-what.

I'd been looking for her, and had actually gone so far as to go out the front door (no one was in the front yard) and walk all the way around the giant house, through the trees that wrapped around it, just in case she'd ended up in the woods and passed out puking or something.

I found her in the backyard, just inside the edge of the trees in the dark, arguing with Seth.

I couldn't tell what they were talking about, but I'd definitely seen her popping pills with him earlier and who knew what the fuck they were on. Jessa had tears streaking down her cheeks, and I'd definitely never heard that sad, terrible, whiny tone coming out of her mouth before.

I stood back in the trees and watched. I was worried about her, but I really didn't know if I should interrupt. I didn't think she was in any danger with Seth; he was definitely the gentle stoner type. But she was definitely wasted and she seemed distraught.

"Nothin' you can do about that."

I looked over as Jude came up beside me. He was holding a drink in his hand, and he was looking at Seth and Jessa.

I hugged myself. It was chilly between the trees. "Do you think she's okay?"

He looked at me in the dark, and I could just make out the stony expression on his face. The one that said, *Like fuck I'd let anything happen to her*.

"I should take her home soon," I said. But I just stood there.

Jude didn't say anything, but he just stood there, too.

So I turned toward him. "How are you?"

He stared at me. "Thought you left," he said, not answering my question.

"I'm right here."

"Yeah." His gaze wandered down my body, and the way his eyes flicked back up to mine, kinda lazily, and he wavered on his feet a bit... I realized he was drunk. He smelled like booze, and I'd rarely seen Jude truly drunk. "You look good, V."

V.

Oh, for the love of Christ. He called me V, like we were still friends or something. Like we were still *us*.

As if there'd ever been any us.

"You look good too, Jude," I said. "Always do."

He did.

He looked exactly the same. Maybe a little bigger. Every time I saw him he was bigger. His hair was a little longer. I knew he'd been patched in as a King, long ago, and I'd seen him wearing his cut with the Nomad patch inside the house. He wasn't wearing it now. Just a black hoodie.

Everything else looked the same.

Everything *felt* the same.

Including my feelings for him, which hadn't cooled, or crawled away and fucking died like I would've hoped they would by now.

Really, I should've known exactly what was coming by the way he was looking at me...

He put his hand on the side of my face. His thumb smoothed over my bottom lip... and the world stopped turning.

Then he leaned in and kissed me.

I closed my eyes, and for one lingering heartbeat I allowed myself to just soak it all in. The faint, woodsy, boozy smell of him, and his crazy-soft, liquor-drenched lips.

Jude and his fucking kisses.

Why was this guy always kissing me out of nowhere?

I pulled away. I pulled my face right out of his hand. Because it was Jude, and the last time he spoke to me, he told me, *You and me, we're not goin' down that road.*

And, because I had a man.

"I'm with Blazer," I told him. I used his club brother's road name because I figured it would have impact.

It did.

His jaw turned to jagged granite. He made a snort-growl noise that was absolutely oozing with contempt—or maybe it was disgust. But I knew this information wasn't new to him. I'd definitely avoided the Kings clubhouse and pretty much anywhere I might run into Jude over the last two years, but I knew he had to have heard at some point that Ben was seeing me.

The ice clinked in his glass. He took a swig, downing the amber liquid. Jude had never been all that much of a drinker, especially in comparison with the company he kept on both the biker side and the rock 'n' roll side of his life.

He was definitely loaded right now.

"What?" I asked him, already feeling exhausted by this game. "You want to fuck me, is that it?" I was only twenty years old and my relationship with Jude—or my non-relationship with him—already felt ancient.

He glared at me. "No."

"That's good. Because I'm not fucking another guy while I have a boyfriend."

"Good for you." He sucked back his ice and crunched on it, and raised his glass in the air like he was toasting nothing. "Good for him." Then he tossed the rest of the ice cubes over his shoulder and started to walk away. "Have a nice life, Roni Webber." He slurred my name, and I grabbed his arm, stopping him.

He did stop. He stopped dead and just stood there with his back to me. My hand dropped away. He didn't turn to face me, but he didn't leave, either.

So I took a deep breath and asked him what I'd wanted to ask him ever since he told me *we're not goin' down that road.*

"If I'd never had sex with Piper, would you have fallen in love with me?"

He turned slowly to face me, weaving a bit before he found his feet.

"Would you have thought about marrying me?" I asked him. "Making me your girl? Going down that road with me?"

He blinked at me, then stared me down with red-rimmed eyes. "You?" He chuckled, an ugly, ugly sound in the night. "You... Veronica Webber... are not the kind of girl a guy marries." He stumbled a bit as he took a step toward me.

I stood my ground.

His gaze fell to my mouth as he loomed over me. "You're the kind of girl some guys fuck on a kitchen counter and forget..." His eyes skipped back up to mine. "And other guys never get over."

I just stared at him.

I felt sick all over.

In that moment, I hated him, and I loved him so, so much. It ripped me right down the middle. I wanted to cry and shove him away and wrap him in my arms.

"Jude!"

Jesse interrupted, throwing his arm around Jude's shoulders. "Brother, where the fuck have you been?" The way he leaned on Jude, I could tell he was drunk, too. "Jessa's trying to leave and Brody's losing his mind and..." He looked up kind of belatedly and seemed to notice me standing there. "Oh, hey, Roni."

"Hey." I looked into the dark, but Jessa and Seth were no longer there in the trees.

"*MOTHAFUCKAAAS!*" Zane, out of nowhere, jumped on Jude's back and stuck a bottle of liquor in his face. Jude stumbled back but caught Zane's legs and held him there, as Zane jammed the bottle into Jude's mouth and poured liquor into him, cackling all the way.

Jude wrenched his head away and spat out liquid. Then he dumped Zane on the ground, snatched the liquor bottle from him and dumped the contents all over him... and Jesse fucking died laughing.

Zane just lay there, laughing like a drunken hyena.

Jesus Christ...

What was I even doing here?

There was no conversation to be had with any of these men tonight.

With Jude, there never really was.

I went back into the house. I tried to find Jessa, but as far as I could figure out, she was most likely in Brody's bedroom—with him—since I couldn't find either of them and it was the only room with a closed door I couldn't get into. Maggie was deep in a conversation with Elle, so I called a cab. I sent Jessa a text to let her know I was leaving, then went home.

I didn't talk to Jude again.

Why would I want to talk to someone who just kept hurting me?

But his words haunted me.

You're the kind of girl some guys fuck on a kitchen counter and forget... And other guys never get over.

Was he seriously never going to forgive that I'd once had sex with his brother—before we'd even hooked up?

And what was he implying? That *he* was never getting over me?

He sure acted like he was over me. Way the fuck over me.

Except for that kiss...

The morning after that party, Dirty headed back out on the road to finish their tour, and Jude went with them again.

While they were away, Jessa finished her first year of college and left Vancouver in pursuit of modeling; her agency sent her to work with their sister agency in New York.

And she never came back.

When she left, I said goodbye to her at the airport. But I was saying goodbye to a lot more than Jessa Mayes. I was saying goodbye to her brother and his whole crew of friends. I was saying goodbye to Dirty.

Because I wasn't under the same illusions that Brody and her brother and everyone else seemed to be. I *knew* Jessa wasn't coming back.

So I hugged her and kissed her and wished her all the happiness she deserved and hadn't seemed to find in this city, and I saw her off.

And I said goodbye to Jude Grayson, because without Jessa around, I knew there was a very real chance I'd never see him again.

CHAPTER TWENTY

Jude

THURSDAY.

It had been a week since I'd fought with Roni and she'd accused me of not wanting her around the club. Since she'd told me she changed her mind about our fuck buddy arrangement, and I walked out.

We still hadn't spoken.

I had no fucking idea how she was feeling, what she might be going through.

All I knew was I was seeing her tonight.

And I wanted to see her.

The documentary TV series that Dirty had shot this summer while searching for a rhythm guitarist, and ultimately hiring Seth back, was starting to air tonight. Brody had decided to host a screening of the first episode. But he was keeping it tight, just the inner circle and their dates.

Maggie had sent me the guest list, and of course Roni was on it. Roni was never all that tight with the band, but she was tight with Jessa Mayes.

Since the screening was at Jessa's house, wasn't much chance I was getting that name scratched off the list, even if I wanted to.

Didn't love that this was how we were seeing each other,

walking into a room of people, instead of alone. But seeing her face-to-face seemed like a better option than a text message anyway.

Better way to approach her and see if maybe she was as unhappy about the way things went down a week ago as I was.

7:22 pm.

I rolled into Brody's place alone. I wasn't the first to arrive or the last, but when I walked into the party room, Roni was already there, helping Brody set up at the bar.

And the feelings I had when I saw her there... Nothing but warmth.

Relief.

A kind of softening of the tension I'd been carrying around.

Good feelings.

All good feelings.

But then I watched as she went to sit down on a couch... and Zane sat down next to her. Elle was on his other side, so it's not like he was sitting down with Roni in particular... But *shit*, did it stick in my throat.

Seeing her sitting next to him like that.

She'd looked up when I walked in. So I knew she knew I was here.

But she didn't come near me.

She smiled at something Zane said, and the ugliness in me crept up. That old voice inside.

The one that wondered if maybe it really was all about sex for her, and always was.

But I knew, I fucking knew that wasn't true.

I endured the screening. The show was pretty damn good, thanks to Liv being a kickass director, even if it had a touch of that cheesy reality-contest-show feel. Zane and Jesse were great. Lots of banter and white-toothed smiles. The usual.

Roni remained on the couch, next to Zane, the whole time. They didn't talk all that much, but the ugliness festered in me until I had to walk out.

I made up some bullshit excuse to take off before anyone else, kissed Jessa and the baby, and drove the fuck home.

When I got there, I dug out some weed. I didn't even bother keeping cream soda stocked at home. Too dangerous.

I went out to my back porch and sat alone in the dark and smoked. I never smoked alone. I rarely smoked at all.

But I smoked in the dark, and I remembered.

Eight long months after I'd told Roni she wasn't the marrying kind and basically made a grade-A drunken asshole of myself, we came back home off the first world tour.

With the wind totally yanked the fuck from our sails.

Seth had been kicked out of Dirty at the end of the tour. Literally on the last night of the tour, after the last show. The band couldn't handle his drug abuse anymore, or the erratic behavior that was a result of it, and he had so much drug debt, so many bad choices dragging him down... no one could save him from himself by that point—even me.

The next day, I'd gotten his ass into rehab. He'd immediately bounced right out, and that was that.

I'd try to help him, get him back into rehab, but not until he came crawling back asking me for help again.

Which he would.

I was pretty damn sure about that.

Until then, nothing I could do.

But it was a shake-up, a wake-up call for all of us. At least, it should've been.

Jessa was still away, modeling, had never come home. Always had some new gig, some contract to fulfill, some reason she couldn't come home to see us.

It bothered Jesse, a fuck of a lot. He still worried about her.

But life rolled the fuck on.

Dirty went pretty much straight into writing mode on their

second album, which they'd already decided would be called *Dead Crazy*, which was pretty much how we all felt at the end of the tour.

I was pretty caught up in trying to balance the high-octane level of life with the band—who were now so famous I went pretty much every-fucking-where with Jesse—and my club responsibilities. By the end of the tour, we had a solid security crew established for the band, and I was managing it. I could've stepped away from the Kings, financially.

But I didn't.

I never would.

I assured Piper of that, in a long and ridiculously fucking heartfelt conversation over a bottle of bourbon, a few weeks after I got back from the tour.

Then, one night, I saw Roni at a party.

The party was at Brody's place, where so many of our band parties were. The guest lists at those things were pretty tight by then, and I always knew who was coming and going. There were always surprises; wouldn't be much of a party without them.

How *she* got in without me noticing, though, I'd never know.

But there she was, standing in the kitchen, talking to Jesse.

My guard was down. I was so caught off-guard, when she saw me and kinda smiled like she couldn't help herself, I actually hugged her. We started talking, and within a few minutes of talking to her, of standing so close to her I could smell her familiar, sexy smell and feel the warmth off her body... my dick was up.

I wasn't drunk, and she wasn't flirting with me, but she was smiling at me, a genuine, wistful sort of smile. And I knew she wasn't with Ben anymore; I'd seen him at the clubhouse and that was pretty clear.

By the time she excused herself to get another drink, I was getting all kinds of wrong ideas.

Not ten minutes later, I saw her flirting with some dude, some promoter Brody had invited. He had his hand on her waist and she was smiling at him.

And my hard-on officially died.

I spent the rest of the night with my arm around some other girl, getting mildly sauced and pretty much avoiding her.

Late in the night, I saw her doing shots with Zane, of all people. I should've known right then what was coming.

But I told myself I was over it.

I wasn't fucking over it.

I wasn't over *her*.

It was definitely easier to put Roni Webber out of my mind when life was busy as fuck and I was traveling with the band and the women were a penny a dozen.

But when she was right in my face... this girl... she drew me like a damn magnet.

So that night, I very purposefully magnetized myself to some other girl.

Roni might've thrown me a few wounded looks over it, but hey, I was over it, right?

The party went late. Like until-early-the-next-morning late. Jesse crashed in one of the guest rooms, so I stayed over too, taking one of the couches in the music room. Figured we'd have breakfast—or lunch—with Brody whenever we got up. I didn't even see Roni leave, told myself I didn't care. But in the morning, I found her.

I found her in bed in the other guest room with Zane.

The kind of rage I felt as I woke her up, hauled her ass out of that bed, shoved her clothes at her and marched her out of Brody's house, was like nothing I'd ever felt before. It was almost like I was floating apart from myself. Like I was boiling alive and completely numb at the same time.

I said all of two words to her.

Get out.

I threw her in a car with Elle and one of her girlfriends; they were just pulling out of the driveway when I flagged them down. Then I stormed the fuck back upstairs to the guest bedroom where Zane was just dragging his sorry, hungover ass out of bed. I knew he was drunk off his ass last night. Maybe still was.

What the fuck else was new?

Somehow, that just made it worse.

"What the fuck was that?" I threw the bedroom door out of my way. It didn't have one of those door stopper things on it, or else I broke it, because the doorknob punched right through the drywall.

"What?" Zane looked at me with his bloodshot eyes and I seriously wanted to punch him. I'd never wanted to punch Zane before.

"I fucking warned you about this shit," I growled, fucking seething. I felt like that beast in the *Looney Tunes* cartoon, the Hyde creature that comes out after the scientist drinks that fucked-up potion.

Must've looked like it too, judging by the look on Zane's face.

"What shit?"

"*This* shit." I grabbed a beer bottle off the bedside table, knocking the other bottles and glasses right off in the process, and smashed it against the far wall.

"Whoa. Whoa, whoa." Brody came up behind me. "The fuck's going on?"

I shrugged him off when he put his hand on my arm, and got in Zane's face. "I told you, you keep down this path, we're puttin' your ass in rehab. Before you end up like Seth."

Zane stayed pretty damn calm. His eyebrows went up, his liquor-drenched brain cells working on overdrive to figure out what the fuck was up my ass.

"This really about me?" he asked me, even as Brody put a hand on my chest and tried to angle in. "Or about Wild Card?"

"Zane," Brody said, "just get your shit and go downstairs."

Zane didn't move.

"I didn't know you were into her, brother," he told me, reading the fury on my face. His eyes on me were pretty steady for someone who was probably still half-cut. "I wouldn't have, if I knew."

I pushed in until my chest bumped his and snarled at him, "I am sick as fuck of cleaning up your shit."

Then I stormed the hell out.

After that, I should've gone home.

I went straight to Roni's.

She'd moved out of her mom's place the year before and I'd never been to her new place, but I knew exactly where she lived. It was an apartment, a basement suite in a house near Kits Beach, shared with a couple of roommates. Fortunately or not, neither of them were home when I hammered on the door and Roni opened it.

"You fucked Zane?" I bowled right past her into the house.

She just stared at me, speechless, for a long moment. Then she shut the door and followed me up the hall, where I was pacing like a pissed-off beast.

She hugged her arms tight around her waist. She'd showered already; maybe I'd gotten her out of the shower. She had on a little silk robe with flowers on it and her hair was wet.

"Why would you care?" she asked.

I advanced on her so fast, she stumbled and almost fell backing up, and I fucking hated myself for it. But I was not a rational human being when it came to this woman. I put her right up against the wall without even touching her, and she didn't even look the least bit scared. Just confused.

"Why can't you just get the fuck out of my life?"

Yeah, I had some balls to say that to her when I'd just barged into *her* home.

It wasn't even my life she was trespassing in, anyway.

It was my fucking *head*.

"I'm not in your life," she said carefully. "I... I sent Jesse a nice photo I saw of Jessa from a shoot she did. I know she doesn't always send them to him, so I did. He thanked me and he told me about the party. I thought that was really nice of him to invite me. So I came." Her eyes were starting to shine, but I couldn't tell if it was hurt or anger. "If you'd rather I didn't come to any Dirty parties, ever again, you can say so and I'll stay away. You'll never have to see me again."

"Good. Then stay the fuck away."

"Fine." She swallowed, and I could see it in her eyes: definitely hurt.

I turned away and stormed toward the door. But when my hand was on the handle, I stopped.

Jesus Christ, what was it with me, with this girl?

I scraped my fingers through my hair, then turned on her. She was right behind me, probably ready to slam the door shut behind my ass as soon as I walked out.

Instead, I grabbed her and kissed her. Crushed my mouth to hers and pretty much ate her face off. She didn't protest. She didn't kiss me back, either, for at least a few seconds.

But then she was right there with me, devouring me back.

Within seconds, we'd fumbled our way into a bedroom. I assumed it was hers. I ripped off her robe and pushed her on the bed. I knelt over her and stripped off my jacket, my shirt. While I did that she took out my dick. She handed me a condom; she had them in singles in a bowl by the bed, which I didn't even want to think about.

I sheathed myself without even taking off my jeans, while she worked them down around my thighs.

Then I fell on her and her thighs went around me. I drove into her fast, spearing her mouth with my tongue as I gave it to her.

That first time we'd fucked had been slow, passionate. Tender, even.

This time, it was the last thing from tender.

It was angry, hurt, bitter, brutal and dirty. I went at her with a groaning, skin-slapping, possibly bed-breaking vengeance until she suddenly shoved at me.

"Pull out," she said.

"What...?" I rolled off, and she immediately went at my dick, tearing off the condom so fast it hurt.

I flinched. "Fuck."

"Sorry," she said, like she wasn't sorry, as she tore off my jeans and underwear.

Then she went down on me.

And fucking hell, could Roni Webber suck cock. I didn't even want to know where she'd learned those particular skills... but I was grateful she'd learned.

Some girls had no sense of dick whatsoever. No idea how to

touch a dick or suck a dick. Roni was all over it like a pro. Working my shaft with one hand, my balls with the other, her mouth devouring me and her tongue ravaging all the sensitive spots.

Then she squeezed the base of my shaft, hard, fucking strangling me, and sucked like hell on my head, like she was trying to pull me apart.

I fucking groaned. I liked it rough. Most girls were too scared or timid or uncomfortable to get rough like that.

Not Roni.

I got up on my knees, somehow, while she was doing her thing, and started fucking her mouth. She sucked me harder, like she was saying *Bring it the fuck on.* So I rammed my hips forward, hitting the back of her throat, and she squirmed, pulling away.

"I don't do that," she gasped, her green eyes flashing up at me.

"What?"

"I don't deep throat."

So I just let her blow me how she wanted, let her control the depth.

"Touch yourself," I ordered her, while she was sucking me off. She ran one hand down between her legs and did that. She shifted to lie on her side on the bed, giving me a front row view of it. "Keep goin'," I told her. "Make yourself come with my dick in your mouth."

She did as I told her to. She moaned as she blew me, and it was kinda torture, but I made damn sure I didn't come.

She did.

And right when she did, I pushed forward, slowly, easing my cockhead into the back of her throat.

Her throat squeezed around me and her eyes met mine, kinda dazed with orgasm. I eased myself out, giving her a moment to push me off. She didn't.

So I eased back in. Then she closed her eyes as my dick cut off her air. Her body writhed beneath me as she kept riding her hand, and then I pulled out, letting her breathe.

She sighed, kinda melting as her hand slipped out from between her legs.

I flipped her over and pulled her hips up, so her shoulders were on the bed and her ass was where I wanted it. I helped myself to another condom from the bowl. I rolled it on and slammed home, filling her slick pussy with everything I had to give her.

I didn't *want* to hurt her, but I was just gonna go ahead and take what I wanted unless she told me to ease the fuck off.

She didn't.

I grabbed a fistful of her hair and yanked her head back. She cried out and said *Yeah* and *Fuck* a lot, so I figured she was as into it as I was. When I let her hair go, my hands dug into her hips as I drilled into her. The sleek curve of her arched back gleamed with fucking sweat. My hands slipped on her skin when I smacked her ass a few times. And I smacked *hard.*

She didn't complain.

She was *sweating* with want for me.

"Give it to me, Jude," she pleaded. And not like some pre-rehearsed line she might use on every guy. Breathless and desperate, like she was aching for it.

Like she'd been aching for it ever since the last time I was inside her.

Three. Motherfucking. *Years*. Ago.

"Darlin', I'm gonna give it to you so good, you're not gonna walk right for a week. You're not gonna forget this day and how good I fucked you, for the rest of your damn life."

All kinds of dirty, stupid shit like that just flew the fuck out of my mouth.

"Good..." she moaned. "Fuck me like that. I like it rough... I want you to fuck me, just like that..."

Fuck...

This girl.

I could feel it as our bodies slammed together...

The deep, primal, animal attraction. Me to her. Her to me.

Had I ever wanted a woman, any woman, like I wanted her?

No.

Fucking sadly... No.

I fucked her until we were both soaked in sweat. Then I flipped her back over so I could see her face while I fucked her. So I could see her face when I came.

She came again when I did, her green eyes locked on mine.

Afterwards, as I got dressed, she sat on the edge of the bed in her robe. "What is this?" She didn't even sound hopeful or expectant or anything other than sad.

"Closure," I said. I pulled on my leather jacket and stared at her. I was still breathing hard. The condom had barely hit the wastebasket under her desk and I had my clothes back on. I waited for her eyes to meet mine.

They did, and she nodded, just barely. "Okay."

I left her there, and I didn't look back.

As I rode home that day, I knew I wouldn't see her again. I knew the next time I saw her at a party, I'd have to walk the other way. I'd have to lose her number, which was still in my fucking phone.

I could not let myself stay hung the fuck up on Roni Webber for the rest of my life.

Because every time I looked at her, I'd just see all that shit I didn't want to see.

It wasn't that she'd betrayed me.

I'd betrayed myself.

I'd broken a promise I'd made to myself, so many years ago, when I knew shit-all about women. When I was thirteen and started getting hard-ons for the girls at my dad's club, and I saw how they bounced from lap to lap.

When I saw how they bounced into my brother's lap.

All I knew was I was never giving my heart to one of those girls. To any girl who was with one of my brothers first.

And Roni Webber had now been with fucking *three.*

Piper.

Ben.

Zane.

That I knew of...

And I was all fucked up over it.

I was pissed that she'd slept with Zane. I was jealous that she'd dated Ben.

I was still sore that she'd fucked Piper.

I truly fucking wished she hadn't... because I truly fucking wished things could've been different between us.

They couldn't.

I knew my reasons for pushing her away were bullshit, in a way.

But they were also a matter of motherfucking pride.

It was the way I was brought up, in my dad's club. I wouldn't even dare go to him with this, ask his advice. If I told him I was all fucked up over a girl Piper had fucked-and-dumped years ago, a girl my brother had already deemed a slut, he'd smack me upside the head.

It was the way things were.

When I was a boy, I was picked on for being too scrawny. Too quiet. Too brown.

So I got big.

I got a loud bike. I hung with a loud-as-fuck band, and loud-as-fuck friends.

I fucked women who wanted me, and I did not take my brother's sloppy seconds.

Any woman I was ever even gonna consider getting serious about was gonna be mine and no one else's.

And Roni Webber had gone ahead and disqualified herself, three times over.

2:06 am.

I was still sitting in the dark, on my back porch. I'd run out of weed a while ago and it was cold as shit out. And still, I sat.

Because six years had gone by since that morning in Roni's apartment, and here the fuck we were.

Time had passed.

Life was lived.

Women came and went.

And I'd grown the fuck up. I'd like to think so, anyway.

I didn't necessarily buy into the club's views of women or the rules surrounding the treatment of them anymore.

I definitely didn't give a fuck what my brother thought of Roni anymore. At least, I sure as fuck didn't care about his approval.

But was I still jealous?

Was I still sore?

More important: was I really gonna let what happened in the past ruin whatever this was between us?

Because of all the things that had changed in all these years, my feelings for her never had.

CHAPTER TWENTY-ONE

Roni

IT WAS the eve of Christmas Eve, and Jude and I weren't together.

I was at a Dirty party at Zane's house in West Vancouver with Jessa and baby Nick.

Jude was who-knew-where.

We still weren't talking, which was probably more my fault than his. I hadn't seen him since the documentary screening at Jessa's a couple of nights ago, where we hadn't even spoken. He'd left early, but he'd texted me later that night. Like around 2:00 am late.

Been thinking we should talk.

I didn't reply.

Really, what did we have to talk about at two in the morning?

I was done with our text-and-meet-up-for-sex relationship. I really didn't want to be Jude Grayson's convenience fuck.

I wanted to be his everything.

Was that so fucking wrong?

As Jessa and I made our way through Zane's house, which was dark and mostly empty of people, to the covered, heated patio out back where everyone had converged around the bar, the pool and the various seating areas, I looked for Jude. But he definitely wasn't here.

We found Zane by the bar, and even though Jessa had told me

No presents, I handed him the bottle of my famous home brew: blackberry vodka, which I bottled every summer during blackberry season and was just ready in time for the holidays.

I knew Zane didn't drink, but I never hit a holiday party without a bottle of my home brew in-hand. People asked me about it year-round; it was that good.

"For your guests," I told him.

"Thanks, Roni," he said, giving me a hug and a kiss on the cheek. Then his ice-blue eyes drifted down my curves. "And, whoa. Hot dress."

It was a hot dress. It was one of Jessa's; one of the ones I liked to call her supermodel dresses, the ones that hung in the back of her closet but she rarely actually wore, and since she couldn't fit into them right now anyway, had offered me my pick of for the holidays. It was short and black with a subtle sparkle and fit me like a sexy glove. Cleavage, leg... this dress had it all.

"*Don't* flirt with her."

Zane's pierced eyebrow rose as Jessa hooked her arm through mine, yanking me away.

"Okay... What was that about?"

"Nothing," she said. "I'm just pissed at him right now."

"Why?"

"I really can't tell you. Let's just say... the way Zane Traynor treats women is fucking asinine."

"Um, we've known that forever."

"True," she said. "And *why* did you sleep with him again?"

I gave an exasperated sigh. "Because I was twenty-one and he was super hot." *And I was super fucking pissed at Jude for making out with some chick right in front of me.* But I kept that part to myself.

We found Brody by the pool; he'd come early, so Bishop had driven us. When he saw Jessa and his son, he lit up like a Christmas tree and pulled them into his arms. I waited while they snuggled and kissed and cooed over their baby together. Then Brody seemed to notice me and cleared his throat.

"Hey, Roni."

"Hey, Brody. Merry Christmas."

"Everything's set for the New Year's Eve show, yeah?"

"Seems that way."

He knew it was. I was pretty sure he was semi-shocked that I'd pulled the whole thing off. I could've given him a laundry list of all the details I'd taken care of since we last spoke if he really wanted one, but I'd learned years ago that talking about business at a Dirty party wasn't really done. Which meant that any second now, someone would cut us off by handing us drinks and changing the subject.

Sure enough, before I could offer another word, Jesse appeared with champagne for me and a sparkling juice for his sister.

I thanked him for the bubbly, gave him a distracted kiss on the cheek—he probably knew where Jude was, and if he was coming, right?—and slipped away to do the rounds a bit. Wished people happy holidays and all that.

Pretty much most of the usual crew were here. It was a great group of people, really, one I'd enjoyed becoming more and more a part of this last year, since Jessa came back home.

It made me sad, actually, to think that if all the shit between Jude and me just didn't work out, I might not really see these people again. If things weren't good between us, I didn't think I could handle coming to these parties or even going to a Dirty show and risking running into him... or not running into him.

At the far end of the patio, Amber had a photo booth all set up, and Shady, Zane's bodyguard and a King I'd known for years, was dressed up like Santa. I was watching Amber take photos of people sitting on his lap when I heard a familiar voice behind me.

"Dylan Cope! Santa's knee, now."

Next thing I knew, Ash brushed past me. He and Dylan converged on Santa, each of them taking a knee. Dylan in red leather pants and the fugliest Christmas sweater of all time, in which he somehow still looked hot (the fashion at this thing went from "red carpet" to "holiday trash"), and Ash wearing nothing at all

Christmasy other than a black T-shirt that said in big white letters *I Saw Mama Screwing Santa Claus.*

Amber took a few photos, her lights flashing.

Katie, who was helping Amber out, took a Polaroid, and I peeked over her shoulder. In the photo, Dylan was feeding beer to Santa; Ash had his eyes half-closed and a joint hanging out of his mouth. Katie handed it off to Amber. "There's one for your Christmas album."

Amber sort of half-smiled and clipped the Polaroid to one of her light stands, where a bunch of others had been hung.

Ash then plucked it off, kissed Amber on the cheek, stuck the Polaroid in his teeth, and disappeared.

Katie and Amber exchanged a look.

Not my business.

"Be right back," I told Katie.

I collected Jessa and once it was our turn, we each took one of Santa's knees, Jessa with baby Nick strapped to her front in his baby carrier. Both of us kissed Shady on the cheek and Amber took a few photos. Katie handed a Polaroid over to each of us.

Jessa and I watched as the images developed, and I got all warm and fuzzy about it when I saw Jessa and her baby and me all snuggled up together on Santa's lap.

"I love you," I told her, overcome with emotion. "I'm so glad you moved back. And I'm really glad you found your way back to Brody."

"Aw, sweetie." Jessa put her arm around my shoulders. "I love you, too." She was looking at me and I avoided her eyes as I stared at the Polaroid in my hand. "How're you doing?"

"Fantastic."

Clearly, she saw right through that. "Is this about Jude not being here?"

I looked at her. "I don't know. I mean, he's not here with me, that's for sure. I don't even know if he's coming."

"He wouldn't miss it, Roni."

"But it's not like he asked me to come with him. Or to spend

Christmas with him. I know we agreed our whole thing was about sex. But it's not. For me... it never was. And now we're both coming to your Christmas Eve dinner tomorrow, and I don't know... I know it's something the guys do every year. Brody and Jude and Jesse and Zane... So I don't even know if I should be going if Jude doesn't even invite me—"

"Okay, stop," Jessa interjected, and the forcefulness of her tone halted my stupid little spiral. "Listen to me right now. I love Jude, but fuck him. *I* invited you. You're coming."

Tears actually tingled in my eyes, and I pulled her close to cover it, giving her and Nick a hug. "Thank you."

"Merry Christmas. Go get drunk and have a good time, for both of us."

"What, are you leaving?"

"I'm not staying long. Brody will stay for a bit, but Bishop will drive me home..." She trailed off, and I turned to look at whatever had snagged her attention.

Jude was standing there, right behind me. Staring at me.

"Hey, Jude," Jessa said.

His dark eyes flicked to her. "Bratface." He cracked a smile. "I mean Jessa. You look pretty."

"Thank you. You look... handsome."

He did.

He always did.

My dark horse... Always showing up out of nowhere, to win the day—and totally fuck with my hormones and my heart. This time, in a thin, body-hugging black sweater and dark gray jeans.

Damn.

His gaze shifted back to me and drifted down my body. "That's one hell of a sexy dress."

"Thank you." I'd worn it *because* it was sexy, I felt beautiful in it... and I wanted Jude to like how I looked in it.

But now that he was here, I didn't even want him looking at me like that—like he wanted to fuck me.

"You didn't answer my text," he said, when his eyes met mine again.

"Um... I'm just gonna go find Bishop..." Jessa tried to slip away, but I caught her arm and held her at my side.

"It's okay. *I'm* going. I'll send Bishop over to get you."

"Where're you goin'?" Jude shifted himself into my path.

I dropped Jessa's arm to cross my arms under my chest. She didn't leave, and I told him, "I don't want to be your speed-dial pussy, Jude," right there in front of her.

Jude's gaze flicked to Jessa, briefly, before meeting mine again, and it really, really rubbed me the wrong way. Like he cared more about her witnessing this, or about what she might think, than about what I was actually saying? What I felt?

"That's not what you are," he said.

"Yes, I am. I don't want to be your fuck buddy anymore, okay?"

I walked away, heading for the house. Or maybe the bar. Wherever.

But then I stopped short.

Some guy was standing right by the bar with Dylan and his bodyguard, Con, and he looked... familiar. Kind of spine-tingling familiar. Which was weird, because I was sure I'd never seen him before.

It was his teeth.

His mouth was the first thing I noticed about him. He was laughing as Con talked, and his teeth were showing. A row of perfect white porcelain veneers—with silver canines. He was cute, in a dangerous sort of way. And he was wearing a Kings cut over his ugly Rudolph-themed Christmas sweater.

I remembered what Talia said about the guy she saw outside my place with the silver canines. I looked around, but I hadn't seen her; I didn't think she was here yet.

"Roni..." Jude had come right up behind me.

"Who is that?" I asked.

"Who?"

I pointed at the dude with the teeth. "That. The guy with the Kings shit and the silver teeth."

I felt Jude's chest rise against me as he drew a breath. "That's Lex."

"Who the fuck is Lex?"

"He's a King."

"I can see that. Who is he?" I turned to face him. "And why did Talia see him outside my place?"

He didn't answer. His dark eyes held mine, and I could see him thinking through whatever shit he was thinking—but not saying.

I turned and walked away.

Jude followed me. Right past Lex—and out of the corner of my eye, I saw Jude give him a shove.

"The fuck are you doin' here?"

I glanced back long enough to meet Lex's eyes and see them go wide.

"I didn't know she'd be here..." I heard him say, before I disappeared into the house.

I heard Jude follow.

I strode right past Zane, Maggie and Elle, who were talking in the hallway, and I heard Jude thunder, "Why the fuck did you invite Lex?"

"Huh?" Zane said, and I paused to look back and listen.

"You don't even like him," Jude growled.

"I invited him," Maggie said, looking from Jude to me. "What? It's Christmas."

I spun on my heel and kept going. I'd made my way into the front foyer by the time Jude caught up. It was kinda dark and no one seemed to be in the house but us. I could feel him, practically on top of me.

"Roni." He grabbed at my elbow but I yanked it away, turning to face him.

"You had that guy watching me? Why?"

He sighed. "Because I wanted to make sure you were okay."

"Okay? Why? Why wouldn't I be okay?"

He was silent.

I waited.

"I didn't trust Taze."

I put my hands on my hips. "You mean you didn't like him fucking me."

"That too."

I started to turn away but he stopped me, his hand gripping my arm. "I was worried about you."

"Why?"

"I told you. He's a bad dude, V."

I shook off his hand. "I *broke up* with him."

"I know."

I made an exasperated sound. "Is that Lex guy still watching me?"

"No." He ran his hand over his face, then sighed again. "There's another guy."

My jaw dropped.

"His name's Bane."

"Jude! You can't have guys following me around. It's fucking *creepy*."

"It's for your safety."

"I'm not with Taze anymore. I haven't even talked to him since the night I sent him that text, when *you* told me to," I jabbed him in the chest with my finger, "and *we* fucked."

"Good."

"So why do you still have someone watching me?"

"It's just for a while. Just a precaution. Until I know he's not gonna try anything."

I frowned, taking a step back. "Try what? Taze wouldn't hurt me."

He went silent again.

I spun around, so fucking frustrated, I could've... "Where's the bathroom in this place? You know, somewhere a girl can lock herself in and scream...?"

"There was an incident," Jude said.

It wasn't so much the words but his low, sober tone that made me turn back to him and listen.

"Between Taze and me. I don't want that blowing back on you. Until I'm sure that's not gonna happen, I want a guy on you."

What?

"You should've told me. You could've told me that, Jude."

"I didn't want to involve you."

"In what?" I fired back, exasperated. "My own life?"

"In anything that could be dangerous. I don't want you hurt, Roni."

"You have to tell me this shit, though. If it's about me, I want to know."

"It's not about you. It's about Taze and me. I just want to make sure you're safe, that's all."

"For how long?"

"Not long. Maybe a few more weeks. I have a guy watching Taze, too. Just making sure he's not gonna stir up shit."

That actually made me pause and take a breath. "You think he will?"

"No. It's not fuckin' likely."

I stared at him, letting the implications of those words sink in...

"Jude. What did you do? Did you hurt him?"

"No. No, I didn't hurt him."

Then it very slowly dawned on me...

"Oh my God. That horrendous bruise on your back?" I took a step toward him, so I could see his face better in the dimly-lit hall. "Your face? That was Taze?"

"It's nothin' you need to worry about, darlin'."

"He hurt you? Because of me?"

"Nothing's because of you," he said firmly. "It's just guy shit. It's got nothing to do with you."

Holy shit.

The thought that Taze had done anything at all to Jude because of me... It *was* because of me. I wasn't born yesterday. For sure, the Sinners and the Kings had some bad blood between them. That wasn't exactly a secret. But Taze and Jude never would've looked at one another twice, probably, if not for me.

If Taze even said a nasty word to Jude because of me, I'd be choked.

The fact that he'd put his hands on him... or a weapon? Whatever had left that horrible bruising on his back...

"Jude..."

"I'll introduce you to Bane." He shifted closer to me, his voice softening. "I'll give you his cell number, so you can communicate with him if you need to. That make you feel better?"

"Fuck, yes."

His eyes held mine, and the tiniest ghost of a smile played at his lips. "Good."

I swallowed, softening a little. "Look... I'm really sorry, okay? For that stupid fight, the other night..."

He shook his head. "You were right. I didn't want you around Piper."

Oh. Well, that hurt.

"You're ashamed of me," I said, quietly. I couldn't even look at him. "Just like you were back then."

He took me by the shoulders and got close to my face. "I am not ashamed of you, Roni. I was never ashamed of you." I looked up into his dark eyes, and he said, "I just don't want to even think about you bein' with anyone else."

What?

"With Piper?" I was so fucking confused. I'd rarely even run into Piper over the years. I'd never even had a real relationship with him, and we'd only had sex once, a decade ago. Piper didn't care about me. I didn't care about him.

Why did Jude still care?

"With anyone," he said.

I took a slow, deep breath, just feeling those words.

"Come on, darlin'," he said, slipping his arm around me. "Let's sit down. We can talk."

He steered me from the foyer into a dark living room and sat me down on the couch. But he didn't sit down beside me. He knelt on the floor in front of me, between my knees... just like he had that first night we'd ever had sex.

And it killed me.

I wished we could just rewind, go back to that night, and start over.

Because that night... it was perfect.

Before we fucked it all up.

"I don't even wanna talk," I whispered.

"What do you want, V?"

"I want to kiss you."

He wrapped his arms around me, pulling me towards him, and I kissed him. He ran his hands down my thighs and then up, under my dress. I put my hands on his, but I didn't push them away.

"Jude..."

It was the feeblest attempt in the world to curb a guy's attempt to get under my dress, and it was quickly abandoned as he slid the sparkly fabric up, exposing my lace panties. They were skimpy and red and had a sparkly little candy cane on the front, right above my clit.

He grinned.

"Merry Christmas?" I whispered.

He chuckled. Then he slipped a finger under the lace, yanked the panties aside, and shoved his face between my legs. I had no choice, really, but to fall back on the couch and enjoy it.

"*Fuck*... ahhhh... Jude... shit, I love it when you go down on me."

"Yeah, darlin'...?"

"Mmm. You've got a magic mouth..."

He said nothing, just used his magic mouth to make my eyes roll back and my pussy clench.

I wanted him to fuck me, but maybe that was too rude? I glanced toward the foyer; I could hear the party, the voices and music in the distance, but no one seemed to be coming.

"Should we... uh... be doing this in here...?"

"Please," he said, between licks. "It's Zane's couch. It would be depressed... if it didn't get any action... at Christmas."

I giggled.

His big hands pressed down on my inner thighs and his thumbs spread me open, and he drilled his tongue into me, making me forget about anything else. Then he lapped his tongue up and sucked on my clit. He kissed me and then sucked on me again, kinda groaning as he did it.

"Jude... you're gonna make me come..."

My whole body was starting to shake.

"Yeah, babe," he murmured, kissing me again. "Missed this fuckin' pussy..." He sucked on me again. His tongue played with my clit and swirled around...

When the orgasm gripped me, I gasped and plunged my hands into his hair. I held him to me as he sucked on me, as the waves of pleasure rolled through my body.

"Yeah..." he murmured. "This pussy is mine..."

I never would've thought words like that out of a man's mouth would turn me on so damn much.

"You can have my pussy, Jude," I said with a sigh, giving in to the fact as I collapsed on the couch. Really, my pussy had never been able to resist him. "But what about the rest of me?"

"Yeah..." he said, his hands sliding up over my curves. He drifted his fingers up my throat and into my mouth; I bit down lightly on his fingertips as his eyes met mine. "That's all mine, too."

CHAPTER TWENTY-TWO

Jude

IT WAS SUNDAY, the morning of Christmas Eve, when I woke up with Roni.

It was the first morning we'd ever woken up together. The first time one of us had spent the night in the other's bed. We were at my place, where I'd brought her after Zane's party last night.

Although... as it turned out, I wasn't exactly in bed with Roni.

Just her candy cane panties and a hint of her sex kitten perfume.

I heard the clinking of dishes and smelled toast.

I got up, pulled on some briefs and a T-shirt, and wandered toward the smell of food. This place had definitely never felt more like a home than when I found Roni Webber in the kitchen, wearing one of my T-shirts, making me breakfast in the sunlight.

"Oh, hey," she said, perking up when I walked in. "You want some toast?"

"Sure."

She grinned and popped a couple of slices in the toaster for me. Then I swept her up in my arms. I kissed her a few times, softly. Lips, cheeks, eyelids, nose.

"Sorry," she said softly, "I'm really not much of a chef and you don't have much for groceries, but I made do. There's some fruit sliced up. And by the way, if you want a girl to make you breakfast after you fuck her brains out, you might wanna buy some eggs or something."

"What can I say..." I kissed her cheek again and let her go. "I eat on the go a lot. I'm not home much. And I don't want girls cooking me breakfast."

Her face fell.

"Shit. Except you, V. I meant, except you."

"Oh." A tentative smile played at her full lips.

"Jesus. Did I just say that shit to you when you're standing in my kitchen wearing my shirt and makin' me breakfast?"

"You did."

"Foot-in-mouth disease. I have it."

"It's okay."

"I'll eat whatever you wanna make, darlin'."

"Cool." The toast popped and she put it on a plate for me. "Butter?"

"Just a bit."

"You want coffee or anything? I couldn't find where you keep it."

"I don't. You need one?"

"No. I'm a casual user." She smiled. Girl was pretty as hell with her unbrushed morning hair and no makeup on her face. "Here you go. Fruit?"

"I'll grab some." I helped myself to some of the apples and strawberries and whatever she'd sliced up into a bit of a fruit salad, throwing it on my plate. Looked like she was already finished her breakfast. "You could've woken me up. No idea why I slept so long. I'm usually up pretty early."

She shrugged. "I dunno. You looked so cozy there, and I was hungry."

"Thank you." I leaned against the counter and bit into my toast. "Best toast any girl's ever buttered for me."

She rolled her eyes. "You're not gonna sit?"

I looked at the chairs around the table, which I rarely pulled out. "Just always stand here to eat breakfast," I said. "Usually I just have a smoothie."

She smiled a little. "You want some jam on that?"

"I have jam?"

"I found this on the porch," she said, pointing out a little mason jar of what looked like homemade jam, on the table. "Went out there with my juice to check out your sad little garden. Someone named Janice left it for you?" She raised an eyebrow as I glanced at the little tag on the jar.

"My neighbor," I said.

"Did you screw her?" She looked away as she sipped her juice. "I'm not jealous. Just wondering. It's good jam." She turned to put the bread away and I wrapped my arm around her from behind.

"I didn't screw her," I whispered in her ear, then bit her lobe a bit. "Why you so interested in Janice? You into athletic blondes?"

She made that throaty little giggle of hers. "Sometimes." Then her eyes met mine, and her face fell. "Kidding," she said. "I didn't mean Taze... or whoever."

Whoever. That meant Piper or Zane, no doubt.

I released her. "Sorry I brought it up."

"I don't have a thing for blonds, Jude."

I didn't say anything.

She stared at me, biting on her plump lip a bit. "You've mentioned it a few times. Said stuff about Taze being blond..."

"Have I?"

"I don't have, like, a blond guy fetish or something."

"Good to know," I said, putting my empty plate down on the counter. "'Cause I'm not blond."

"No. You're..." She looked at my hair. "Dark."

I drank my juice.

"Hawaiian, Brazilian... English and Swedish."

Good memory. Couldn't even remember telling her all that, but I must've, at some point.

"So is Piper," I said. "Think there's some Norwegian in there, too."

"And you look it. All of it." She stared at me. "He does, too, kind of. Just... differently."

"Uh-huh."

She seemed to be about to say something else, but turned away to put her plate in the sink instead. Then she turned back to me, suddenly, like she'd just gotten the nerve to say what she wanted to blurt out. "Do you want me at the dinner tonight?"

I stared at her. *Huh?*

"I mean, Jessa invited me, but I know it's a traditional thing you guys do, and... I don't have to come. Really."

I knew Jessa invited her, and I'd just assumed she was coming.

"Yeah," I said. "I want you there."

"Oh." She seemed to relax a bit, but still looked kinda on-edge. "Okay." She turned away.

Then she turned right back again.

"Is that... like... a weird thing for you? That... your brother's blond? And you're... not?"

"Well. It wasn't *not* weird when I was a kid, tell you that." I finished the rest of my juice and looked at her.

"Oh," she said. "But. I mean... obviously, you know you're gorgeous, right?"

Right. I knew that like she knew I wanted her to come to this dinner.

"Knowing isn't the same as feeling, darlin'."

Her brow scrunched up a bit. "I guess..." She picked up our juice glasses, slowly, as she thought that through.

"Put the glasses down."

She put them in the sink.

I took hold of her hips and turned her to face me, smashing my mouth down over hers and giving her a long, steaming-hot kiss. And I was patient as fuck about it. I kissed her and kissed her until she let the rod drop out of her ass and she relaxed back into her curvy, confident self in my arms. I could feel the shift, the way she suctioned her body up against mine and kissed me back.

When I finally broke away, I told her, "That's how much I want you at the dinner tonight."

"Okay," she said, her voice all throaty with lust; way more convincing.

"I'll be there around three," I told her, releasing her.

"Oh. We're not... going together?"

"I've gotta head out to Piper's first. He's deep frying the turkey. Told him I'd give him a hand with the deep fryer. Bringin' it over in his truck."

"Oh. Right."

"So?"

"So what?"

"What time are you gonna be there?"

"I don't know. Maybe four? To give Jessa a hand if she needs it."

I watched her as she cleared the breakfast shit off the table. "I'll need to head out soon. You want a shower first? The shower in the master bathroom is shit, so we gotta use the one down the hall."

She looked at me sideways and smiled softly. "Why do you live here?"

"You don't like my place?" I looked around. Yeah, it was old. Smallish. But it was clean. Simple. I liked simple.

"I just mean, it's not your place. It's a rental, right?"

"That obvious?"

"You could afford much nicer, I'm sure."

I shrugged. "Better things to spend my money on."

"Such as?"

"Bikes. Travel." I checked out her bare legs. "Women."

She rolled her eyes. "You go shower. I'll finish cleaning up."

"You really don't have to do that, darlin'."

"Just go." She was fussing over the dishes in the sink, and I slipped my hand around her hip to her stomach, that slight curve of her belly that fit right into my hand. I brushed her hair out of the way with my chin and kissed her temple.

"Yes, ma'am."

I left her there. I could feel her pulling away a bit, but fuck if I knew why. I told her I wanted her to come to the dinner. If she was nervous about seeing Piper or something, not sure what I was supposed to do about that.

I was uneasy about it myself.

I'd told Jesse at the party last night that I wouldn't be coming by his place this morning to work out, and he'd definitely seen me leave with Roni. So he could connect the dots there.

Other than that, I hadn't said shit to anyone yet—including Piper.

Was definitely gonna fill him in that I was seeing Roni when I went by his place today, though, *before* he ended up in a room with her and a beer in his hand and said something stupid.

No idea what he'd make of it. Really didn't care. As long as Roni was mine, we'd work the rest out.

And last night, when I screwed her on Zane's couch in the dark, I'd definitely told her she was mine.

She didn't argue.

As I got into the shower, I realized I wasn't even sure what time it was, which was fucking rare. Something about Roni, about spending time with her... She sucked up my focus, made all my attention converge on her.

Made the clock in my head shut the fuck up.

And I liked it.

I figured I had enough time, though, to get cleaned up, very possibly screw the hell out of her again, and head out to Piper's place, with time to spare.

This Christmas Eve dinner thing—the Orphans' Potluck, we called it—had been a tradition between Jesse, Brody, Zane and me, ever since we were about twenty. We'd started the tradition when the four of us were renting that shitbag apartment together. The year Jesse's mom died.

We called it the Orphans' Potluck because none of us had parents to spend Christmas Eve with. Jesse's and Zane's were dead,

Brody hated his, and my dad lived out of town. My mom lived in the city but she always spent her Christmas Eve at church, so I'd see her on Christmas Day. Back then, Jesse and Zane would spend Christmas Day with Zane's grandma, Dolly, Brody would spend it with his parents—when they managed to force him to—or at Dolly's, or he'd come with me to my mom's.

Couple of years after that, Brody's dad died anyway and his mom fucked off to wherever with her new husband.

So, Orphans' Potluck.

We still did it every year on Christmas Eve. Each year, one of the four of us guys took our turn hosting. We kept the invite list pretty tight, just the inner circle, but everyone brought food to contribute and it was always one hell of a feast.

As for Christmas Day nowadays, we all had family we loved, to celebrate with. I still had my mom and my brother. Zane still had Dolly. But Jesse now had Katie and her family, and Brody had Jessa and Nick.

Actually, it definitely felt like this year, with Jessa back and a new baby in the mix, we all had a little more to celebrate.

And now... I had Roni.

When I stepped out of the shower, I wrapped a towel on, loosely, and wandered out into the hall, just in case she felt like celebrating the holiday season again. But she dashed right by me and into the bathroom. "Thanks," she said, "I won't be long." Then she shut the door in my face and turned on the shower.

Guess that meant I wasn't joining her in there.

As I dried off and got dressed, it was sinking in that she was definitely acting a little off. It wasn't like I knew what she was like in the morning, exactly. Some people were groggy in the morning, or short with their words or just plain out of it until they had a coffee. But this wasn't that.

Maybe she was put off by the fact that I'd asked her to meet me at Brody and Jessa's place—instead of asking her to go *with* me?

If so, I really wasn't sure how to make up for it, other than pull out her Christmas gift a little early.

When she got out of the shower, I had it sitting on the kitchen table. I was dressed, but she'd taken it to the next level. Clothes on, purse on her shoulder and jacket in hand, like she was ready to leave a trail of dust. When she saw the gift box, though, she stopped.

She looked at me, then looked at it again.

"Another gift from Janice?" she asked me, completely deadpan.

Jesus, the girl had sass.

"Read the damn card."

She set her jacket and purse down and carefully nudged open the little folded tag that I'd barely been able to write on, it was so damn tiny.

"*Veronica*," she read aloud. "*Merry Christmas.*" She turned it over. "Hmm. It's not signed by anyone."

"Must be from damn Santa Claus."

"Guess he came early?"

"Don't be a brat."

A smile spread, tentatively, across her face. Her cheeks were kinda flushed from her shower, her black hair a little damp, but she still didn't have any makeup on, and I had this weird thought that she was gonna look really beautiful when she got old. One of those women who just got better with age. Her black hair turning gracefully to silver and then white, and her pale skin just suiting her and all the old guys hound-dogging all over her.

Jesus.

The fuck was wrong with me?

The holidays were making me sentimental as fuck, or something.

I watched as she very carefully, almost timidly, slipped her fingers under the tape and gradually peeled open the silver wrapping paper with the little bells all over it. The woman at the store chose it, and by the way Roni was treating it like it was fine-spun gold, I figured it was a good choice. She finally unwrapped the white box inside, then started the process all over again with the tape that was holding the box together.

"While we're young, sweetheart. Christmas is gonna come and go."

She threw me a quick glare and resumed peeling. When she'd worked the lid open, she pulled it back, exposing the silvery-gray tissue paper inside. She plucked at it gently, loosening it from the gift in the box.

"You're killin' me."

She smiled a little, then finally peeled the tissue paper back enough to work her hands inside. She grasped her gift and pulled it out, holding it in her hands. It gleamed in the morning sunlight.

She cocked her head and looked at me kinda sideways.

"It's a vase," I said, like an idiot.

"For a second," she said, "I swear to God, I thought it was gonna be a gun or something. You know, for my 'protection.'"

"That why you were handling it like a bomb about to blow?"

"I just wanted to savor it," she said, looking embarrassed. She gazed at the vase. "It's beautiful, Jude."

"You know, to replace the one I broke."

Her green eyes hit mine, and it shocked me, deep, like it often did. "We broke it together."

"Yeah." I cleared my throat. "It's not a big deal. Jessa helped me pick it out. She said you'd like it."

She was turning it over in her hands, carefully. "It's crystal."

"There's a gift receipt inside. If it's not what you want."

She tucked it carefully back into the box. Then she gripped the back of my neck and stood up on her toes to kiss me. My arms went around her, holding her up, and my mouth slammed over hers, and what was probably meant to be a sweet *Thank you for the gift* sort of kiss turned into the deep, dirty, nasty, wet sort of kiss they put at the beginning of a really good porno.

"It's the best... present... ever..." she said, in-between sucking face with me. "And now you can buy me more flowers... to go in it..."

Then her phone started buzzing.

She ripped away, her lips swollen and wet. She frowned a bit. "Damn."

"Ignore it?" I held her against me, but she tried to wriggle away, looking apologetic. I released her and she fished the buzzing phone out of her purse.

"Shit," she mumbled, as I adjusted my hard-on in my jeans, "it's my mom."

"You're not gonna answer it?"

She raised an eyebrow, like *Maybe not.*

"It's Christmas Eve," I reminded her.

She kinda grumbled under her breath—something about *And now he's Mr. Nice Guy...?*—and finally picked up the phone. "Hey, Mom."

I listened, and even though I'd never met Roni's mom, the way the conversation rolled, Roni's end kinda clipped and guarded, I figured out a whole lot of shit about their relationship, fast. At least, Roni's side of it.

"Yeah. I'm not sure yet, Mom. I was maybe gonna meet up with Jessa..." Her eyes met mine.

When? I mouthed at her.

Tonight! she mouthed back.

I shook my head at her, slowly.

She turned away. "Yeah, I'm here. I can maybe let you know—"

I plucked the damn phone out of her hand.

"Cindy?" No, I'd never met her, but I knew the woman's name. Knew a lot about her, actually.

"Hello?" Roni's mom said. "Who's this?"

"This is Jude. I'm a friend of Roni's." I glanced at Roni, who was standing there in shock.

"Oh?" Roni's mom said.

"Sounds like we've just confirmed our plans for tonight," I informed her. "Havin' dinner over at Jessa Mayes' place. Kind of a pre-Christmas thing. Few people. You're welcome to join, if you're free."

Roni's mouth floated open.

"Oh. Well... yes. That would be nice. I haven't seen Jessa in a long time."

"I'm sure she'd love it if you came. Have you met the baby yet?"

Roni snapped out of her shock and made a grab for the phone. I held her off with one arm.

"No," her mom was saying. "No, Roni mentioned she had a little boy, and I sent a card, you know, but I haven't seen her in so long..."

"Great. I'll let her and Brody know you're coming." I gave her the address, then hung up and handed the phone back to Roni. "That so hard?"

She glared at me. "What did you just do."

"I invited your mom to Christmas Eve dinner."

She sighed and started typing on her phone.

"What're you doin'?"

"I'm telling her it's a potluck, so she better bring something nice." She sent the text and stuffed the phone back in her purse.

I studied her.

"You don't want to see your mom at Christmas?"

"You don't understand. She made no plans to see *me*."

"At Christmas?"

"Jude." She looked up at me, hands on her hips. "This is what she does. Whatever plans she had for tonight must've fallen through. And I promise you, if she did have plans, they were with a man. I'm her last minute backup on Christmas Eve. I'm always her last minute backup."

"You don't know that."

"Trust me. I know. If there was any chance she was getting laid tonight, she wouldn't be calling me."

I took hold of her and gathered her into my arms. Girl looked frazzled as fuck, and I'd really never seen Roni frazzled. "She's your mom, Roni. It's Christmas Eve. Maybe she'll surprise you."

She laid her head on my chest. "No. She won't. She will be incredibly unsurprising."

"Maybe she'll surprise me." Roni peered up at me and I grinned. "I've never met her."

"There's a reason," she muttered. "Do you have any idea what you've just initiated? Cindy Webber in a room full of rock stars? Christ."

She looked exhausted just considering it.

I gave her a squeeze. "I work security for Dirty, babe. Think I can handle one randy woman in a room full of rock stars."

She looked at me like I was an idiot. "You haven't met this one."

"If she's anything like you, darlin'," I said, with a healthy dose of sarcasm, "putty in my hands."

CHAPTER TWENTY-THREE

Roni

AS IT TURNED OUT, I went over to Jessa's place earlier than I'd expected because she called me all in a twitter, asking for help.

Since she so rarely asked for help, I took it as a compliment and got my ass over there.

I wore a soft, hunter-green sweater with a beaded black pattern of leaves on one shoulder and my black leather leggings, and I put soft curls in my hair. I'd given myself smoky eyes with a little sparkle and soft red lips with gloss. Of all types of parties, I *adored* holiday parties. The festive feel. The food. The cozy feeling of being in a warm house with friends.

And knowing I'd get to enjoy this one with Jude didn't hurt.

I packed a small overnight bag just in case, left my car at home and took a cab. That way, I could drink or stay as late as I wanted and not worry about it. I'd maybe even stay over if that was best.

Or stay over at Jude's again.

It took a while to get through downtown and over the Lions Gate Bridge; it was snowing out, lightly, and the roads were starting to get bogged down. But I was still the first to arrive.

Brody was in the kitchen, basting the giant ham he was baking with pineapple rings and cloves stuck to it, and the house smelled amazing. I gave him a warm Christmasy hug and a kiss on the cheek.

"Aren't we in a festive mood," he commented, and I just grinned.

Jessa was downstairs in the party room, where one long table had been set up and beautifully decorated with a red-and-green plaid tablecloth and matching place settings. There was a massive Christmas tree in the corner by the big windows and Christmas music was playing, and Jessa was fussing over her seating arrangement, baby Nick strapped to her front in his carrier thing.

I gave them both a kiss and asked where I could help.

"I'm stuck on the social politics," she said, chewing at her bottom lip. "Like where to seat everyone. I had it worked out, but then with adding your mom in, I had to change some things around... We always split the couples up, to make it more mingly, and do a boy-girl-boy-girl arrangement, if possible. But I can't seem to make it work."

"What politics?"

"You know, Katie and Elle, Dylan and Amber and Ash..." Her voice dropped to a whisper. "Brody and Seth..."

"So? Just do the best you can," I told her, as I glanced at the pretty little place cards she'd made and set out. "We're all adults here—Oh sweet mother of fuck. For the love of all that's good and holy on Christmas Eve, do *not* seat my mom next to Zane."

"Why?" Jessa's eyes went wide. "You think he'll be rude?"

"Um, no. That's not what I was thinking." I plucked the place card with *Cindy* written on it from the table and handed it to her. "Have you met my mom?"

"I have." She seemed to be getting the drift, and plucked a few place cards, rearranging things. "Okay. Let's put your mom next to Jude." She looked at me. "At least you can pre-warn him, and you can trust him, right?"

"Yeah. He's been warned."

"Okay. So she'll go between Jude and Jesse. She already knows my brother decently well, so things will be less... unpredictable."

"Yeah. Other than that time her swimsuit top 'accidentally' popped off in front of him at that barbecue."

"That was, like, twenty million years ago." She glanced at me and grinned. "Maybe she's matured?"

"Maybe we should cancel this whole thing and I'll just go home."

"Moving on," she said sharply. Jessa was really adapting to life as a mommy; already had a little more authority in her voice. It was impressive. "I'm putting Piper between you and Maggie. He knows you both well enough, I'm hoping he'll behave."

"What about Katie?" I suggested. Katie was practically Piper's sister-in-law.

"I have her between Ash and Seth. Oh for Christ's sake, do I need to move Katie and Zane farther apart...? Because that would put Amber next to Ash, which would be weird, because Dylan's all the way over there..."

"Why can't Katie and Zane be close?"

"Because he always flirts with her to piss Jesse off, and if my brother's in a bad mood it's really gonna ruin my Christmas."

"Why would he be in a bad mood?"

"I don't know. He's all annoyed that one of the songs he wrote isn't going on the album now because everyone likes one Zane wrote better..."

"Oh."

"I don't want to put Piper next to Amber. She's new and I don't want him to scare the shit out of her. So." She rearranged a couple more place cards, putting me between Seth and Piper. "That's good, right? You and Piper are cool?"

"Yeah," I said. "Of course we're cool."

Really, I hadn't seen Piper in years, so I had no idea how "cool" we were. Jessa, of course, knew about my entire obsession with him, years ago, and she also knew at some point I'd completely stopped obsessing about him.

I never told her that was because he'd fucked me and then blew me off.

She also knew I'd dated his friend for a long time, on and off. And was now screwing Jude.

So maybe she was right to worry.

"It'll be fine," I assured her. "We'll all be on our best behavior. And if Zane starts any shit with Jesse, we'll just, I don't know, change the subject."

She looked incredibly skeptical, but finally sighed and said, "Okay. I think that's the best we can do."

"Seriously, babe." I put my hands on her shoulders and gave her a steady look. "Trust your friends and family to act like the adults they are. You can't babysit everyone at once."

"I give you that same advice right back, about your mom."

"Fuck." I sighed, and we took one last look over the table. "It's perfect."

Honestly, I had no idea if it was perfect. But last thing I needed to do was heap more drama on Jessa's plate by refusing to sit next to Piper because I was worried Jude might be jealous or something. I didn't want her stressing and rearranging the place settings ad infinitum. She was hosting this thing with a newborn hanging off her boob, for Christ's sake.

"Let me help you with those," I said, taking the stack of fancy snowflake-shaped napkins from her hand and laying them out on the plates like she'd been doing.

I knew most Dirty parties these days were at least somewhat catered, but not the Orphans' Potluck. Everybody was responsible for showing up with something to contribute, food-wise, but obviously that still left a shit-ton of preparation for whoever was hosting.

"I just hope everything turns out well," Jessa said with a little sigh as she stroked Nick's head. "I literally had to tell Zane what to bring, lest he show up with a loaf of bread and a couple of hundred-dollar bills."

"He's done that?"

"He's done that. The man is truly clueless in a kitchen. This year I just went ahead and put him in charge of cranberry sauce and gave him the names of a couple of good delis where he can get some. If he fucks that up, we can probably live without it."

I grinned. "Yeah. But I do love cranberry sauce..."

Gradually, people started showing up, and the room filled around us as the scents of food permeated the house. Dean Martin was singing "Let It Snow! Let It Snow! Let It Snow!" and the tree was all lit up with twinkly lights. It definitely felt like Christmas.

Especially when Jude arrived—and the whole room warmed right up. Or maybe it was just me. He popped his head into the party room and saw me having a drink with Katie, came right over and gave me a hug and a kiss on the cheek. He smelled like snow and fresh winter air and truck exhaust.

"Gotta fry up the turkey," he said, gave Katie a kiss on the forehead, and disappeared outside where the guys were wrestling the deep fryer off Piper's truck. They set it up on the back patio and gathered around it like a bunch of cavemen who'd just discovered fire, while the ladies congregated in the kitchen and party room, prepping the other food and making drinks.

Besides Jesse and Katie, Maggie, Dylan and Amber showed up pretty early. Zane came shortly after that, with a shitload of cranberry sauce and a big tray of Christmas cookies that Dolly had made. Seth and Elle arrived next, then Ash showed up, just when Dylan had started texting him to find out where the fuck he was. When he walked in, he was already drunk, but a few other guests were on their way there too, so no biggie.

It was the holidays after all.

I had one or two before dinner to take the edge off, but after that, I stuck with the non-alcoholic cider that Katie had made—likely, she'd made it in an effort to be thoughtful to Elle and Jessa, who were pregnant and breastfeeding, respectively, because that was just Katie's way.

My mom showed up last, not too long before dinner, so at least there wasn't much time for her to wander the room causing trouble before we'd all be corralled into our pre-assigned seats.

I heard Zane ask Brody who the fuck she was and why she was here, and when Jude cut in and said, "She's Roni's mom and I invited her," Zane got a big-ass grin on his face and looked over at me.

Because obviously there was only one reason Jude would invite my mom to dinner. I figured this was as close as we were getting to Jude admitting he was screwing me.

I just smiled back and sipped my cider.

My mom had dressed, as usual, like a woman two decades younger than she was, a woman who was planning to have Christmas Eve dinner at a sleazy strip joint—you know, before hitting the stage to do her thing. Granted, Cindy Webber looked pretty damn good and a wee bit younger than her forty-nine years, but she also definitely looked—and behaved—overly *available* in a room full of men who were largely non-single.

I had to hand it to her, though; she did have incredible radar when it came to single men and quickly horned in on the only men in the room who weren't here with dates—namely Zane, Piper, and Ash. And immediately got her flirt on. I could hear her loud, ingratiating laugh across the room. And I definitely saw her hands all over Zane, seeking out places the sun didn't shine. Even he looked slightly uncomfortable.

Wasn't sure I'd *ever* seen Zane Traynor uncomfortable.

Ash, on the other hand, seemed to think my mom was a riot, and before long, they were doing shots together.

It really didn't help my outlook for this event.

When Brody told us it was time to put our asses in our seats, we all found our little handmade place cards with our names on them and sat.

It was the first time I'd actually been close to Piper. He'd been out on the patio dealing with the turkey most of the time and drinking beers with Brody, and as soon as he'd walked into the party room, my mom had cornered him by the Christmas tree and peppered him with questions about his Kings cut, which he was wearing over a black sweater. I couldn't remember a time when I'd seen Piper without his cut; it was kind of like a second skin.

Jude definitely hadn't worn his to Christmas Eve dinner.

"Everyone just dig in while it's warm," Brody instructed, "and pass shit around. We'll do a toast and stuff later."

Fine by me. The fuller my mouth was with food, the less I'd have to make small talk with Piper, and the sooner I could get the meal over with and maybe go snuggle up with Jude under the mistletoe.

"Merry Christmas," I said, as we both sat down.

"Merry Christmas..." Piper said, kinda narrowing his eyes.

"Roni," I supplied. Sweet baby Jesus, did he actually forget my name?

"Roni." He smiled a little, and I had no idea what he was thinking. Hopefully it didn't involve a kitchen counter. "I was gonna say Veronica, right? Ben's girl."

Right. So that's what he was thinking.

"Yes, Veronica," I said. "And no, not Ben's girl."

I glanced at Jude. I was on Piper's left, and Jude was seated across from him and two over to the right. Between my mom, on his right, and Brody, who was at the head of the table. Definitely not so far away he couldn't hear us if he wanted to, even though my mom seemed to be talking his ear off already.

He was looking right at me.

"You were seein' him for a while, few years back," Piper said. He passed me the cranberry sauce, and I daubed a bit of it onto my plate.

"I was. Many years back. How is he?"

"Good. He's moved back from Kelowna."

"I didn't even know he was living there."

Damn. Couldn't he make conversation with Maggie? I glanced past him, but Maggie was chatting with Dylan, on her other side.

I could feel the weight of Jude's gaze. I glanced at him and smiled, and mouthed, *Yams*, pointing at the bowl of yams, then at myself. I'd made them and they were awesome, whipped with butter and nutmeg, cloves and cinnamon. I'd gotten the simple recipe from Jessa, and I was thrilled it had turned out perfectly.

Jude's mouth quirked in a tiny smile and he reached for the bowl of yams.

"So," Piper said as I filled my plate. "You seein' my little brother now?"

"Define seeing."

And *little*? I wasn't sure Jude Grayson could be referred to as *little* in any context.

Piper cracked a smile and his gorgeous dimples popped. So like his brother's. Other than their physiques—though Piper was bigger—their damn gorgeous smiles were the most similar things about them.

"Seein' as in seein' him next to you when you wake up in the morning feelin' satisfied."

"Yeah." I looked up into his blue eyes. "Something like that."

"Yeah? You seein' anyone else like that?"

Seriously? He was questioning my loyalty? My intentions with his brother?

Right here and now?

And why was it starting to make me sweat?

It definitely wasn't because I'd had sex with *him*. The fact was, I'd had sex with three men at this table. (Him, Jude and Zane.) I'd made out with two others, too. (Dylan and Ash.) I was really no stranger to sex, casual or otherwise.

It wasn't even the fear that he might say something awful and out-of-line to me, right now.

It was the fear that he might say something awful *about* me—to Jude. That maybe he didn't approve of me. That he might somehow turn Jude against me or something. That this was why Jude didn't want to take me to parties at the clubhouse.

Because Piper might be bothered that I'd once screwed him, and was now screwing his brother?

When I looked at Jude again, he was watching Piper, who was saying to me, "Heard you been rollin' with the Sinners."

When I glanced at Piper again, he definitely wasn't smiling anymore. And I definitely got the feeling he hadn't learned that information from Jude.

I swallowed the lump of turkey and yams that was in my mouth.

"The turkey's fantastic," I told him. "Really juicy."

"I asked you a question."

"No. You didn't. It was definitely more of an accusatory statement."

"You bangin' any Sinners? That's what I'm askin', case it wasn't clear."

"The fuck?" That was Jude, from across the table, and the conversation around us kinda died down. He and Piper locked eyes. "Pipe, *lay off.*" That was pretty much a growl, so yeah, he'd definitely heard what Piper said to me.

Piper kinda chuckled next to me but he went back to his food, as did I, and gradually everyone else did, too.

I chatted a little with Seth on my other side, asked him how the new album had turned out, that kind of thing. The next time I dared look up, my mom and Ash, who were sitting at basically opposite ends of the table, were somehow doing shots together.

They got everyone else raising a toast, and Ash said something boozy about his love for everyone at the table. I really didn't hear it all. I was looking at Jude, who was looking at his brother like he wanted to throttle him.

Then Brody took over the toasting and thanked us all for being here and all that good stuff, and we all cheered and drank.

Piper got talking with Maggie and I ate the rest of my meal in silence, occasionally joining into Jesse and Amber's conversation across the table from me.

Everything seemed to be moving along decently well, and for a few short minutes I allowed myself to think we might actually get through this little Orphans' Potluck without serious incident.

I made eye contact with Jessa, who was seated at the end of the table opposite from Brody, and smiled as if to say, *See? No drama.* She raised her cider to me as if to say, *Thank Christ,* and sipped.

Then things really fell apart.

Piper had turned back to me, and out of nowhere he said, "You look good."

"Thank you."

Then his blue eyes trailed right down my face and deep, *deep* into my cleavage, and he said, "Remember you."

Oh, *fuck*.

Were we doing this?

Really?

His eyes met mine again. The scar down the side of his face made him look extra sinister in the twinkly Christmas lights, and the cranberry sauce and meat in my belly congealed into a brick of dread.

Sweet Jesus. I'd been so worried about my mom doing something horrific, I hadn't even seen *this* coming.

"Noticed they got a decent kitchen counter in this place. Wonder if it's seen any action lately."

Holy. Fuck.

Did he just say that to me?

His face was pretty close to mine, and there was really no mistaking it. The words. The tone. The inference.

Was he actually coming on to me?

Or was he testing me? Checking to see if I'd actually screw him at this dinner party?

And screw over his brother?

I sipped my drink, just trying to stuff down the ugly anger and humiliation that was broiling up in me, sickening and quick.

No. He wouldn't screw Jude like that.

I was pretty damn sure about that.

Which meant he was definitely testing me.

Or maybe Jude was testing me?

I glanced over at Jude. Was there any chance that he'd asked Piper to do this? Put me on the spot like this and test me?

Jude was staring at me, and he did not look happy. The volume of the noise around the table had risen as people gradually finished eating and started drinking more. I had no idea if he'd heard every word Piper just said to me or not.

"You want," Piper said, right close to me, "we can go check it out. If memory serves, you were all too willing last time."

"Pipe. Shut the fuck up."

That was Jude.

"Just askin', brother," Piper said, returning his brother's dead-eye look. "Can't fault a guy for askin'."

"*Stop*," Jude growled.

"Stop what? Just makin' conversation with your girl."

"Stop talkin' to Roni if you can't show respect."

"Guys..." Jesse said.

"Didn't realize I needed your permission to talk to her, brother."

"Maybe you guys want to discuss this outside," Brody said evenly.

"Yeah. Fighting over a woman at the dinner table is so... gauche," Ash said, and threw back another shot.

"Said the man wearing the shirt that says *Jingle My Bells for a White Christmas*," Elle said dryly.

"Not another word," Jude growled at his brother. "Or you can leave."

"Jude..." I said, but he didn't even seem to notice I'd spoken. I felt sick, horrified and humiliated, and he wouldn't even look at me.

"Jude, man," Jesse said. "Pipe, let's go get some air."

"You're kiddin' me," Piper said, making no move to get up. He grinned at his brother, completely undaunted, ignoring Jesse. "You're really sweet on her. Again."

"Get the fuck up from the table before I make you."

"Jude!" I slammed my fork down on my plate, and finally, he looked at me.

It was like a record had stopped, like the needle had scratched its way across the surface and everyone had gone stone silent.

Except that Dean Martin was still crooning out Christmas carols in the background.

I turned to Piper and asked him, very calmly, "What would you like me to do? Go back in time and unfuck all those other guys? You? Ben? Everyone I ever fucked but your brother?"

"Oh my goodness, Roni," my mom slurred, as if I was embarrassing *her*. "Language..."

"I would, you know," I went on, "if it meant I could have him. If it meant he'd stop holding it against me."

Any lingering conversation or attempts to interject had completely died off. I wasn't speaking loudly, but my voice sounded loud in the room.

I looked over at Jude. "Is that what you'd like me to do?" I asked him. "Magically change history so you can get over it?"

"Can we talk about this later?" he said, in a low but softer voice.

"No. I wasn't a virgin when we first got together or even when we first met, and you knew that. You're not exactly a virgin yourself. For all I know you've fucked ten times as many people as I have, but have I ever given you a hard time about it, even once? I haven't. Because I don't care. If you actually care about me and you're done fucking other people, I don't care about your past."

We sat there facing off across the table. In utter, uncomfortable silence.

Dean Martin crooned away.

Someone cleared his throat. Dylan, maybe.

Baby Nick squealed and started crying in his bassinet, and Jessa hurried to attend to him.

"Holy fuck," Zane said. "Please. Someone tell a dick or fart joke, quick."

Maggie sighed.

Jude said nothing.

I tossed my snowflake napkin on the table and walked out.

CHAPTER TWENTY-FOUR

Roni

I GRABBED my jacket and boots and pulled them on, but I didn't head out the front door. Nothing that dramatic.

I just went upstairs, all the way up to the second floor and down the hall to Jessa's writing room. The room Brody had furnished and decorated for her with such love. I pushed through the glass door to the rooftop patio and walked the length of it in the cold.

Snow was falling, but just in sparse, floaty flakes.

I stood by the fire, which wasn't lit, and stared into the little pile of burnt wood feeling sick about that whole ugly scene. *Fucking Piper.*

And Jude... Jude was so damn private about his personal stuff... and here I'd just gone and spilled all our private shit right in front of his friends.

I wasn't sure what to do or say to smooth things over or whatever.

I wanted him to stop holding me at arm's length, treating me like I was just his fuck buddy and all that crap. Tell me and everyone else how much he actually cared about me, if he did. If he really wanted me to be his.

Or maybe just let me fucking go if he didn't.

I also wanted his brother to eat a bag of dicks.

Was there a Christmas card for that? Because Piper Grayson sure deserved one.

I heard footsteps squishing in the inch of snow on the patio and turned to find Jude coming toward me. He'd followed me out from the writing room.

"Sorry," I sighed, because of all things, I really didn't want to fight with him, no matter how upset I was. "For, you know, causing a scene."

"Yeah." He stopped a few very generous feet from me and put his hands in his pockets. Not a good sign. "I'm not a real fan of that. But from where I was lookin', my brother started it."

"Are you really so upset because I had sex with him? I get that he's your brother, but it happened a *decade* ago. I was young. Didn't we both do stupid shit when we were young?"

I stared him down, because for fucking sure he did stupid shit when he was young. Like telling me *we're not goin' down that road* and pushing me away as if I meant nothing to him, *because* I'd fucked his brother.

When he didn't speak, I went on. "Yes, I pursued him for a year. And then he fucked me on the kitchen counter at a party, and that was it."

"I know."

"Well, then... maybe you also know that he made it clear, right afterward, that he wasn't interested in me. And believe me, with that move, I wasn't interested in him anymore either. But yes, your brother touched me. I mean, whatever cooties he left on me are probably long gone by now, but does that make me used goods or something? Forever? Am I just too dirty for you?"

"You're not dirty, Roni."

"Then what's the problem? Why am I being accosted by your brother at Christmas dinner?"

He shook his head. "I'm gonna talk to him about that. He's got no business—"

"Yeah, he does," I said. "If he really thinks he's looking out for you. Saying the shit to me that you should be saying yourself."

He drew a deep breath.

"If you've got a problem with me, Jude, you need to just say it already."

I hugged myself against the cold as he stared at me.

"You think it's about the guys you've been with," he said, slowly. "It's not. It used to be about that. It's not about that anymore."

"Then what is it about?"

He was silent for a moment as the little flakes of snow fluttered down between us, just looking at me.

Then he said, "I once saw Brody's dad punch him."

I stared at him, stunned and a little confused. "What?"

He looked away. "He *tried* to punch him. Took a swing. A good swing. But Brody was sixteen and pretty built by then, so you can guess how that turned out for his dad."

"Yeah..." I said, hugging myself tighter. "I guess."

Jude's dark eyes met mine again. "I know kids are abused every day, Roni. I've seen abuse. I've seen violence. I've caused violence. But I've never seen a more disturbing abuse of power than a grown man who should've been a father figure and a protector physically shoving a teenage girl away from him and out the door of her own damn house like she was nothing to him, shoving her down the stairs and shuttin' that door in her face."

As he spoke, tingles skittered through my body in a slow, slow shiver. And it wasn't from the cold. I really wasn't sure what he was talking about. Not exactly. I didn't remember, exactly. But I *knew*.

I knew he was talking about me.

"I know you were pushed around," he said. "I saw your mom's boyfriend shove you out that door. And right in front of Jessa." He took a step closer to me and stopped. "Maybe there was worse abuse than that. Maybe you'll tell me about it sometime. That's up to you. But what I saw that day... it was enough to stay with me for the rest of my damn life. To shape how I saw you, what I thought about you and how I felt about you. But I still can't imagine how it felt for *you*."

I was speechless. Totally stunned.

I had no idea he'd ever seen anything like that or knew a thing about what went on in my home. Of all the things I'd ever confided in him, that was not one of them.

"I don't remember that," I confessed. It wasn't something I'd ever really talked about. But I was grown-up now; I could talk about it, with him. "There *were* other times. I don't even remember that specific time, that's how many times there were."

Yes, kids were abused. I was one of them. But the abuse was never severe. I rarely went to school with hidden bruises. Not all of my mom's boyfriends were cruel to me. It didn't affect me long-term. It didn't inform my choices with men, the types of men I chose or how they treated me... And there were a million other excuses I made to convince myself that it wasn't that bad, it didn't matter, it didn't mark me. I wasn't eternally damaged. It was in the past.

And yet, here we were.

"You asked me if I ever lied to you," he said. "Then you told me you weren't afraid of me. When are you gonna stop lyin' to me?"

I didn't say anything. I didn't even know how to answer that.

He was right; I was totally fucking afraid of him... and what he could do to me.

"You've spent all your life tryin' to prove to everyone around that you're a tough girl. I know you're strong, Roni. You don't have to prove that to me."

I said nothing.

"Maybe you've just never let yourself consider that we could have a relationship where you don't end up gettin' hurt."

"Maybe," I said, my voice small.

I knew I was getting hurt. No matter how this played out, I was getting hurt, right?

I knew he was leaving soon, that after the New Year's Eve event I might never even see him again. That in the New Year he'd be leaving on tour.

That there would be other women for him.

I'd always known that. His life was with the band, the MC.

But there would be no one else for me. I knew that by now; that he was the only man for me.

If I couldn't have him, what then? A life of empty loves with the wrong men, my mom's fucked up life?

"Maybe you don't have to try so hard to protect yourself from me."

Yeah. Maybe that too.

"Maybe you could let me in."

I just stared at him.

"I've grown up," he said. "Somewhat."

"I know that."

"I'm never gonna push you around, Roni, in any way."

"I know that, too." My voice actually trembled. "But... don't you know there are worse ways you can hurt me than that?"

He didn't answer that.

"That man who pushed me out the door?" I said. "I didn't love him."

Jude took another slow step toward me.

"I know I've walked away from you, more than once," he said. "And that cut you. I meant it to cut you. But like I said, I grew up. I'm here, but you've gotta meet me in the fuckin' middle, V. You've gotta step into it. You can't lie to me. You can't stand there and act like you don't need me. Like I'm not the one for you, if that's what I am. Like you're never gonna give me a chance to win back your trust."

I knew I'd been doing that. Holding myself back. Withholding my trust.

But I just didn't know he knew it.

I'd never lied to myself about my feelings for him.

But I'd definitely lied to him.

"I want to be with you," he said. "I want *you*. I've always wanted you. Like you have no idea how fuckin' much. But I gotta tell you, I would never take anything less than all of you, V."

Oh my God. Warmth flooded me, hearing those words...

I want you.

I've always wanted you.

I'd been waiting so long to hear those words out of Jude's mouth... it was like I'd been waiting my whole damn life.

It felt like I'd forgotten to breathe for a while, so I sucked in some air. Then I took a tentative step toward him.

"Okay. So... this is all of me. I do trust you. I trust you with my life," I told him, and it was the truth. "I guess it's just my heart I'm a little more precious about."

"Yeah." He smiled a bit, but it was a sad smile. "I got that."

"And you've gotta step into it, too," I told him. "I want all of you, and then some. I want everything you've got and everything you didn't even know you had to give. I want it all, and I want it now. I'm greedy, and I'm not a patient woman, Jude Grayson."

"Yeah." His smile deepened. "I got that, too."

"I don't want to spend the rest of my life waiting for you."

"I know. I'm here, darlin'. I'm in."

I nodded, absorbing that.

I'm in.

Holy shit...

I took another deep breath. I was shaking a little, all over. Still scared, maybe, that he was going to change his mind and push me away—again. "I can learn to trust, Jude. Maybe it just doesn't come so easily for me or my heart."

His smile faltered, his eyes softening in a way that made me totally melt. "I'm sorry I broke it."

"You did," I said, and the tears welled up in my eyes so fast I couldn't stop them.

He started to reach for me and I knew he was gonna pull me into his arms. But before he could pull me close, I took that final step and wrapped my arms around him instead.

He hugged me tight as I put my head on his chest. He rested his chin on my head and said, "You broke mine too, V. I know you didn't mean to, but you did."

"I'm so sorry."

"No sense bein' sorry for something that was never your fault."

"I should've seen it sooner," I said, shaking my head.

"Seen what?"

I looked up into his face, into his gorgeous dark eyes. "That you were the one."

He kissed me then, softly and without any tongue. I could feel his heartbeat in his lips against mine. He tasted of bourbon and pineapple and cloves.

"I take it you liked the ham..." I murmured.

I peeked up into his face and he raised an eyebrow at me.

"You are the one, Jude Grayson."

I pressed my body up into his to keep warm, and as his gaze held mine, I felt that undeniable spark between us catch fire... seconds before he slammed his mouth down over mine. And this time, there was a *lot* of tongue.

"You still cryin'?" he asked me after a few minutes of making out. "'Cause I'm gettin' turned on, and I don't wanna be that guy."

"I'm not crying. I'm horny." I kissed him again. "I don't do the crying thing very often. Horny is more my style."

"Good. 'Cause I really don't wanna see you cry." He wiped the remnants of a tear off my cold cheek with his thumb. "C'mon. Let's go inside before we turn into snowmen."

We headed through the nearest doorway seeking warmth—which happened to be the French doors that led into Jessa and Brody's bedroom. As soon as we were inside and slipping off our jackets, I grabbed his arm, tugging him back. "We don't have to go back down right away though, right? I mean, I'd pretty much finished my dinner."

"Me too."

I tugged him into the en suite bathroom and we shut the door, and he immediately yanked my leather leggings down around my ankles. By the time he'd done that, his dick was in his hand, hard and ready.

"Damn, you work fast."

He grinned his gorgeous, rare grin. "Aim to please."

Before he got all cocky about it, I informed him, "You know, you look like your brother when you grin."

The smile faltered and his eyes narrowed at me. "Do not talk to me about my brother when my dick's out."

I grinned and kissed him, kicking off my boots, then shimmied my panties down around my ankles, pulling both feet completely free of the leggings and panties. I wrapped one naked leg around his hip as he put on a condom. "I love it when you come all prepared like a Boy Scout."

"I know you do." Then he shoved into me. He gripped my ass with his big hands, hiking me up on his hips, and I wrapped both legs around him. He carried me toward the counter, looking for somewhere to put me.

"Oh. Please don't do me on the counter," I said. It was just too reminiscent of the whole Piper thing, the conversation too fresh. He seemed to understand, and put me up against the door instead. He hooked his arms under my thighs and looked in my eyes.

Then, just when I'd braced myself, expecting him to start pounding, he kissed me instead, slow and deep.

Then he eased his cock into me, filling me slowly... and a warm rush that felt like love and lust all mixed up together spread through my body.

I closed my eyes, just savoring it.

"I ever tell you I love you, Roni Webber?" Jude murmured in his low, rough voice.

I opened my eyes. He was looking at me, his gaze intent on my mouth.

"Not in so many words. Or any words, really. But... I kinda knew. For maybe five minutes. You know, before you broke my heart."

His dark eyes met mine. "I love you."

Then he kissed me, hot and deep, as he fucked me against the bathroom door. It was slow but it was passionate and it was Jude, so at some point I definitely heard the door or the door frame crack behind me.

"Oh, *shit*..." I was right on the edge of orgasm when it happened. "I think... baby, I think we broke the door."

"Mmm," he said, kissing my neck as he thrust into me one last time—and I fell apart. The pleasure slammed through me... Christmas fireworks gradually fading to yuletide logs sparking in the night.

My legs quickly turned to jelly, so I had to unwrap them from his hips and put my feet on the floor. I shoved gently at his chest. "Lie down."

He lay down on the floor and I climbed on, ramming my hips against him as I took him in a fast, hungry pace... gasping and sweating until we both went over, together.

As I sat on top of him, my hands on his chest, panting and slowly rocking my hips, we both kinda floated back to reality. I asked him, "Did I mention that I love you, too?"

"You inferred."

"Great. Then I guess you don't need to hear it..."

He ran his hands up under my sweater and squeezed my breasts through my bra. "Don't be a brat. I wanna hear it."

"I love you, Jude."

"Say it again, darlin'."

I reached to place my hands on the floor on either side of his head, and lowered my chest down to his. He extracted his hands from my sweater to bury them in my hair. I whispered, "I. Love. You. Jude." I put a kiss on his face between each word.

He smoothed my hair back from my face and we kissed for a couple of minutes. Just kissed, over and over.

Then he sighed, a deep, satisfied sigh. "Guess we should get up. Floor's cold, and you know I gotta go pound my brother's head into the concrete now."

"Why?"

"For bein' rude to you."

I smiled. Then, just to be certain... "You really didn't put him up to that?"

"Fuck, no. You think I'd let anyone talk to you like that?"

Guess not.

"Please," I said softly. "No head pounding on my account. But...

I wouldn't be totally opposed to you bitch slapping him in front of everyone. I mean, if you think it's necessary."

He grinned. "I'll seriously consider that."

When I walked back down to the party room, Jude right behind me, Jesse was standing there at the bottom of the stairs like he'd been waiting for us.

"All good?" he asked.

"Yup," Jude said. We'd stopped, but we stood about a foot apart. I wanted to slip my arm around his waist, but something held me back.

Despite his declaration of love to me in a bathroom, while his dick was in me, I still wasn't exactly sure if he'd want me to.

Men could be weird like that.

"Pipe's out back," Jesse said, "having a beer with Brody."

"Yeah. Let him stay there. Hope his nuts freeze off."

Jesse smirked, then looked at me. "You want a drink, Roni?"

And that small kindness from Jude's best friend went straight to my heart. "Yeah. I'd love that. One of those delicious ciders your wife made. With some booze in it."

"You can get me a bourbon or something, since you're gettin'," Jude said.

"Coming up."

And just like that, Jesse Mayes, rock star, headed off to get me a drink.

"You okay?" Jessa approached and ran her hand down my arm, giving me her worried mommy look.

"I'm good."

"She's perfect," Jude said. "Think I broke your bathroom door, though. Tell your man to send me the bill." Then he slipped his hand into mine.

Jessa saw it. "Okay, then." She looked at me and when I smiled, she gave me a dorky smile right back, one that reminded me of when we were teenagers.

"Don't look now," I said, giving Jude's hand a little squeeze as Jessa turned away, "but you're holding my hand in front of everyone."

"Yup. Got a problem with it?"

"Nope."

"Good. 'Cause I'm about to drag you under that ball of mistletoe over there and kiss the fuck out of you, too."

"That one?" I pointed at the mistletoe that hung over the windows, by the tree.

"That one."

"Everyone's gonna see it."

"Which is exactly why I'm gonna do it."

And that was exactly what he did.

CHAPTER TWENTY-FIVE

Jude

I WALKED BACKSTAGE, feeling the electric energy of the crowd building out front. The opening band had finished their set a little while ago and everything was set for Dirty to take the stage.

Everyone who was supposed to be here was here, and so far the New Year's Eve event was rolling smoothly along.

Jessa and Nick had come by early, before the opening band went on, to take a look around and fawn over Roni's success. Then Bishop had taken them home.

I'd already been here for hours doing my thing, and so had Roni. And every time I glimpsed her across the room, or down some hall, talking to people and looking like she did... I got proud. I got a soft, warm feeling in my chest that I liked, a fuck of a lot.

On Christmas Day, I'd taken her to Christmas dinner at my mom's place, and if there'd been any shred of doubt left in my mind that Roni Webber was the woman for me (there wasn't), seeing the instant mutual affection and respect between her and my mom would've erased it. I couldn't think of much that would make me melt more than the two most important women in my life getting along.

Piper had even managed to dig up some manners and generally keep his mouth shut.

In the small area right behind the stage and off to one side, I found the band hanging out; just Brody and the members of Dirty. This was their sacred space where no one else would be allowed to join in. This was how it'd been on the first world tour, and we'd decided it was a good practice to bring back. Give the band a few minutes together before they went onstage, with no one else in the way. No one but me and Brody. Maggie was welcome too, but knowing her, she'd stay out of the way anyway, unless she was needed.

I could see down behind the stage to a hall that ran underneath, where a bunch of crew and security were hanging out. And there was Roni, looking gorgeous as fuck in her black silk blouse, tight black skirt and fuck-me heels, her black hair all smoothed down and her lips a glossy red that I was gonna enjoy seeing all over my dick later.

"She did great, yeah?" Brody said, beside me.

"Yeah," I said. "She did incredible."

Then Brody shook my hand and pulled me in for a hug, because that's what he always did before a show.

I moved over to Jesse, and when he saw me, he nodded over toward Elle and Seth. Elle was looking curvy, the little baby bump in her belly showing through her short, gold-glitter dress.

"The fuck are we gonna do without her?" Jesse said.

"Don't know. Gotta say, it's not gonna be the best." I couldn't really see anyone else onstage with Dirty playing bass. Elle had been with the band since the beginning. "You all need each other to make this thing what it is. What it's supposed to be."

"Yeah. Kinda makes the having-Seth-back thing a little anticlimactic. Won't be the five of us up there."

"Yeah, but tonight it will. So... enjoy it." I clapped him on the shoulder, and he gave me a big-ass hug. I couldn't even imagine what it would've been like if I'd told him *I* wasn't coming on the tour. Jesse had never toured without me.

Even if I'd ever told him I was *considering* not coming on the tour, he'd probably have thrown a world class hissy and trashed the place.

I went to check on Dylan and Seth and Elle. Dylan was kicked back in his kilt, one foot up on his other knee, drumming on his boot. His usual pose before a show. Seth and Elle were standing next to him, his arm around her waist.

"You good?" I asked Elle. Not like I'd know what to do if she wasn't; the baby in her belly was more of a lady issue than I was accustomed to handling. But I'd get Maggie on it quick, if she needed anything.

"I'm good. I'm sad," she said, right through her soft smile. I could see it in her eyes. She was torn. We were all torn about her leaving the tour.

"Well, we'll take care of you on the road, you know that. Whatever you need, you'll have it. Keep you comfortable while your man does his thing."

"I know that," she said, and gave me a hug and a kiss on the cheek. "Thanks, Jude."

Then I shook Seth's hand. "It's gonna be a good year, brother," I told him, looking him steady in the eyes. Of all the men in our little family, I was pretty sure I was happier than anyone, save maybe Zane, that Seth was back with the band.

"Yeah," he said, "it is." Then he pulled me in for a hug.

"You gonna play 'Blackout' for me tonight?" It was my favorite song from the new album; the heaviest song.

"Yup," he said, and I patted him on the back.

Then I dropped down into a squat next to Dylan. "You good?"

"Yeah, man. How's it look out there?"

"Looks like a bunch of horny kids lookin' to party. Few MILFs, few hipsters, few bikers, the usual."

He grinned.

"Saw Ash out there with some piece," I told him, and I watched his smile kinda fade. "Lookin' pretty rough."

"Yeah. I saw him."

"That kid gonna be okay?"

"He's fine."

"You know," I said, "you ever want him to stop comin' to Dirty shows, you just gotta say the word." I felt like it needed to be said. I had no problem with Ash. But if he was causing problems for Dylan, for his performance, or just fucking with his head, that wasn't gonna stand.

And definitely, something had been fucked up since whatever went down between them. According to Con's intel, they'd both been fucking Amber, then only Dylan was fucking Amber and Ash had turned into a one-man gong show overnight, drinking and fucking his way through the Lower Mainland.

I'd been meaning to check in with Dylan on this for a while now. But ever since a certain sexy-as-fuck woman had pretty much hijacked my attention, there'd been a few conversations I'd been meaning to have that had fallen by the wayside.

"No," Dylan said. "It's not like that. If Ash wants back later, just let him in."

"Alright, brother. Felt like I had to mention it."

"Appreciate it."

I wasn't sure he did. He might actually be a little pissed at me for even suggesting Ash might be unwelcome, but oh-the-fuck-well. It fell under my job description to make sure no one unwelcome was welcomed. But I was only gonna mention it once.

This moment on, I'd happily keep my nose the fuck out of Dylan and Ash's bromance unless Dylan ever brought it up.

I clapped him on the shoulder as I stood up and headed over to check on Zane.

He was standing just off to the side, behind a wall of amps, smoking weed—alone.

I happened to know that no one in the band mind-fucked themselves before a show like Zane did. It was why he pretty much always smoked up right before he went onstage. I wouldn't call it stage fright, exactly. More like he psyched himself out somehow, tore himself down, right before he built himself back up. Nerves, maybe. Some kind of self-doubt.

He never talked about it, but I could see it.

I wasn't even sure if the rest of the band really saw it. It wasn't something I'd mention to Jesse. Jesse and Zane liked to needle each other's weak spots, and Zane didn't need any needling over this.

Brody saw it, and the both of us did what we could to make sure Zane was solid before he went onstage. For my part, that meant clearing people the fuck out of his space to give him room to deal with whatever shit was going on in his head, have his smoke, and mentally get where he needed to get.

"Happy fuckin' New Year," I said, giving him a little punch on the shoulder. "You ready for this or what?"

"Always ready, brother," he said, but he looked distracted as fuck. "Who's that guy?" He tipped his chin and I followed his gaze, down behind the stage... and saw Maggie standing with some of the crew and a couple of my security guys.

"Maddox. He's with me tonight." I looked at Zane, watching him watch Maddox and Maggie talking. "He's a King. You've met him."

"Right." He smoked his joint, his jaw kinda rigid. "Keep an eye on her, huh?" He didn't say her name, but I knew who he meant.

I watched as he put out the joint on the side of an amp and flicked it into the dark—just as the lights out front dropped and the crowd noise swelled.

"You know," he said, "lots of fucking drunk assholes at this thing."

"Sure, brother."

He turned toward the stage just as Jesse walked by, smacking me on the shoulder and giving Zane a shove.

Zane shoved back, just lightly. Jesse had his guitar slung on and did a little air guitar riff on it, then walked out onstage. The crowd exploded. Dylan and Elle followed him out. Seth went next, and I patted him on the back.

"Hey," I said, as Zane started after them. When he glanced back at me, I told him, "Make 'em happy out there."

It was pretty much what I told him before every show. Since day one, that was pretty much the summary of Zane's job at a Dirty show.

Make the crowd happy.

And Zane Traynor was damn good at his job.

"Always do," he said.

Then he headed out onstage.

I sighed.

It wasn't exactly the first time Zane had asked me to keep an eye on Maggie at a show or wherever. Or asked me about some guy she was talking to.

Who the fuck is that dickwit?

Did you see that fuckwad with Maggie?

Can you tell that asshat to move the fuck along?

I was getting used to these questions.

I didn't love what they told me, because they told me shit I really did not want to know.

Shit I did not want to have to deal with.

I watched from the side of the stage as the band kicked into "Get Made." Great, heavy, sexy song to start their set off and set the tone for this event.

Then I headed off to do my rounds.

Later, while Dirty was still onstage and I was still doing my rounds, I headed out back to find Piper talking to a few of my guys in the alley. He was wearing a plain black motorcycle jacket, and I pulled him aside.

"Thanks for leavin' your colors at home," I said, with somewhat mock gratitude. "I know it fuckin' pains you."

Fuck if I could remember the last time I'd seen my brother wear any kind of leather without Kings shit all over it—but last thing I needed was him or anyone else showing up in Kings colors, drawing attention, twitching up the police and causing drama at Roni's event. She'd worked too hard for that shit.

"Thanks for invitin' me," he said, with the same mock gratitude right back. He was smoking a joint and offered it to me, but I declined. "Your girl put together a good show?"

"Yeah. Band's happy. Brody's happy. Everything's goin' smooth."

"Good."

I took a big breath. No point dragging out the small talk. "I'm stayin' Nomad. If you guys'll let me."

Piper stared at me. And right now, seeing him like this, just kinda dressed like a normal dude... he seemed just like some normal dude, and not the VP of the West Coast Kings.

My brother.

"You know we'll let you, brother."

"I'm goin' on the road with Dirty."

"Yeah." He looked fucking disappointed. Sad, actually. I hated putting that look on his face. "Not like I didn't know."

"You knew?"

"If you were staying, you would've told me long ago."

Well, fuck.

He shrugged, as if to say *Whatever*, but I knew this was important to him. Piper had done about everything over the years, short of actually chaining me to the floor, to make me stay. "I know it's a tough decision."

"It is."

He looked at me for a minute, considering. "You're not stayin' for her?"

I gave him a dark look that said, *None of your fucking business.*

But truth was, I was *going* for her.

Roni was one of my primary reasons for going on the road with the band. Because stepping into it with her—bringing her into my life—meant I had to protect her from MC shit in every way I could; same as I did with Jesse. She'd be welcome at the clubhouse. She'd be *with* me in every way.

But the less *I* was involved in Kings shit, day-to-day, the better it would be for both of us.

And the safer it would be for her.

"She'll be on the road with me," I informed him, "sometimes. And when she's not, she'll be here. And if I ever call you up and ask you to look in on her or help her out with something—"

"Then I will," he said, in all seriousness. "You know I will."

"And you'll drop your attitude toward her."

His eyes narrowed. And yeah, I knew people didn't talk to Jeremy "Piper" Grayson this way. But he was my brother, and I did when necessary.

"Just lookin' out for you, brother," he said.

"She's not the enemy."

"Yeah."

"And you're not gonna disrespect her or call her a slut or make any mention of the time you fucked her at that party and then tossed her away like trash."

"Brother—"

"She wasn't trash. She was seventeen. I don't wanna hear you say an ugly word about her, ever. She's with me now. She's not public property and she's not some club slut you think you can pass around. She's mine."

"You done?"

"For now."

Piper tossed his joint into the shadows. "Am I allowed to take bets on how soon she ditches your cranky ass?"

"No."

"Then I guess I'll see you both at the table next Christmas."

"Yeah. If your ungrateful ass gets an invite."

His eyebrows went up, and amusement flickered over his face. Piper always came to the Orphans' Potluck, and no way Mom was gonna ban him on Christmas Day, so it was an empty threat. He knew it. But he got my meaning.

"How 'bout I apologize to her for bein' a dick. That increase my odds?"

"Be a start," I grumbled.

Piper grinned, his dimples slicing into his cheeks.

What the fuck now.

I turned to follow his line of sight... where Roni had just popped out the back door to talk to Con and Bane, looking hot as hell in her silky blouse and tight skirt and high heels.

"Just surprised you managed to lock that down, little brother. Wild Card Webber," my brother mused. "She get prettier? Or did I just get more sober?"

"Christ, you're an asshole," I muttered, starting to walk away. "And don't go smilin' at her. Keep your damn dimples to yourself."

11:58 pm.

"Come on! Are you kidding me?" Roni scolded me, waving me over as I strolled toward her. "I thought you were gonna miss it."

"No chance."

I'd just walked into the VIP room, where she was waiting on me. It was an enclosed room with a giant one-way window overlooking the nightclub floor and the stage below. The lights were off so we could see everything down in the club, and we were the only ones in the room. Because that was part of Roni's deal when she planned out this event.

The VIP room was closed.

When Dirty went offstage, they'd go park their asses in the club right alongside the fans. We'd roped off some tables for the band members and their dates and a few other guests, a seriously limited VIP section, right down beside the dance floor, and I had a whole team of guys down there, some in security shirts and some in plain clothes. So it would feel like everyone in the room was partying with the band.

All Roni's idea, and it was a good one.

As I approached the window where she was waiting and practically bouncing up and down, Dirty had just rocked out the last notes of their final song of the night. A Dirty classic, "Dead Crazy."

Some lights had come up over the stage, illuminating the band as they put aside their instruments and hugged each other. Dylan tossed drumsticks into the crowd. Zane peeled off his sweaty shirt and tossed it to his admirers.

The show was done.

The crowd was going crazy.

Total success.

I glanced at my girl, who was applauding even though no one could hear her or see her but me. The lights spilling over us from the club lit her up in a sexy red, violet and blue glow, flickering over her pale skin and dark hair. And the world's happiest grin curved those sexy lips.

So gorgeous.

Zane grabbed his mic and asked what time it was, and people screamed. Elle held up her iPhone so he could see the screen and Zane shouted, "GET READY TO KISS SOMEONE 'CAUSE THIS SHIT IS GOING DOWN, FUCKERS!"

Someone backstage was handing bottles of champagne to Dylan, and he handed a couple to Jesse.

Seth took Elle's hand.

I grabbed Roni's hand and pulled her close to me. She beamed her gorgeous smile on up at me.

"HERE. WE. GO!" Zane shouted.

And then a shitload of voices joined in as he started counting down.

"Ten! Nine! Eight! Seven! Six!..."

But I didn't need a countdown. I just laid a kiss on Roni.

"Five! Four! Three! Two! One!"

Midnight.

"HAPPY MOTHERFUCKING NEW YEAR MOTHERFUCKERS!"

Zane's voice roared through the room. I was still kissing Roni.

I heard some laughter and mic feedback and no doubt the band was hugging and kissing and dumping champagne on each other.

Then I could feel the shift as the lights started to go down again; even though my eyes were closed, I could tell the whole club got darker. But this was no "Auld Lang Syne" moment. Almost immediately, a deep, resonant, repetitive beat started rising.

Roni broke our kiss and bounced excitedly. "Oooh, here she comes!"

I followed her gaze to the stage. The band was just clearing out, bodies disappearing into the dark as the lights gradually dropped off. Until only one light, a cluster of spinning beams, shot down through a sudden, rising fog—on Zane, standing center stage. He was spraying champagne on the front couple of rows of screaming fans.

"You're in for a treat, kids," he growled into his mic. "The beautiful, unstoppable DJ SUMMER." Then he tossed the mic and disappeared into the rising fog as he headed offstage.

There was a screech of feedback, then someone turned off the mic.

A repeating echo of Zane's voice rumbling *DJ SUMMER* faded out, as a couple of famous lines from one of Dirty's biggest party anthems, "Love Struck," rose, louder and louder, along with a heavy Jesse Mayes guitar riff; it was Elle's voice, then Zane's voice, repeated over and over...

Good girls?

We got any good girls here tonight?

Good girls?

We got any good girls here tonight?

The beat kept rising, Elle's and Zane's voices looping around and around, and the crowd kept screaming. A woman's silhouette appeared and then Summer ran up the steps to her deck, which had been set up at one side of the stage.

She wore a silver bodysuit, unzipped low, with some generous cleavage, white fur boots and a sleek white sparkly wig. She raised her hand high in the air and the crowd did the same, clapping and screaming. She curled her hand into a fist and the fist stayed up in the air, holding, holding, as the voices kept looping...

Good girls?

We got any good girls here tonight?

Then Summer dropped her fist like a hammer and the house

exploded with lights and a heavy-as-fuck, insanely cool beat on a remix of "Love Struck."

Roni started rocking her sexy body in my arms.

"I'm not gonna pretend to understand the whole DJ thing," I said in her ear, but I pulled her round ass against me as she moved.

Roni looked at me over her shoulder like I was crazy.

I shrugged. "Not really my kinda music."

"Just give her your ears," Roni said, "for the next three hours, and trust me, you'll get it." She looked out into the club. "Summer's a master. She's gonna mix in bits of songs you recognize, working her way into some really dirty, danceable ghetto funk, sampling in some rock to punch up the energy. Then when everyone's danced their asses off to the point that she knows they never want to stop... she'll hit them with some *really* heavy bump 'n' grind, so they wanna fuck right on her dance floor."

"Other than the fuckin' part, I have no idea what you just said."

She laughed. "Think of her as, like, a mad conductor. She'll read the vibe of the room, the energy and response of the crowd. Pretty much like at a rock show, but she can adjust as she goes. She'll pull back when it feels right, push harder when it feels right, bring the whole room along with her. It'll all build to this ecstatic peak, and then she'll run them right off the cliff with her when it's time." She turned in my arms and slipped her arms around my neck, pressing her curves against me. "It's why people do certain drugs at a show like this. You pop a few pills at the right time, the high hits you right as the music peaks. And it's like one giant orgasm."

"Huh. I'm startin' to see the appeal."

"Plus, you get to dance."

"Nope. Sorry, babe. I do not dance."

"Is that right?" She pushed me back toward a couch. "Well, I do. Sit your ass down."

I sat.

She then started twisting her hips to Summer's remix of "Love Struck," which was full-on pumping through the club now, and the way she rolled her hips... Jesus and fuck. Girl could move.

"Yeah?" she said, watching me as she ran her hands down her body. "You like that?"

"Yeah. I like that."

"Then don't move."

I wasn't going anywhere.

She swiveled her hips in little figure-eights and started unbuttoning her shirt. She did it slow, but there weren't many buttons to delay the inevitable. She turned and peeled the shirt off one shoulder, then the other, peeking at me over her shoulder... and my cock swelled.

She stripped the shirt completely off and tossed it at me. I caught it and as she turned back to me, smoothing her hands over her bra, she laughed at what had to be the stunned look on my face, losing her rhythm.

"Wait, wait," she fumbled, giggling, "I can do this." She caught her rhythm again and I was hypno-fucking-tized.

It was her hands that really did it. They wandered over her body, smoothing over her curves, and my dick hardened in response. The smile was gone from her face and her eyes locked onto mine as she drifted nearer.

She hooked her thumbs inside the waist of her skirt and shimmied it down over her hips, let it drop and stepped out of it. Then she tossed that at me too. I caught it and held onto both of them, her shirt and her skirt, as she worked her way closer.

When she was halfway to me, she turned around and bent over, her perfect ass in the air, and grabbed her ankles.

"Damn," I said.

She came back up, arching her back and tossing her hair down her back.

I had to shift my hips to try to find more room in the front of my jeans. *Jesus Christ.* Where did she learn moves like this?

Then she smoothed her hands over her panties and did a slow, hip-swiveling turn to face me. Her hands continued down her thighs, down to her knees, and the next thing I knew she was on her knees, crawling toward me, hips rolling all the way, like a cat in heat.

Her eyes were locked on mine and her cheeks were flushed. She looked amused… and turned on.

As she reached my feet, she put her hands on my knees, bit her plump bottom lip and spread my legs with force. The aggressive move sent a fiery signal straight to my balls.

I balled up her clothes in my fists. Then she pushed herself into me and up, dragging her chest against me from my spread thighs all the way to my face.

Then she burst out laughing. "Something like that. I can't remember all the moves." She stood up and tussled her hair. "I took a class a while ago, just for fun. This is the first time I actually tried the moves out on a man."

"You kiddin' me?" I tossed her clothes aside and got up, my ego swelling—right along with my dick—that she'd never done that for anyone else. I walked her right up against the window. "You are not done. You do not get to talk to me about musical orgasms, then wiggle that ass all over the place for me like that, shove your tits in my face and just stop."

I put my hands on her hips, hooked my thumbs into her panties, and started taking them right off.

"Oh… well… I… oh, *damn*… Jude… "

Roni's feeble protests and her soft little hands kinda pushing at me but not pushing at me when I got down on my knees and started eating her pussy were adorable.

"But… I should… *oh, fuck*… go down and… you know… talk to the band and… stuff…"

"Later." I swirled my tongue around her clit, getting her all wet and trembling, then dug the condom out of my pocket. I'd put one in every fucking pocket I had, optimistic as fuck about bringing the New Year in together with a bang. Or several bangs.

I worked my jeans down and got the condom on while I lapped at her pussy, just teasing her a bit, and she struggled, maybe trying to get comfortable while her legs wanted to give out.

Then I got to my feet, hiked her legs up around my waist and buried myself in her... so fucking hot and tight... and fucked her right there against the giant glass window.

Her bare ass squeaked against the glass as I rammed into her. She giggled her throaty laugh, even as she groaned in pleasure. She wrapped her arms tight around my neck, holding on. "Oh, *shit*... it feels... like I'm gonna fall..."

"I got you."

"I feel like... everyone can see my... everything..."

"Yeah. And you fuckin' love it."

I fucked her with the music thumping and the bass vibrating the glass until we'd smeared the window with sweat, and we both came.

She went first.

I went with the feel of her pussy squeezing my dick, her throaty screams in my ears, her sweat-damp body wrapped tight around mine.

Maybe I didn't know shit-all about Summer's style of music, but hey, it got me laid. I wasn't complaining.

Then my knees started wanting to fold. I set Roni back on her feet, planting a kiss on her head. "Get dressed."

"What, now you're modest?" She swatted my bare ass just before I pulled up my jeans. "Three seconds ago you couldn't have cared if they projected us over the stage down there."

"That was when my dick was up."

She laughed and got dressed, buttoning up her blouse. "Damn, I'm all sweaty." She smoothed her hair. "Totally worth it, though. I so needed that."

"What, that?" I gestured at the window.

"Yeah. That was maximum tension relief. I was *so* nervous tonight."

"Couldn't tell," I said, honestly. "Don't think I've ever seen you nervous."

"Yes, you have. That night when I was eighteen, at the Back Door, and you blew me off." She glanced at me around the curve of her black hair. "I was nervous as hell."

I finished pulling on my shirt. She was slipping her high heels back on.

I walked over and as she stood up, I got close to her face. "V..."

"What?" She blinked her green eyes at me. "I still remember every word you said. How it made me feel. *You and me, we're not goin' down that road.* You took my hand and that's what you said to me." She swallowed and gazed up into my eyes in a way I probably didn't deserve for that bullshit. "But... I would've gone down any road with you."

I took her hand and twined my fingers through hers, just like I did that night. I still remembered it, too. How soft and small and warm her hand felt in mine. How much it killed me she'd been with my brother. How much it killed me to push her away.

And I felt the connection between us now, just like I did then. The want I had for her. For *more.*

More of her.

More of *us.*

So this time, I told her the truth.

"You and me, darlin', we're goin' down the longest road there is."

CHAPTER TWENTY-SIX

Roni

"HEY YOU. WHAT TIME IS IT?"

Jude looked over at me, in no particular hurry. "It's Saturday," he said. "Who the fuck cares?"

He was just finishing hanging up the big black-and-white photo on canvas of him and Piper with their dad—on my living room wall.

I smiled and went to grab my phone from my purse. "Just want to make sure I give myself enough time to get ready. You're coming tonight, right?"

"Yup. Gonna swing by with Jesse and Katie to catch the end of the set and pick your sexy ass up." He stood back and examined his hanging job. "This look straight to you?"

"Hmm." I came to stand next to him and looked at the photo, tilting my head at various angles, considering.

"Are you shittin' me?"

I grinned. "It's straight. Finally." Then I popped up on my tiptoes and kissed him on the cheek. "Nice work."

"Gotta say. It looks good over your girly-ass couch."

"My girly-ass couch is an antique and I'll have you know it's gorgeous."

"It's alright," he said, sitting down on it to start unpacking what looked like motorcycle magazines and random handfuls of paperwork he probably needed to sort through. "Could be softer. It's stiff as fuck."

I just smiled and went back to what I was doing—sticking push pins into a map of North America that now hung on the dining room wall next to my desk. I was pleased as shit that Jude was moving his stuff into my place before he left on tour. He'd given up his rental place, parked his car over at Jesse's and his bikes at Piper's, dumped some of his giant dude furniture at Piper's too, and brought all his personal stuff here.

Which meant that even when he wasn't here, his stuff would be... and I would know he was coming back.

Totally worked for me.

Plus I could open my closet and touch his clothes, and smell his woodsy man-musk and swoon and all that.

I was staying in Vancouver to work; I was optimistic about being able to quit my day job, soon, and focus on promoting events. After the New Year's Eve event, Summer and I had talked about doing a couple of shows in the spring when she was back from a short tour she was doing down the coast. And I had a pretty big event tonight that she was gonna do a little impromptu guest appearance at, which I was super excited about.

Once I was promoting events for her, it would just open more doors.

And in-between all the fabulous parties I'd be throwing, I'd be visiting my man on the road. Maybe I'd even drag him out clubbing with me in some of the bigger cities, to get ideas and make contacts.

"I'm just gonna cherry pick the places I want to go, and forget the others," I told him. "Fargo? No thanks. Austin, yes please..." I already had the tour schedule pinned on the wall next to the map, with the dates I was planning to join him on the road highlighted in pink.

"Can't blame you," he said.

"Three shows in New York... I'm totally coming for that." I turned to look at him, sitting on my girly-ass couch beneath his photo. "And while you're gone, I'll just gaze at your picture..."

He glanced at me, raising an eyebrow, and I batted my eyelashes. He grinned halfway. "Still can't believe you really want that thing in here."

"What thing?"

He pointed his thumb over his shoulder at the giant black-and-white photo.

"Seriously? It's gorgeous." I took a few steps closer, crossing my arms as I gazed at it. "Just look how fucking cute you are, peeking out from behind your dad's leg with your little mop of dark hair... and those *eyes*... What were you, like four?"

"Something like that."

"That makes Piper, what, nine or so?"

"Yeah."

I looked closer at the older boy in the photo, standing next to his dad with his chin tipped high. "He looks like a little blond shit."

"He was."

"Cute blond shit," I muttered. "Worst kind."

"Yup."

I stared at the two boys in the photo and their handsome father in his leather jacket and faded jeans, his blond hair kinda ruffled up in the breeze. The deep lines around his eyes from squinting into the sun. Piper looked a lot like him, even at nine. "What the hell was I even thinking?"

"Huh?"

"You know. When I was all enamored with your brother. I must've been seduced by all the badassery. I mean, he had a scar on his face. I don't think my hormones could see past that when I was a teenager."

"Uh-huh."

"Seriously. You were always so much cuter than him."

"I've spent my life in Pipe's shadow. You think I don't know where I stand?"

"You stand next to me."

He stopped sorting his papers and stood up, walked over to me and kissed me for that.

I slipped my arms around him and he did the same to me. "You're my favorite Grayson brother by miles," I told him, gazing up into his eyes. "You always were. Don't ever forget that."

"Always?"

"Always."

"What about your sexual bucket list?"

My jaw dropped. "You know about that?"

"I know everything, darlin'."

"Uh-huh. Well. I wanted him from a distance. It's not the same thing. When I got close, Piper wasn't very nice to me, Jude."

"He didn't respect you."

"No shit."

"You know..." He leaned in close, his lips brushing mine. "I gave him a nice fat lip for that. When I found out what he did to you at that party."

Whoa. That surprised me.

I knew how close Jude and his brother were. Ben used to mention it; how much it bothered Piper that Jude was always on the road with the band.

"You hit him?"

"Would've done worse, but all I could land was one blow. He was bigger than me. Always has been."

"But you've got the bigger heart. And, quite frankly, the bigger dick. From what I remember. Though to be fair, I never got quite as personal with his..."

"Spare me the details or he's gettin' another fat lip next time I see him."

"Aw, baby." I leaned up and kissed him again. "Don't you know? Women always like the brother with the bigger dick."

He grunted. "Women like blond and dangerous."

Right. Blond and dangerous.

Piper. Zane. Taze.

All the guys I'd fucked when I should've been fucking *him.*

And maybe for the first time I was really starting to understand what a sore spot that was. That maybe Jude had *always* felt like he was in his brother's shadow in some way.

Standing in Dirty's shadows couldn't have done much to dispel that feeling over the years.

Jude Grayson had strength and confidence and charisma; those were three of the things I'd always been most drawn to in him. But he was human. He was full of contradictions, weaknesses and insecurities, just like anyone.

He was a man who'd once let himself start to fall for a girl he thought chose his brother over him. A brother he loved and looked up to, which probably just made it worse.

"Women like dark and mysterious, too," I told him. I ran my hand down the side of his face, over his soft stubble, looking in his dark eyes.

"True. Pretty sure Jesse gets laid once in a while."

"Women like devoted," I told him, in all seriousness. "Women like respect. Women like to be loved."

His eyes softened as he gazed at my lips. "That so?"

"Women like men who make them feel like the only woman in the world."

"Mmm." He walked me slowly back until we bumped up against my desk. "I don't think I've respected you on this desk yet," he murmured, brushing his lips over mine again... and sending a shiver of desire through me, so strong.

Then he curled his hand around the back of my neck and pulled me to him for a toe-curling kiss... while his other hand roamed down my body and started peeling off my clothes...

And he made me feel like the only woman in the world, the way only he knew how.

EPILOGUE

Maggie

"SHIT..."

I opened my front door to Jude. I'd glimpsed him through the peep hole, standing at my door on a Sunday morning—mere days before we left on tour.

He hadn't called me first and he hadn't texted. I'd had no heads up whatsoever that he was coming by or even that he wanted to speak with me.

Whatever this was, it wasn't good.

My breakfast roiled in a glob in my stomach as I swung the door wide and put on a smile, like I was delighted by this little surprise.

I was not delighted.

"Hey, good morning! What are you doing here?"

My discomfort must have sang right through, because his eyes narrowed at me.

"Brought you a coffee," he said. "It's mocha."

Then, without being invited, he walked right in.

"Cool. You coming from Jesse's?" I closed the door behind him and tried not to panic. I tried to convince myself that this could actually just be a pleasant social call.

As if Jude ever made those to my place.

I knew he spent his early mornings with Jesse, working out. So maybe he'd just finished up there and thought he'd drop by, see how I was doing, if I was all packed up and ready for the tour...

Nope. Who the fuck was I kidding?

He turned to me and fixed me with his impermeable security-guy stare-down, and held out the coffee cup.

I took it. "Thanks. Double mocha? I only drink it if they put the chocolate whip on top." I was kidding, but hey, I said stupid shit when I was afraid my entire life might be about to crumble right out from under me.

"Triple," he said. "I had them put the chocolate syrup on too."

"Oh. Well, thanks."

That was Jude; always one step ahead of you.

Really, Jude Grayson and his no-bullshit work ethic was a massive factor in why I'd always stayed on my toes. If I'd ever slacked off, Jude would've noticed even if Brody didn't. And last thing I needed was Jude growling in Brody's ear that I couldn't hack it.

I never let Jude see me vulnerable. Which meant my personal shit stayed the hell out of the realm of the band and away from his sweeping radar.

Even so, I didn't doubt he knew things about me that I'd never told him.

It was pretty much his job to know.

But I was terrified that the reason he was here, right now, was because he knew *everything*.

"You want to come in, sit down?" I asked. It only seemed polite.

"No, thanks," he said, looming in my front hallway. "Won't be stayin' long."

Oh, God.

It really didn't take long to swing an ax, right?

Jude was the ax man, and we all knew it. It was Jude who'd been sent to fire Seth—both times.

But *me*? Would Brody really be that cruel?

"Okay..."

"Zane asked me to keep an eye on you."

My veins turned to ice water. I felt like that chick in *Frozen*, the world around me suddenly turning all to ice.

I couldn't move as he spoke.

"At the New Year's Eve party. Somethin' about too many drunk guys around."

He stared at me, like he was waiting for *me* to fill in the blanks on that.

"What guys?" My voice sounded huskier than usual; felt like a shard of ice was lodged in my throat.

"Don't know. He wasn't specific."

He just kept staring me down, his dark eyes like the gates to hell —wherein judgment and fiery punishment awaited.

"I don't get it..."

"Nothing to get," he said. "Zane's gettin' uncomfortable seein' you talk to other guys... seems pretty fuckin' obvious to me."

"What is?" I said, too quietly.

"Maggie. I see how you've been acting. The both of you."

Oh, for the love of fuck...

Here it comes.

"Is this gonna be a problem on tour?" he asked me.

And shocked the hell right out of me.

He *wasn't* here to drop the ax on my career with Dirty?

The ice in my throat melted and I swallowed.

"Is... *what* gonna be a problem on tour?"

Jude drew a deep, rough breath, then let out a silent sigh. "You really think I don't know about Vegas?"

Oh, Christ.

Jude knew about fucking *Vegas*?

The whole place was an ice palace, the coffee was hot in my hand, and I was just kind of floating in-between. I couldn't even feel anything. Just hot and cold. My whole body was covered in goosebumps.

"You think I don't know where Flynn was," he said, "where *you* were, that night? You think I don't see? You know I always know where my guys are."

I swallowed again. The ice was recrystallizing in my throat.

"You've been acting squirrelly as fuck whenever Zane's in the room. Avoiding the studio on this album. Makin' yourself scarce. That's new."

"I mean, if you think I should be—"

"Zane hasn't exactly been chasin' skirts like a drunk frat boy on Spring Break, either. That's definitely new."

He waited, letting that sink in.

I didn't know what to say. Didn't know what I *could* say to fix this.

And Zane hadn't been... *what*?

Since *when*?

"Zane needs to get onstage and perform, Maggie. And I need to have his back. You know there'll be pressure. You know there'll be women. You know what it is to be on tour."

"I do."

"So. Is this gonna be a problem for Zane?" There was a weird emphasis on the word *this*, which I interpreted as: *Are YOU gonna be a problem for Zane?*

"*No*," I said, pretty fucking offended that he would ask me that.

And yet. He had every right.

As Dirty's head of security.

As Zane's friend. The friend who'd gotten him into rehab all those years ago, helped him get sober. The one who had his back at every turn. The one person Zane trusted most, literally, with his life.

Honestly, the worries I now saw in Jude's eyes were mere reflections of my deepest fears.

"Is this gonna be a problem for *you*?" he asked me.

"No," I said. Reactive. Defensive.

Fucking scared.

I just wanted this conversation over with. Because it made me feel horribly exposed.

I'd been living this lie, this secret, for so long now, I'd gotten weirdly used to the constant discomfort of it all. The guilt. The pressure. The small, almost daily deceptions. And maybe I'd convinced myself I could just stay used to it.

As long as it was kept a secret.

I'd convinced myself, maybe, that no one would ever know.

That we'd figure things out, somehow, before anyone ever had to find out.

But we hadn't figured things out.

We hadn't figured anything out.

I'd refused, flatly refused, to move forward with our so-called "relationship." And Zane had refused to give me an annulment or a divorce. We were still secretly married but not married. Both of us holding onto something so stubbornly, so defiantly and so tightly, it was bound to break.

And yet, it couldn't break.

Not in the middle of a world tour.

Too many people were involved. There was too much pressure, too much expectation. Too much money already invested, too much time already put in, too much work already done.

Too many people counting on this.

To break was not an option.

So I stood strong, like I always did, and I told Jude what he needed to hear.

"Everything will be fine," I told him. "The tour will be incredible," I assured him. "There will be no problem between me and Zane."

But I really didn't know if any of that was the least bit true.

THANK YOU FOR READING!

Turn to the end of this book to read an excerpt from Zane and Maggie's story, the next book in the Dirty series...

Dirty Like Zane

I ~~shouldn't~~ ~~can't~~ ~~won't~~ love him.

ACKNOWLEDGMENTS

Thank you to my incredible and ever-growing ARC Team. And all my friends and family who continue to support me in what I love to do. I couldn't do this without you all.

Thank you to Guin for beta reading. And big love to Brittany for the inspiration, and sending love right when I needed it most.

A huge thank you to my family, Mr. Diamond and our little girl, for holding down the fort while I worked on this one, on a ridiculously intense schedule. Let's not do that again. But thanks to all your love, support and devotion, we did it!

This book was an incredible uphill climb in writing and would've been impossible without the support I had from my man. All those intense hours pushing onward at the coffee shop with my earbuds in and music playing, immersed in Jude and Roni's world—while you pulled daddy duty so I could dive deep with the muse—will forever be written on my heart.

Pressure creates diamonds; we've always said so and it's never been truer than with this book, and very possibly, my favorite book hero of all time. There's just something about Jude.

To my readers: THANK YOU for reading this book! I'm so honored that you chose to read this love story; my intent as a romance author is to spread love. If you've enjoyed Jude and Roni's story, please consider posting a review and telling your friends about this book; your support means the world to me.

With love and gratitude,
Jaine

PLAYLIST

Find links to the full playlist on Spotify and Apple Music here:
http://jainediamond.com/dirty-like-jude

Dirty Deeds Done Dirt Cheap — AC/DC
Run Right Back — The Black Keys
Rusty Cage — Soundgarden
Lean On (feat. MO & DJ Snake) — Major Lazer
Strange Times — Riff Raff, Goody Grace & DJ Afterthought
Sexy Boy — Air
Sweet Nothing (feat. Florence Welch) — Calvin Harris
In the Light of the Moon (feat. lil aaron) — Goody Grace
#1 Crush (*Nellee Hooper Mix*) — Garbage
Lonely Boy — The Black Keys
Die, Die My Darling — Metallica
Help I'm Alive — Metric
Can I Sit Next to You — Spoon
Two Shots (feat. gnash) — Goody Grace
Sativa (feat. Swae Lee) — Jhene Aiko
On Call — Kings Of Leon
Love Her Madly — The Doors

Blood Sugar Sex Magik — Red Hot Chili Peppers
Dreams — Fleetwood Mac
I Wanna Get Lost With You — Stereophonics
D'yer Mak'er — Led Zeppelin
Loud Love — Soundgarden
Promises — Calvin Harris, Sam Smith
Piece of My Heart — Janis Joplin
Dakota — Stereophonics
Little Cream Soda — The White Stripes
Hope (feat. Brave) — Tim Legend
Personal — Emotional Oranges
Tearing Me Up — Bob Moses
I Kissed a Girl — Katy Perry
Closer — Tegan and Sara
Open Wide (feat. Big Sean) — Calvin Harris
Conquest — The White Stripes
Claudeland — Highly Suspect
High And Dry — Radiohead
I Want It All — Arctic Monkeys
Sex with Me — Rihanna
Love Is Madness (feat. Halsey) — Thirty Seconds to Mars
Man In Black — Goody Grace
Roots, Rock, Reggae — Bob Marley
Cold Hard Bitch — Jet
4 In The Morning — Gwen Stefani
Sober (feat. JRY) — DJ Snake
Verona The Hellcat Ft. Jessie Reyez — Allan Rayman
505 — Arctic Monkeys
Don't Play No Game That I Can't Win — Beastie Boys & Santigold
Faking It (feat. Kehlani & Lil Yachty) — Calvin Harris
Beast Of Burden — The Rolling Stones
Let It Snow! Let It Snow! Let It Snow! — Dean Martin
The Only One — The Black Keys
Miss You — The Rolling Stones

Glass House — Kaleo
Crash 2.0 — Adventure Club & DallasK
Love Is Strong — The Rolling Stones
Only Girl (In the World) — Rihanna

EXCERPT: DIRTY LIKE ZANE

Dirty Like Zane

A secret marriage romance,
featuring a bad boy hero who's trying to be good,
and a kick-ass heroine whose only weakness
is the man she can't resist.

CHAPTER ONE

Maggie

All you have to do is avoid him.

That's what I'd been telling myself in preparation for this day. This tour.

Just keep it platonic.

Keep it professional.

And when all else fails... Avoid.

I took a sweeping glance across the parking lot; the members of Dirty were meeting up behind their former rehearsal space, which was now Jesse's wife Katie's art studio. There was room for a few of the tour buses to pull into the lot, but the sporting goods store across the alley had a larger lot where the rest of the buses had filed in.

It was a commercial-industrial neighborhood and not much else was stirring; it was ungodly-early for a January morning, the sun just starting to lighten the sky, and I could see my breath as I looked around.

I glimpsed a few of the band members. Jude's security team. A few of our road crew milling about, those who hadn't already headed south yesterday with the trucks. Our tour manager, Alec, counting heads, his assistant passing out coffees.

Not one sign of Zane.

All clear.

I raised my mochaccino to Alec; he waved back, and I turned to head across the lot.

"Hey, Maggie." Zane's bodyguard loomed in front of me, and I almost pissed myself. For a giant man, Shady was incredibly light on his feet. He eased back, seeming to realize he'd almost literally scared the piss out of me. "Uh... good morning?"

"Hey, Shady," I mumbled, dashing past him.

I waved a hasty hello to my bus driver, who was talking on her phone, and beelined for my bus. I'd already glimpsed it across the alley, parked behind Katie's studio. While the rest of the buses were silver-and-black, mine had a purple swirl down the side.

I turned to cut between two of the massive buses.

And there was Zane.

I stopped so suddenly, I almost spilled coffee all over myself. It slopped out the sippy hole in the lid and burned my hand.

Fuck.

I licked the coffee off my skin and glanced up.

Zane hadn't seen me. His left side was turned toward me.

I wasn't even sure what he was doing.

He was just standing there, alone, in the shadows between the buses, staring at the ground and kinda muttering to himself... like he did when he was nervous before going onstage, or when he was working on a song in his head.

Then his hand raised to his mouth, trailing smoke. He was smoking a joint—because, you know, that was a normal thing to do at the ass-crack of dawn.

If you were Zane Traynor.

He wore biker boots and fitted jeans with the knees ripped out, a white Henley shirt with pushed-up sleeves and one of his trademark black leather vests. He had maybe a week's growth on his jaw and his blond hair had been freshly buzzed on the side into a swatch of velvet, the long part on top falling forward.

Gorgeous.

Dangerous.

Dirty's lead singer.

My legal husband.

Technically, he was also one of my employers. And the one man I'd have to avoid as much as humanly possible on this tour, without making it totally obvious.

Because no one was supposed to know about *us*.

About the fact that we'd secretly gotten married in Las Vegas almost two years ago.

Or the fact that he made my heart race and the backs of my knees sweat... and occasionally made me spread my legs for him and scream like I'd never screamed for any man before.

To all the world except for the very few people who knew the truth about us, I was simply Maggie Omura, Dirty's assistant manager, and he was Zane Traynor, Dirty's lead singer, and we were nothing more to each other than co-workers and, on a good day, friends.

We definitely weren't a married couple who weren't really a couple but who occasionally fucked, fought, and generally had a totally fucked-up relationship.

I just stared at him, afraid to move and not breathing at all. My heart was beating too hard and several parts of my body were starting to sweat, right on cue.

Zane tipped his head back and ran a ring-laden hand through his hair, smoothing it back from his face as he looked up at the sky. He took another drag from his joint... and I slowly backed up.

I got the fuck out of there before he caught me staring at him.

I pretty much ran for my bus, and when I got there, I frowned to see Jesse's guitar tech, Jimmy, stepping out. Jimmy was definitely one of the good ones; he'd carried my bags for me, whisked them away before I was even out of the taxi—but still. He was a dude.

I gave him a look and pointed at the pretty pink sign I'd posted on the window of the front door yesterday, when I'd personally decorated the bus. It said, in giant silver glitter letters: NO DUDES.

Jimmy smiled sheepishly. "Your bags are inside, Maggs."

I gave him a curt, "Thank you," then disappeared up the steps inside. I set my coffee down on one of the tables in the lounge, glanced around and called out, "Hellooo?" But clearly none of the other girls were here yet.

There was a loud, staticky *blip* that almost made me jump out of my skin—apparently, I was that tense—and a voice spoke over the walkie that lay on the table.

"Hey, Maggie. You there?"

I picked up the walkie and replied cheerily, "Hey, Alec!"

"You seen or heard from Zane or Dylan yet this morning?"

"Nope!"

Half-true.

I'd definitely seen Seth, Elle and Jesse in the lot. I hadn't seen Dylan, but our drummer was pretty much always late, so no panic there just yet.

And Zane, well... Alec would find him soon enough.

"Oh, here's Dylan," he said. "Hopefully Zane checks in soon."

"Uh-huh. You know, we can always roll out without him. If he misses the Seattle show, Jesse can cover his vocal parts, right?"

"Uh... okay?" Alec chuckled. "Just let him know I'm looking for him if you see him?"

"Will do!"

I tossed the walkie on a couch with my leather jacket and

headed down the back hall, where the bunks were. I supposed Alec didn't share my little theory that we didn't really need our lead singer, but this was his first Dirty tour. Maybe his opinion would change; Zane had that effect on people.

Either way, no way was I holding Zane's hand—or anything else —through this tour. If he couldn't "check in" with Alec, not my problem.

After stashing my pretty makeup bags full of toiletries and cosmetics in the washroom, I started unpacking and putting away some of my clothes in my designated closet/locker. Then I made up my bunk with the bedding I'd brought; soft sheets, velvety-soft blanket and a multitude of cushy pillows. There was no window by my bunk, but there was air and temperature control, some recessed lighting and a little cubby where I could store a few things.

Comfy enough.

This would be my home for the next four months while we toured North America, before we headed overseas to continue Dirty's *Hell & Back* world tour. We rarely traveled by bus on other continents but here at home we had so many tour dates, especially in the U.S., that it made the most sense, both economically and comfort-wise, to travel by bus.

These days, every member of Dirty had their own luxury bus—except for Elle and Seth, since they were a couple. Our road crew traveled on other buses with a bunch of bunks in them. Once we rolled into a city, the band and management would stay in a hotel, but for the most part everyone preferred traveling this way—for each of us to have our own space, with our own stuff, set up the way we liked it; a home-away-from-home that rolled right along wherever we went.

For my part, I was already in love with my bus.

The Lady Bus.

It was the bus for the female crew, and there really weren't many of us.

There was me.

There was my assistant, Talia, whom I'd begged to come on the tour at the very last minute. Since my boss, Brody Mason—Dirty's manager—had a new baby and wasn't coming on this tour full-time, he'd offered me both a promotion and an assistant. I was pretty sure he did it out of guilt when he saw how stressed I was leading up to the tour, but he really didn't need to feel guilty. My stress had little to do with my workload.

I'd turned down the promotion, as usual, but jumped at the chance to take on an assistant, and Talia was my first choice. I was actually afraid she might say no since she was in school, but as it turned out, the opportunity to go on tour with Dirty—one of the biggest touring rock bands in the world—was too much to pass up.

Lucky for me.

I adored Talia. She reminded me of a younger, blonde—and very possibly hotter—version of me. She had a work ethic to rival my own and, in my opinion, the fact that she was a babe with impeccable fashion sense was just a point in her favor.

It had always irked me when certain men in this business—and there were a lot of them—took one glance at me and assumed I didn't belong here, or worse, that I was just some fangirl. If you asked me, women could be pretty, sexy, fashionable—or anything else they damned well wanted to be—and kick ass.

I'd spent the last eight years of my life proving that was true. In high heels and a manicure.

Talia and I would be joined on the Lady Bus by Elle's assistant, Joanie. I liked Joanie, too. No bullshit, great work ethic, and she'd been working closely with Elle for years. She knew the lay of the land.

Bonus: I'd never seen Joanie or Talia so much as bat an eyelash in Zane's direction. When Zane Traynor walked by, women tended to get starry-eyed, stupid, and slutty.

Myself included, unfortunately.

But not these women.

And then there was Sophie, our newish merch girl; girlfriend of our longtime merch guy, Pete. On the last Dirty tour, Sophie had proven herself an asset; tons of fun, zero drama. She had an easy, hearty laugh, and though I was pretty sure she was devoted to Pete in every way, she tended to laugh heartily at pretty much everything that came out of Zane's mouth.

Nobody's perfect, right?

Pete was riding on one of the crew buses, and while Sophie really could've stayed on there with her man, I'd definitely upsold her on the perks of riding on the Lady Bus.

Perks that included pretty decor, cleanliness and a fresh, unoffensive scent.

So, along with our female driver, Bobbi, we had five ladies traveling on a luxury six-bunk bus—just enough for me to convince Brody that we needed our own bus.

Thank God.

No way was I ending up on a crew bus crowded with farting, snoring men. Been there before, repeatedly, and paid my dues in full.

And no fucking way was I ending up on a rock star's bus.

Elle and Seth had Flynn and Bane, their bodyguards, on their bus. Jesse and Katie had Jude, our head of security and Jesse's best friend and bodyguard on their bus. Dylan had his girlfriend and our tour photographer, Amber, with him, as well as his bodyguard, Con.

And Matt, the bassist we'd hired on for this tour, had his own people.

Which left Zane, who had nobody on his bus with him except his bodyguard, Shady. Our ADHD-afflicted lead singer was the one rock star on this tour who probably needed some kind of assistant-slash-life-manager-slash-therapist on his bus. For a biker, Shady was a lovely man, but I'd literally had to teach him how to open an email so he could access the tour schedule; no way he was gonna assist Zane with anything other than watching his back and maybe rolling him a joint.

I was organized as hell, and while I certainly *could've* helped Zane sort out his clusterfuck of a life, *fuck that.*

Brody knew nothing about my fucked-up secret marriage to Zane, but he did know, possibly better than anyone, what a lunatic

Zane Traynor could be. And he respected me, deeply. I really didn't *think* he'd suggest that I bus with Zane, but there was no way in hell I was willing to risk that conversation.

The Lady Bus was my insurance policy and my sanctuary.

My dude-free safe haven, as indicated by the NO DUDES sign.

There was also a large pink neon sign in the shape of the female symbol that I'd hung on the wall of the lounge (overkill much?), and an overabundance of fresh flowers to welcome the other ladies onboard.

Whatever.

I surveyed my work and I was pleased. The Lady Bus was warm and welcoming, cozy and comfortable. For the next four months, it would feel like home. We'd have girl talk and peace and quiet, a dude-free zone where we could escape all the madness of touring...

I sighed with satisfaction and turned toward the door.

And Zane was there.

I froze. My entire body immediately broke out in goosebumps, and not because he'd startled me.

My nipples actually hardened.

He stood at the top of the steps, all six-foot-whatever of his tall, built, Viking body filling the entrance to the lounge.

I crossed my arms over my chest as his ice-blue eyes wandered over me, and a hot-cold flush skittered through my body; I was starting to sweat again.

He'd let himself right onto my bus. Did he not see my sparkly sign?

Yeah. He saw it.

"I thought you were Talia," I said stupidly, as if to explain my staring.

"Nope," he said.

Then he just stood there.

And I just stared.

Shit. Where the hell were my ladies?

Through the front window, I could see Bobbi over with some of the other drivers, chatting, drinking coffee. But the rest of the girls?

Fucking late, that's where they were.

I glanced at my watch.

When I looked up again, Zane had cocked his evil-gorgeous pierced eyebrow at me. He definitely hadn't missed that I was wearing the watch he'd given me for my last birthday—when he was in hardcore trying-to-win-her-over mode.

With Zane, there were exactly three modes—where I was concerned.

Trying-to-win-her-over mode.

Trying-to-fuck-her mode.

And pissed-off-at-her-and-fucking-other-women mode.

All equally devastating for different reasons.

I would've given the watch right back, but since it was the only ridiculously lavish gift he'd ever tried to give me—other than the engagement ring he'd tossed my way the morning after we got spontaneously, stupidly married—and it was actually practical, I kept it. It was Cartier, definitely worth more than my car, and perfect for me; silver with a touch of pink gold on the face and a subtle ring of diamonds.

But mainly, it would be useful on tour.

Or so I'd told myself.

"*Fuck,*" I muttered, starting to panic as he took a step deeper into the lounge—and every hair on my body stood on end. "Everyone's late."

"I'm not."

"Yeah, but you're not supposed to be here. See the sign? *NO DUDES.*" I gave him the fakest smile in the history of smiles. "That means *ever*, and that means *you.*"

Zane appeared totally unfazed by my sign or my attitude. "We're not even on the road yet, Maggs. Come on, I wanna see your bus." Then he shouldered past me with his broad man-shoulders.

"For fuck's sake. We're leaving soon."

"Got twenty minutes."

"Alec's looking for you."

"Just saw him."

I huffed a sigh and stood in the middle of the lounge with my arms crossed, waiting for this to be over as he poked around. Then he disappeared down the back hall.

When he reemerged, he looked around, his gaze lingering on the flowers and the strings of twinkly lights I'd hung, the fluffy pink pillows and the neon lady symbol on the wall. "So, no dudes, huh?"

"Yup."

"Why?"

"Because," I told him as icily as I could, "dudes ruin things."

His eyelids dropped a little, and his gaze drifted south of my waist. I was wearing jeans and a little sleeveless top, both were tight, and now I was wishing I'd worn a much longer, baggier shirt. Or maybe a garbage bag. "What things?"

"For one, you're smelling up my Lady Bus with your man smell."

His eyes met mine again and the corner of his gorgeous mouth twitched.

And my knees wobbled a little.

It was true; I could totally smell him. He smelled like pot, a bit. But then there was that heady, sexy scent of his that had always driven me fucking crazy. Or driven my sex parts crazy. I was pretty sure the mere smell of this man had made me spontaneously ovulate a time or two. And by now, I knew exactly what it was; this spiced-chai bodywash he used combined with the leather vests he pretty much lived in... and *him*. Yup. Zane just smelled *that* good.

Totally unfair.

When Zane Traynor walked into a room—or in this case, my tour bus—he came armed with an array of weapons: his bad-boy blond hair, his ice-chip blue eyes, his devilish smile, his smoky voice, his rock-hard body... and that pussy-wetting smell of his... to name a few.

You know, like any natural predator.

While I felt like some poor, soft snail caught without its shell, utterly defenseless as he sauntered over to me, his eyes locked on mine.

"You can smell me?" he asked, in that lazy, suggestive way of his when he got close. "Over all that potpourri shit?"

"Potpourri?" I glared at him. "What is this, 1983 at your grandma's house? It's incense, it's Fresh Rain scent and you're ruining it."

He stared at me, his tongue swiping slowly over his bottom lip, and my eyes tracked the movement. I couldn't stop staring at his mouth.

Maybe because I knew exactly how that tongue and those soft lips felt... all over me.

He nodded toward the back hall. "You got a bunk back there?"

I tightened my arms over my chest, even as my stomach dropped.

Fuck. Me.

I was so woefully ill-equipped to handle this shit.

I needed to avoid this man like I needed my next breath. Because whenever he got near me, he hacked my feeble defenses right down to the quick. And when he got my defenses down, he got me alone.

And when we were alone, like this... he could do *anything*. Because no one was here to see it, and I'd be unable to stop it.

He could get in my face.

Mess with my head.

Put his hands on me.

And once he did that...

"Well," I said cooly, "I don't sleep hanging from my feet like *The Lost Boys*, so yeah, I've got a bunk."

Attitude.

Denial.

Avoidance.

These were about the only defenses I'd ever had when it came to Zane, and as time wore on, they'd only grown less effective.

Avoidance; total avoidance was the only defense I really had left.

If I couldn't avoid him, I was screwed.

Literally and often.

"Which one?"

I just glared at him. *So* not his business.

"Lemme guess. The one with the pink velvet blanket and the military corners. And the five hundred pillows."

"It's not velvet," I said, my tone frigid.

"Felt like velvet."

Fucking great. He'd fingered my bed. It probably smelled of him now, too.

"It's pretty small," he observed. "You know... you ride on my bus with me, you get a whole bedroom with a giant bed."

"Mm-hmm. Which I get to share with you."

"That's just one of the perks, Maggs." He said that slowly, his blue-eyed gaze drifting over my face and lingering on my lips. "No one else on my bus but Shady. It's gonna get pretty quiet."

I said nothing.

"A guy might get lonely..."

"I'm sure you'll find someone to keep you company," I told him, deadpan.

I was sure. Women would be lining up to warm Zane Traynor's bed on this tour, just like they did every other day of his life.

"Should really be my wife," he said, his tone sharpening.

"If you had one."

He stared at me.

I glared right back.

"You ever want to come check it out, door's open."

"I'm sure it is."

He didn't respond to that. He didn't get mad or defensive or argue. He didn't crank up the trying-to-fuck-her charm.

"So let's just be clear about this," he said, in his low, dead-sexy voice. "I'm offering to share my bus with you. And you're turning me down."

I looked away. "I'm not turning you down, Zane. I have my own bus."

And we already talked about this... ad nauseam.

He didn't say anything.

But he was so close to me now, there was nowhere for me to look to avoid his chiseled, gorgeous face, but *down*... at his chiseled, gorgeous body. The Henley shirt, closeup, was thin, stretched over his sculpted muscles. The leather vest was narrow and open; I could see his left nipple and the piercing in it poking against the almost see-through white fabric. The shirt was haphazardly tucked into his jeans in one spot, the rest slopping out, but it definitely did nothing to cover the insane bulge in the front of his jeans.

Was he already hard? I couldn't exactly tell. Zane had a huge dick, and while he usually wore loose-fit jeans, these ones were pretty snug.

I didn't want to stare.

I really didn't.

But there was nowhere else to look. He was *everywhere*.

Then his hand, suddenly, was on my face. Just lightly cupping my cheek, his warmth radiating into me.

I jerked back, startled, and butted up against the partition between the lounge and the driver's seat. He'd cornered me—and as usual, I didn't even notice it was happening.

The fact was, anytime Zane had gotten me alone he'd been able to corner me.

And fuck me.

At least, since we'd been married.

There were really only two reasons we hadn't been fucking *daily* since our wedding night.

One, he let me off the hook a lot. Stayed away when I asked him to. Respected my boundaries, for the most part.

And two, I'd managed to avoid him a hell of a lot. I'd worked my ass off to keep a physical distance between us, most of the time. Because I knew anytime he got me alone... it was only a matter of time.

A few tense moments. A few hungry glances. A few heated words...

And it was all over.

He'd corner me.

I'd somehow let him.

And his giant dick would be in me.

Before I knew it I'd be halfway to my next screaming, scorching, mind-fucking orgasm.

I allowed myself to look up into his waiting eyes… and a wave of longing rocked through me.

I bit down on my tongue.

He stroked his thumb over my cheek, lightly, and over the corner of my mouth, tugging on my lip. I felt the urgent thud of my pulse between my legs, and I sucked back a breath. Then I held it, tight, like it was my life. Like if I let it go, I'd die.

"We're gonna get through this," he told me, in a low, rough, almost-whisper. "Together, Maggie."

Then his lips met mine.

Warm.

Soft.

He gave me the most feather-soft, barely-touching kiss… and the floor dropped out from under me. The world turned upside-down and my throat constricted.

My heart pounded right to a stop.

I didn't move.

I couldn't.

I knew I was a masochist when it came to Zane; that had already been established. I was a strong woman, but I was weak when it came to him.

I was just trying not to be a total moron and fuck him on day one of this tour.

We cannot fuck around on this tour, I'd told him, the last time we were alone together. Two months ago.

And again only three days ago, over the phone.

Yeah, Maggie, he'd said. *We sure as fuck can.*

Which meant we were at a stalemate.

Again.

Always.

His hand dropped away, his lips left mine and he brushed past me, leaving me with a whiff of his sexy man-scent. Then he dropped down the steps and off the bus, and he was gone.

I exhaled hard… then inhaled, deep. My lungs ached from not breathing for so long.

At least my heart had started beating again; pounding. I could've sworn it'd really stopped for a minute there.

And my pussy *ached.*

Truly, one of the worst problems with being madly, insanely, stupidly in lust with a man whom I firmly, deeply, to-the-marrow-of-my-bones believed I could never be with was that it made it difficult to be with anyone else. Impossible, actually. Which meant that I hadn't been. With anyone.

Anyone but *him,* since we were married.

Almost two years ago.

And it was slowly killing me.

I, Maggie Omura, was suffering a slow, slow death by desire.

Unsated desire.

Or at least, rarely-sated desire.

It dawned on me, too slowly, that the blinds were open on the lounge windows… and panic hit me like a lightning bolt to the spine. *Shit. SHIT.* Did anyone see that shit?

Jesus, what the fuck were we doing?

I walked straight to the back, to the bunks, and rolled into mine. And then it really sank in.

Oh dear God.

How the hell was I gonna get through this?

Hiding from Zane the entire tour… Was that really my plan?

I stared at the ceiling, which was actually the underside of Talia's bunk, and sighed, because yeah. That was my plan.

My ridiculous, futile plan.

I heard someone come onboard and I didn't even poke my head out to see who it was. I just lay here, breathing slowly in and out, my head still reeling from that kiss.

"Good morning! Why's Zane on our bus?" Talia appeared. "I thought it was no dudes allowed."

"It is," I said, sitting up. "It most definitely is. He's got the memo on that now. Feel free to kick his ass out if you catch him sniffing around."

"Okay," she said, though she sounded uncertain. Probably didn't love the idea of having to tell our lead singer to take a hike, but she'd learn; sometimes telling Zane Traynor to fuck off was the only sensible move a girl could make.

"Where've you been? We leave in like fifteen."

"I was here half an hour ago." She looked stricken, worried she was in trouble. "I was just talking to the crew..."

"Oh." I slid out of my bunk and stood up. "Sorry. I didn't sleep much last night..." I muttered a lame apology and headed out to the lounge. Talia followed. "Can you find Joanie and Sophie, and get them in here? We should have a quick meeting before we roll out."

"Of course. I just saw Joanie pop into Elle's bus, and Sophie was with Pete. I'll get them." She dashed out the door.

So... my ladies weren't late.

Well, good.

I forced myself, again, to breathe. Why was it so damn hard just to breathe?

It was like Zane did something to the oxygen, made the environment inhospitable to female life.

I sipped my mochaccino and tried to regroup. To start this day over again. Just pretend Zane's little invasion into my sanctuary had never happened.

But it did.

He'd touched me.

He'd kissed me.

On day fucking one—no, moment one—of the tour

And now my whole system was out of balance.

I lit more incense to burn away the lingering smell of him. A little meeting with my lady crew to start this tour off right was what I needed—so I could go over the rules of the Lady Bus with them.

Rule number one: *No dudes.*

That meant any dudes, for any reason.

Boyfriends.

Hookups.

Pushy lead singers.

Unless this bus caught on fire and we needed someone to ax us the hell out... from this moment on, absolutely no dudes were setting foot on this bus.

Only problem with that plan was I couldn't exactly hide in here forever. And I'd still have to deal with Zane *out there*.

I'd have to see him, talk to him, work with him.

Every. Day.

And the truth was I *wanted* to see him.

I hugged myself as I looked around the bus, at this pretty little cocoon I'd created to insulate myself from the world outside. From him.

And I knew; the purpose of the Lady Bus wasn't to keep Zane away from me.

It was to keep me away from him.

ABOUT THE AUTHOR

Jaine Diamond is a Top 5 international bestselling author. She writes contemporary romance featuring badass, swoon-worthy heroes endowed with massive hearts, strong heroines armed with sweetness and sass, and explosive, page-turning chemistry.

She lives on the beautiful west coast of Canada with her real-life romantic hero and daughter, where she reads, writes and makes extensive playlists for her books while binge drinking tea.

For the most up-to-date list of Jaine's published books and reading order please go to: jainediamond.com/books

Get the Diamond Club Newsletter at jainediamond.com for new release info, insider updates, giveaways and bonus content.

Join the private readers' group to connect with Jaine and other readers: facebook.com/groups/jainediamondsVIPs

goodreads.com/jainediamond
bookbub.com/authors/jaine-diamond
instagram.com/jainediamond
tiktok.com/@jainediamond
facebook.com/JaineDiamond

Made in the USA
Coppell, TX
05 December 2024

41782516R00215